LESS THAN A GENTLEMAN

By Kerrelyn Sparks

LESS THAN
A GENTLEMAN

KERRELYN SPARKS

AVONIMPULSE
An Imprint of HarperCollinsPublishers

Excerpt from *The Mad Earl's Bride* copyright © 1995 by Loretta Chekani.

Excerpt from *Wanted: Wife* copyright © 2013 by Gwen Jones.

Excerpt from *A Wedding in Valentine* copyright © 2013 by Gayle Kloecker Callen.

EPub Edition JULY 2013 ISBN: 9780062128799

Print Edition ISBN: 9780062128805

10 9 8 7 6 5 4 3 2 1

To my mother, Charly,
who has waited ten years for this story to be published.
Of all my books, this is her favorite.

ACKNOWLEDGMENTS

Less Than a Gentleman began in 2002 as a manuscript titled *Taking Liberty*. Although I failed back then to sell the original manuscript, it served a good purpose at the time, for it inspired my agent, Michelle Grajkowski of Three Seas Literary Agency, to take me on as a client. She has always loved this story, so she is celebrating its release as much as I. Thank you, Michelle, for believing in me before I entered the world of vampires.

I would also like to thank my dear friend and critique partner, Sandy, who spent hours going over the manuscript.

My thanks also to Avon Books of HarperCollins, and most especially my editor, Erika Tsang, who has brought *Less Than a Gentleman* to life, when most publishers would reject a romance set in Colonial America during the Revolutionary War.

And finally, a big thank you to my readers who are willing to leave the vampire world they know and follow me into the unknown. You won't find any vamps or shifters in these pages, but the laughs are still waiting to catch you by surprise, the action is still intense, and the romance is still hot. As always, love is at stake!

CHAPTER ONE

South Carolina
Friday, August 25, 1780

Captain Matthias Murray Thomas tugged at the ropes that bound his hands behind his back. The gradual lightening of the night sky, visible through the open window, warned him he was running out of time. With the coming of dawn, he and his companions would be marched to their death.

His movements caused a drop to trickle down his arm. Either blood from his shoulder wound or sweat, he could no longer tell, for the hot, humid air was thick with the scent of both. Mosquitoes hummed over them, enjoying the feast of defenseless men.

The call of a wood warbler claimed his attention and brought back memories of his youth. His family would spend the summer months in Charles Town, then return to the plantation in the fall, where the song of the wood warbler would greet him. Every year the birds rested for the autumn months in the South Carolina marshlands before continuing their migration south.

The warbler's song pierced the air, jolting him back to the present. He and the other captured soldiers were being held in an abandoned house just north of Nelson's Ferry on the Santee River. In August.

The first rays of dawn crept through the open window, giving shape and form to the huddled mass on the floor. His fellow prisoners lay sprawled around him, either snoring or moaning from untended wounds. As the ranking officer, he had stayed awake all night to watch over his doomed men.

The youngster beside him whimpered in his sleep. Fourteen years old, the boy had said. Too young for a soldier and far too young to hang as a traitor.

Matthias searched the blue uniforms to locate his cousin and winced at the sight of Richard's blood-crusted face. Two English guards, equipped with bayonet-tipped muskets, stood at the door, their red coats easy to spot in the dim light.

The boy beside him flinched.

Matthias nudged him with his boot. "Simon."

The boy awoke with a shout.

The sound drew the attention of the guards. They frowned at Matthias, apparently holding him accountable for the sudden noise.

"You'll hold your tongue if you know what's good for you," the taller guard warned him.

Matthias shrugged his uninjured shoulder. "It was a bad dream. I'm afraid of the dark."

The guard snorted. "Yankee cowards. I've seen how you turn tail and run."

A low rumble of curses grew as the prisoners sat up and responded to the insult.

"Dammit, Greville, don't get them riled up," the second guard warned his companion.

"Are you all right?" Matthias whispered, his voice masked by the grumbling of the prisoners.

Simon struggled to a sitting position. "I dreamed about the battle."

Matthias nodded. The battle at Camden had been one of the worst in his experience. "Was it your first?"

Simon's eyes filled with tears, and he blinked to keep them from falling. "I didn't turn tail and run."

"No, you fought bravely."

"You saw me?"

"Yes, I did," Matthias lied. "You held your ground."

A hint of a smile crossed Simon's face, then disappeared. "What will they do to us in Charles Town?"

Either kill us slowly in prison or quickly by the gallows. "We're not there yet." Matthias planted his feet on the floor, and bracing himself against the wall, he pushed to a standing position. He ambled toward the guards—the tall one named Greville and a shorter, freckle-faced one with carrot-colored hair.

"Halt," Greville ordered.

Matthias motioned with his head to the chamber pot in the corner. "I need to relieve myself."

The freckle-faced guard shrugged. "Then do it."

"Regrettably, in my current condition, I find myself unable to unfasten my breeches or . . . handle the equipment. If you would care to assist me?" Matthias arched a brow at him. "Seeing that you're English, you might enjoy it."

"The hell you say." Freckle-face pointed his bayonet at Matthias. "Greville, tie his hands in front."

Matthias watched calmly as Greville eased a long, gleaming knife from his leather scabbard. "Hmm, an Englishman with ten inches. Do I dare turn my back?"

"Shut your foul mouth, Yankee." Greville jerked at his arm to spin him around.

Matthias gritted his teeth as more blood oozed from his shoulder wound. He surveyed his fellow prisoners. Dried blood and dirt etched their weary expressions with shades of rust and brown, but the early sun caught the glimmer of hope in their eyes. They were counting on him. Better to die, providing their escape, than to march with them to the gallows like obedient sheep.

Greville sawed through his ropes. "Turn."

He pivoted and stretched his hands forward so the guard could loop more rope around his wrists. Greville's knife rested in its leather-tooled scabbard, so damned close Matthias's fingers itched to grab it.

Click. Freckle-face cocked his musket.

Patience, Matthias reminded himself. *Timing is everything.* He sauntered to the corner and relieved himself. After buttoning his breeches, he leaned over.

"What the devil are you doing?" Greville demanded.

Matthias turned slowly, clutching the edge of the chamber pot in his bound hands. Freckle-face had assumed a firing stance.

"The thunder mug is full, and the men will need to use it. I thought I'd empty it out the window." Matthias offered the malodorous pot to the guard. "Of course, if *you* prefer to do it—"

"Dump it," Greville ordered.

"As you wish." Matthias paced to the open window and peered outside. Only one soldier guarded the front of the house. Damned arrogant redcoats.

"What are you waiting for?" Greville muttered.

"For the guard to pass," Matthias said. "Or would you prefer that I douse him with *eau de toilette*? It could only improve his smell."

The prisoners hooted and pounded the floor with their booted feet.

"Cease your noise!" Freckle-face aimed his musket at the prisoners.

They grew quiet, but their sudden misbehavior had been heard by the guard outside. He sprinted toward the window, and Matthias showered him with the contents of the chamber pot.

"Aagh!" The man jumped back. "Shit!"

"Not exactly." Matthias hurled the pot at the redheaded guard.

Freckle-face raised his musket to deflect it, but not quickly enough. The flying pot smacked him in the face and he tumbled backward, firing into the ceiling. Flakes of plaster rained down, and the pot shattered on the floor.

"Damn you!" Greville seized his musket and rushed toward Matthias, clearly planning to skewer him with the bayonet.

Matthias leapt to the side, grasped the musket's barrel,

and wrenched the weapon from Greville's hands. With the butt end, he smashed his attacker in the face. Greville collapsed, crying out as blood gushed from his nose.

Matthias trapped the musket between his feet, bayonet pointed upward, so he could slice through his ropes. "Richard, watch the window. The guard outside is a trifle pissed."

With a snort, his cousin scrambled to his feet.

Just as Matthias finished freeing his hands, he noted Greville attempting to sit up. He knocked the guard out with another blow to the head, then yanked Greville's knife from the scabbard. Possibly a family heirloom, with its ornate handle inlaid with ivory, but still a weapon he couldn't afford to leave with the enemy.

"The other guard!" one of his men shouted.

Pottery shards crunched as Freckle-face stumbled to his feet. His musket had discharged, but it still possessed the deadly bayonet. With an angry roar, he attacked.

Matthias jumped aside as he threw his newly acquired knife. It lodged with a hideous thunk in the redcoat's chest.

Freckle-face halted, his eyes wide with shock. He crumbled to his knees, still focused on Matthias's face. The disbelief in his eyes glazed to a pained acceptance as if, for a brief moment, he mourned his own passing.

Squashing any sort of emotional reaction, Matthias checked the musket he'd taken from Greville. He had to remain focused until his men were free.

"Matt!" Richard lunged to the floor.

The drenched guard stood outside, his musket aimed at the window opening.

Matthias dropped to the floor a second before the shot

exploded. He rolled toward the window, jumped to his feet, and pointed his musket at the guard's face.

With a loud gulp, the guard stepped back.

"You think this is frightening, you should see what's behind you," Matthias said.

"Ha! You think I'll fall for that old trick?" The guard glanced over his shoulder, then looked again as a group of armed Colonials charged toward him. "Bloody hell!" He dropped his firearm and lifted his hands in surrender.

Matthias removed the bayonet from his musket. "Stand up, Rich, and I'll cut your ropes."

Richard glanced out the window as he scrambled to his feet. "Who are those men?"

"Local militia, from the looks of their clothing." Matthias cut through his cousin's ropes, then handed him the bayonet. "Release the others."

Grins and shouts of victory spread amongst the soldiers.

Matthias exchanged a smile with young Simon before aiming his musket at Greville, who was regaining consciousness. "This one is still loaded."

Grimacing, Greville touched his broken nose. "You damned Yankee, you cannot hope to succeed."

"We already have." Matthias heard the tramping of feet as the militia moved through the house. "I'm afraid we must decline your offer of hospitality in Charles Town."

Greville continued to curse as he sat up, but ceased abruptly when he spotted his comrade's body. His face paled. "You *killed* him."

Matthias winced inwardly. They were at war. It was self-defense. He'd had no choice. War was hell. There was a whole list of justifications that he repeated to himself every night so he could sleep. And be at peace. Sometimes he slept. He'd given up on peace months ago.

Greville touched his empty scabbard. "You used *my* knife. On my best friend." He shifted his gaze to Matthias. "You bastard. I swear you will pay for this."

I probably will. Matthias turned as the door burst open and militiamen marched in. "Good morning, gentlemen. This room is secure."

A short, swarthy man in the Colonial uniform of a lieutenant colonel shouldered his way into the room. "I heard a weapon discharge in this room. What happened?"

Matthias motioned to Freckle-face. "He fired it, sir. I . . . handled the situation."

The lieutenant colonel glanced at the dead redcoat, then inspected Matthias. "And you're the one who splattered the guard outside?"

"Yes, sir."

"Do you think so highly of yourself, Captain, that you were prepared to take on twenty-five redcoats single-handedly?"

"I knew you were outside, sir."

The lieutenant colonel narrowed his dark eyes. "How? The redcoats didn't hear us. We took them by surprise."

"Apparently they're not acquainted with the migratory habits of the wood warbler."

The officer's mouth twisted with a wry smile. "I could use a man like you. I'm Francis Marion. And you, Captain?"

"Matthias Murray Thomas, sir."

"You're under my command now." Marion turned to a man who had just entered the room. "Report."

Dressed in the tattered and bloodstained uniform of a major, the man towered over the smaller lieutenant colonel. "We released over a hundred lads from the other rooms," the major replied with a Scots accent.

Marion nodded. "And the British?"

"Twenty-one prisoners." The major hooked a lock of graying auburn hair behind his ear. "Five wounded, one dead."

"Make that two." Marion gestured to the knifed redcoat.

"He has a name, damn you." Greville spat a glob of blood in their direction. He glowered at Matthias as a militiaman hauled him to his feet and tied his hands behind his back. "I heard *your* name, Matthias Murray Thomas. I won't forget it."

The militiaman dragged Greville out the door.

"Where are you taking the prisoners?" Matthias hoped it was far away.

"North Carolina," answered Marion. "There's no point in staying here. After Gates's defeat at Camden, South Carolina is lost."

"But there's still hope," Matthias protested. "Colonel Sumter is doing well in the west. We should rendezvous with him."

Marion shook his head. "You haven't heard. Sumter was defeated two days after Gates."

Matthias's mouth dropped open. Gates and Sumter both defeated?

Marion motioned to the Scotsman. "The major here was with Sumter. He escaped capture and met up with us."

A chill stole over Matthias as his spirits plunged. His men were free, but South Carolina was indeed lost. "There's no one left."

The Scotsman snorted. "And what are we, lad? A pack of ghosts?"

Marion paced toward the window. "Unfortunately, we'll have to disappear like ghosts. Once the British learn of our little escapade here, they'll retaliate. And they'll most likely wreak their vengeance on the known patriots in the area."

Matthias felt a twinge in his gut at the thought of his mother alone on the plantation. Unprotected. His stomach churned even more when the Scotsman leaned over Freckle-face and yanked the knife from his chest.

"Ready your men, Captain," Marion ordered. "We march for North Carolina immediately."

Matthias cleared his throat. "With all due respect, sir, many of my men are wounded and would not survive the journey."

"Do you have an alternative?"

"We could hide in the swamp. Some of the wounded live nearby. I could deliver them home at night. Then they can rejoin us once they've recovered."

Marion frowned as he considered. "Very well. We cannot fight the British with dead soldiers. Take care of your men."

"Thank you, sir."

"I expect you to be more than a nursemaid, Captain," Marion continued. "Your objective will be to sever the British lines of supply and communication between Charles Town and General Cornwallis in the west. Burn the bridges and the ferryboats. And lose your uniforms."

"Yes, sir."

"Use Snow's Island as your base," Marion referred to

a river island in the midst of the nearby swamp. "I hope to return in a few weeks. Until I do, South Carolina is in your hands."

"I understand." Matthias swallowed hard at the lump in his throat. He and his men would be the only resistance left in the area. And they were a sorry lot.

"Good luck to you, Captain." Marion bowed his head, then strode from the room.

The Scotsman handed the knife to Matthias. "I believe ye dropped yer wee blade. I wiped it clean."

"Thank you." Matthias wedged the knife under his belt. "Why did you come east? You had to know you were going further into enemy territory."

"I had my reasons." The major examined Matt carefully. "I havena met many a man as strapping and fearless as you. I have two daughters. Ye may be just the man for them."

Matthias groaned. Hadn't he endured enough match-making schemes from his mother? "I have no intention of marrying, sir."

The Scotsman snorted. "As if ye were good enough for either of them. My lassies are the reason I came this way. I need to know they're safe. The last I heard they fled Charles Town and were living in a cabin off the Pee Dee River."

"You wish me to provide them with protection?"

"Och, just try it, laddie. My daughters will roast you over an open fire. All I ask is that ye tell me they're safe. Send a message to me, Jamie Munro."

"And your daughters?"

"Virginia Stanton and Caroline Munro."

"I'll take care of the matter, sir."

"Aye, I believe ye will." With a smile, Major Munro strode from the room.

Matthias shrugged his uninjured shoulder. He'd faced the enemy in battle for four years and survived. How difficult could a pair of females be?

Blackened timbers lay strewn across the ground. The house had been small. Only the stone fireplace remained standing as the sole testament to a family's former hopes and dreams.

Matthias tied his horse to the nearest surviving tree, then picked his way across the ruins.

"There's nothing left worth stealing." A young man stepped from the woods, leveling a musket at Matthias.

"I'm not a thief." Matthias wiped the soot from his hands, leaving black streaks on his buff-colored breeches. In his new role as partisan leader, he now dressed to blend into the surroundings. "Is this your home?"

"Aye, what's left of it." The man lowered his weapon. His wife emerged from the woods with two young children clinging to her skirt.

"I've been traveling down the Pee Dee," Matthias explained. "This is the fourth burnt home I've found, but you're the first people I've seen. What happened?"

The man removed his tricorne to wipe sweat from his brow. "The British did it, those accursed devils."

"When?" After the rescue at Nelson's Ferry, Matthias had remained in the swamp for a week, taking care of his men. Last night, he and his cousin had traveled to the upper Pee

Dee to visit Richard's parents. Then today, he had ventured downriver in search of the major's daughters.

"The redcoats were here yesterday," the man answered. "They started on the coast in Georgetown and worked their way up the Pee Dee, burning everything in sight."

Matthias grimaced. This place had to be nearly seventy miles from Georgetown. Seventy miles of burnt homes.

The man sighed. "They said we deserved it for helping the partisans free some prisoners at Nelson's Ferry, but I had no part in it."

Matthias flinched as if he'd been hit with the blunt end of an axe. It was his rescue that had caused this? His heart squeezed at the sight of the children, wide-eyed and silent, their faces smudged with soot. On their cheeks, little trails of cleaner skin had been left behind by their tears.

He reached into his shoulder bag and removed the loaf of bread his aunt had given him. "'Tis not much, but it is all I have with me."

"Thank you, good sir." The wife accepted the loaf.

"No thanks are necessary, I assure you." Matthias swallowed a knot of guilt. "If you travel upstream another twenty miles, you'll reach my uncle, the Reverend Nathaniel Thomas. He'll be able to assist you better than I."

The man nodded. "Thank you."

"I'm searching for two women who live along this river. Perhaps you know them? Virginia Stanton and Caroline Munro?"

"Aye." The man accepted a piece of bread from his wife. "But we haven't seen them since the redcoats came through."

The woman passed out pieces of bread to her children.

"Poor Virginia is expecting in about a month. 'Twould be her third."

They have children? Matthias loosened his neck cloth. The major had neglected to tell him that small detail. "Their father, Major Munro, asked me to locate them."

"They live about five miles south of here." The woman's eyes filled with tears. "That is, they did." She turned away as if to escape the bleak possibility that remained unspoken.

The two women and their children could be dead.

Chapter Two

Monday, September 4, 1780

The drum of horse hooves drew closer.

Caroline exchanged a worried look with her older sister. Virginia touched her swollen belly with a protective gesture and eased to her knees behind the tall thicket of sweet pepperbush.

They were a pitiful bunch, Caroline thought, glancing from Ginny, who was beginning her ninth month of pregnancy, to her young nephew and even younger niece. Their few belongings filled the sacks that straddled an old brown horse.

The thundering noise grew closer. In their hiding place, four-year-old Charlotte huddled beside her mother. Edward sidled closer with a defiant look, as if daring anyone to say he was afraid.

The horse pawed at the spongy, black earth, sensing the vibrations of approaching horsemen. More than one, Caroline could tell. The rumor she had heard last week flitted through her mind. Redcoats had invaded a home, found a pregnant woman, and stabbed her and the unborn child with their bayonets. Then they had written a warning above the bed. *Thou shalt not give birth to a rebel.*

She glanced at her expectant sister and murmured a silent prayer. Then, in case God was occupied elsewhere, Caroline lowered herself to one knee and lifted the loaded musket to her shoulder.

She eased the tip of the barrel between leafy branches of sweet pepperbush. The strong scent of the spiky white flowers itched her nose. *Blast.* This would be a bad time to sneeze. The horsemen dashed by in a dusty blur of black, brown, and dirty homespun. Colonials, four of them. Caroline caught her breath and stood.

"No," Virginia whispered. "They could be British deserters. They could be desperate, even ruthless. We trust no one."

Caroline refrained from mentioning their own desperate situation. Eventually, they might have to trust someone. "The danger is over for now. We should press on."

For five days, they had traveled south through the Black Mingo Swamp, winding their way around bogs and hiding from anyone who ventured close. They planned to reach the Black River and follow it westward 'til they located Colonel Sumter's army, where their father was stationed.

Caroline walked in front of their group, carrying their one musket. She glanced back to check on the children, who rode. Nine-year-old Edward nodded in the saddle. Seated behind him, Charlotte rested, her arms wrapped around her brother. *Poor innocents.* Father had been right. The price of freedom would be paid by all, including the children.

Virginia led the horse by the reins. She gave Caroline a tired smile.

Caroline smiled in response, then faced front with a jerk. Dear God, what if her sister went into childbirth? In the middle of a swamp with enemy redcoats all around?

She swallowed hard at the panic rising in her throat. *Face the facts, Caroline. You're the only able-bodied adult in the group. It is up to you to make sure we survive.* By her calculations, they were now close to the Black River. If they found passage upriver, they could be reunited with Father in a few days.

"What is that smell?" Virginia asked.

Caroline sniffed. *Not again.* The air along the Pee Dee had been thick with the smoke of burning homes. Had the British burned along the Black River, too?

"I smell fire," Edward announced.

"Mama, I need the potty," Charlotte whispered.

"Do you see a chamber pot around here?" Edward muttered.

"Don't fret, sweeting," Virginia told her daughter. "We'll stop soon."

Caroline strode around a bend in the path and slowed to a halt. The path widened and sloped down to the Black River. Here the land had been cleared of vegetation, but as the river snaked into the distance, tangled vines hugged its banks. The horse path continued on a parallel course to the river. In front of her, smoke curled into the air from the charred remains of a rowboat. A boat they could have used.

She groaned. How could it get worse than this?

Virginia stopped beside her. "We'll figure out something."

"Can I get down now?" Charlotte asked.

Caroline propped the musket against a tree, then lifted her niece off the horse. Virginia led Charlotte behind some bushes.

"Godsookers! Look at that." Edward slid off the horse and ran down to the water's edge. "They set it on fire while it was still in the water. I didn't know that was possible."

Caroline frowned, gazing at the blackened remains of the ferry that floated on the far side of the river. "Ships burn at sea all the time." She winced inwardly. *Blast!* She'd done it again and blurted out something dreadful. Edward's father, a blockade runner, had been missing at sea since last April.

Luckily, Edward didn't seem to notice. He had picked up a stick and was prodding at the burnt remains of the rowboat.

"Edward, we are the ablest amongst our group. Your mother and sister are counting on us. We mustn't let them down."

He stabbed the boat with his stick. "Fear not, fair maiden. I shall defend us to the death!"

Caroline sighed. She was definitely on her own.

"What do you want here?" a man's voice shouted.

Caroline spotted a log cabin a short distance away. A man leaned against the door frame, watching them with the bloodshot eyes of a drunkard. The ferryman, she assumed.

"Good sir," she greeted him with a forced smile. "How are you today?"

"I'm ruined." The man lifted a jug for a long drink. Wiping his mouth with a grimy shirtsleeve, he stumbled a few steps toward them. "I've been put out of business by my own neighbors, the scurvy bastards."

Edward snickered at the man's choice of words.

Caroline frowned at her nephew, then tied off the horse so she could join the ferryman close to his cabin. "It was your neighbors who burned your boats?"

"Aye. Now that they're militia, they think they can do whatever the hell they want. Said they had to burn all the boats to hurt the British."

"Oh, I'm sorry for your loss." Caroline suspected it could have been the group of men who had passed them on the horse path. As much as she applauded anyone's efforts to bedevil the British, the militia had also made matters difficult for them. "We're attempting to rendezvous with Colonel Sumter. Do you have any other boats?"

"'Twill do you no good." The man upended his jug, discovered it was empty, and tossed it onto the ground. "The armies are gone."

"*Gone?*" A chill prickled the skin on her arms. "What do you mean?"

"I mean the armies with Gates and Sumter. The British killed them all."

Caroline gasped. *Papa.* She looked at Edward to see if he had heard. No, he had moved to the river's edge to poke his stick in the mud. Good Lord, what should she say to Ginny? Perhaps nothing for now, until she knew for sure. "Surely some of the men escaped?"

The ferryman scratched his dirty shirt. "I suppose. Shall I feed your horse for you?"

"Ah, yes, thank you." Caroline's mind raced as she considered their dilemma. Where should they go? The Munro family home in the foothills of North Carolina was too far away. Virginia would never make it there in her current condition. Was Ginny's husband, Quincy, still alive? Was their father still alive? What if Jamie Munro was lying in a field somewhere, alone and wounded? How could she ever find him? How could she take care of her family all alone?

The ferryman untied the horse, then scrambled onto the saddle and rode away.

Caroline stood, transfixed with disbelief.

Edward threw his stick at him. "You scurvy bastard!"

"Edward James Stanton!" Virginia marched from the bushes. "I will not tolerate such language."

"But he stole our horse!" Edward shouted.

Caroline emerged from her state of shock and dashed after the thief. She ran, her heart pounding and filled with dismay as she watched the last of their belongings disappear down the horse path, gone forever. Breathing heavily, she slowed to a stop.

You fool! She had wondered how it could get worse. Now she knew. They had no transportation, no destination, no money, no food. Not even a change of clothes.

She trudged back to where her sister and the children waited. "I'm sorry."

Virginia nodded and sat beside the dirt path.

"'Tis all right, Mama." Charlotte tugged an object from her apron pocket. "I still have my book from Papa. See?"

Virginia's eyes glimmered with tears. "Yes, sweeting."

"What a bufflehead," Edward muttered.

"Hush," Caroline warned her nephew. "I want to take a look in the ferryman's cabin. Will you come with me?"

She and Edward rummaged through the filthy cabin and

located several useful items—a knife, a horn of gunpowder, a tinder wheel, a block of cheese, and a sack of figs.

As they feasted on cheese and figs, Caroline attempted to come up with a plan. If they continued west, there was no guarantee they would ever locate Father. She couldn't even be sure he was alive. But if they went east, they would end up in British-held Charles Town. She stood and brushed the dust from her skirts. "I believe we should travel westward."

"I agree." Virginia packed their meager supplies in the empty sack.

Caroline retrieved the musket and led the way up the horse path. The sun began its final descent and still they trudged along. Her hopes of finding decent shelter dwindled with each step. Would they be forced to spend another night sleeping under the trees?

Finally, they reached a clearing. No cabin in sight, only a pier that stretched into the river.

"Godsookers, would you look at that?" Edward pointed.

Caroline's mouth dropped open. On the opposite bank of the river, a green lawn spread before an enormous white house in the Georgian style.

"Perhaps they will take us in for the night," Virginia suggested.

"But how do we get there?" asked Edward.

"There must be a way." Caroline ventured onto the pier. A second pier on the other side of the river taunted her. So close and so far away.

"There should be a boat of some kind," Virginia said. "They obviously cross the river to use this path."

Caroline scanned the riverbank. "There, I see it!" She pointed downstream to a rowboat partially hidden by cattails. Thank God it was on their side of the river. She strode to the river's edge to retrieve the boat.

It was stuck in shallow, muddy water. As she waded in, the mud sucked her feet down and filled her shoes. She grimaced at the cool, squishy sensation. With effort, she dragged the boat to the pier. It was a small boat, too small for them all to cross at once.

"May I row?" Charlotte asked when her mother helped her board the boat.

"No," Virginia replied. "Let your aunt row. And keep your hands inside the boat."

"Why?"

Edward climbed aboard. "Because an alligator will bite your fingers off!"

Charlotte squealed and rocked the boat.

"Enough, Edward." Caroline rowed the children across to the opposite pier and ordered them to remain there. Then she returned for her sister.

"Don't fret," Caroline told her sister as she rowed. "I shall speak to the owner of this place and procure us lodging for the night."

"Have a care what you say. They could be Loyalists."

"I know I tend to say unfortunate things at the wrong time, but I will succeed in this. I promise." Caroline tied the boat off and helped Virginia climb onto the pier.

She passed the musket and supplies to Edward. "Hide these over there." She pointed to the nearest grove of lobloly pines. Before leaving the boat, she untied her apron and dipped it into the river so she could clean her face and hands.

Leaving the dirty apron in the boat, she stepped onto the pier. "There. How do I look?"

"Allow me." Virginia retied the ribbons that gathered Caroline's red curls behind each ear. "There. You look quite . . . presentable."

Charlotte gave her a dimpled smile. "Like a princess."

Having just returned from his task, Edward glowered at his sister. "Don't be silly. Princesses aren't covered with mud."

"Thank you, Edward. I needed that." Caroline faced the house and took a deep breath. She marched forward, squishing in her muddy shoes.

White columns supported the deep porch and second-floor balcony. Caroline ascended three brick steps and paused in front of a wide double door, flanked with narrow windows. She knocked. Nothing.

She knocked again. Was the place deserted?

Footsteps sounded on the other side of the door. A young woman peeked out the window, her face pale and frightened. Strands of lank brown hair had escaped her cap and dangled around her thin, narrow face. She turned away.

Caroline heard voices inside the house. Female voices. She glanced back. Virginia and the children had followed her and waited at the porch steps.

An older woman peered out the window. A lacy mobcap perched on her blond, gray-streaked hair. She smiled.

Caroline smiled back. So far, so good. She heard the scrape of a bolt. The young woman opened the door. Dressed in the plain clothes of a servant, she bobbed a curtsy, then stepped back so her mistress could greet them.

The older woman hesitated in the doorway. "Forgive us for taking so long, but one must be careful these days."

The scent of rose water and freshly laundered cotton presented Caroline with a painful reminder that she was in dire need of a bath. "I apologize for my appearance. 'Twas a difficult journey."

"I see. Still, you arrived sooner than I expected."

Caroline blinked. "I have?"

"Of course. I only received your letter last week. But never fear. All shall go according to plan."

Caroline opened her mouth to speak, but hardly knew what to say. "I . . . you're very kind."

"No, no. 'Twas kind of *you* to accept my proposal. I've waited so long for my son to marry. I'm quite convinced this is the only way to manage it."

"I beg your pardon?"

"Oh, you brought your family with you?" The woman peered around her.

"Ah, yes." Caroline turned slightly to make the introductions. "My sister, Virginia, and her children."

"How delightful! I adore little ones." The woman turned to the young servant. "Betsy, prepare all the guest beds, including the ones in the nursery."

The servant nodded and left.

The woman clasped her hands together. "This is wonderful. With a full house, we shall have a genuine wedding party."

"Wedding?" Virginia gave Caroline a worried look.

Caroline cleared her throat. "Is the groom here?"

"Matthias?" the woman asked. "No, I'm afraid not. The

last time I heard from him, he was with Gates's army north of here. But I hope he'll come home soon."

Caroline's chest tightened. This poor woman hadn't heard about Gates's defeat. Her son could be a prisoner or . . . he could have died in battle. *Just like Father.*

"You look sad." The woman's blue eyes clouded with worry. "Are you having second thoughts?"

Caroline blinked away tears. "I'm fine. I'm . . . greatly relieved to be here." She didn't know this woman, but she already felt a deep connection to her. They could both have their hearts shattered by this war.

The woman gave her a hopeful look. "Then you haven't changed your mind about marrying Matthias?"

Caroline had no idea who this Matthias was, but she seriously doubted he would be returning home anytime soon. If ever.

She glanced back at her sister and the children. The perfect solution had fallen into her lap. All it required was a lie. A horrible lie but a possible one, for there could never be a wedding without a groom.

Virginia frowned at her and shook her head.

"I'm not mistaken, am I?" the woman asked. "You are Agatha Ludlow?"

Food and clean beds for the children. A safe place for her sister to give birth. How could she refuse? Their survival depended on her.

With a weak smile, Caroline curtsied. "Yes, I am."

CHAPTER THREE

The woman took Caroline's hand in both of hers. "I'm delighted you're here. You'll make a lovely bride."

Caroline's smile wobbled.

"Ca—" Virginia covered her mouth and coughed. "Excuse me, ah, Agatha, *dear*." She gritted her teeth. "May I have a word with you?"

Caroline gave her sister a pointed look. "Later. After we've settled in."

Charlotte tugged on her mother's skirts. "Mama, may I change my name, too?"

With a nervous laugh, Virginia pulled her daughter close, smothering her face in her wide skirts.

"Bufflehead," Edward growled at his sister.

"Mind your manners." Virginia glared at her son.

With a sullen frown, Edward bowed to their hostess and muttered, "I am delighted to make your acquaintance, madam."

"Why, thank you, sir." Smiling, the woman motioned for them to enter. "Welcome to Loblolly Plantation. I'm Jane

Murray Thomas, but I hope the little ones will call me Aunt Jane."

Caroline strode into the entrance hall, relieved to have heard the woman's name. It would seem suspicious if she didn't know. Her shoes clunked with a resounding echo on the polished floor. Glancing back at the muddy trail she had made, she winced and slipped out of her shoes.

Virginia stopped beside her and introduced the children to Jane Thomas. "I believe they should retire for the evening. Is it possible for them to bathe and have a bite to eat first?"

"Of course. And you and Agatha will wish to bathe, also. I'll arrange for it at once." Jane hurried down the hall and out the back door.

The children wandered to the base of the stairs. Wide with elegantly carved balusters, the staircase curved gracefully up to the second floor.

"Godsookers," Edward whispered.

Virginia faced Caroline. "Have you lost your senses?"

"No. Under the circumstances, I believe I have taken the most sensible recourse available."

"Mrs. Thomas seems like a kind woman. If you had told her the truth, I doubt she would have turned us away."

"I didn't want to take the chance." Caroline lowered her voice. "I'm doing this for you, Ginny, and the children."

"I know. That's why I feel so guilty about it. And what if your so-called groom shows up?"

"I don't think he will. Mrs. Thomas said he was with Gates, and I happen to know that army was defeated."

"Oh, no." Virginia grimaced. "Are you sure?"

"The ferryman told me about it before he stole our horse."

Caroline hoped her sister wouldn't ask about Sumter and their father. She hated to add to Ginny's worries.

Virginia sighed. "I'm concerned how this ruse of yours will affect the children."

"They'll have food and clean beds."

"Yes." Virginia nodded. "I'm grateful for that, but they will have to lie, too."

Caroline winced. Once again, she'd blundered ahead without thinking everything through. "I'm sorry."

"'Tis done." Virginia walked toward the children. "Sweetings, we're going to play a game for a few days and call Caroline Aunt Agatha. Do you understand?"

They nodded.

Jane Thomas sauntered back into the hall. "My servants are heating water in the kitchen. 'Tis the only hearth that is lit during the hot months."

"Of course. We can bathe there if it is more convenient," Virginia offered.

"As you like," Jane answered. "We have a small room off the kitchen with a tub. Did you leave your trunks on the pier? I can have a servant fetch them for you."

"I'm afraid we have none," Caroline admitted. At least part of her story was true. "We were robbed on our way here."

"Gracious! You poor souls." Jane studied the children. "There are some old clothes in the nursery that belonged to my son. They might fit young Edward. And Matthias wore some simple gowns before his breeching that will suit Charlotte."

"That would be wonderful." Caroline strode toward the stairs. "I'll bring them. Where is the nursery?"

"The third floor. Look for an old trunk."

The *third* floor? Caroline had never stayed in such a grand house before. "I see."

"Come along." Jane motioned for Virginia and the children to follow her. "I'll show you to the kitchen."

Caroline ascended the stairs in her stocking feet. On the second floor she paused at the large open window that overlooked the back of the house and the garden below. Rectangular in shape, the garden was lined along its perimeter with thick hedges of Carolina jasmine and climbing roses.

She took a deep breath and let the sweet scent of roses fill her senses and calm her frayed nerves. How lovely it would be to rest on one of those stone benches, surrounded by blooming flowers. In the center of the garden, a small reflecting pool caught the rays of the setting sun and sparkled like diamonds.

So beautiful. A place untouched by war. The perfect place for her family. She'd made the right decision when she'd lied. And she'd keep telling herself that 'til she believed it.

Behind the garden, rows of trees formed an orchard. To the right, she spotted the kitchen garden. Mrs. Thomas was ushering Virginia and the children into a brick building next to it. The kitchen.

Guilt nagged at Caroline as she started up a narrow staircase to the third floor. She shouldn't have lied to Mrs. Thomas. The woman deserved better than that. It was surely a blessing from above that they had discovered a safe haven in the midst of war. So in turn, she would try to repay Mrs. Thomas by being a blessing to her and helping her any way she could.

The nursery consisted of two rooms, one for the children

and another she presumed for the nursemaid. She searched through several trunks, located some suitable clothes, then found her way to the kitchen.

After they had all bathed and supped, they took the children to the nursery to put them to bed. Virginia tucked Charlotte in and gave her a kiss. Edward had immediately fallen asleep.

"I cannot thank you enough, Mrs. Thomas," Caroline whispered.

"Please call me Jane. And I should thank you. It has been so long since there were children here." Her eyes shimmered with unshed tears. "Now if you and your sister are ready to retire, I'll show you to your room."

Virginia rubbed the small of her back. "If you don't mind, I'd prefer to stay in the adjoining room. My children might need me during the night. After all they've been through . . ."

Caroline couldn't help but admire her older sister. Even though Ginny had to be exhausted, she still worried about her children first. "Do you want me to stay here with you?"

Virginia hugged her. "No, I'll be fine. Sleep well."

"Good night, then." Jane smiled, then led Caroline down the stairs to the second floor. "There are four rooms on this floor, one in each corner. My husband and I use the two bed-chambers facing the front balcony."

"Is your husband here?" Caroline asked.

"No." Jane paused beside a door. "He was in Charles Town last spring, fighting the British. Now he's a prisoner."

"Oh, I'm sorry. I hope he'll return to you safely." Caroline cringed inside. What if Jane lost both her husband and her son?

"I think you'll be more comfortable in this room than the guest room. The bed is larger." Jane opened the door. "I hope you like it."

Caroline wandered into the bedchamber. Centered against the far wall was a large, four-poster bed. Mosquito netting cascaded from the ceiling to encircle the bed. "'Tis beautiful."

Jane smiled. "I'll fetch you a night shift."

"Thank you." Caroline ambled to the glass-paned doors and peered outside. A small balcony overlooked the back of the house. When she opened the doors, a breeze swept in, caressing her with floral scents from the garden below.

She breathed deeply. At last, a night of peaceful slumber.

"Boy, don't you come in my kitchen smelling like a swamp rat." Dottie wagged a plump finger at Matthias.

Ignoring her warning, Matthias strode inside and gave the old woman a hug.

"Shoo! You'll get me dirty." Although Dottie fussed, a wide grin spread across her brown-complexioned face. "Didn't I teach you better than that?"

"You're the best, Dottie. Do you have the medicine and bandages ready?"

"I see right through you. I always did." She planted her hands on her wide hips. "Buttering me up you are, just to get what you want."

He smiled. "I'm very grateful. My men wouldn't have healed so well without those concoctions of yours."

Her brown eyes danced with humor. "I make more than medicine, you know."

With a grimace, he waved his hands. "No special potions for me. Just some bread and stew, if you have it." He straddled a stool at her table.

She set a bowl of stew and loaf of bread in front of him. "I had a feeling you might come tonight."

"Hmm." He spooned hot stew into his mouth. "Do you have any ale?"

She placed a cup and pitcher of ale on the table. "You still haven't been to see your mother."

"I know." He gulped down the ale and poured some more. "I've been busy." After delivering more of Dottie's medicine to his men, he needed to resume his search for Major Munro's missing daughters.

Dottie sat across from him. "The Great House is only thirty yards from here. You should let your mother know you're alive."

"What?" Matthias ripped a piece of bread from the loaf. "You didn't tell her I was all right?"

"And hurt her feelings? How could I tell her you came to see an old slave woman and not your own mother?"

He frowned. "You know what happened the last time I went home."

It had been a year ago when the southern colonies had felt safe from the ravages of war. His mother had arranged a ball in his honor. Twenty-five young ladies she'd invited. And their conniving mothers. No men whatsoever. Matthias had felt like a sweetmeat on a silver platter, inspected and picked over by a pack of voracious females.

It wouldn't have been so bad if they had hungered for him personally. He'd never been one to object to a woman's charms. But he knew the truth. It was the grand house and the plantation he stood to inherit that whetted their appetites.

He sopped up the last of his stew with a hunk of bread. "I need to be going."

"You're seeing your mother tonight," Dottie announced. "And you're taking a bath before you do."

He popped the bread into his mouth. "I don't have time."

"You'll do it, or you won't get any medicine from me."

Matthias chewed his food slowly. "Since when did you become a tyrant?"

Dottie grinned and rose to her feet. "I'm already heating the water. I brought some of your clothes from the Great House and stashed them in the cupboard over there."

He glowered at her. "How did you know I was coming tonight?"

"I have my ways. Do you want more stew?"

He blinked at his empty bowl, slowly becoming aware of an odd, light-headed sensation. "You put something in it, didn't you?"

She cleared the table. "It was in the ale. A restorative. To bring joy back into your life."

He snorted. "Joy in the midst of war? I've seen more people die, buried more bodies than I care to remember. I appreciate your concern, Dottie, but 'twill take much more than a potion to bring me joy."

"You could be right." She regarded him with wise, old eyes. "And it might happen sooner than you think."

Washed, dressed in clean clothes, and his stomach full for the first time in months, Matthias had to admit he did feel better. As he strode through the flower garden in the moonlight, there was an extra spring to his step. And the blooming flowers in the garden seemed particularly fragrant. Comforting.

That was what he needed. A little comfort. How long had it been since he'd slept in a real bed? Months? A year? His men wouldn't begrudge him one night away from the swamp.

The back door wouldn't budge. His mother must have bolted it from the inside, something she never did before the war. He tried the servants' entrance, hidden behind a frame of latticework. Bolted, also.

So how was he supposed to see his mother if he couldn't get in? She'd probably bolted the front door, too.

Matthias gazed up the lattice to his balcony. As youngsters, he and his cousin had used the lattice to sneak out at night to go fishing. Of course the doors had not been bolted back then, but climbing down the lattice had seemed more exciting.

Matthias wasn't sure the lattice would now hold his weight, but with Dottie's restorative coursing through him, he felt eager to give it a jolly-good try. Halfway up, a thin board cracked beneath his shoe. He shifted his weight and found another foothold. The last thing he wanted was to slip and tear Dottie's stitches in his shoulder.

He swung his legs over the balcony railing and landed with a soft thud. *How odd.* His door was open. Of course, he reminded himself. Dottie had gone there to fetch his clothes. She must have opened the door to air out the room.

He slipped inside. Moonlight filtered into the room, glimmering off the white mosquito netting. He strolled over to his secretaire, then kicked off his shoes and dropped his breeches. When he draped his breeches on the back of the chair, he noticed something was already there, something thick. He ran his fingers over the folds of cotton. The scent of roses drifted up to his nose. His mother's perfume. Why would she leave one of her gowns in his room?

Odd. He pulled off his stockings. He'd talk to his mother in the morning. For now, he simply wanted to sink into a mattress and forget about the war.

He unwrapped his neck cloth, then removed his shirt and undergarments. How could he forget the war when he had so much to do? Ferryboats to burn. Supplies to capture. He untied the bow from his hair and dropped the thin leather thong on the desk. And those two missing females. Where the hell could they be?

He strode to the bed and slipped under the netting. With a sigh of contentment, he stretched out between the clean cotton sheets.

The bed shifted.

He blinked, staring at the ghostly netting overhead. He hadn't budged an inch. There was only one explanation.

Slowly, he turned his head and peered into the darkness beside him. The counterpane appeared lumpy as if— He listened carefully. Yes, soft breathing.

He sat up. A soft moan emanated from the form beside him. Female. His heart started to pound, his body reacting instinctively. Good God, it had been too long since he . . .

What the hell? He drew his racing libido to a screeching halt. This had to be another one of his mother's plots to force him to marry! Even Dottie was in on it. She had insisted he bathe and go to the Great House. Then they had locked up the house, so he would be forced to climb the lattice to his bedchamber. Straight into their trap.

He scrambled out of bed, batting at the mosquito netting that still covered him.

The female gasped and sat up. "Who's there?"

"Bloody hell," he muttered. His mother's scheme had worked perfectly. He was alone and naked with whomever she had chosen for his bride.

Another gasp and a rustling of sheets. The woman climbed out of bed. Damn! She would run straight to her witnesses to inform them that he'd bedded her.

"No!" He leapt across the bed and grabbed her. "You're not getting away." He hauled her squirming body back onto the bed. Her sudden intake of air warned him of her intent to scream.

He cupped a hand over her mouth. "Don't."

She clamped down with her teeth.

"Ow!" He ripped his hand from her mouth.

She slapped at his shoulders.

He winced as she pounded on his injury. "Enough." He seized her by the wrists and pinned her arms down. "No screaming. And no biting. Do you understand?"

Her breaths sounded quick and frightened.

He settled on top of her, applying just enough pressure to keep her from escaping. "I know what you're after. You think to trap me in wedlock so easily?"

"*What?*"

He could hardly see her pale face in the dark. His damp hair fell forward, further obstructing his view as he leaned closer. The scent of her soap surrounded him. Magnolia blossoms. His favorite, and Dottie knew it. This was a full-fledged conspiracy. "I assume you brought witnesses with you?"

"Witnesses?"

"Of course. Why would you want me in your bed if there's no one to see it?"

"My God, you're perverse."

"You're hoping I am, aren't you?" He stroked the inside of her wrist. "You're hoping I'll be tempted by your soft skin."

She shook her head and wiggled beneath him.

He gulped. She was definitely not wearing a corset beneath her shift. "You think I cannot resist a beautiful, womanly form?" Damn, but she *was* hard to resist.

"Get off of me," she hissed.

"I beg your pardon? That's hardly the language of a seductress. Didn't they coach you better than that?"

"Damn you, release me."

He chuckled. "You're supposed to coo in my ear, not curse me. Come now, let me hear your pretty little speech. Tell me how much you want me. Tell me how you're burning to make love to me."

"I'd rather burn in hell, you demented buffoon."

He paused, wondering for the first time if he had misinterpreted the situation. "You're . . . not here to seduce me?"

"Of course not. Why would I have any interest in a demented buffoon?"

He gritted his teeth. "Then who are you and why are you in this bed?"

"I was in bed to sleep, which would be obvious if you weren't such a demented—"

"Enough! Who are you?"

She paused.

"Is the question too difficult?"

She huffed. "I . . . I'm Agatha Ludlow."

He reeled back. Agatha Ludlow? He'd rather share a bed with a swamp snake.

"Who are you?" she asked. "Are you Mrs. Thomas's son?"

He bolted out of bed, flung aside the mosquito netting, and grabbed his breeches. "No, I'm not." Hopefully Agatha wouldn't know who he was, and he could escape. He stuffed his legs in the breeches and fumbled with the buttons.

"You're not Matthias?"

"No, I'm a . . . a servant. Absolutely penniless." He pulled on his shirt.

"Then why are you here? I'm fairly certain this is not a servant's bedchamber."

She had him there. "I was late returning, and . . . Why are you in Matthias's bed?"

"I didn't realize I was." She heaved a sigh. "Thank God you're not him."

She was relieved? That didn't sound right. Agatha Ludlow would jump at a chance to trap him in marriage. He gathered up his stockings and shoes. "I apologize for frightening you. Good evening, mistress."

He strode to his mother's room to inform her that her latest scheme had failed.

CHAPTER FOUR

"Mother, you put a woman in my bed."

With a gasp, his mother sat up in bed. Her book tumbled onto the floor. "Matthias, is that you?"

"Yes." He closed her bedchamber door. One lit candle illuminated the area around his mother's bed, but the rest of the room lay in shadow.

"Matthias! You're alive!" Jane scrambled out of bed and ran toward him. "I was so worried."

"I'm fine." He embraced her. "I've been hiding in the swamp from the British. Any news from Father?"

"No, I'm afraid not." She skimmed her fingers over his face. "It is really you. Thank God."

"Why would you lay a trap for me in my own—"

"You're hiding in the swamp?" Jane regarded him with a worried look. "Why? What happened to the army?"

"We lost at Camden." When his mother gasped, he continued, "You didn't know?"

"No. Oh, dear." She stepped back, clenching her hands together. "This is terrible."

"Yes. Speaking of terrible, there's a—"

"Are you truly all right? You weren't injured in any way?"

"A bullet grazed my shoulder, but Dottie sewed it up, and 'tis much better now."

Jane's eyes widened. "You've been home before?"

"Well, yes. I was in pain, and Dottie helped—"

"You didn't come see me?" Jane lifted a hand to swat his shoulder, then stopped herself. "How could you? Don't you know how much I worry about you?"

"I'm sorry, but I was afraid you would host another ball, where a horde of grasping young ladies and their greedy mothers swarm the house like a plague of locusts."

"Don't be ridiculous. I couldn't have a ball in the midst of a war." She waved a dismissive hand. "I would have arranged a smaller, more intimate gathering."

"Exactly. You never cease with the matchmaking."

"I would gladly cease if you would just marry."

He snorted. "This latest scheme of yours is beyond my patience. Planting a woman in my bed—"

"You went to bed?"

"Yes. And if you think to force me into marriage, let me assure you that nothing happened."

"Oh, dear." Jane clutched her hands together. "That poor girl."

He scoffed. The poor girl sported some vicious teeth. "I cannot, for the life of me, fathom why you continue with these plots of yours. *You* were forced into an arranged marriage and have been miserable every day of it. Why would you wish me to suffer the same?"

"I want you to be happy."

"Then let me choose my own wife!" He took a deep breath and shoved his hair back from his face.

With a sigh, Jane perched on the edge of her bed. "I fear you will never marry."

"Not as long as the war continues, no."

Her shoulders slumped. "I want grandchildren. A house full of them. Do you have any idea how awful it has been for me? Three babies I buried. Three."

"I'm sorry." Matthias didn't need reminding that he was the only child to survive. He'd heard it all his life. The future of Loblolly Plantation would rest entirely on him. At the age of ten, he'd been escorted to his grandfather's deathbed, and there, his grandfather had insisted Matthias swear a sacred oath to protect and nurture Loblolly.

He'd felt trapped ever since.

His mother heaved a dramatic sigh. "I've waited so long for you to be old enough to have children of your own."

He sat on the end of the bed. "One thing I have learned as a soldier is that timing is everything. This is *not* the right time. I have buried children. I will not father any until this war is over."

"But they would be safe here. The war hasn't touched us here."

"No place is safe." He gritted his teeth. "Even my bedchamber boasts a hotbed of deadly peril at the moment."

"You exaggerate, surely."

"I have the teeth marks to prove it."

Jane gasped. "She bit you?"

"Aye. I can only pray the wench is not rabid."

"Don't be ridiculous. She must have been frightened out

of her wits, poor child. You—you didn't take liberties with her?"

"No! Nothing happened. Besides, I apologized."

"Oh, dear." Jane slanted him a suspicious look.

He scowled back with indignation. *He* was the victim tonight. "How could you, Mother? Of all people, Agatha Ludlow? How low can you go?"

"I thought you liked her. You said so after the ball."

"I said she was the only one I could tolerate, and only because she's honest about her ambitions. The others simpered and pretended to be enthralled by me. Agatha is blatant when it comes to greed. She wants wealth and will do whatever it takes to get it."

"Gracious, she didn't strike me that way. She seemed very kindhearted."

He scoffed. So kindhearted that she had repeatedly called him a demented buffoon. "Why is she here?"

"I invited her."

"And put her in *my* bed?"

His mother lifted a hand to rub her brow. "I didn't know you would come tonight. Believe me, I expect you to wed a woman before bedding her."

"There will be no wedding or bedding."

Jane leaned toward him, touching his arm. "If you would just stay a few days, you might like her. She seemed very sweet to me. And the children are so precious."

"What children?"

"Her sister brought her children. They're in the nursery."

While Jane described each child in minute detail, Matthias searched his memory. As far as he could recall, Agatha

Ludlow had no sister. The only daughter of a Charles Town merchant, she was spoiled and vicious. She also had a rather thin, nasal voice. The woman in his bed had possessed a gentle, melodious voice, in spite of the disparaging words that had passed from her luscious pink lips.

He stiffened. Agatha Ludlow had a mouth like a dried-up prune. And if Agatha had suspected who he was, she would have welcomed him with open arms.

"I'm sure if you had children," Jane continued, "they would be just as adorable as Edward and Charlotte."

"Mother, Agatha Ludlow doesn't have a sister."

"Of course she does. They look so similar. They must be sisters."

"I'm saying this woman cannot *be* Agatha Ludlow."

"Ridiculous. Why would she lie?"

He shoved his hair behind his ears. "Does she look like Agatha?"

Jane shrugged and gazed across the room. "She's very pretty. I'm sure you'll approve."

Was his mother avoiding eye contact? What was she up to? "What did you tell this alleged Agatha?"

"That I hoped you two would marry."

"Bloody hell." He stood and paced across the room. "Whoever this woman is, she wants the plantation."

Jane rose to her feet. "Why do you say that? You're a handsome man. A woman could easily love you for yourself."

"Women like Agatha don't even see me. They cannot see past this house and all the beautiful gowns and jewelry you own."

Jane frowned. "I wish you would at least give her a chance."

"I have no time for it. I leave at dawn."

"So quickly?"

"Yes. Good night, Mother. I'll come again in a few days."
He kissed her cheek and left the room.

On the second-floor landing he paused outside his bedchamber door. Was the woman inside Agatha Ludlow or an
imposter? Should he barge inside and confront her?

No, not at night when she was barely dressed. Besides, he
would easily recognize Agatha in daylight. All he had to do
was remain here until morning.

But if she were a stranger and he met her as the heir to
the plantation, would she tell everyone he had attacked her in
bed? Better to play it safe as the penniless servant.

He ascended the stairs to the third floor. The servant
quarters were there, and he'd be able to find the appropriate
clothing and an unoccupied bed to sleep in.

If the young lady was Agatha, she would recognize him at
once. But if he was right about her being a fraud, he wouldn't
have to say a word. Her failure to recognize him would be as
good as a confession. Yes, by morning, the mysterious woman
would be exposed and sent packing.

Caroline opened her eyes the next morning to see someone
peering down at her. "Oh, Edward, you startled me."

"What are you doing in Charlotte's bed?" he asked.

"I came up here to sleep with your mother." Caroline sat
up in the narrow bed. "But Charlotte was already in bed with
her."

"She joined me early in the evening," Virginia explained as

she brushed four-year-old Charlotte's hair. "What happened? Were you lonesome down there all by yourself?"

"Not exactly."

"Perhaps she had a bad dream," Charlotte suggested.

"More of a nightmare," Caroline muttered.

"Tell us about it," Edward bounced onto the bottom of her bed with an excited expression. "Was there a horrid monster?"

"You could say that." Caroline climbed out of bed. "You're sitting on my gown, Edward." She had grabbed her clothes and vacated the bedchamber immediately after her mysterious visitor had disappeared. The nursery had seemed the safest place to go.

Caroline and her family dressed and descended the stairs in search of breakfast. They peeked into the rooms overlooking the front porch. One was a large parlor; the other, a library. They located the dining room at the back of the house, behind the library. It boasted a long table that would seat twelve. A large silver epergne rested on top, reflected on the polished surface.

"Godsookers," Edward whispered. "Are we eating in here?"

"Wherever we eat, you two mind your manners," Virginia whispered to the children. "And don't wolf down your food like last night."

"We were hungry," Edward spoke in their defense.

Virginia smiled. "I know, sweeting. You've both been wonderfully brave. I'm very proud of you."

"Ah, there you are," Jane called to them from across the hall. "Come this way. I thought the morning parlor would be more cozy."

They filed into a smaller room. Its windows gave a cheerful view of the garden. An upholstered settee rested between two windows. A sideboard and armchairs lined another wall. In the center of the room, a round table was surrounded by five chairs.

Betsy was setting the table.

"I cannot tell you how happy I am to have company." Jane smiled at them, then turned to the servant. "Betsy, you may bring the food now."

The young woman nodded and passed by them, her eyes downcast.

"Good morning, Betsy," Caroline whispered.

Betsy glanced at her, then hurried from the room.

"Come and sit." Jane took a seat at the table.

Virginia sat to her left. "Thank you for loaning us these gowns. 'Tis fortunate you kept your lying-in clothes, or I fear I would be dressed in a bedsheet."

"I'm delighted to see them put to use after all these years." Jane motioned for Edward to sit at her right. "But it was such a shame you were robbed."

"I threw a stick at him, the scurvy bas—" Edward noticed his mother's piercing glare. "Uh, bufflehead."

Caroline sat next to Edward so she could kick him if needed. It would be difficult, she realized, for the children to maintain her falsehood. Too many lies would confuse them, so the truth should be told whenever possible. Besides, Jane didn't appear to know Agatha Ludlow very well. She certainly didn't know what the woman looked like.

"We didn't lose a great deal to the thief," Caroline explained. "Most of our belongings were already lost. The British set fire to our house. In fact, as far as we could tell, they were burning all the homes along the Pee Dee River."

Jane shook her head, frowning. "How dreadful."

"They burned our house in Charles Town, too," Edward said.

Jane touched his shoulder. "I'm so sorry."

Caroline unfolded her napkin. "We decided the best course of action was to flee."

Charlotte, seated between her mother and aunt, frowned at Caroline. "I don't want any fleas."

Edward made a face at her.

Jane smiled. "Of course not, dear."

Betsy entered with a large covered platter in her hands. She set it on the sideboard and slowly approached Jane.

"Where is the coffee?" Jane asked.

"Begging your pardon, ma'am, but the coffee is coming." Betsy shoved a strand of brown hair back from her face and glanced nervously toward the door. "The . . . the butler is bringing it."

Jane sat back. "Butler? But we haven't had a butler since—"

"Haversham," Betsy interrupted. "'Tis Haversham, ma'am. He's back."

Jane's eyes widened. "From the dead?"

A tall man strode into the room bearing a tray with a silver coffee service. "I'm feeling much better, thank you."

Jane gasped. Her hand fluttered at her throat. "Good Lord, what are you doing?"

"Serving you as always, madam." He set the tray on the sideboard with a clunk.

Caroline wondered why Jane was so obviously agitated with the manservant. All she could see was his back, a straight back with broad shoulders. A white wig on his head made it difficult to estimate his age, but his bearing and determined stride suggested a young man. A very healthy young man.

Jane pressed her hand to her chest. "This is outrageous."

"I agree, madam." The butler advanced toward the table, the silver coffeepot clutched in his hand. "I was not informed that we have guests."

Not too young, Caroline thought. Close to thirty years, and not privileged ones at that. He had the tanned, stern features of a man who had dealt with hardship and survived. A strong man with a keen intelligence. She wasn't sure how she knew that, but she did. For some reason, all her senses had suddenly gone on alert. And her heart was thudding in her chest.

The butler's gaze circled the table and stopped briefly at Virginia. He tilted his head, apparently noticing her state of pregnancy. Immediately, he focused on Caroline.

It was more than a simple look; it was an examination.

She lowered her gaze to her hands as her heart pounded. Why would he stare? Unless . . .

Could he be her assailant from last night? A penniless servant, the man had said. But this man was far from weak and humble. On the contrary, he exuded power and confidence.

She ventured a peek. His uniform of pewter-blue velvet fit snugly. Too snugly. Long legs, strong thighs, trim waist. If memory served her correctly, the man last night had possessed similar attributes. Heat rushed to her face as she recalled the way he had pinned her beneath his body. His naked body.

She lifted her gaze to the butler's hands. It seemed odd for a manservant not to wear gloves. She noted his firm grip on the coffeepot. Was it the same hand that had circled her wrist and stroked her skin?

Her gaze drifted past his broad shoulders to his face.

He slowly smiled.

He knows. Her cheeks blazed and she looked away. What should she do? Tell Jane that her butler accosted women in the middle of the night?

"Are you planning to serve that coffee today?" Jane glared at him.

"Yes, madam, forgive me." He filled her cup before moving on to Edward to fill his.

Edward, unaccustomed to coffee, gave his mother a questioning look.

Caroline gripped her hands together, determined not to show any reaction when he approached her. She stared at the pink rosebuds on her china cup as he poured coffee into it. Surely he was standing closer than necessary. Her gaze drifted to his hand.

Teeth marks, clear and red. She stiffened with a gasp. Good Lord, she'd really sunk her teeth into him.

"Is something wrong?" He had completed his task, but remained standing close to her.

"No." Caroline turned away, determined to ignore him.

"Miss Agatha Ludlow, I presume?"

"Yes."

"Interesting." He eased around her, too closely, and tilted the coffeepot over Charlotte's cup.

"My daughter doesn't drink coffee," Virginia said.

"Oh. Of course." The butler moved on to fill Virginia's cup.

"Haversham." Jane observed him with a disapproving frown. "May I have a word with you in private?"

"Later. I must attend to my duties first."

"I don't like my name anymore," Charlotte announced. "Can I change it, Mama?"

With a wince, Virginia exchanged a frustrated look with Caroline.

Jane smiled at the little girl. "What name did you have in mind, my dear?"

Charlotte wrapped a glossy black curl around her finger while she considered, then perked up with a dimpled smile. "I want to be Princess of the World."

Edward snorted. "There's no such thing, you bufflehead."

"You will apologize at once." The butler's voice was low, but commanding.

Edward's mouth dropped open.

Haversham regarded the young boy with a grim expression. "A man does not insult a lady in such a fashion."

"She's not a lady. She's my sister."

Haversham cocked an eyebrow.

Edward gulped. "I . . . I apologize."

Without a word, Haversham swiveled and returned to the sideboard.

Caroline marveled at the butler's effect on Edward. It hadn't occurred to her 'til now that with Ginny's husband gone, Edward would be in need of male guidance.

And the butler was certainly male. Very male. She had pounded on those broad shoulders, felt his bare skin hot against her hands. She dragged her gaze off his strong back and vowed once again to ignore him. After all, the rascal attacked women in their beds. He was the last man on earth who should be lecturing Edward on how to treat a lady.

"I think Charlotte is a lovely name," Jane said.

"I used to like it," Charlotte explained. "I was named after Charles Town because I was born there. But I don't like it now because the bad British men came and burned our house."

"I see." Jane nodded. "Don't worry, dear. We'll chase them away soon enough."

Sugar bowl in hand, Haversham approached the table. He strode straight to Caroline and set the bowl beside her. "Sugar," he whispered.

His voice tickled the back of her neck. She refused to acknowledge him and spooned sugar into her coffee. Then she passed it on to Edward.

Haversham returned to the sideboard.

"All the ladies in my family are named after the place they were born," Charlotte continued. "My mother was born in the conoly . . . colony of Virginia."

Caroline winced and nudged Charlotte with her foot.

Her niece looked at her. "Didn't I say it right?"

Haversham paced straight toward her, a creamer in his hand. "And where, pray tell, is the colony of Agatha?"

Caroline lifted her chin. "There is a small town that bears the name."

"Indeed?" He stopped next to her.

"The town is in a very remote place. No one's ever heard of it."

He remained standing there, close to her elbow. She considered elbowing him firmly in the groin, but decided not to give his body parts further thought. He leaned over and set the creamer beside her plate.

She dared a glimpse at his face.

He appeared to be focused on the low-cut bodice of her gown. Her cheeks heated up. The scoundrel! She should have elbowed him.

His eyes met hers. "Cream," he whispered.

She sucked in a breath between clenched teeth. *Blast the man!* How could his eyes be such an angelic shade of blue when he was clearly far from innocent?

Jane cleared her throat. "Haversham, will you get on with it, please?"

"Yes, madam." He returned to the sideboard.

Betsy removed the cover from the tray she had brought in. Steam rose from a heap of scrambled eggs and bacon.

"I'll take it." Haversham plunked a serving spoon on top of the food and brought the tray to the table.

He set it next to Jane.

She gave him a wry look. "How do you explain your remarkable recovery, Haversham? I could have sworn you were ready for the grave."

"A restorative, madam, from Miss Dottie." He spooned eggs onto her plate.

Standing at the sideboard, Betsy smothered a giggle with her hand.

"Really?" Jane asked. "It must have been very powerful."

"Indeed. I daresay I feel like a new man." Haversham hesitated with the spoon poised over the bacon. He set the spoon down, grasped some bacon in his hand, and tossed the slices onto Jane's plate.

Charlotte giggled, then stopped when her mother gave her an ominous look.

Jane heaved a resigned sigh.

The butler picked up the tray and proceeded to a smiling Edward.

"Godsookers." Edward peered at the man's hand. "Did something bite you?"

Caroline sank deeper into her chair. Would they notice if she completed her meal under the table?

Using the spoon, Haversham piled eggs onto Edward's plate. "I was attacked last night by a wild creature."

Edward's eyes widened. "What kind of creature?"

The butler tossed bacon onto the boy's plate. "A vixen, the red-haired variety."

Caroline eased her fingers around her fork.

"What's a vixen?" Charlotte asked.

"A female fox," Edward answered. "How could you tell it was female?"

With the hint of a smile, Haversham brought the tray to Caroline. "She wiggled like a female. In all the right places."

She raised the fork in her clenched fist and gave him a look of warning.

The glint of amusement in his eyes told her he was unaffected by her threat. He spooned eggs onto her plate.

"Oh, I love foxes," Charlotte announced. "I like their bushy red tails."

His mouth twitched. "Indeed."

Caroline aimed close to his hand and stabbed a slice of bacon with her fork. He didn't flinch, blast him. "As for myself, I can hardly sleep at night for fear of being rudely awakened and attacked by a loathsome pest."

Haversham dropped two more slices of bacon onto her plate. "How about a lovable pest?"

She gave him an icy glare. "I could never consider an annoying bedbug to be lovable."

"Then you should try a man."

Her mind went blank. Unable to think of a reply, she realized she was even finding it difficult to breathe. His blue eyes remained steadfastly focused on her face.

Jane's voice sounded strained. "That is enough, Haversham."

"Yes, madam." He moved on to Charlotte and ladled eggs onto her plate.

"I don't like eggs very much," Charlotte mumbled.

He placed bacon on her plate. "Breakfast is good for you, Princess of the World."

With a giggle, Charlotte grabbed her fork and dug into the eggs.

Virginia smiled at her daughter, then glanced at Caroline with a questioning look.

Caroline knew her sister was wondering about her behavior with the butler. She'd have to explain later. If she could. Meanwhile, Haversham heaped eggs onto her sister's plate.

"Oh, I'm sorry," Virginia said, grimacing at the huge pile of eggs before her. "I meant to tell you. I'm unable to eat eggs in my condition. They don't agree with me. But I'll have some bacon, if you don't mind."

Haversham paused as if uncertain what to do. Then he picked up Virginia's plate and dumped the eggs back on the tray.

The children giggled.

Jane rubbed her forehead. "That is enough, Haversham. You and Betsy may leave us now."

Frowning, he deposited bacon strips on Virginia's plate. Without a word he pivoted and left the room. Betsy grabbed the tray's cover and darted after him.

After a few bites, Jane scraped back her chair and stood. "Please continue without me. I have a matter I must attend to." She exited the room.

"I think she's mad at the butler," Charlotte whispered.

"Do you think she'll give him the sack?" Edward asked.

"I hope not." Charlotte munched on a piece of bacon. "I like him."

Caroline pushed her eggs around the plate. "He's a demented buffoon."

Virginia leaned toward her. "Is there something going on between you and him?"

"No. I have no interest in him whatsoever."

Frowning, Virginia picked up a slice of bacon. "You seem to be forming a bad habit of late."

Caroline reached for her coffee cup. "What habit would that be?"

"Lying."

The cup slipped in her hand, splashing coffee onto the pink rosebuds of the matching saucer.

CHAPTER FIVE

"What on earth are you doing, Matthias?"

"Eating breakfast." He stuffed the serving spoon, full of eggs, in his mouth.

"I don't mean *now*." His mother stood in the kitchen doorway, glaring at him. "I mean that ridiculous charade of yours in the parlor. Whatever possessed you?"

"Must have been the ghost of Haversham." He pointed the spoon at the breakfast tray. "Betsy, do you want any of this?"

She shook her head. "I already ate."

Dottie chuckled as she scrubbed a pot. Matthias spooned more eggs into his mouth.

His mother strode into the kitchen. "I expect an explanation."

He nodded as he chewed.

With a sigh, his mother removed his white wig. "You make a terrible butler."

"Hmm? I served the food, didn't I?"

"You were arrogant and insolent."

He shrugged. "Positive traits for a butler."

"You insulted my guests."

"They deserve to be insulted. They're liars."

She dropped his wig onto the table next to the breakfast tray. "You're the one lying, Matthias. Pretending to be Haversham, of all people. A sham, indeed."

"It was the only uniform that fit." He brushed off a velvet sleeve. "I thought I carried it off very well. What do you think, Betsy?"

She exchanged a grin with Dottie.

His mother's wry expression made it clear she disagreed. "I thought you were leaving at dawn. Why are you still here?"

He bit off a piece of bacon. "Has my welcome run out so soon? I'm devastated."

"You would be most welcome if you behaved yourself."

"Don't worry. I'll slink back into the swamp as soon as I finish eating. But before I go, let me tell you about the redheaded vixen in there with the sharp little teeth."

"I don't want to hear it." Jane waved a hand in dismissal and headed back to the door. "She's been through enough hardship. Someone robbed them on the way here. And the poor girl must have suffered a terrible fright last night when you—you—whatever you did to her."

"I did *nothing*! Nothing happened."

Jane paused at the door. "Then why did she feel the need to bite you? That is hardly the ideal beginning of a courtship."

"I'm not courting that fiery little hellcat!"

"I say you are. I like her." Jane stepped outside.

"How can you like her?" Matt grabbed another slice of bacon and paced after his mother. "She's a liar."

"She's a pretty, intelligent, well mannered—"

"Liar," he repeated. "She is *not* Agatha Ludlow."

"Fine." His mother swiveled to face him. "You didn't want Agatha anyway. Perhaps this one will suit you."

"You would saddle me with a deceitful wife?"

"She's trying to protect her family. She's willing to do anything for them, even if the price is a betrothal to a total stranger. I believe her ability to love that deeply makes her an excellent choice for a wife."

He blinked with a sudden realization and pointed his bacon strip at her. "You're not surprised, are you? You knew all along she wasn't Agatha?"

Jane shrugged. "I suspected."

"Why didn't you demand the truth?"

"She's a guest. It would be rude to ask if she were lying."

He laughed. "So you plan to let her manipulate you?"

His mother frowned at him. "I do not feel manipulated, Matthias. Not when I know the truth."

"You don't know who she is."

"I don't care. I'm enjoying their company. I've been alone here for six months." Jane narrowed her eyes. "Do you understand how lonely I am?"

"I'm beginning to. I'm sorry."

"I'm sure she'll tell me the truth once she learns to trust me. She's not a very good liar."

He snorted and muttered, "She's one hell of a biter."

"That would be a desirable quality in a wife, don't you think?"

"Sharp teeth?"

"No! Pay attention." His mother swatted his arm. "It would behoove you to have a wife who is a poor liar."

"Well, I think I'd rather have one who didn't lie at all." He jammed the rest of the bacon in his mouth.

Jane smiled. "You couldn't take your eyes off of her."

"I had to look at her to make sure she wasn't Agatha."

"Ah. Are they similar in appearance?"

"No. Agatha's somewhat pretty, but this one—" He stopped himself when he noticed the gleam in his mother's eye. "I've seen possums that are more appealing."

She swatted him again. "I expect you to be cordial to her."

"I won't be here. I have business to take care of."

His mother sighed, then stood on tiptoe to kiss his cheek. "Very well, Matthias. Be careful, please."

"I will."

"And one more thing, Haversham." She headed back to the Great House.

"Yes?"

She glanced back with a smile. "You're dismissed."

Matthias eased his horse into the shallow river. Midstream, the water rose to his knees. He didn't mind wet stockings. It helped to keep him cool. The summer had been long and steamy, and the arrival of September had done little to ease the heat.

As he approached Snow's Island, the sun glinted off something metallic in the swamp holly. A musket. The sentries were charged with the task of keeping the hideout a secret.

He raised a hand and shouted the agreed upon phrase to identify himself. "How do you catch an alligator?"

Young Simon stood and delivered the response. "Use a lobsterback for bait."

Matthias urged his horse up onto the bank. "How is everything?"

"Quiet, sir." Simon held the bridle as Matthias dismounted.

"Matt!" Richard strode toward them. "What happened? We expected you back last night."

Matthias smiled in spite of the guilt he always felt at seeing the red scar on his cousin's face. "I went home for more supplies from Dottie. And I saw my mother."

"I should have gone with you. How is Aunt Jane?" Richard was especially fond of Matthias's mother. She had invited him as a youngster to live at Loblolly during the winter months. There, he had shared the nursery and private tutor with Matthias.

"She's fine. She's . . . entertaining some guests." Matthias lifted his shoulder bag over his head. "I brought medical supplies and loaves of bread. Can you pass them out, Simon?"

"Yes, sir." Simon accepted the bag with a shy smile. "And I'll feed your horse, sir."

"Thank you. Tell the men that as soon as they're done eating, we ride." Matthias watched the boy walk toward camp, leading the horse by the reins.

Richard lowered his voice. "You realize, don't you, that you're the boy's hero?"

Matthias winced. "Has he mentioned anything yet about his family?"

"No, not a word." Richard took a deep breath. "What are the plans for today?"

"We'll break into small teams. I want every ferryboat along the Lynches and Black rivers burned. And all the bridges except for the one at Kingstree. We'll blacken it a bit, so it will look like we meant to destroy it but somehow failed."

"Why?"

"'Twill be the only way across the river. The British will be forced to use it to move their supplies. And we'll be ready for them."

Richard frowned. "An ambush? Do we have enough men?"

"There's only one way to find out." Matthias pushed his tricorne back from his brow and wiped his forehead with his sleeve. "Hopefully, a few more volunteers will show up."

"Oh, that reminds me." Richard removed a letter from between his shirt and waistcoat. "This arrived while you were gone. News from North Carolina. One of the redcoat prisoners from Nelson's Ferry escaped."

The memory of that morning weighed heavily on Matt's mind. As a victory, it should have evoked feelings of pride. But instead, he felt guilt. Their escape had caused so many families along the Pee Dee River to lose their homes when the redcoats had retaliated. And the knife he'd used to kill the freckle-faced guard was still wedged beneath his belt. Greville's knife.

"Marion is rebuilding the army," Richard continued. "He plans to return here in a few weeks."

"That's good." Matthias unfolded the letter. No doubt, the redheaded major would be returning and wanting to know about his daughters, Virginia Stanton and—

"Damn!" He crushed the letter in his hand. *Virginia*. The little girl had said her mother was born in Virginia and that they bore the names of their birthplace.

"What?" Richard snatched the letter back. "It seemed like good news to me."

"*Virginia*. I should have known." It was right there in front of him, and he had missed it. Two homeless women. Both with red hair like their father. The woman on the Pee Dee River had said Virginia was expecting her third child. How could he have been so blind?

Richard scanned the letter. "I don't see anything about Virginia here."

"Not the colony. The woman! Bloody hell, why didn't I see it?" Matthias gritted his teeth. He knew damned well why he'd missed the clues. He'd been too occupied ogling and tormenting the false Agatha to see the obvious.

All he had seen were her emerald-green eyes that switched from ice to fire so fast a man could be burned if he wasn't careful. And he'd had an insane desire to play with fire.

She had smelled like magnolia blossoms. He'd wanted to stick his nose in her fragrant curls and feel them soft upon his face. Too much exposure to the sun had given her a youthful appearance with a few freckles across her nose, but one look at the rest of her and there was no doubt of her maturity. Her skin looked soft as cream. Delicious—

Richard's laugh interrupted his thoughts. "A woman? Has the mighty Matthias finally fallen?"

"No! Not to that conniving little she-demon." The father had said they could take care of themselves. They sure the hell could. A week after losing their home on the Pee Dee, they were on the Black River, living in luxury and spinning their lies to deceive his mother. And all this time, he'd feared the worst for the poor innocent women. Innocent, ha! "I'll wring her neck. I'll go back tonight and . . ." Would she be in his bed again?

"And what? You would never hurt a woman and you know it."

"She's not a woman. She's a vixen with sharp little teeth."

Richard chuckled. "Her name is Virginia?"

"No. Virginia is the sister." Matthias took a deep breath to calm his racing pulse. "I should confirm my suspicions before contacting Major Munro, but I believe I have found his daughters."

"Really? Where are they?"

Matthias smiled at the memory of the vixen's warm body beneath his in bed. "They're safe . . . for now. Until I have a little chat with one of them tonight."

"Virginia?"

"No. Her name is Caroline. Caroline Munro."

CHAPTER SIX

Caroline admired the crocheted edging on the pillowcase. "'Tis lovely. I've rarely seen such a fine set of childbed linen."

Jane rummaged through the trunk. "I haven't looked at these in years. After I lost my third child, I couldn't bear it."

"I'm so sorry." Caroline folded the pillowcase. "Perhaps we should put them away."

"No. I've hidden them here long enough." Jane looked about the nursery. "I wanted to fill this room with children." Her gaze rested on Charlotte. "God works in mysterious ways."

"Indeed. You're a godsend to us." Caroline returned the pillowcase to the trunk.

Virginia eased onto Edward's bed. "I'm so sorry for the ones you lost, Jane. I cannot imagine carrying one full-term and then losing it." She smoothed a hand over her belly, and her eyes glimmered with tears. "I've been fearful for this one."

"You'll be fine." Jane perched on the bed beside Virginia. "And so will the child."

"Godsookers!" Edward skipped toward them with a tin box in his hands. "Look what I found. There must be a hundred of them."

"Oh, gracious." Jane picked up one of the pewter soldiers from the box. "I'd forgotten about these. Matthias and his cousin loved playing with them."

"May I play with them?" Edward asked.

"Of course." Jane placed the soldier back in the box.

"Come, Charlotte." Edward dumped the soldiers on the floor.

Jane leaned over and pulled another item from the trunk. "Ah, I remember this one. A white bed gown of silk damask." She passed it on to Virginia.

Virginia fingered the expensive lace. "These should remain in the family. I don't feel right about using them."

"Nonsense." Jane waved a hand in the air. "You *are* family. Your sister . . . Agatha has agreed to marry my son."

Caroline attempted a smile.

Virginia bit her bottom lip. "What if . . . Agatha and Matthias do not suit each other?"

Smiling, Jane selected another item from the trunk. "I believe they will do quite nicely together."

Caroline groaned inwardly. What if this Matthias suddenly returned home? And worse, what if he liked her?

At the age of twenty-six, she'd accustomed herself to the prospect of remaining a spinster. Finding a suitable man was difficult in these times. All the strong and healthy young men had volunteered for the army. And many, like Roger, never returned. The familiar twinge of guilt pricked at her once more. *Forgive me, Roger, for sending you to your death.*

Charlotte stamped a foot, jolting Caroline from her thoughts. "I don't want to be the British. The British are bad."

Edward stretched out on the floor, lining up a row of soldiers. "You have to be the British. I'm going to be the Continental Army."

"I hate the British!" Charlotte screamed. "They want to kill Papa!" She crumbled onto the floor, crying.

With a gasp, Virginia struggled to get off the bed.

"I'll get her." Caroline ran to her niece and gathered her up in her arms. "Shh, sweeting. Your papa is fine."

Edward rose to his knees. "I'm sorry, Charlotte. I'll be the British and let you beat me really bad."

"I don't want to play war," Charlotte cried.

"Of course not." Caroline hugged her tight. "Edward, put the soldiers away."

"All right." He gathered up a handful and dropped them into the tin box with a noisy clatter. "You know Papa is all right, Charlotte. You said he would always be all right as long as you had the book he gave you."

Charlotte sniffed. "You told me that was nonsense."

"I was wrong." Edward dumped the rest of the soldiers in the box. "I believe it."

"So do I." Virginia reclined against the pillows and closed her eyes. "I've always believed that if something happened to Quincy, I would know. Somehow I would feel it."

Caroline's heart ached for her sister. They had been visiting Aunt Mary in Boston when Ginny had fallen in love with the dashing sea captain, Quincy Stanton. Caroline knew firsthand how much Ginny adored her husband. How did she survive each day not knowing how he fared?

It was just as bad for their mother in North Carolina. Mama fretted over both her husband and her son. Fergus had gone over the mountains to join the frontier militia, and they'd received no news from him in months. Caroline could only pray that her brother was still alive. And her brother-in-law. And her father. She also prayed that her niece and nephew would survive without being physically or emotionally damaged for life.

That was more than enough anxiety to live with each day. She would not add to it and suffer like her mother and sister, constantly worrying that their beloved husbands could be dead. She'd learned that lesson too painfully with her fiancé, Roger. Never again would she love a man who was involved in the war.

If only there was someone safe to love. Someone who wouldn't put on a uniform, line up before the British, and invite them to shoot at him. Someone like . . . a *butler*?

She flinched and caught her breath. How could she even consider the scoundrel? She pushed the errant thought from her mind as she set her niece on the floor next to Edward. "Shall we go outside for a walk?"

"All right." Edward jumped to his feet.

"I want to stay with Mama," Charlotte whispered.

"Of course." Caroline smoothed back her niece's black curls. Charlotte might have inherited her father's dark hair, but her fair complexion and pale green eyes were Ginny once again. And the tears in those eyes tore at Caroline's heart.

Edward skipped onto the pier. "Can I go out in the rowboat?"

"Not by yourself." Caroline stopped beside her nephew and pointed upstream. "Is that smoke in the distance?"

"Godsookers. Are the British burning homes again?"

"I hope not." She eyed the black clouds of smoke rising into a clear blue sky. "It might be the militia burning more ferries."

"Let's take the rowboat and have a look."

"No. We'll stay here, where it is safe." She turned away and wandered downstream along a path lined with swamp rose and sweet bay.

Edward joined her. "How long will we stay here?"

"Until your mother has recovered from her lying-in."

"What about our plan to find Grandpa?"

What, indeed? Was Father still alive? Caroline halted under a sycamore tree. "I wish he'd stop fighting."

"Grandpa likes a good fight." Edward jumped, making a grab for the lowest tree branch.

"There's no such thing as a good fight."

"Of course there is. We're fighting for freedom." Edward braced his feet against the trunk, then swung a leg over the branch.

Caroline sighed. It was hard to remember the cause was noble when so many loved ones were in danger. With her nephew happily climbing the tree, she wandered to the riverbank. There was a large gristmill almost a mile downstream. The waterwheel rotated slowly with the sluggish current. This must be where the plantation produced its flour.

Could Haversham be working there? She shook her head. Why did he keep invading her thoughts?

On her way back to Edward, she paused by a small tree. "Look at this. A dogwood."

"So?" Edward's voice emanated from behind a cover of leaves, clearly unimpressed.

She pulled a branch of the dogwood toward her. "The twigs can be used for cleaning our teeth."

"So?"

"I need a knife."

"Oh." Edward dropped onto the ground, suddenly interested in the conversation. "I know where there's a knife. In the bag I hid by those trees." He pointed to the grove of loblolly pines.

"Excellent." Caroline accompanied him to the grove.

He brushed off the pine needles he had heaped on top of their meager supplies. "What about the musket?"

"Let's leave it here for now." She rummaged through the bag and removed the knife.

"Can I take the tinder wheel and candles to our room? I can light the candles at night so Charlotte can see her book."

"Fine." Caroline returned to the dogwood tree, where she cut four twigs. She frayed the ends of the twigs with the knife.

Meanwhile, Edward entertained himself with the tinder wheel. He stuffed dry leaves into the tinderbox, then wrapped the string around the steel wheel. With a yank on the string, the wheel spun against the flint. Sparks flew, igniting the tinder, then sizzling out.

His eyes lit up. "Zounds, this is better than a top."

"'Tis not a toy. You must be careful with it." Caroline slipped the knife and dogwood twigs into her skirt pocket, and they headed toward the house.

Inside, she passed the twigs to Edward. "Take these to the nursery, so you and Charlotte can clean your teeth." Edward made a face, then scampered up the stairs carrying the tinder wheel, candles, and twigs.

Caroline strode out the back door to the kitchen. She'd met Miss Dottie the night before when she'd bathed.

"May I help with the cooking?" she asked.

"No, child," Miss Dottie replied as she chopped some onions at the long table. "Betsy and I will do just fine."

"But you have more mouths to feed now," Caroline insisted. "Please allow me to assist you in some way."

Betsy glanced up from the table where she was peeling potatoes and smiled shyly.

Dottie chuckled. "We heard you had a visitor late last night."

With warm cheeks, Caroline quickly looked about, but Haversham was nowhere in sight. Where could he be? "May I at least take care of the nursery while we're here? I would hate for our presence to burden you in any way."

Dottie studied her a moment, then mumbled softly, "That boy would be a fool to let this one get away."

What boy? Was she referring to Haversham?

"Help yourself to an apron and some cleaning rags." Dottie motioned to a cupboard.

"Thank you." Caroline slipped on an apron and filled a small bucket with water from the pump. With a handful of rags and the bucket, she returned to the nursery, where she enlisted the help of her niece and nephew. They cleaned the entire nursery while Ginny rested.

"Can we play now?" Edward asked for the tenth time.

"Yes." Caroline used her apron to wipe the perspiration from her forehead. "Let's go to the garden."

With a cheer, Edward and Charlotte clambered down the stairs. Caroline followed at a slower pace, carrying the bucket and rags.

A breeze welcomed her at the back door, surrounding her with the scent of roses. She set her cleaning supplies down next to the latticework. Glancing up, she spotted the balcony to the bedchamber where she'd been so rudely awakened. Had Haversham climbed the latticework to sneak into the room? Where was he now? The rascal had disappeared after breakfast.

She groaned. Once again, she was thinking about him. Firmly shoving him from her mind, she strolled into the garden. A tall metal device at the end of the garden pool drew her attention. Strips of metal formed a hollow sphere with Roman numerals embossed inside. An arrow shot through the center. She surmised it was some sort of sundial.

Charlotte and Edward skipped around the reflecting pool, then leaned over to dangle their hands in the water. She avoided looking in the pool, not wishing to see how many new freckles she had acquired on her journey from the Pee Dee River.

Jane emerged from the back door, a large bonnet atop her head, thick gloves on her hands and a basket in the crook of her arm. "Ah, there you are." She dropped her basket in front of a bed of blooming marigolds. "I thought I would do a little work in the garden."

Caroline joined her. "May I help you?"

Jane motioned to her apron. "Betsy told me you were cleaning in the nursery. There's really no need. You're my guests here."

"We don't wish to be a burden." Caroline knelt in front of the flowerbed. "And I enjoy gardening. I did most of it at our home in Charles Town."

Jane gave her an amused look. "I'm surprised, Agatha. I thought your family had quite a few servants."

"Oh, well, times have been difficult lately." Feeling her cheeks grow hot, Caroline looked away. She could hear the children laughing, but they were nowhere in sight. "Where are Edward and Charlotte?"

Jane removed a small cushion from the basket and knelt on it. "It sounds like they're in the pergola."

"Oh." Caroline scanned the three borders of the garden. She had assumed the climbing roses and jasmine covered walls, but instead, they formed hollow tunnels. "You have a marvelous garden."

"Yes, it has been my one joy in life. Other than Matthias, of course."

Caroline dug her fingers around the prickly base of a dandelion and yanked it out. "'Tis a large garden for you to tend by yourself."

"Yes. I fear we're very short on help these days." Jane used her shears to snip off dead flowers. "My husband went to defend Charles Town and took quite a few of the men with him. I suppose they're all prisoners now. At least the ones who survived."

"I'm so sorry."

With a sigh, Jane moved her pillow down to the next group of flowers. "Then we suffered an epidemic of smallpox and lost half a dozen farmhands."

"How terrible." Caroline pulled another weed. "What do you grow here? Indigo?"

"Yes." Jane wrinkled her nose. "If you had come a few weeks earlier, you would have smelled it a mile away. It causes an awful stink when they cook it down to bricks. I always spent the summer months in Charles Town to escape the smell, but of course with the British there, I was forced to remain here."

"I see."

"I've been alone here for months. Matthias is not able to stop by very often."

Caroline added another pulled weed to her growing pile. "He must be very busy with the war. You said he was a soldier?"

"Yes, a captain."

Was he still alive? Caroline hoped so, for Jane's sake, but prayed she'd be gone before he could return.

Jane sighed. "There's too much here for me to keep up with. Dottie and Betsy are the only servants in the kitchen and the Great House. Betsy's indentureship will be over in another year. I don't know what I'll do then."

"I would be happy to help. And you also have Haversham."

Jane winced as she accidentally snipped off a live flower. "I . . . uh, had to relieve Haversham from his duties as a butler."

Caroline's mouth dropped open. "Oh." The colors of the flowers wavered before her eyes, and she blinked. She'd been laboring in the heat for too long.

"Are you all right? You look a little pale."

"I—I'm fine. I hope my behavior this morning didn't cause ..." Her voice drifted off. Why did she feel so odd, so empty? She hardly knew the man.

Jane watched her closely. "He's a handsome man, don't you think?"

"I ... suppose. What will happen to him?"

Jane smiled. "Don't worry, dear. He'll return soon. He's rather ... attached to this place."

Did that mean he was an indentured servant like Betsy? What were his duties exactly? He certainly didn't appear to have any experience as a butler. As curious as Caroline was, she was reluctant to ask Jane about him. She didn't want to admit how much he dominated her thoughts.

Her gaze wandered to the latticework that he'd climbed the night before. She hadn't dared tell anyone that she'd found herself wrestling in bed with a naked man.

"I've been meaning to apologize," Jane said softly. "I understand you were rudely awakened last night."

Caroline gasped. Had Haversham confessed his crime? Surely he hadn't mentioned the part about their wrestling?

Jane concentrated on her garden gloves as she removed them. "He assured me that nothing happened."

"Exactly. Nothing happened. And Haversham apologized." Heat flooded Caroline's face. Why was she defending him?

Jane gave her a sympathetic look. "Still, after all you've been through, it must have frightened you." She dropped her gloves into her basket. "These are dangerous times, so we lock the house up at night. The only way Haversham could enter was to climb the latticework. He thought the bedchamber was unoccupied."

"I see." Though Caroline wondered why he had jumped to the conclusion that she was there to trap him into marriage.

"I wanted to warn you," Jane continued. "He may need to enter that way again."

"I understand," Caroline assured her. "I'm perfectly happy to sleep in the nursery."

Jane shook her head. "It would be too crowded. We'll move you to the guest room." She motioned to the small balcony above the morning parlor. "It has a smaller bed, but I believe you'll be quite comfortable there."

The room overlooked the garden like Matthias's room, but there was no latticework below the balcony. No way to access the room from outside.

Caroline smiled. "It looks perfect. Thank you." At last she could look forward to a night of peaceful slumber.

Chapter Seven

An hour after sunset, Matthias eased into the kitchen, surprising Betsy and Dottie as they ate their evening meal. "I hope you have some stew left for me."

Dottie grunted as she hefted herself to her feet. "Didn't you say you'd be gone for a few days? I should have known better than to believe a rascal like you."

Matthias grinned as sat at the table. "How could I stay away from your cooking?"

Dottie's mouth twitched as she ladled the last of the stew into a bowl. "Somehow I don't think it's my cooking that's brought you here."

No, it wasn't. All day long Matthias had looked forward to confronting the little vixen who had wheedled her way into his house with her lies and deception. By God, he would wring a confession from her before the night was through.

Betsy set a square of cornbread in front of him. "You smell like smoke."

"Aye. We've been burning boats and bridges." He slathered some butter on the cornbread and took a bite. It melted in his mouth. "Damn, Dottie. You're the best."

She snorted as she handed him a bowl of stew. "That is true, but I can't take credit for the cornbread."

He glanced at Betsy, and she shook her head.

"Miss Ludlow made it." Betsy poured him a mug of ale.

"The false Agatha?" He looked askance at the cornbread and nudged the saucer away. "Did she put poison in it?"

"Don't be silly, boy." Dottie sat down to resume her eating. "Why would that sweet girl do something like that?"

"*Sweet?*" Matthias gulped down some ale to wash away the taste of the vixen's cooking. "She's a liar. With sharp teeth."

"I like her," Betsy said quietly as she sat across from him. "She doesn't act as if she's better than us."

"Yep." Dottie buttered her cornbread. "She's a sweet girl, all right."

"She's deceiving my mother," Matthias growled.

"She's made your mother very happy," Dottie argued.

"She's made us all happy," Betsy added. "She cleaned the nursery today, so I wouldn't have to. And she helped your mother in the garden."

"More proof that she's lying," Matthias grumbled. "The real Agatha Ludlow would never engage in physical labor."

Dottie snorted. "So now you find fault with her for working hard?"

Actually, he was impressed, but since he didn't want to admit it, he ate his stew in silence.

"She helped us cook dinner," Dottie continued, "even though I told her she didn't need to."

Betsy nodded. "And she helped me carry all the dishes to

the Great House. She doesn't want her family to be a burden on us."

So the little vixen had a guilty conscience and was trying to atone for her crime with hard labor. Did that mean she regretted her lie? Matthias shoved that thought away. He couldn't allow himself to feel sympathy for her.

But if she had behaved like the real Agatha, she wouldn't have helped the servants. She would have made them miserable with her selfish demands. What if Caroline Munro was actually a kindhearted person?

He finished his stew and eyed the cornbread. It would be a shame for it to go to waste, especially when there was so much hunger in the world.

"Eat." Dottie shoved the saucer closer to him.

He took another bite. Damn, it really was good. And if she was making his mother happy . . .

He shook his head. He wouldn't excuse her deceit. Even if she was beautiful. And hardworking. And kind and helpful to the servants. He'd still wring a confession from her tonight. Before he was done with her, she'd know the full power of his wrath.

He smiled as a vision flitted through his mind. She would fall to her knees, begging forgiveness, and he, being a gentleman, would be merciful and allow her to remain at the house. In gratitude, she would sink into his arms, and he would hold her close to comfort her. With a gentle sigh of surrender, her pretty mouth would open, and he would . . .

He winced, quickly reining in his errant thoughts. Apparently, he was less than a gentleman.

Dottie gathered up the dirty dishes. "If you spend the

night here, I can make more bread in the morning for your boys in the swamp."

He nodded. "Thank you. I'll do that."

Dottie smiled, then motioned toward the bathing room. "You should wash up before seeing your mother. There are some clean clothes in the cupboard."

Ten minutes later, he stood in the garden, studying the balcony to his bedchamber. The window was slightly ajar. Most probably, Miss Munro was sleeping in his bed again.

As hard as she had worked all day, she might be sound asleep. Was it necessary to confront her tonight? He could unmask her in the morning just as well. And he should do it with his mother present. That way he wouldn't be tempted to hold her. Or comfort her.

Aye, the more he thought about it, the more certain he was that being alone with Caroline Munro was dangerous. He shoved his damp hair back from his brow and entered the house through the back door. Betsy usually locked up before retiring to her small room on the third floor, but she was washing dishes now in the kitchen. The arrival of Miss Munro and her family had increased the workload for Betsy and Dottie, but they didn't seem to mind. They liked her. Even though they knew she was lying.

He strolled up the stairs to his mother's bedchamber, then knocked on the door and peered inside.

"Matthias!" Jane whispered excitedly as she climbed out of bed and rushed toward him. "I didn't expect you back tonight."

"Disappointed?"

"Don't be silly." She looked him over. "Are you all right?"

"Yes. I came back to confront the false Agatha. I'm reasonably certain I have discovered her true identity. She's—"

"Don't tell me," Jane interrupted.

"Don't you want to know who is sleeping in your house?"

"She'll tell me when she's ready. I want her to trust me."

He scoffed. "How can you trust *her* when you know she's lying?"

Jane gave him an annoyed look. "Have you even attempted to see this from her perspective? She's trying to take care of two children and a sister who's about to give birth. The British burned their homes in Charles Town and on the Pee Dee. The poor girl is desperate to provide a safe haven for her family. Desperate enough to agree to marry a man she's never met. A man, who could, as far as she knows, be an absolute monster."

"Why, thank you, Mother."

She huffed. "You know what I mean. Under the circumstances, I find her quite admirable."

He shifted his weight. Had she really agreed to marry him? In that case, the little vixen might actually be a fortune hunter after all. "She knows me as a penniless servant. I would like to remain so."

Jane gave him a wry look. "If you persist in lying to her, you can hardly object to her lies." She wandered back to her bed and perched on the edge. "Do you know if she's from a good family?"

"Her father's a major in the army."

"Ah." Jane's eyes gleamed in the candlelight. "Then she's an excellent match for you."

He frowned. "I told you. I will not marry as long as—"

"Are you staying for the night?"

"Yes." He sighed. "I suppose she's in my bed again."

Jane smiled. "The guest room will suit you nicely."

A sliver of moonlight shone through the open window in the guest room, casting a silver sheen over the mosquito netting that draped the bed. Matthias kicked off his shoes as he closed the door with a slight click.

The sound of rustling sheets emanated from the bed.

He turned, narrowing his eyes.

"Is someone there?" a female voice whispered.

He scoffed. His mother was up to her old tricks. At least tonight he wasn't naked. "I beg your pardon, Miss . . . Ludlow. I'll be on my way." He stuffed his feet back into his shoes.

"Haversham? Is that you?"

"Aye. I'll leave—"

"Oh, thank goodness."

The netting swayed, and the scent of magnolia wafted toward him, tempting him. In the dim light, he caught a glimpse of her white nightgown as she slipped out of bed.

"I was afraid you had lost your employment. Although Jane mentioned that you were somehow attached to this place."

"Aye. I'm afraid she's stuck with me." He fingered the door latch, debating whether to leave. Was there any harm in merely talking to her?

"Then you're an indentured servant? Like Betsy?"

Her question caught him by surprise. So she thought

he was not only a penniless servant, but an indentured one. "Would you think less of me if I were?"

"No, of course not. My father came to the New World as an indentured servant."

"He did?" Matthias had a hard time imagining the huge Scotsman as a servant.

"Aye. 'Tis nothing to be ashamed of. Father always says a man can succeed in America if he's willing to work hard. Though I have to admit, my father didn't serve the entire seven years."

"Why not?"

"'Tis a long story. Were you intending to sleep here? I could move to the nursery." She passed through a beam of moonlight.

Matthias caught his breath. She was in a dark corner now, where she'd left a bundle of clothes on a chair, but for a few glorious seconds he'd seen her clearly. She'd looked like an angel with the moonbeam glowing around her and her hair tumbled about her shoulders in curly disarray.

His voice sounded choked. "Don't go."

"'Tis late," she whispered from the dark corner.

"I know. I'll sleep elsewhere." He hesitated with his hand on the door latch. What had happened to the confession he had wanted to wring from her? Suddenly, he couldn't bear the thought of anyone mistreating her. No longer did he want to intimidate her. He wanted her to trust him. "I would like to hear more about your father."

"You would?"

"Aye." He wandered toward the window and looked out at

the garden below. Moonlight sparkled on the pond. "When did your father come to America?"

"In '47." She wandered toward him, clasping a shawl around her shoulders. Her nightgown, most probably borrowed from his mother, wasn't long enough for the length of her legs, so he was afforded a view of shapely calves, delicate ankles, and slender feet.

He sucked in a deep breath. Could an angel affect a man like this?

She stopped next him and peered out at the garden. "Father's ship landed near Williamsburg, and he was purchased by a professor from the College of William and Mary. The professor was an excellent teacher, but not very good about practical matters. It wasn't long before my father was entrusted with all his business affairs."

"And then?" Matthias grew increasingly curious. He might actually know the professor. Before joining the army, he had studied at the College of William and Mary.

"Since the professor's wife had died, his daughter was running the household," Miss Munro continued. "She and my father fell into a struggle over which one of them was actually in charge. And at the same time they were falling in love. She's my mother, of course. And Grandpa gave my father his freedom as a wedding gift."

"Who was the professor?"

"Tobias Oglethorpe."

Oglethorpe was her grandfather? Matthias leaned against the wall just beyond the beam of moonlight. Oglethorpe was the best teacher he'd ever had. "That's a good story."

"I've always liked it. When I was young, I would beg Mother to tell it to me, over and over."

"Of course, most people in Charles Town would know that Agatha Ludlow's father was never an indentured servant."

Miss Munro winced, then gave him an injured look. "Is that why you encouraged me to tell the story? So you could trap me?"

"No. I liked your story. But shouldn't you be honest with Mrs. Thomas?"

A pained look crossed Miss Munro's face. "Jane has been so kind to us. I feel . . . terrible." She turned abruptly and headed back to the dark corner.

"Then tell her the truth." He grabbed her arm and spun her around to face him. The tears in her eyes made his stomach clench. "Tell me."

A tear rolled down her cheek. "I don't know whom to trust anymore."

"You can trust me." He smoothed away her tear with this thumb. "Mrs. Thomas will not make you leave. You're safe here."

Another tear escaped. "That was all I wanted. A safe place for the children. And my sister."

"I know." He held her gently by the shoulders.

She clutched her shawl tightly as she searched his eyes. He stared back, willing her to trust him.

"My name is Caroline. Caroline Munro."

A sensation of victory burst inside him. "Miss Munro."

"Yes?"

"A pleasure to meet you." His gaze lowered to her mouth.

"I . . . appreciate that, sir."

He leaned closer.

She jumped back. "I should go now, so you can sleep."

"No. Stay. I'll go." He hurried to the door and closed it firmly behind him. Good God, he had almost kissed her! He must be losing his mind.

He bounded up the stairs to Haversham's old room on the third floor. As he undressed, he found himself smiling. He hadn't needed to force a confession from her. She'd trusted him enough to tell him the truth. Even though she thought he was a penniless, indentured servant, she trusted him.

And it felt damned good.

CHAPTER EIGHT

Caroline was relieved the next morning when Haversham did not appear at breakfast. Simply thinking about him made her heart thud wildly in her chest. She hardly knew the man, yet she had conversed with him at length, alone in a bedchamber. Wearing nothing but a thin nightgown that was much too short.

She'd allowed him to hold her. She'd confessed her true identity. Was this madness, or something else? She slanted a look at her sister across the breakfast table. There had been times when Ginny was falling in love that Caroline had thought her sister was behaving irrationally. Even recklessly. Was she doing the same?

Could she be falling for Haversham? She couldn't deny feeling attracted to him. The man was extremely handsome. But was she simply reacting to the first available man she'd met in months who fit her criteria? Single, healthy, and not involved with the war. Those were good things, but they hardly constituted a basis for a serious relationship.

He'd wanted to kiss her. She was almost certain of it.

Every time the memory crossed her mind, her heart pounded. And her face grew warm.

Sleep had been nigh impossible last night. She'd been tormented with the memories of how handsome he had looked in the moonlight. Without a jacket or cravat, he'd been dressed simply in tight breeches and a homespun shirt. His dark hair had been wet and loose about his shoulders. His shirt had outlined every muscled contour of his broad shoulders. Dark whiskers had shaded his strong jaw. He had looked dangerous. Strong. Exciting.

And he'd wanted to kiss her. Her cheeks grew hot again. How much sleep had she lost, imagining what might have happened if she hadn't jumped away?

"My dear, are you all right?" Jane asked. "You seemed flushed."

She stiffened and pushed her eggs around her plate. "I'm afraid I'm not very hungry this morning."

Jane nodded. "The heat affects my appetite, too. Did you not sleep well?"

The memory returned—Haversham's hands on her shoulders, pulling her closer as he leaned in for a kiss. "I—I have a great deal on my mind."

Jane gave her a sympathetic smile. "Don't worry, dear. It will all work out for the best."

"Thank you." Caroline wondered for the hundredth time if she'd made a mistake trusting Haversham. But if Jane trusted him, then he had to be dependable, didn't he?

Where was he this morning? Perhaps she should see him after all. It might help her make sense of the confusing thoughts and feelings that had plagued her all night.

When Betsy returned to take their dishes to the kitchen, Caroline insisted on helping.

The kitchen was full of the enticing aroma of freshly baked bread. But no Haversham in sight.

"Have you seen the butler this morning?" she asked.

Dottie chuckled as she wrapped some loaves in squares of cotton. "I suspect he's gone to the stable. But he'll be back for this bread before he leaves."

Caroline swallowed hard. "He's leaving?"

Dottie smiled. "Don't you fret, child. He'll come back. He's just feeding the hungry today."

The tightness in Caroline's chest dissipated. Surely he was a good man if he was engaged in charitable works. "Have you known him for very long, Miss Dottie?"

"All of his life." Dottie's eyes twinkled with humor. "Have you taken a liking to him?"

Caroline's face heated with a blush. Even Betsy looked amused. "I wouldn't phrase it that way. I'm simply . . . curious. I was wondering how trustworthy he is."

"Then maybe you should ask him." Dottie motioned to the door.

Caroline whirled about. *Good Lord.* How long had he been standing in the doorway?

He bowed his head. "Good morning."

"Good morning." With her face downcast and burning with heat, she slipped around him and headed out the door.

"Miss Munro, will you take a walk with me?"

She hesitated. "My sister might need me."

"I won't take much of your time. I was hoping to say good-bye before I leave."

She ventured a quick glance at his face. He looked so sincere with his angelic blue eyes. Last night in the moonlight, his hair had appeared black, but now, in the sunlight, she could see it was actually a rich shade of brown. "I can spare a few minutes, I suppose."

"Thank you." He motioned toward the kitchen garden and led her down a path between two rows of carrots and parsnips. "I'm not sure I apologized properly for barging into your room last night."

"'Twas an accident."

"We seem to have those often." He smiled.

Her heart squeezed in her chest. *Don't think about how handsome he is. Remember how little you know of him.* "Why are you leaving?"

His eyebrows lifted as if he were caught off guard. "Do you ask because you're simply curious? You're wondering how trustworthy I am?"

She winced as he repeated the words she'd said earlier. "It has occurred to me that I don't know you very well."

"You trusted me last night. Have I changed since then?"

No, of course he hadn't. Why was she having second thoughts? The answer hit her hard enough to make her stumble.

"Are you all right?" He grabbed her by the elbow.

She gave him a wary look. Last night, she had trusted him with her identity. Today, she was wondering if she could trust him with her heart. It was a frightening thought. "Why are you leaving?"

He paused. "Business."

"You attend to matters of business for Mrs. Thomas?"

"Yes." He led her into the orchard. "I'll be gone for a few days."

"I see." She would miss him.

"Will you miss me?"

She gasped. Was the man a mind reader? She pivoted, surveying the rows of trees. "What a beautiful place."

"You should see it in the spring when the trees are in full bloom."

She nodded. "I'm sure it is lovely."

"You didn't answer my question."

"I don't recall a—"

"Are you lying again?" he asked softly, his eyes twinkling with humor.

She scoffed. "You might find this hard to believe, but I am not a habitual liar."

"But what if that was a lie? Perhaps I should be concerned about how trustworthy *you* are."

She huffed. "I'm a paragon of virtue."

"You called me a demented buffoon." He gave her an injured look. "Three times."

Her mouth twitched. "You kept count?"

"Aye. I was wounded to the core."

She snorted. "Look who's lying now."

"You bit me, too."

"Only once. Do you have a habit of accosting women in their beds?"

"Only once." He grinned. "Only you."

For some odd reason, she was happy to hear that. "You're the only person I've ever bitten."

"I'm honored."

She bit her lip to keep from smiling.

"Admit it. You'll miss me."

With a shrug, she sauntered down the path. "Perhaps."

"Vixen," he muttered behind her.

She grinned. She might not know a great deal about Haversham, but she did enjoy his company.

He ran to catch up with her, and they strolled side by side for a while.

"Are you going to tell Mrs. Thomas the truth today?" he asked.

"Yes." She took a deep breath. "Wish me luck."

"You'll be fine. Mrs. Thomas likes you."

"Did she say that?"

He nodded, smiling.

Caroline smiled back, then wandered into the shade of a peach tree. Her father had planted five of these at home. Was he alive? How would she ever find him? How was Mama surviving each day, not knowing if he would ever return? How could Ginny endure each day, wondering if her babe would be born without a father?

Caroline's fleeting moment of happiness crashed around her as reality returned. Tears burned her eyes, and she turned away so Haversham wouldn't see. She had to stay strong, no matter what. And she had to count her blessings. How fortunate she was to have found this piece of heaven on earth.

"Is something wrong?" he asked behind her.

She blinked away the tears. "I cannot tell you how relieved I am that my sister can give birth here, and my nephew and niece have food to eat and real beds to sleep in. The war has taken a terrible toll on them."

"I'm sure it has."

"And Ginny's been so worried about her husband. We haven't heard from him since last April."

"He's a soldier?" Haversham rested a palm against the tree trunk. "What's his name?"

"Quincy Stanton. He's a blockade runner. But with the British in Charles Town, I'm afraid he's been cut off from us."

Haversham frowned. "That's a dangerous business he's in."

Caroline sighed. "We know."

"His name sounds familiar. Is he involved with Stanton Shipping?"

"Aye. You've heard of it?"

Haversham nodded. "This plantation transported indigo with Stanton Shipping before the war."

"I see." Caroline glanced up at the canopy of green leaves above them. "I feel so helpless sometimes. All I can do is hope and pray. Will all three survive?"

"All three?"

"Ginny's husband; our brother, Fergus; and our father. With so many to worry about, I've made a vow never to involve myself with a soldier."

Haversham stiffened. "But they're fighting for freedom."

"And some are dying." Like poor Roger. She closed her eyes briefly. If only she had kept her mouth shut. "You asked if I'm a habitual liar. I'm not, but I do have a terrible tendency to say the wrong thing at the wrong time."

"We all do that occasionally."

She shook her head. "Not as badly as I."

"May I ask where you were headed when you ended up here at Loblolly?"

"We were traveling down the Black River, in hopes of finding my father with Sumter's army. But then I learned they were defeated. I don't know if my father . . ." Tears blurred her vision.

Haversham muttered a curse and strode away a few steps. "Bloody hell," he whispered, then turned to her. "I . . . I know a few soldiers in the area. I could ask if they know anything."

Her breath caught. "You could?"

"Aye." With a grimace, he clenched a fist. "'Tis the least I can do."

"Oh, thank you!" Caroline rushed toward him. "His name is James Munro, a major." She touched his shoulder. "Thank you so much."

"Don't mention it." Haversham bowed abruptly. "Good day, Miss Munro." He sprinted back to the kitchen.

"Good day," Caroline whispered. What had happened? He'd run off as if the devil were on his heels.

Matthias cursed himself all the way back to the camp on Snow's Island. He should have realized she'd be as worried about her father as her father was about her. She'd been battling tears, fearing that her father was dead.

He could have relieved her fears. He could have told her he had met her father. But how could he admit he was in the army when she was determined never to involve herself with a soldier? And if he admitted his true identity, she would know he was the heir to the plantation. Dammit, he liked being Haversham, the penniless servant. It was the only way he could be sure that she liked him for himself and not for his wealth.

He pushed those thoughts aside. Why was he concerned whether she liked him or not? He'd made his own vow not to marry as long as the war continued. Caroline was right. It was absolute folly to become romantically attached during these perilous times.

And it was dangerous for him to allow a woman to distract him from his work. If he lost his focus and let his emotions reel out of control, he could end up dead.

It was better this way. His guilt would serve a purpose by forcing him to put some distance between them. After a few days away from her, he'd forget the pain that glimmered in her eyes. He'd forget his desire to protect her and comfort her.

He was a soldier first.

He groaned. He was an ass.

All day long, Caroline waited for a private moment with Jane so she could confess her true identity. It was difficult, though, with the children always underfoot. Even now, they were chasing each other around the reflecting pool while she helped Jane in the garden.

As she knelt in front of a flowerbed, Caroline realized this might be her best opportunity. She wrenched out a weed growing next to a rosebush. "I cannot thank you enough for the kindness you have shown us."

"Posh, my dear. I am the grateful one." Jane cut off a long-stemmed rose and added it to her basket. "You and your family have brought me great joy. And I'm very excited over the prospect of having a newborn babe in the house."

Caroline nodded. "I've been very concerned about my sister."

"No need to fret. You will be relieved to know that Dottie is an excellent midwife."

"Oh. Thank you." Caroline took a deep breath. "But I must admit there is another matter that has been weighing heavily on me. I'm afraid I—"

Charlotte's scream interrupted her confession. She jumped to her feet just in time to see Edward fall into the reflecting pool with a noisy splash.

"Edward, of all the silly things to do." Caroline frowned at him as he sat in the water, grinning.

Jane laughed. "He reminds me of Matthias. I cannot tell you how many times my son landed in that pool."

Water dripped from Edward's clothes as he scrambled out of the pool. "Give me a hug, Charlotte!" He made a grab for her.

Charlotte squealed and dashed around the corner of the house with her soggy brother in pursuit.

"Excuse me." Caroline followed them, wiping her dirty hands on her apron. As she came to the front lawn, she noticed the children had frozen in their tracks.

Down at the wharf, a barge had docked. Three British soldiers stood on the pier. Their red coats clashed with the pastoral scene as if an artist, bored with peaceful shades of green and blue, had splashed angry red marks across the canvas.

A chill ran down Caroline's back in spite of the late afternoon heat. She should have known. There was no escape from the war.

Their paradise was lost.

The children gazed at her, their eyes saucer-wide. Charlotte's bottom lip trembled.

"Come." She reached for them, and they ran into her arms. She ushered them quickly to the back of the house. "Jane! We have visitors."

"Visitors? Who?" Jane strode toward her.

"Redcoats."

Jane stumbled to a halt. "Oh, dear. What shall we do?" Her hands shook as she removed her gardening gloves.

"We'll have to speak to them." Caroline knelt in front of the children. "Go inside. Tell your mother what has happened and stay in the nursery."

They nodded and ran into the house.

Jane dropped her gloves on the grass and smoothed out her skirts. "Come with me, please."

"Of course." Caroline accompanied her to the front lawn.

The soldiers were approaching the house. A white-wigged officer escorted a young lady. His tall, gaunt appearance was further accentuated by his companion's short, well-rounded form. Dressed in coral silk with a matching parasol, she released a high-pitched giggle that carried across the lawn.

"How do you do?" the officer called to them. "I'm Captain Ezra Hickman. I'm on my way to General Cornwallis in Camden."

The captain's accent sounded familiar, like those heard in Charles Town. He must be a Loyalist, Caroline thought, an

American willing to kill his neighbors for the glory of a king three thousand miles away. Or so the Loyalists claimed. She suspected they had other motives—revenge and greed.

"How do you do? I'm Jane Murray Thomas." Jane's curtsy faltered.

Caroline stretched out a steadying hand, and Jane gave her a grateful look.

"'Twill be all right," Caroline whispered. She faced the newcomers, and to her dismay, discovered the captain was eyeing her with interest. His female companion took one look at her and dismissed her with a sniff. Apparently, she looked like a servant with her sunburned face and dirty apron.

"As I was traveling from Charles Town, I happened across this admirable young lady in need of an escort." The captain bowed his head at the woman on his arm. "She assured us you would be most hospitable."

Jane glanced at Caroline with a worried look. "Yes, of course."

"Mrs. Thomas, so good to see you again." The woman stepped forward, closing her parasol. "Surely you remember me? I'm Agatha Ludlow."

CHAPTER NINE

Caroline flinched.

This was it. The unmasking.

Jane would demand that she and her family leave at once. Good Lord, Jane could have the soldiers arrest them. Caroline risked a glance to see how angry Jane was, but she had turned away to climb the steps to the front porch.

"Welcome to Loblolly." Jane hesitated at the front door as if reluctant to open it.

"Thank you." Agatha Ludlow swished past Caroline without a second glance. "Captain, would your men fetch my trunks, please?"

"Of course." Hickman motioned to the other soldiers. They paced back to the river, grumbling under their breath.

Agatha lifted her skirts with a gloved hand as she ascended the porch steps. "I simply adore this house."

Instead of joining the ladies on the porch, the captain stepped back and examined the house. He glanced over his shoulder at the river. "Mrs. Thomas, is your husband home?"

Jane visibly paled. "No, he's . . . away on business."

Captain Hickman tucked his tricorne under his arm. "Then you are alone."

"I have guests staying with me." Jane glanced at Caroline.

Although Jane's expression conveyed more of a plea for support than an angry accusation, Caroline still struggled with the guilt of her deception. She remained standing on the lawn, uncertain what to do but convinced that at any moment, the earth would crack open, flames would belch forth, and the devil himself would appear with a personal invitation for her to join him in the bowels of hell.

Captain Hickman turned to her and smiled. A cold, lifeless smile that chilled her to the bone, a smile like a wolf baring its teeth when it had selected which sheep to cut from the herd. Caroline steeled her nerves to keep from shuddering. A fleeting thought skittered through her mind—perhaps the devil preferred ice to fire.

The captain inclined his head. "At your service, mistress. May I inquire your name?"

"Miss Munro. Caroline Munro." She gave Jane an apologetic look. "I'm so sorry. We'll be on our way now."

Jane frowned. "Do you truly wish to leave?"

Where could they go? Tears of despair blurred Caroline's vision. She shook her head. "No."

"Then you will stay." Jane opened the door.

Agatha Ludlow followed her into the house. "I was so delighted to receive your invitation. I have such fond memories of this house. Do you still have that marvelous harpsichord in the parlor?"

Caroline trudged up the porch steps, her heart heavy. She should feel relieved. The truth was out, and she and her family still had shelter. But she felt guilty for not confessing the truth to Jane before it was too late.

Captain Hickman touched her elbow with his bony fingers. "You look sad. I trust it is not due to our arrival."

"No, not at all." Caroline forced a smile.

"Then you will be pleased to do your duty for your king." Hickman tightened his grip on her elbow. His gaze wandered down to her low neckline, then back to her face. "I expect to be made . . . comfortable."

She swallowed hard. Rumors had abounded in Charles Town of soldiers abusing their power with helpless women. "This way, please." She eased away from his grasp with the pretense of leading him into the foyer.

The captain's booted steps echoed on the polished floor. How could his blue gaze seem so cold when Haversham's blue eyes had twinkled with warmth?

"Such a horrendous journey." With languid, graceful motions, Agatha Ludlow loosened the coral silk ribbons that tied her bonnet beneath her chin. "We were halfway here when my manservant took off with my maid."

"Oh, dear," Jane murmured. "How dreadful."

"I was devastated!" Agatha removed her bonnet and shook out her glossy brown sausage curls. "They abandoned me in a godforsaken inn by the river. Thank goodness Captain Hickman came along when he did."

The captain bowed. "My pleasure." He accepted Agatha's offered hand and kissed her gloved fingers.

Agatha blushed prettily. "Such a relief to know gallantry has survived in these perilous times." She withdrew her hand slowly with a coy smile.

Caroline breathed easier, relieved to see Hickman's interest shift to Agatha where it appeared welcome. But why would Agatha flirt with other men when she had journeyed here to marry Jane's son? And there was another problem. Agatha gave every indication of being a Loyalist. Why would she agree to marry a captain in the Continental Army?

Agatha tilted her head toward Jane with a helpless look. "I do hope you will have a maid available for me?"

"I'm afraid we're short on help these days," Jane confessed.

Agatha shuddered. "'Tis this dreadful war to blame. I wish they would hang all the rebels and be done with it."

Hickman bowed his head. "Your wish is my command."

With a giggle, Agatha deposited her hat on a bombé chest. She gazed in the mirror above it and patted her hair into place.

"If you will excuse me." Caroline sidled toward the stairs. Her sister would be waiting to hear what was happening.

Agatha turned and inspected Caroline, looking down the considerable length of her nose. "What lovely fair skin you have. Though I suggest you use a parasol from now on. It would do wonders for deterring those ghastly freckles."

Caroline bit her lip. She would have to be courteous. Agatha had been invited here, not her.

Jane eased closer to her. "Caroline?"

"I must apologize," Caroline whispered.

"We'll talk later." Jane touched her shoulder. "For now, would you please go to the kitchen and ask Dottie to prepare tea for our guests? And have Betsy prepare the bedchambers."

"Oh, yes. Please do." Agatha covered her mouth with a

gloved hand as she delicately yawned. "I must rest before dinner."

"Very well." Caroline headed for the back door.

"One moment." Hickman raised a hand to stop her. "My men won't be needing a room. They'll remain by the barge tonight. The cargo I'm transporting is extremely important. It cannot be left unprotected."

Caroline nodded. "I understand." At least there would be only one redcoat in the house tonight.

Hickman continued, "I require a bedchamber overlooking the river, so I can keep an eye on the situation."

"May I ask how long you will be staying?" Jane asked.

Hickman cocked an eyebrow as if he found the question impertinent. "We leave at dawn."

Caroline exchanged a glance with Jane, knowing they were both relieved, but unable to show it.

"I prefer a bedchamber overlooking the garden." Agatha flicked her fingers at her as if dismissing a maid.

"As you wish." Caroline gritted her teeth as she strode to the back door. This was the woman Jane had chosen for her son? Had Matthias approved of the engagement?

Halfway to the kitchen, she halted with a sudden thought. What if Jane's son returned home tonight? He wouldn't stay alive long enough to court Agatha. Three redcoats would be here to greet him.

Her sudden stop had caused the contents of her skirt pocket to knock against her hip. The knife. She'd been using it to prune rosebushes in the garden. She could only hope she wouldn't need it for protection.

Captain Ezra Hickman filled his glass from the brandy decanter Mrs. Thomas had brought to his bedchamber. A shame it hadn't been the flame-haired Miss Munro or flirtatious Miss Ludlow, for he would have asked either one of them to stay.

Miss Ludlow would possibly agree, but Miss Munro was more of a challenge. He had attempted to engage her in conversation at dinner, and she had barely managed to remain civil.

She had to be a Colonial sympathizer. Ezra smiled, then took a sip of brandy. Watching the rebels squirm was the only bonus to this disastrous assignment. He enjoyed seeing the fear in their eyes whenever he made his appearance, and what a delight to watch them swallow their pride in order to appease him.

Brandy glass in hand, he paced to the window overlooking the river. His men had built a campfire close to the pier to guard the cargo. He wrenched open the glass-paned door and strode onto the balcony.

The Black River lapped lazily against the sides of the barge, the sound carried to his ears on a gentle breeze. He studied the clear night sky, brightened by a full moon. An excellent night for travel. And those damned partisans tended to strike at night. Cornwallis would have his neck if he lost any of the precious cargo.

Ezra gulped down more brandy. If the partisans knew what he was transporting, they'd laugh all the way back to their stinking swamp. A man of his abilities, transporting wigs, furnishings, and lacy white bed linens. What a ridiculous waste of his military skill.

Of course, only a good officer could be trusted to oversee the transport of the general's personal items, but the assignment was a dead end. He had only two men to command. No chance for glory, no opportunity to shine on the battlefield. Damn, at this rate, he would still be poor and landless at the end of the war. His uncle, a wealthy merchant in Charles Town, would offer him employ as a lowly clerk. Then his cousins would come in their fancy clothes and carriages to gloat.

Damn it to hell! Ezra tossed the rest of the brandy down his throat. He needed a new assignment. Something important. Something that made him stand out.

Lieutenant Colonel Banastre Tarleton. Now there was a man who was making a name for himself. And what a name—the Butcher. Tarleton was famous after his slaughter of rebels at the Waxhaws. He'd probably end up with a title and land in England.

Wouldn't that be splendid? Ezra wandered back inside and refilled his glass. If only he could distinguish himself in battle, then perhaps he could acquire a title, too. Or at least some land where he could rub his cousins' noses in the dirt.

There was no doubt about it. The best way to make a name for himself would be through Tarleton. The British lieutenant colonel led a mounted troop of dragoons, all in coats of green.

Once the barge was safely delivered to Cornwallis, Ezra would request a transfer to Tarleton's troop. But how could he convince the pompous old windbag of a general to agree?

Ezra paced back and forth, sipping the brandy and devising his strategy. First, he'd emphasize the need to eradicate the local militia. He would describe the destruction he had seen along the Black River. The partisans had burned so many bridges and boats that the only way to move supplies would be by barge.

Of course. Ezra halted in mid-stride. They'd have to move all the supplies by barge. Cornwallis would be looking for a way station halfway between Charles Town and Camden.

Ezra smiled. He had the perfect solution.

Cornwallis would be pleased. Then, in gratitude, the general would honor his request.

Ezra downed the last of the brandy and let the rich liquor linger on his tongue. This was the sort of life he deserved. He ambled toward the large four-poster bed. Mrs. Thomas had said it was the master's bed. Master of a plantation. That would be title enough for him.

He pulled off his wig and draped it on the bedpost. Then he sat and yanked off his boots. With a yawn, he stretched out on the comfortable bed.

These accursed rebels. How could a pack of uneducated, backward peasants live so well? And what made them think they had some God-given right to it, as if their damned feelings were some sort of justification for treason. Oh, they had *rights.*

They had the right to die, every last one of them.

Late that night, Matthias left his horse in the stable and made his way to the kitchen. He hadn't intended on coming back so soon. He had thought that his burden of guilt would lighten as the day wore on, but on the contrary, it had grown worse. He'd found it nearly impossible to concentrate, knowing that Caroline was here, suffering needlessly.

He ducked into the kitchen. The sound of snores emanated from Dottie's room in the back. In the bathing room, he washed off the grime and smell of smoke. The dirty clothes he had left two nights ago had been washed, so he slipped them on and hurried to the Great House. He glanced up at the balconies that overlooked the garden. Which bedchamber was Caroline sleeping in tonight?

The back door and servants' entrance were bolted, so he climbed the lattice to his balcony and slipped inside the room.

The sound of soft breathing came from beneath the mosquito netting. He smiled to himself, liking the thought of Caroline asleep in his bed.

He drew closer, and his heart began to pound. In the dim light, he could barely make out the rounded form under the white bedsheet. He ducked under the netting and sat beside her. Slowly, he stretched out his hand to where the sheet displayed the widest curve. Her hip, soft but firm. The instant reaction in his breeches caught him by surprise, and he removed his hand.

She moaned softly.

"Vixen," he whispered, fisting his hands to keep from touching her. "Wake up."

She gasped. "Captain? Is that you?"

He stiffened. How did she know he was a captain? His mother must have told her who he was. *Damn.* Now she would know he was heir to the plantation. "Yes."

"Captain, you naughty man." She sat up. "But I have to admit I'm not surprised. I knew you would come to me."

She was expecting him? "We . . . need to talk."

"Talk? Is that what you call it?" She giggled and eased closer to him. "This happens to me all the time. Men fall under my spell. They cannot help themselves."

"Amazing." What the hell was she talking about?

"Yes." She sighed. "'Tis the curse I must endure for being so beautiful."

He shoved his damp hair back. This didn't sound like the vixen. In fact, her voice seemed entirely different. A bit nasal and . . . annoying. He squinted to see her face in the dark. "And your name is . . . ?"

Her high-pitched giggle grated his ears. "Agatha Ludlow, you silly man. You know who I am."

He clenched his teeth. "Have you taken up lying again?"

"Excuse me? Oh, I see." She sidled up close to him and skimmed her fingers up his arm. "You've caught me, Captain. I'm a very naughty milkmaid. What will you do? Spank me?"

What the hell? Matthias scooted out of her reach. "I'm not going to hurt you. Who do you think I am?"

"Captain Hickman, of course." With a gasp, she moved back. "You are Captain Hickman, aren't you?"

Hickman? Who the hell was he? Did the vixen invite lovers into his house and entertain them in his bed?

"Oh, dear." She retreated to the far side of the bed. "Your voice does sound a little different. Who *are* you?"

"Who are *you?*"

"I told you. I'm Agatha Ludlow."

Matthias lunged back. Mosquito netting tangled around

his head and shoulders like a trap falling into place. *Damnation!* His mother was at it again.

"Who are you?" Agatha asked again.

"A . . . a nightmare." He fought his way free of the netting and ran for the door.

CHAPTER TEN

"Mother, you put *another* woman in my bed."

"Matthias, is that you?" His mother sat up in bed, dropping her book onto the floor. A lit candle revealed the shock on her face. "Good God, why did you come here?"

"I thought I lived here."

Jane scrambled out of bed and ran to the shut door. She pressed her ear against the wood to listen. "You shouldn't have come," she whispered.

"I wish I hadn't. This time I found the real Agatha Ludlow."

"Oh, no. Did she recognize you?"

"No, it was dark and she thought I was someone else. Can you believe the woman comes here to wed me and consorts with other men at the same time?" Matthias retrieved his mother's book from the floor and placed it on her bedside table. "I see you're reading the Bible. If you're searching for moral guidance, I could offer you some useful advice. Stop planting women in my bed."

"Keep your voice down." Jane dashed to the balcony door. Hiding behind the curtains, she peeked out. "'Tis not safe."

Matthias strode toward the balcony. "What's wrong?"

"You shouldn't have come tonight. Can you sneak out the way you came in?"

"Hell, no. I came through my bedroom and Agatha is there." He peered through the glass-paned door and spotted the glowing coals of a dying campfire down by the river. In the moonlight, he could make out a few bodies on the ground close to the fire. "Who are they?"

Jane whisked the curtains shut, blocking his view. "Don't look at them. They might see you." She gave him a worried look. "They didn't see you when arrived?"

"No. I rode in from the back. Who are they?"

Jane paced to her bedside table and ran her fingers over her Bible. "They're redcoats."

"Damn," Matthias whispered.

"They're guarding a supply barge at the pier."

He peeked out the curtains. "How many are there? Do you know what kind of supplies?"

"Don't you even think about causing trouble. The last thing we need is the British exacting revenge on us."

Matthias studied the scene in the distance. "They're not very good guards. They appear to be sleeping."

"Good." Jane sighed with relief. "The potion is working."

"Potion?" He pivoted to face his mother.

"Yes. Dottie mixed a sleeping potion into a bottle of rum, and then Caroline gave it to the soldiers outside."

"Caroline? Then Miss Munro finally told you her name."

Jane nodded. "After the real Agatha showed up, she could hardly continue with the pretense."

He snorted. "She waited until she was caught before she confessed?"

"Don't be harsh on her. I don't know how I would have survived the day without her. She helped me mix some sleeping potion into your father's good brandy, and I gave it to Captain Hickman." Jane shuddered. "He's a Loyalist."

"Bloody turncoat," Matthias muttered. "Where is he?"

"Hopefully, he's sleeping in your father's bed."

A Loyalist redcoat sleeping in his house. Matthias cursed silently. He could hardly confront a sleeping enemy. "'Tis a shame the bastard's drugged."

"'Tis a blessing. We were frightened out of our wits. Betsy dropped the soup tureen at dinner, she was so afraid. She ran to the kitchen in tears, and Caroline took over her duties."

"Miss Munro waited on you?"

"Yes, she's been very helpful. It was her idea to drug the soldiers. And I readily agreed. If you'd seen the way that captain was looking at her—"

"What?"

"Shh." Jane frowned. "He might still be awake."

Matthias balled his fists. "Did the lobsterback have his claws on her?"

"He flirted with both the young ladies," Jane muttered. "Agatha enjoyed it, but I could tell Caroline was nervous."

"She should have bitten him." Frustration boiled inside Matthias. How dare the redcoats invade his house and frighten his mother, her servants, and his . . . vixen. He paced the floor. "How long do they intend to stay?"

"They're leaving at dawn."

"If they're able to wake up. I hope the potion has no side effects that will make them suspicious."

Jane winced. "Dottie said it was a light potion."

"I hope you're right. Try to sleep." He kissed her cheek.

"Are you leaving?"

"I dare not leave you here unprotected. I'll stay close by until the redcoats are gone."

"Please don't tamper with their cargo. Captain Hickman would blame us."

He groaned inwardly. As much as he'd love to set the barge on fire, he couldn't risk endangering his mother. Or her guests. "All right."

"Thank you." His mother hugged him. "The third floor should be safe for you. Why don't you use Haversham's old room?"

"Very well. Good night, Mother."

Moonlight shone through the large window on the second-floor landing, lighting the way up the stairs. The third-floor hallway was dark, but Matthias knew his way. He had slept in Haversham's room the last two nights.

The door opened an inch, then knocked against a piece of furniture. A soft feminine gasp greeted him.

Damn. Set up again. His mother had lured him to the vixen's lair.

"I'm warning you." Miss Munro's voice sounded strained. "I have a knife."

Matthias snorted. "Is it as sharp as your teeth?"

There was a pause. "Haversham? Is that you?"

"Yes. Who else barges into your bedchamber every night?"

"Oh, thank God. For a moment, I thought you were one of the redcoats."

Did this mean *he* was welcome in her bedchamber? Or did she merely consider him safe compared to a redcoat? *Damn.* He was tempted to let her know he could be just as dangerous as the next man. If he wanted to be.

He shoved at the door, reached inside to yank the chair out from under the latch, then invaded the dark room.

She gasped. "I—I was going to let you in."

He spotted the form of her white nightgown across the room. The scent of magnolia blossoms drifted toward him, almost as if she had reached out to touch him. Blood surged to his groin. Damn, he could barely see her and he was reacting to her.

"Are you still by the door?" she whispered.

"Yes." He closed it behind him.

This was the east side of the house, directly under the apex of the roof. The wall to his left boasted a window in the shape of a half circle. Moonlight spilled through, creating a shaft of misty light that cut the room in half.

On each side of the light, darkness reigned. He was on one side; she on the other. The shaft of light reached the wall to the right, illuminating the clothespress where he had found Haversham's uniform. Next to it sat a wooden chair where Miss Munro had spread her gown and white petticoats.

He clenched his fists, fighting an urge to cross the room and pull her into his arms. "Forgive my intrusion."

"No, forgive me. I'm afraid I've taken over your room. We didn't expect you back for a few days."

He stepped closer to the shaft of light. "I couldn't stand the thought of you worrying. I have good news for you."

"Yes?" The white form of her nightgown moved closer.

"Your father is alive and well."

She gasped. "He is?"

"Yes. He survived the battle—" He stopped when a white blur ran toward him, crossing the shaft of light. With her arms outstretched, she bumped into him in the darkness, throwing her arms around him as he steadied her.

"Oh, thank you! Thank you, Haversham!"

His groin tightened at the feel of her body pressed against his. "Miss Munro."

Sniffing back tears, she reached up to touch his cheek. "Thank you so much."

He swallowed hard at the guilt stuck in his throat and placed his hand over hers. "Caroline."

Her hand tensed. "I—I beg your pardon." She retreated a step, withdrawing her hand.

He was sorely tempted to pull her back into his arms, but no doubt, she would be shocked by the growing problem in his breeches.

She clutched her hands together. "How did you find out so quickly?"

"Your father was looking for you and your sister, so he left word with the partisans in the area."

"Is he nearby?"

"He went to North Carolina with Francis Marion, but they're expected back soon."

"I see. Thank God he's safe." She stepped back into the shaft of light, clasping her hands together at her chest. Her hair was loose about her shoulders, and her eyes glimmered with unshed tears. He'd never seen such a beautiful sight.

"I needed good news." She lowered her hands to her sides. "Thank you."

He gulped. In the light, he could see the outline of her breasts. He stepped back. "I should be going now."

"No! I'm the one who should leave. I've taken your room."

"There are other servant rooms."

"But this one is yours." She dashed to the chair and picked up her gown.

"I don't want you wandering about the house, not with a redcoat here."

She hesitated, clutching the gown to her chest.

"You don't feel safe with them here, do you? That's why you're sleeping with a knife."

She sighed. "They came with Miss Ludlow."

He moved closer to her, staying in the dark. "Mrs. Thomas told me how helpful you've been. Thank you for that."

She waved a dismissive hand. "I'm glad to help. Jane has been so kind to us."

"That must have been shocking when the real Agatha showed up. I would have liked to have seen your face."

She shuddered. "I thought I was going straight to hell. But from what I can tell, it is a blessing not to be Agatha Ludlow."

He chuckled. "That is true."

She smiled. "Well, thank you for coming back to give me the news. I'll take my leave now. Good night." She stepped toward the door.

"Go back to bed, Miss Munro." He moved into the light to block her.

Her eyes widened. "I'm not throwing you out of your room."

"Caroline." He grabbed her by the upper arms.

She stiffened. "I—I shouldn't sleep in your bed," she whispered.

"I can no longer sleep there."

"Why not?"

"I would be tortured by the scent of magnolia blossoms and lie awake all night, thinking of you."

"I—I find that hard to believe."

He moved closer. "Do you know your eyes are the bright color of a magnolia leaf just as it unfurls?"

"No."

"And your skin, I wager it is as soft as the flower petals."

"I wouldn't know."

"Then we should find out." He grazed her cheek with his fingertips. "I was correct."

She drew in a shaky breath.

He skimmed his fingers down her neck to her shoulder.

"Haversham," she whispered. "Are you trying to seduce me?"

"Do you think I could?" He slid his hand to the back of her neck.

She shook her head. "No."

Indeed? The vixen might as well have issued a challenge. "There's only one way to find out."

CHAPTER ELEVEN

Caroline gulped. Haversham meant to kiss her.

And she wanted it. She closed her eyes and lifted her chin. He pressed his lips against hers, then released her and backed away.

She took a deep breath and opened her eyes. *That was it?* It wasn't bad, but somehow she had expected a cannon to fire in the distance.

She moistened her lips and adjusted the gown against her chest. Then she ventured a glance at Haversham's face.

He was studying her, his eyes glimmering in the dim light. A chill prickled the skin on her arms. Whatever was he thinking to cause him to stare at her so much? "It seems odd for me to call you Haversham. What should I call you?"

"Lover would do."

Surprised, she gave a nervous laugh. "I think not."

"I see I'm out of practice."

She smiled. Somehow, the thought of a man this strong and handsome being less than expert appealed to her. "Well, I wouldn't fret about it if I were you."

He raised one eyebrow.

"It was rather . . . pleasant, actually. Considering you're out of practice. I—I rather enjoyed it."

"How kind of you to notice." He stepped closer. "There *is* a remedy, you know."

"Excuse me?"

His gaze lowered to her mouth. "More practice."

"Oh. I supp—" She gasped when he pulled her against him. Before she could catch her breath, his mouth was on hers.

Stunned, it took her a moment to realize everything he was doing. His lips were opening, closing, pressing, nibbling, molding against her lips in a way that made her mouth move with his. It was shocking. Intriguing. She'd never known there could be so many subtle maneuvers involved in a kiss. She could hardly think. Hardly stand.

She grabbed at his shoulders to steady herself. He tightened his arms around her. With the gown sandwiched between their bodies, she slid her hands up to his neck.

He groaned and abandoned her mouth. He moved down her throat with tickling, tasting kisses.

With a moan, she tilted back her head. This was far better than she had ever imagined. Was that a rumble deep in his throat or had the cannons fired in the distance, shaking the walls of the house?

"Was that an explosion?" she whispered.

"Not yet, but damned close." He nuzzled her ear, then traced it with his tongue.

She shivered, too muddled in her mind to think clearly. She only knew she wanted more. She splayed her fingers into his thick, damp hair. Loose from its tie, his hair was shoulder-length and soft against her cheek. He smelled of soap and sun-dried linen.

He slid his hands to her waist and pressed her against him. Something jabbed at her, sharp and sudden.

"Ow!" She jumped back. The gown dropped to the floor.

"Are you all right?" he asked.

"Something poked me in the stomach."

He stepped back into the shadows. "I—I beg your pardon."

"It seemed awfully sharp." She rubbed her belly. "And pointed."

"*Pointed?*"

"Yes." She considered the gown on the floor at her feet. "Oh, I know what it was." She plucked the dress off the floor. "See the pin? Jane's gown was too big around the waist for me, so we pinned it."

"I see."

She suddenly felt the full impact of what she'd been doing with this man she hardly knew. Her face flooded with warmth, and she gave him a nervous smile. "I'm sorry. I didn't mean to . . . end things so abruptly."

He remained silent, hidden in the shadows.

"I'm quite all right," she assured him. "'Twas naught but a small prick."

"You don't say."

She wondered why his teeth sounded clenched.

"I bid you good night, Miss Munro." His footsteps tapped sharply, headed toward the door. Then she heard the door close.

He was gone.

Caroline draped the gown over the chair, pondering his hurried exit. Had she angered him? Or perhaps she had not excited him enough.

He certainly had excited her. Dear Lord, the man had nearly made her swoon with excitement. With a sigh, she returned to bed. At least she could face her spinsterhood knowing she'd been thoroughly kissed. By a butler, no less.

She smiled. Haversham was not like any butler she'd ever met. She wasn't quite sure what he was. An indentured servant? A man of business? He was confusing—attentive one moment, running away the next. But one thing was very clear.

Haversham was not in need of practice.

Matthias rolled over on the narrow cot in an empty servant's room next to the nursery. The air was stuffy and hot. The lumpy mattress smelled of mildew. Still, for a man accustomed to sleeping in the swamp, these problems should be minor. He knew exactly what was keeping him awake.

Naught but a small prick.

Bloody hell. He'd been close to bursting his breeches and all she had felt was a tiny pin lodged in a gown? And that first kiss she had dismissed as merely *pleasant*? He had purposely restrained himself for fear of offending her with too much lust and too big a bulge. As if she'd notice.

Oh, she'd *enjoyed* it, she said. No doubt, she'd also enjoy a ride in the park or a shiny new ribbon for her bonny red hair. *Damn it to hell.*

He punched his moldy pillow. It was just as well. He had

no intention of involving himself with a woman, not even the tempting Caroline Munro. The timing was wrong.

Slowly, he became aware of a strange odor. Was something burning? He slipped on his breeches. Fumbling with the buttons, he paced toward the door in the dark.

"Ow." He found the door by ramming his big toe into it. Outside in the narrow corridor, he sniffed to determine the origin of the smell.

The nursery.

He burst open the door. He had a quick glimpse of Edward sitting cross-legged on his bed with a lit candlestick in front of him. He held something over the fire, melting it. "What—"

Edward jumped and dropped whatever he was melting. It knocked over the candlestick. Instantly, his blanket caught fire. The boy yelped and leapt out of bed.

Matthias lunged forward, grabbed the pillow, and smothered the flames. "What the hell are you doing? You want to burn the house down?"

"I'm sorry." Edward's voice sounded shaky in the dark. "I didn't mean to."

"Haven't you been told not to play with fire?"

"I . . . I thought I could control it."

"Edward?" Charlotte's sleepy voice came from across the room. "Who are you talking to? Is it Papa?"

Matthias winced. "I'm not your father."

"Are you his ghost?" Charlotte whispered.

"Don't be silly," Edward growled. "If he were Papa's ghost, then Papa would have to be dead."

"Oh. Then whose ghost is he?" Charlotte asked.

"Enough." Matthias gritted his teeth to keep from shouting. "Both of you, go to sleep. Now."

"He sounds like Papa," Charlotte mumbled.

"Good night, Princess. And you, Edward," Matthias turned to the boy. "No more playing with fire."

"You're not my father. You cannot order me about."

"*You* cannot stop me. I'm bigger than you." When Matthias was satisfied the boy was going to remain quiet, he pivoted toward the door. "Good night."

Back in his room, he stretched out on the cot. His mother certainly couldn't complain about being lonesome now. There were a greedy strumpet and a drugged redcoat on the second floor, a redheaded temptress and a pregnant woman on the third, and in the nursery, a little princess and a boy who played with fire.

The next morning, Matthias sat up with a gasp. A thin layer of perspiration coated his skin. With a muttered curse, he shoved his hair back from his face. *Damn it to hell*. It was back. The nightmare. He thought he had outgrown such nonsense.

Four years in the army had given him a ready supply of wretched memories, but none of those tortured him in his sleep. In fact, he couldn't recall any nightmares since he'd left home. It was only at Loblolly where this one childish memory continued to torment him.

The sounds next door in the nursery alerted him that the guests were up and about. Soon they would be having breakfast, but with Agatha in attendance, Haversham could not appear. She would recognize him as Matthias in a second.

A shame, though, that he would miss seeing Caroline. Was she remembering their kiss? Or trying hard to forget?

And what about the drugged soldiers? He dressed quickly and made his way to the nearest dormer window. Yes! The barge was gone, and the British with it. Only a blackened circle marred the green lawn where the campfire had been.

So the women were now safe and he could return to Snow's Island. He would have to exit the house without Agatha seeing him. The simplest solution was the servants' stairway.

Years earlier when Grandfather had built Loblolly, his Quaker upbringing had made him uncomfortable about owning slaves. Not that it had stopped him. To alleviate his guilt, Grandfather had built the house with a hidden passageway so the servants could move about unseen. That way, he was spared the humiliation and discomfort of passing a slave in the hall or on the grand staircase.

Grandfather's sons had contrasted sharply in their opinion of slaves. Whereas Matthias's father, the elder son, accepted slavery without question, Richard's father became a minister who preached against the evils of bondage. Even so, Uncle Nathaniel had swallowed his ire and allowed Richard to live at Loblolly during the winter months. That way, Richard had been able to share Matthias's tutor and acquire a fine education.

Matthias recalled playing with Richard in the hidden corridor. If memory served, the passageway began in a storeroom on the first floor. It ran between the library and dining room, then continued up a narrow staircase to the second floor.

There, the corridor ran between his bedchamber and his father's, with doors leading into both rooms. He had positioned a clothespress over the door to his room to block it off. But the servants had used the door to his father's bedchamber. Unlike Grandfather, Father was quite comfortable around slaves. Particularly the young maids.

Matthias located the door that accessed the passageway. Disguised as part of the wall, it opened with a hidden latch beneath the chair rail. He clicked the door open. Before him, a narrow staircase descended into darkness. He closed the door and felt along the wall as he stepped blindly down the stairs.

On the second floor, he moved silently in case Agatha was still in his bedchamber. He descended to the first floor and stopped at the entrance to the library. His father had installed peepholes at each door so a servant could look before entering. He had always suspected this was his father's way of keeping his lecherous activities from being interrupted.

The small sliding door was situated above a row of books in the bookcase. He pushed it to the side and peered through the open rectangle. The library was empty.

The door was part of the bookcase, hinged to swing back into the secret corridor. It opened with a creak. At the desk, he grabbed a piece of paper and dipped a quill into the inkwell.

Dear Caroline,
I must leave for a few days to attend to business.

He hesitated, tempted to write that he would miss her, but decided against it. She didn't want to get involved with a soldier, and he didn't want to marry as long as the war continued. In a moment of weakness, he had kissed her, but it would be better from now on to keep a cordial distance from her.

Wishing you and your family good health and happiness.

He signed it with an *H*, then, letter in hand, he returned to the passageway and pushed the bookshelf door shut. At the end of the corridor, the final door opened into a storage room. He cracked it open.

Betsy was stacking plates on the center table.

"Betsy," he whispered.

She yelped and spun around.

"Shh. Someone might hear you." Matthias eased inside and shut the door.

"Mr. Thomas! You gave me such a fright." Betsy gave the secret door a curious look. "What were you doing in there?"

"I'm sneaking out so Miss Ludlow won't see me."

"Oh. I wish I could avoid her." Betsy shuddered. "She brought those awful redcoats with her."

"They're gone now. You're safe." Matthias folded the letter he had written in half. "Will you give this to Miss Munro? And don't tell her who I really am."

Betsy gave him a quizzical look and stuffed the letter in her apron pocket. "Isn't it dangerous for you to be here?"

"Yes, but I'm leaving now." He strode to the other door that opened into the dining room. "Where is everyone?"

"In the morning parlor."

"Good. Take care of yourself, Betsy." Matthias dashed across the dining room and exited the house through the servants' entrance.

As he entered the kitchen, he spotted Dottie in front of the great hearth, sliding loaves of bread into the brick oven. "Good morning, Dottie."

"Morning. Your mama told me you were here, so I started making some bread for your boys." Her round face glistened from the heat of the kitchen fire. "Can you wait 'til it's done?"

"Aye, I'll wait. Thank you." Matthias filled a bowl with hot water from the kettle so he could wash and shave. Steam rose up to his face. "Your sleeping potion worked well on the redcoats."

Dottie nodded. "Poor Betsy couldn't do a thing with them around."

Matt rolled up his sleeves. "I noticed she seemed edgy."

"More like terrified." Dottie broke eggs into a skillet. "And with reason. She lost her father and two brothers in battle. Then her mother died. She couldn't keep the farm going by herself and ended up selling herself to your mama."

"Damn." Matthias touched the water to test its temperature. "I never knew."

"You never asked." Dottie carried the skillet to the hearth and set it on a three-legged trivet.

He'd never asked. Matthias stared at the bowl of water, listening to the sounds of Dottie's cooking. Her spoon scraped against the cast iron. The fire crackled. Sausages in another skillet sizzled. "I never asked if you have family, Dottie."

She snorted. "Do you think I came from a cabbage patch?

Of course I had a mother and father. And brothers and sisters. Haven't seen them since the master brought me here."

Matthias swallowed hard. Dottie had been at Loblolly for twenty years. He washed and shaved in silence.

Dottie heaped eggs and sausages onto a plate. "Come and eat."

"Thank you." He sat at the kitchen table. "I'm sorry, Dottie. About your family."

"I know." She patted his shoulder. "You're a good boy. Always have been."

With a frown, he began eating. If he was good, he wouldn't have made Caroline wait for the news that her father was well.

As he finished the last bite, Betsy walked in with a tray of dirty dishes.

"They finished eating in the Great House." She set the tray next to the dishpan. "Miss Munro said she was taking the children to the garden."

Caroline. Maybe he could see her before he left. He handed his empty plate to Betsy. "Is Miss Ludlow with them?"

"Lord, no." Betsy scoffed. "She doesn't care for the young'uns."

Matthias shrugged on his plain brown coat. "I'll return for the bread in a little while. Betsy, can I have that letter back?"

When she passed him the letter, he tossed it into the fire. With a grin, he headed for the garden. And Caroline.

Chapter Twelve

As he exited the kitchen, Matthias glanced around to make sure he wasn't seen. He dashed to the pergola, and instantly, the temperature dropped as he was surrounded by green, living shade. The sun pierced through the vines here and there, dappling the ground with spots of light.

He heard the children talking. Grasping a vine in his hand, he opened a peephole. There she was, in jasmine-yellow cotton, her red curls gleaming in the morning sun.

"Miss Munro," he whispered.

She glanced over her shoulder.

"Over here."

She squinted in his direction. He crooked a finger through the opening.

She approached, a smile spreading across her sunny face. "Is that Haversham or a hedge that beckons me?"

"Come in," he whispered.

As he walked to the entrance, he could spot her yellow gown on the other side of the vines, moving on a parallel course. She reached the entrance. He grabbed her hand and pulled her into the cool, leafy tunnel.

She laughed. "Whatever are you doing here? Where were you at breakfast?"

"I don't work in the house anymore." Still holding her hand, he backed into the pergola, taking her with him. "In fact, I have to go away for a while."

"You have more business matters to attend to?"

"Aye."

"How long will you be gone?" She moved closer to him. A ray of sunshine shot through the vines, lighting her face. Tiny freckles dusted her little nose.

Freckle-face. Memory of the dead redcoat flashed through Matt's mind. He released her hand. He had no idea how many men he'd dispatched in the heat of battle. Who had time to think about it when fighting for survival? But Freckle-face was the last man he'd killed, and he'd watched the light extinguish in the soldier's eyes.

What the hell was he doing, flirting with Caroline? He'd made his decision in the library to keep a distance from her. But it was damned hard to honor that decision when he was in her presence. The minute he saw her, he wanted to hold her and kiss her. But he had vowed to remain unattached throughout the war. *Timing is everything*. And this was the wrong time.

He stepped back. She must have noticed something in his expression for her smile faded.

He took a deep breath. "Miss Munro, I must apologize for last night."

"Oh?" Her eyes darkened with a wary look.

"I took far too much liberty. It won't happen again."

Her back stiffened. "I see."

"I can explain."

"There's no need." She brushed back a curl with an impatient gesture. "I understand."

"I'm not sure—"

"'Tis simple enough," she interrupted him. "I may have enjoyed it, but you were eager to leave. And now you no longer wish to see me. I understand perfectly. Good day." She swiveled and headed for the pergola entrance.

"Bloody hell, I liked it. Too much."

She halted.

Damn. What was he doing? He should have let her go. "'Tis a matter of timing. I'm not . . . free at this time."

She turned slowly. "Because of your indenture? I thought you understood. I don't care about that."

Was it possible that she could love him for himself? Not for the house, the land, or the wealth. He clenched his fists. He'd be a fool to give her up.

But what choice did he have? He could be dead in a week, a month, a year. He couldn't make promises he wasn't sure he could keep.

He had to withdraw. "I shouldn't see you again. Times are too dangerous because of the war."

Her eyes reflected the hurt he caused. She wrapped her arms around herself as if she'd taken a chill. "I would agree if you were involved with the war. I vowed never to love a soldier again for that same reason. But you're—"

"You loved a soldier? When was this?"

"Three years ago. He died at Brandywine. I never want

to endure that pain again." She wandered toward the hedge and fingered the small jasmine leaves. "You're not a soldier. I thought you would be safe."

Matthias paced toward her. "Is that why you kissed me? Because I'm *not* a soldier?"

She shrugged with a bewildered look. "I wouldn't have kissed you if I wasn't fond of you. But I've avoided soldiers like smallpox for three years. I wouldn't have talked to you if you were a soldier. I would never have let it progress to the point that we . . . kissed."

He cursed silently. He would have never believed that masquerading as a butler could cause such a mess. If he confessed to being a soldier, would she spurn him? It provided a way for him to end their relationship, but he damned well didn't want to take it. She was so tempting. And she thought he was safe to fall in love with.

God help him, he wanted that love. He wanted her.

Suddenly, her answer was paramount. "What if I decided, now, to join the army? Would you refuse to see me again?"

Her eyes glistened with tears. "I would beg you not to join."

"But if I did?"

She took a deep, shuddering breath. "I—I'm not sure what I'm feeling. Everything is happening so quickly. I hardly know you but . . . I don't want to lose you."

"I don't want to lose you, either."

Her eyes locked with his. He knew the instant she understood the desire he struggled with. Her gaze lowered to his mouth with a languid, sensual, green-eyed invitation.

He pulled her into his arms. She pressed against him,

grabbing his shoulders. Their mouths met in a frantic reen-actment of the evening before.

He devoured her lips. He nibbled her neck. He savored the taste of her skin. She smelled of sunshine and magnolia, and felt warm and willing. She melted against him.

And still, it wasn't enough. He returned to her mouth. This was even better than last night. With her hands wrapped around his neck, she was kissing him back. He felt the tight-ening in his breeches. With a groan, he invaded her mouth with his tongue.

She started and pulled back. "What was that?"

"A kiss." He leaned forward, wanting more.

She stepped back. "Is that allowed? I mean . . . you meant to do that?"

"'Twas no accident."

"Oh." Her face grew pink. "Of course. People don't acci-dentally stick out their tongues."

He grinned. "True." So this soldier from her past had never given her a truly passionate kiss. The thought glad-dened his heart.

"When I was a little girl, I thought such things were—Never mind." She shook her head. "I've said enough. My tongue is my worst enemy."

"It tasted friendly to me."

With an exasperated look, she gave his chest a playful push that didn't budge him.

He chuckled. "At least you didn't bite me."

"Well, I wasn't sure you were doing it on purpose." Her blush deepened. "When I was young, I heard some women in the village talking about a woman named Polly. She went into the forest with a man and nine months later, *voilà*—a baby. So I thought it *was* some sort of accident."

"Like falling into a pond?"

She laughed. "I suppose."

He gathered her back into his arms. With a shy glance at his face, she rested her hands on his chest.

"Caroline." He leaned forward to nuzzle her neck. Her scent and the softness of her skin made him instantly hard.

"Hmm?" She skimmed her hands up to his neck.

With each breath, her breasts rose toward him, enticing him to have a taste. He leaned her back.

"Ow!" She jumped. "What was that?"

He straightened. "Excuse me." She must have felt the bulge that time.

"Something jabbed me." She pivoted. "Oh, no wonder. I backed into a stem from this climbing rose."

He glared at the rosebush. How come she never felt him?

"I'm all right. 'Twas naught but a tiny twig."

"Bloody hell," he muttered.

"I should check on the children." She peeked through an opening in the hedge. "Oh, dear, they're digging in Jane's flowerbed." She turned to him with apologetic smile. "I should go before they destroy the garden."

Matthias peered through another peephole and spotted a blue parasol. "Miss Ludlow is coming." *Damn.* How could he return to the kitchen without her seeing him?

Caroline looked again through the hedge. "Another parasol? She must have one to match every gown."

Agatha sauntered into the garden and stopped at the sight of the children. "Oh, my, whatever are you doing?"

"We're digging." Charlotte rose to her feet and wiped her soiled hands on her gown. "Want to see what we found?"

Agatha shuddered so hard her parasol shook. "How disgusting. What filthy urchins."

"They're not urchins. They're earthworms," Edward announced.

Agatha snorted. "Silly child, I was referring to you and your dirty sister."

Caroline stiffened. "I'm going to stuff that parasol down her throat and open it," she muttered.

"Wait." Matthias looped an arm around her shoulders so she wouldn't leave, then pushed back more vines to give them a better view.

Charlotte lifted her chin. "I am not a worm. I'm a princess."

Edward jumped to his feet with an eight-inch earthworm in his hands. "Zounds! This is the biggest one yet!"

Agatha jumped back. "A *snake*!"

"'Tis not a snake." Edward walked toward her, stretching the slimy worm out to its longest length. "See?"

Agatha lunged back. "Keep that away from me."

"But, miss," Edward said. "You should look behind—"

"Stay away!" Agatha leapt back. She teetered on the edge of the reflecting pool, her parasol waving frantically in the air. With a screech, she tumbled backward into the water.

Caroline gasped and whispered, "Oh, no!"

Matthias grinned. "Oh, yes."

Agatha floundered about, slapping lily pads and splashing water all over herself. Her curls drooped on each side of her head like long dog ears. "Blast you, you bloody beggar! 'Twill be your fault if I drown in here."

Edward kicked off his shoes. "I tried to warn you." He jumped into the pool and waded to her. The water only reached his knees.

"Keep away from me!" Agatha shouted. "This is your fault."

"I just want to help you up." Edward leaned over her.

She swatted his hands away.

"Oh, no, you made me drop the worm." Edward inspected her gown. "There it is!" He pointed at her bodice.

Agatha spotted the worm slithering up her gown toward her breasts and let out a window-shattering screech.

Matthias bit his lip to keep from laughing. "Bravo, Edward."

"'Tis not amusing." Caroline grinned.

"Falling in a pond." Matthias slanted her a wry look. "I wonder if she's with child."

Caroline elbowed him in the ribs. "I'd better go."

He grabbed her hand and kissed it. "I'll see you in a few days."

With the chaos surrounding Agatha, Matthias found it easy to escape unnoticed. But he couldn't escape what he had done. He had failed to end the relationship with Caroline.

The trap at Kingstree would be ready within a week, and though he hoped the ambush would go smoothly, bloodshed was always possible. He shouldn't have kissed her again. Not when his next mission could be dangerous.

Chapter Thirteen

Kingstree, South Carolina
Saturday, September 16, 1780

"Move your damned horse," the British officer commanded.

Matthias squatted behind his reclining horse, his musket on the ground by his feet. From his position in the middle of the road, he'd watched the redcoats cross the bridge. There were only five of them—two soldiers on the wagon, two more on foot, and the impatient lieutenant on horseback.

Rubbing his horse's neck, Matthias gave the officer an apologetic look. "I'm afraid he's gone lame, sir."

"He's blocking the road." The lieutenant wiped the sweat from his brow with a lacy handkerchief, his woolen uniform obviously uncomfortable in the noonday heat. "Shoot the beast. My men will help you haul it to the side."

"Aye, sir." Matt picked up his musket and stood.

"Quickly, man. We haven't all day." The officer stuffed his handkerchief up his sleeve. "Aim for the head."

"As you wish." In seconds, Matthias had his musket raised and aimed. Directly at the lieutenant's head.

"What the hell—" The officer's eyes widened.

The other redcoats scrambled for their weapons, then halted as two dozen partisans appeared from the cover of bushes and trees, all with muskets trained on them.

The lieutenant's face reddened with anger. "This is an outrage!"

"No, this is an ambush." Matt whistled. His horse rolled to a standing position and cantered off.

The lieutenant's gaze darted nervously along the line of armed partisans. "If you deny us passage, you will all be guilty of treason."

Matthias kept his musket aimed at the officer. "If we kill all of you, who will be left to report it?"

The British soldiers gave their commanding officer a frantic look for guidance. The partisans slowly advanced.

With a clenched jaw, the lieutenant addressed his men, "Lay down your weapons."

Matthias breathed easier. Over half of his men were out of musket balls and powder, but the bluff had worked.

As planned, the partisans ushered the redcoats into the nearby woods. Simon scrambled onto the supply wagon and drove away. Ten militiamen mounted their horses and rode escort. Matthias and Richard tied the five British soldiers to trees while the rest of his men stood guard.

"Make yourselves comfortable. You may have a long wait," Matthias advised the sitting soldiers. He would send a man to Kingstree to arrange for the townspeople to discover the redcoats and release them the next morning.

"We'll come after you," the lieutenant warned. "We'll hunt you down."

Matthias tightened the knot around the lieutenant's

ankles. Using his knife, he cut off the excess rope. "You could wander the swamp for years and not find us."

"They'd probably drown in a bog," Richard added.

"Traitors," the lieutenant growled. "I'll see you hang."

"Then perhaps I should adjust your eyesight, now." Matthias lifted his knife so the blade caught the sunlight and cast a glare across the officer's face.

The lieutenant paled.

Matthias leaned closer. "How many homes have you burned to the ground? How many children have you left to starve?"

"This is war," the redcoat whispered. "We do what we must."

"Aye, we do." Matthias straightened. "A shame you have no way to defend yourself. 'Twill be a long night."

"Aye." Richard nodded with a twinkle in his eye. "The snakes are bad this close to the river."

Matthias wedged the knife under his belt. "Did you know that alligators are attracted to the color red?"

"Really?" Richard smiled. "How interesting."

Ignoring the frightened protests from the captured redcoats, Matthias mounted his horse. With the rest of his men, he rode back to Snow's Island.

Another week passed, and Matthias stayed at the campsite with his men. Luckily, the supplies they'd captured contained weapons and ammunition they sorely needed. He was careful to ration the wine and rum, and doubled the guard in case the British attempted to locate them.

It was nigh impossible to live each day surrounded by green vegetation without recalling Caroline's green eyes. And he couldn't pass a sweet bay magnolia without longing to bury his nose in her scented curls.

The evenings were worse. The men sat around the campfire and reminisced about their wives and children. And he would remember how she had melted in his arms, how she had returned his kisses, how her eyes had glimmered with tears at the thought of losing him.

"Roasted potatoes again?" Simon sat cross-legged, staring glumly at the potato on a slab of bark. "You know what I'd like, Captain? More of that bread you bring from your home."

The men murmured in agreement.

Richard gave him an amused look. "You haven't been home in a fortnight."

"I'm not hungry." Matthias passed his potato to Simon before walking away.

He settled under an ash tree and swatted at the buzzing mosquitoes. The humming sound of locusts grew louder as the sun descended. A marbled salamander scurried into a clump of marsh fern. Why had he told Caroline he'd be back in a few days? He closed his eyes and muttered a curse.

"Sounds like a woman," Richard said.

He opened his eyes to glare at his cousin. "Sounds like someone prying into my business."

"A bit grumpy, are we?" Richard sat beside him. "The men are laying bets as to why you've been growling so much."

Matthias ground his teeth. "I'm not growling."

"Right." Richard smiled. "So is it a woman? The one you called a 'conniving little she-demon'?"

"No."

"The one you called a 'vixen with sharp little teeth'?"

"Go to hell."

Rich laughed. "The wound's a little tender, huh?"

"What wound?"

Rich's face grew serious. "She wasn't interested, I take it. That's why you're staying here."

"She *is* interested. That's why I'm staying here."

"And that's supposed to make sense? You've been breathing in swamp gas?"

Matthias shot his cousin a wry look. "You know how I feel about this war. 'Twould be foolish for me to marry and father children when I could die any day."

Rich tugged a leaf off a nearby pepperbush and dissected it slowly. "You've given thought lately to marriage and children?"

Matthias shrugged. "The timing is wrong."

Richard tossed the mangled leaf to the ground. "What if there was no war?"

"There's no point to this. Go away."

"Answer me. If there were peace, would you pursue her?"

If there were peace, Richard wouldn't have that blasted red scar down his face. Matthias rubbed his brow. "You could have peace, Rich. You could go home and forget about this nonsense."

"'Tis not nonsense."

Matthias sighed. Richard's father, the Quaker minister, had opposed his son's entering the army. But as soon as Matthias had joined, Richard had followed suit. And Matthias knew his uncle blamed him for leading Richard into the war.

"You didn't answer my question," Richard persisted. "If there was no war, would you pursue her?"

Matthias leaned his head back and gazed at the darkening sky. "I suppose I would."

"You suppose?"

Matthias shrugged.

"I've known you all your life. 'Tis not like you to be indecisive. What's wrong?"

Matt gave his cousin an annoyed look. "I'm not sure. I cannot decide."

Richard rubbed at the scar on his face. "I know. There's something wrong with her."

Matthias scoffed. "I think not."

"Oh, there *must* be. Because if you thought she was perfect for you, you wouldn't let anything stand in your way. Is she ugly and scrawny?"

"No!"

"Then she's stupid."

"No, dammit. And stop insulting her or I'll bash your teeth in."

"Ah, so you *do* care for her." Richard grinned with triumph.

Matt glared at his cousin. "Very clever."

"Perhaps you're afraid."

"Bullshit."

"No, I mean it. Your parents have a miserable marriage. Are you afraid you'll have one?"

"No. My parents' marriage was arranged. I shall choose my own wife. And she'll need to love *me*, not the plantation."

Richard's eyes narrowed. "You're expected to settle down at Loblolly and breed more heirs for the little kingdom."

Matthias gritted his teeth. "I know. What's your point?"

"You were never happy there. You hated the way your father was treating—"

"I don't want to talk about it."

Richard rose to his feet and brushed off his breeches. "I think you're avoiding the truth."

Matthias snorted. "The truth is we're at war."

"And it makes the perfect excuse for you not to marry. How convenient."

"War is never convenient." Matthias scowled at his cousin as Richard wandered back to camp.

At General Cornwallis's headquarters, Captain Ezra Hickman checked the polish on his boots and tucked his tricorne under his arm. A week had passed since he'd made his recommendation, and now the general wished to see him.

The door opened, and Cornwallis's chief aide motioned for him to enter. Ezra strode inside and stood at attention. The general fumbled through papers on his desk.

As Ezra waited to be acknowledged, he chanced a few furtive glances at the other occupants in the room. Next to him stood an ashen-faced lieutenant who looked ready to lose his dinner. Against the far wall, he spotted Lieutenant Colonel Banastre Tarleton. Yes! The general was planning to honor his request. Soon, he'd be trading his red coat for the green one of a dragoon.

"Hickman, is it?" Cornwallis scratched his chin, not bothering to look up. "I expect you know the lieutenant colonel."

"Yes, sir." Ezra bowed to Tarleton. "I am honored, sir. Your reputation is legendary."

Tarleton snorted. "I'm not interested in legends. I want results."

"Yes, sir." Ezra felt his face redden.

Cornwallis waved a pudgy hand. "Don't mind him. He's been in a foul mood ever since the incident at Nelson's Ferry."

Tarleton stalked to a window and stood there, looking out at the rows of tents. "That bastard Marion cannot hide from me forever."

"I saw a report on Marion this morning. Where the deuce is it?" Cornwallis thumbed through a stack of papers and called to his aide, "George, who was the man who filed that report?"

"Greville, my lord," the aide replied with a stony expression. "Do you request his presence?"

"Yes. Right away." Cornwallis motioned for his aide to go. "Now where were we?"

Tarleton turned with an annoyed expression. "We were discussing the debacle at Kingstree. I wanted to have the lieutenant here flogged."

"I believe a loss in wages will suffice." Cornwallis looked at the lieutenant. "What say you, Rooster?"

"Brewster, sir." The lieutenant bowed his head. "I will gladly forgo my wages, sir."

"You deserve worse." Tarleton strode toward the lieutenant. "Losing your supplies to a pack of ruffians? You're lucky I don't whip the skin off your back."

"Yes, sir," Brewster replied with a strained voice.

"Why did you cross at Kingstree?" Tarleton demanded.

"It was the only bridge. The partisans burned all the others."

"And that didn't seem suspicious to you?" Tarleton's eyes blazed with anger as he turned to Hickman. "And you, did you lose your shipment as well?"

Ezra stood stiff at attention. "No, sir. I arrived without incident."

Tarleton examined him. "You speak like a local."

"I come from Charles Town, sir."

"Do you know your way around the swamps?"

Ezra hesitated. His knowledge was limited, but he didn't want to admit it.

Cornwallis leaned back in his chair. "Hickman recommends we move our supplies by barge. In fact, he knows a perfect place halfway to Charles Town. What was the name of that plantation?"

"Loblolly, my lord," Ezra answered. "On the Black River."

"Your suggestion has merit," Cornwallis continued. "And since you are already acquainted with the house and its occupants, I'm putting you in charge."

Ezra's mouth dropped open. *Damn.* He would be far from the battle lines and entirely forgotten.

Cornwallis smiled as he poured a crystal glass full of wine. "You're a lucky devil, Hickman. You'll be eating well and living in comfort while the rest of us suffer."

The general didn't look like he was suffering or missing any meals, Ezra thought. "My lord, I was hoping for something more—" He noticed a hard glint in the general's eyes. This was not the time. "I am delighted to be of service, my lord."

The door opened behind him, and the aide spoke. "Greville, sir."

A tall soldier marched in and stood at attention.

"You're the soldier who escaped from the partisans?" Cornwallis asked.

"Yes, sir," Greville replied, his eyes gleaming with pride. "I escaped five days ago in North Carolina. I made it back here last night."

Tarleton advanced on the soldier. "You were captured at Nelson's Ferry?"

Greville's face reddened. "Yes, sir."

Tarleton gritted his teeth. "Where is Marion now?"

"He was in North Carolina when I escaped, sir. I believe he is still there."

Tarleton turned to Lieutenant Brewster. "When was the ambush at Kingstree?"

"A week ago, sir," Brewster answered.

Tarleton stepped closer to the lieutenant. "Who was the leader of the ambush?"

A drop of sweat ran down the lieutenant's cheek. "I don't know his name, sir. He had dark hair—"

"So does Marion," Tarleton interrupted. "Was he a short, swarthy fellow, in his forties?"

"No, sir," Brewster answered. "He was young and tall. He threatened to cut my eyes out with that vicious knife of his."

"Wait." Greville held up a hand. "He has a knife?"

"Yes, a long, wicked one with a handle inlaid with ivory."

"That's my knife," Greville insisted. "After the bastard broke my nose, he stole my knife to murder one of our soldiers at Nelson's Ferry."

"Make a note," Cornwallis addressed his aide. "I want a bounty on this man's head. A handsome reward should help us nab him. Do you know his name, Greville?"

Greville's crooked nose made his smile appeared lop-sided. "Aye, I'll never forget. He's Captain Matthias Murray Thomas."

Ezra's breath caught. The mistress of Loblolly had introduced herself as Jane Murray Thomas. She had to be related. His heart started pounding, and he stiffened, carefully keeping his face blank.

"I mean to apprehend this Captain Thomas," Tarleton announced. "Since you know him, Greville, you will ride with me."

Greville's eyes lit up. "Thank you, sir."

Ezra remained wooden, not letting anyone know how excited he was. That hefty reward could be his! He could still attain his dream of being a wealthy man. All he had to do was turn in the wanted rebel leader Matthias Murray Thomas.

CHAPTER FOURTEEN

Monday, September 25, 1780

After Caroline had completed two rows, she passed the knitting needles and yarn to her niece.

Charlotte accepted them with a frown. "Do I have to?"

"Aye." Virginia lowered her ever-expanding form onto Charlotte's bed in the nursery. "Jane was kind enough to give us needles and yarn, so you should practice."

With a huff, Charlotte sat beside her mother. "I wager Miss Ludlow doesn't knit her own stockings."

"Don't you want to be able to take care of yourself?" Caroline asked. "And you, Edward, I'm sure you can find something more useful to do than playing with soldiers."

"I like playing soldier when Mama and Charlotte are knitting." Edward stretched out on the floor. "I pretend the clicking noises are their swords clashing."

Caroline plucked one of his soldiers from the floor. "What happened to this one? His head looks melted."

"'Tis nothing," Edward mumbled.

Charlotte paused in her knitting. "He's punishing the red-coats."

"What?" Virginia asked.

Edward glared at his sister. "Tattler."

Caroline inspected the British army. Several soldiers bore mutilated heads. "Edward, what have you been doing?"

He sat, crossing his legs. "I burn them. They deserve it. They burned our house in Charles Town and our cabin—"

"I don't care!" Caroline gathered up the melted soldiers. "These don't belong to you. You have no right to destroy someone else's property."

"But armies do it all the time." Edward gestured to the soldiers on the floor. "And these are armies."

"These are toys." Caroline dropped the soldiers into the tin box. "And they belong to Jane's son, Matthias."

"Aunt Jane said I could have them. I told her I'd be ten years old tomorrow."

Caroline winced inwardly. She had no gift for Edward's birthday. "This is hardly the way to repay her kindness."

Virginia struggled to her feet. "When are you burning them, Edward?"

"He does it at night when you're asleep." Charlotte tugged at her yarn, and the ball rolled off her lap onto the floor. She set down her knitting to run after it.

"How are you starting the fire?" Virginia asked.

"The tinder wheel," Edward mumbled.

Caroline set the tin box of soldiers on the bookcase. "You told me you would light candles so you could read."

Having retrieved her ball of yarn, Charlotte proceeded to

wind it back up. "He caught his bed on fire once, but the ghost put it out."

Edward glowered at her. "Don't you know when to hush?"

Caroline strode to Edward's bed and inspected the pillows. One was scorched. "Where's your blanket?"

"In that trunk." Edward pointed. "It has a black spot."

"So you hid it?" Virginia regarded him sadly. "Edward, you could have burned the house down."

"No, he won't." Charlotte sat on her bed next to her mother. "The ghost will stop him."

"He wasn't a ghost, you bufflehead," Edward growled.

"Don't insult your—" Virginia paled. "There was a man in here? At night?"

"He was a nice ghost," Charlotte insisted. "He put out the fire and fussed at Edward. Then he vanished."

"He went out the door," Edward said.

Charlotte assumed a superior look. "Did you see him?"

"No." Edward wrinkled his nose in disgust. "It was dark because he put out the fire."

"Enough!" Virginia raised her hands. "Give me the tinder wheel. Now."

Edward trudged to his bed, retrieved the item from underneath, then handed it to his mother. "I'm sorry."

Caroline noted her sister's weary expression. Poor Ginny tired so easily these days. And she was growing increasingly worried about her missing husband. At least now, thanks to Haversham, they knew that their father was safe. "Why don't I take the children outside while you rest?"

Virginia nodded. "Stay away from Miss Ludlow."

"We will." Caroline ushered the children from the room.

The sounds of the harpsichord echoed through the house. Agatha was in the front parlor, entertaining Jane once again, so Caroline and the children slipped quietly out the back door. Since Agatha also frequented the garden, Caroline headed to the path along the river.

The sparkling water and blooming swamp rose comforted her frayed nerves. "No more destroying property, Edward. There is enough destruction in this world without us adding to it."

Edward shuffled his feet. "I said I was sorry."

"You'll have to say it again when Jane's son comes home."

Charlotte slipped her hand into Caroline's. "Do you think he'll marry Miss Ludlow?"

"I don't know." Caroline enjoyed the feel of the little girl's hand, so small and delicate. "I suspect he'll find Miss Ludlow even more distressing than his melted toys."

Charlotte giggled.

Edward raced ahead. "I'm going to hide. I bet you won't be able to find me."

For a moment, Caroline considered the benefits of never finding Edward, then chided herself for mean thoughts. She'd have to ask Dottie to bake something special to mark his tenth birthday.

Her thoughts returned once again to Haversham. It had been over two weeks since she'd last seen him.

She chewed her bottom lip, unsure what to think. She was obviously attracted to him. She'd practically thrown herself at him in the pergola. He was a strong and handsome man of wit and intelligence, but that hardly constituted a reason to kiss him. There was something more, something hard to define, but she sensed that he understood her, that he somehow needed her.

So where was he? Putting out fires in the middle of the night? "Charlotte, this man who was in your room, did he know you and Edward by name?"

"I think so. He called me Princess. At first, I thought he was Papa, but he said he wasn't."

Caroline recalled Haversham using the name Princess for her niece. "When did this happen? Was it the night before Miss Ludlow fell in the pond?" The night he'd first kissed her?

Charlotte nodded. "Yes, I think so."

"Have you seen him since then?"

"No. He disappeared."

Caroline sighed. "I'm afraid he has." Her greatest fear was that he'd left to join the army. Her heart squeezed, and she shoved the worrisome thoughts away. Haversham was big and strong. He would survive, no matter what he was doing. And he would return. He had to.

Down the path, she saw the leaves of the sycamore tree tremble in the sun. A branch dipped slightly. No doubt, a long-legged bird had come to roost.

She stopped before a slender young river birch, not much taller than herself. With her hands on her hips, she glared at its leafy canopy. "Edward, I know you're in there. Come down this instant."

Charlotte grinned. "Edward's not there. That tree is too small."

"Hmm." Caroline scanned the surroundings and located an anthill at the base of a pine tree. "There you are, Edward. Come out of that hole this instant."

Charlotte burst into giggles.

Edward dropped from the sycamore tree. "Here I am!"

"Oh, my!" Caroline gasped. "I would have never guessed."

Edward laughed and ran down the path. "I'm going to hide again."

"Me too." Charlotte dashed after him.

Smiling, Caroline ambled after them. The game continued until they reached the gristmill. The children skipped down to the riverbank to observe the waterwheel.

"Careful," Caroline warned them. "Don't get too close."

"Can we go inside the mill?" Edward asked.

Caroline looked about. About fifty yards back from the river, a cabin rested on a hill in the shade of old oak trees. Flowerbeds surrounded the whitewashed walls. The sun glinted off the glass windows.

"Maybe the miller lives there. We'll ask him." Caroline approached the house. She knocked, but no one answered.

"Godsookers."

She heard Edward's voice on the side of the house. She joined him there and stopped short.

The hill provided an overlook to the south, where fields of indigo stretched far into the distance. A dusty path led down the hill to a row of shabby wooden cabins.

"Who lives there?" Charlotte asked.

"The slaves, I suppose." Caroline lifted her hand to her brow to shield her eyes from the sun's glare. In the distance, she spotted men and women working in the fields.

"Can I help you?" a man's voice asked from behind.

Caroline spun about. For a moment, spots of light danced before her eyes from having peered into the sun. The man seemed familiar. Her heart beat faster. "Haversham?"

"No, I'm Jacob. I apologize for taking so long to answer the door. May I help you?"

As her sight cleared, Caroline realized her mistake. At first glance, this man's height and bearing were almost identical to Haversham's, but he possessed a darker complexion and brown eyes.

"I'm sorry if we disturbed you. I'm Caroline Munro." When she extended her hand, the man hesitated a moment before taking it. "This is Charlotte and—"

"Edward." Jacob smiled. "I've heard all about you from Dottie. Would you like something to drink? Some cider?"

"Thank you." Caroline followed him with the children. "We were admiring your house. Do you live alone here?"

"Yes." He opened the front door and motioned for them to enter. "My mother died about six months ago."

"Oh, I'm so sorry." Caroline walked into a sunny parlor. The plastered walls had been painted light yellow. White curtains adorned the windows. The mirror over the hearth had a hairline crack down the middle.

"I like your house." Charlotte wiggled onto a plain wooden settee.

"Thank you." Jacob retrieved four pewter mugs from a cupboard and set them on a pinewood table. "My mother used to cook here, but now I go to the kitchen and eat with Dottie."

Caroline suspected he still grieved for his mother and was

lonesome living by himself. "We've been enjoying Dottie's cooking, too." She sat next to her niece on the wooden settee. "Unfortunately, we've made more work for her and Betsy. I help when I can, but Dottie tries to shoo me away."

Jacob handed mugs of cider to her and Charlotte. "She knows you're guests."

"Yes," Caroline conceded, "but we weren't exactly invited."

"So I hear." Jacob smiled as he sat next to Edward at the table.

"Are you in charge of the mill?" Caroline asked.

"Yes. I've been in charge of most everything at the plantation since last April." Jacob pointed at the pile of paperwork on the drop-leaf desk.

"Can we go inside the mill?" Edward asked him.

"I have some work to finish, but if you come in a few days, I'll take you on a tour."

"Thank you." Edward gulped down some cider.

"The mill has some interesting mechanical devices inside," Jacob continued. "My father and I installed them."

"Really?" Edward leaned forward. "How do they work?"

"I'll show you later." Jacob sipped from his mug. "Father and I have always shared an interest in scientific properties and mechanical engineering. We built the armillary sphere in the garden."

"You mean the metal contraption at the end of the reflecting pool?" Caroline asked.

"Yes." Jacob nodded. "We spent hours working on all sorts of projects. Now he's . . . gone."

"I'm so sorry." His father must have passed away, too, Caroline thought. Jacob was an interesting man. Of mixed race, yet well educated. Friendly, but apparently lonely. And quite busy from the looks of his desk.

She rose and set her empty cup on the table. "We should let you resume your work, but we'll come again. Thank you for the invitation. And the cider."

"It was good to meet you." Jacob stood. "I'll walk you back."

Halfway to the Great House, they discovered Jane Thomas scurrying toward them.

"There you are, Caroline. I've been looking all over for you. Oh." Jane glanced at Jacob, then quickly away. "I—I didn't realize you knew each other."

"We just met." Caroline noted the frightened glint in Jane's eyes. "Is something wrong?"

"Yes." Jane motioned toward the river. "They're back. They're docking at the pier right now."

"Who is back?" Jacob asked.

"Agatha is delighted they have returned." Jane clenched her hands together. "I should have never invited her here. She is increasingly hard to bear. She knows only two pieces of music, and she plays them over and over."

"You can hide in the nursery with us," Charlotte suggested.

Jane laughed nervously. "I may do that." She led them toward the pier. "I was afraid this would happen. The captain mentioned before that he was impressed with the house and its location."

They rounded the bend, and the pier came into view. The children gasped. Jacob cursed softly.

Two large barges had docked at the pier. British soldiers unloaded crates and horses.

"They're moving in?" Caroline whispered.

Jane nodded. "Will you come with me to greet them?"

"No!" Charlotte seized Caroline's skirt. "Don't let them come! They're bad men!"

The fear on the little girl's face pierced Caroline's heart. Her first instinct was to take the children and run. But Jane was afraid, too. She couldn't repay Jane's hospitality by leaving her alone to face the British. And she couldn't expect Virginia to travel during her last weeks of pregnancy. There was no choice but to stay.

"I'll come with you," Caroline told Jane, then she knelt in front of the children. "Listen to me. We will have to be brave. Remember to be courteous at all times, and you must never mention that your father or grandfather are fighting with the Continentals. *Never*. Do you understand?"

They nodded.

"Edward, take your sister through the trees to the back of the house. Then go to the kitchen and tell Dottie what has happened. Stay there 'til I come for you."

"I'll take them," Jacob offered. "They'll be safe with me."

"Thank you." Caroline watched Jacob lead the children through the trees that bordered the front lawn. "He's a nice man. I'm glad he's here."

Jane sighed. "We all have our crosses to bear."

An odd thing to say, Caroline thought, though Jane might be referring to the redcoats who were taking over her house. "We'll have to pray they won't stay very long."

"Oh, no." Jane pressed a hand to her chest. "What if my son returns now? This is terrible."

"We must hope for the best." Caroline studied the redcoats in the distance. "Now that I think about it, if there are officers living here, they might know a great deal. And there could be quite a few messages that pass through the house on the way to Cornwallis."

"What are you saying?" Jane gave her a horrified look. "Are you suggesting we spy on them?"

Caroline swallowed hard. She'd merely been thinking out loud, but her thoughts were definitely leading her toward espionage. Did she dare?

Jane grabbed her arm. "You mustn't. 'Tis far too dangerous."

Caroline recognized Captain Hickman amongst the soldiers. He would make a likely target. "With a little flirtation, I might learn something important."

Jane shook her head. "You're frightening me."

She was frightening herself. Caroline steeled her nerves. She could do this. Her sister had been successful as a spy in Boston. Haversham had said there were patriot soldiers in the area. Any useful information she gleaned could be passed on to them. "Don't worry, Jane. I'll be careful."

Chapter Fifteen

Matthias knew something was wrong the minute he rode into the stable. It was highly doubtful the new horses had arrived at Loblolly on their own.

He sprinted from the stable to the side of the kitchen, then peeked in the kitchen window. Only Dottie was inside. He edged to the corner of the building, his back pressed against the brick wall.

There was just enough moonlight to see the British foot soldier on patrol. Matthias waited for him to round the corner of the Great House, then he dashed into the kitchen and rolled a barrel against the door.

"How many redcoats are there?" he asked as he wolfed down a bowl of stew.

"Six." Dottie poured him a mug of ale. "Captain Hickman and five soldiers. Three of them will be leaving in the morning."

"But the captain is staying?" Matthias ripped a biscuit in two. "For how long?"

"Could be a long time." With a sigh, Dottie sat across

from him. "I considered putting something in the food as a welcoming present, but I didn't want to make the ladies ill, too."

Matthias snorted. "Have a care with your potions. We don't want them angry with my mother. How is she doing?"

"She's nervous. Thank goodness she's already hidden most of the silver. Her greatest fear is that you'll show up. She wants you to stay away from the Great House."

Matthias munched on half the biscuit as he considered. The servants' passageway would be safe enough, but hardly a decent place to sleep. "I could stay on the third floor."

"No. The foot soldiers are rooming there."

"Damn." The redcoats were too bloody close to Caroline. "Can I sleep here tonight?"

"I wouldn't recommend it." Dottie propped her feet up on a neighboring chair. "The soldiers come in every now and then for a nip of rum. The safest place for you is with your brother."

Matthias tossed the last of his biscuit onto his plate. "I don't have a brother."

"Your half brother, then."

"I'll sleep in the henhouse if I have to."

"Why are you so stubborn? Jacob is a good man. You should get to know him."

Ignoring her, Matthias stood and stretched. "I need to bathe. Did you wash those clothes I left here before?"

"Yes." Dottie scowled at him. "They're in the cupboard in the bathing room."

Aware that Dottie was continuing to glower at him, he carried water to the tub in the small adjoining room.

Dottie paced to her private room. "Why bother to bathe if you plan to sleep in a henhouse?" she muttered, then shut her door with more force than necessary.

As Matthias washed, he weighed the dangers of seeing Caroline. First he'd have to make it past the redcoats on the third floor. Then he'd have to deal with her sharp teeth. Would she be angry that he'd stayed away for so long?

Dressed in clean clothes, he located an oil lamp and lit it from the kitchen hearth. The lamplight would be too noticeable outside, so he draped a towel over it. He rolled the barrel away from the door, waited for the guard to pass by the kitchen, then dashed to the Great House.

The doors were not barred, probably so the guards could come and go. He slipped through the servants' door, passed through the dining room, then entered the storeroom. When he removed the towel from the lamp, the flame leapt to life. China and crystal gleamed on the shelves, but gaps remained where his mother had once displayed her silver.

The door to the passageway was disguised to look like part of the wall, the latch embedded under a chair rail. He opened the door, wincing at the noise it made. The hinges needed to be oiled. With the lamp in hand, he entered the passageway.

It was filthy. His last visit had been in the dark, but now he could see the white walls were festooned with cobwebs. Footsteps from his last visit were still imprinted on the dusty floor.

He stopped at the entrance to the library and listened. Male voices rumbled inside, too muffled to decipher, but he would be able to hear if he opened the peephole.

Quietly, he set down the lamp and extinguished the flame.

To keep his steps silent, he removed his shoes. In the dark, he located the peephole door at shoulder level and eased it open.

It squeaked.

"Did you hear that?" a voice asked with a colonial accent. "Check the door, Pugsley."

Matthias heard footsteps. He hunched over to peer through the peephole, but the rectangular opening severely limited his view. He could see the desk, the settee across from it, and the window behind the settee. The curtains were drawn shut. A redcoat officer sat at the desk, his back visible to Matthias. This must be the Loyalist Captain Hickman. He wore a white-powdered wig with a red bow to match his uniform. He held a glass in a bony hand. The contents gleamed like liquid gold in the candlelight.

A door creaked. "There's no one there." Pugsley's British-accented voice came from the direction of the door, out of Matthias's view.

"I want a lock installed on that door in the morning," the captain ordered. "I suspect some of the inhabitants of this house are Colonial sympathizers."

"Yes, sir." Pugsley wandered into Matthias's view. He was a short, square man with a broad face. "Bloody Colonials. I wouldn't trust any of them."

The captain cleared his throat. "I trust you are not including Loyalists in that statement."

Pugsley gulped. "Ah, no, sir. I was referring to the damned partisans who burned all the bridges and ferries."

"They're a pack of fools." Hickman leaned back and propped his booted feet on the desk with a resounding thud. "If they hadn't been so efficient in their destruction, we wouldn't be here in this comfortable home, enjoying this fine brandy. Help yourself, Pugsley."

"Thank you, sir." Pugsley wandered out of Matthias's sight, though he could hear the clunk of glass against the sideboard and swish of brandy being poured.

Matthias drew back from the peephole with a sick feeling in his gut. With the land routes destroyed, the only alternative was to use barges for the entire length of the river. He clenched his teeth. Why hadn't he foreseen this? He had caused the British to take over his own home.

Now his mother, Caroline, and her family were all in danger. He rubbed his brow. The enemy was outmaneuvering him.

Dammit, you have to fight back. He took a deep breath and steadied his nerves. The war wasn't over yet. He bent over to watch the enemy through the peephole.

"I believe I'm going to enjoy my stay here." Hickman finished his brandy. "The ladies are quite lovely."

"Yes, sir." Pugsley sipped from his glass. "You have your choice of pretty wenches—a redhead or a brunette."

Matthias gritted his teeth. Of course they would be interested in Caroline. But luckily, he knew she wouldn't encourage them. She had good reason to hate redcoats.

"Fill my glass again, won't you?" Hickman passed his empty glass to the foot soldier. "I have to say Miss Munro's behavior tonight came as quite a surprise."

"How is that, sir?" Pugsley strode toward the sideboard.

"When I was last here, she hardly spoke to me. I could have sworn she was a rebel sympathizer, but now, I'm not so sure. She was practically in my lap at dinner."

Matthias flinched. The lying swine! Caroline would never—

"Perhaps she's come to her senses," Pugsley said. "If she knows a shilling from a sixpence, she'll realize the rebel cause is doomed."

"I don't care what she realizes as long as she does it in my bed, eh?" Hickman chuckled.

Matthias's blood heated to a full boil. It raced to his head, screaming behind his ears. He flattened his palms against the wall and dug in his fingers.

Hickman accepted his filled glass from Pugsley and slid his booted feet off the desk. "For tonight, I'm taking this brandy to bed." He stood, his glass in one hand and the candlestick in the other. "Check on the barges before you turn in."

"Yes, sir." Pugsley set down his glass and followed the captain toward the door.

They walked out of Matthias's range of vision. As the door creaked shut, the light disappeared.

He was alone in the dark with only the sound of his breathing, fast and shallow. He rested his forehead against the wall, willing himself to think, but the image of Caroline climbing into Hickman's bed circled in his head like a hawk hunting for its next kill.

"Damn it to hell," he muttered. If he caught Hickman so much as touching her, he'd want to kill the scrawny bastard. Had she actually flirted with Hickman at dinner?

He turned and leaned his back against the wall. What a fool he was. He'd spent over two weeks in the swamp, convincing himself not to pursue her, when all along she was pursuing other men.

And it hurt. Damn her, she had the power to hurt him. How had he become so attached when he'd tried so hard to forget her?

God help him, he was hooked like a fish, and no matter how hard he squirmed, the hook remained snared in his heart. *Bloody hell*. As Richard enjoyed putting it—the mighty Matthias had finally fallen.

He'd leave in the morning without seeing her. In fact, he'd be sure never to see her again. After all, he had other matters to attend to. More important matters. For example, he ought to look at the captain's papers on the desk. He twisted the latch to open the bookcase door. It swung back into the passageway.

Halfway to the desk, he heard the creak of a floorboard outside the library door. The redcoats must be returning.

He dashed back into the passageway and shut the bookcase door. Just in time, for he heard the library door open and shut. Through the peephole he saw a faint light. Whoever had entered the library had a candle.

The light grew in brightness as the person approached. Matthias caught a glimpse of white—a nightgown, shawl, and mobcap. The woman moved behind the desk, her back to him. The candlelight shimmered off her hair. *Red*.

It was Caroline. His heartbeat quickened, and he chastised himself for growing excited. As far as he knew, she had come hoping to see Captain Hickman.

She set the candle on the desk and thumbed through the stack of papers. What the hell was she doing? If a redcoat found her doing this, she'd be in deep trouble.

She had to be stopped. He twisted the latch on the bookcase door. With the door opened an inch, he hesitated. Did he really want her to know about the secret passageway?

The floorboard outside the library creaked.

Caroline gasped and blew out the candle.

Matthias closed the bookcase door. *Damn!* He should have nabbed her when he had the chance. What if a redcoat found her?

The library door opened, and another light appeared. Someone was entering with another candlestick.

Matthias searched for Caroline through the peephole. She was nowhere in sight, but the curtains swayed ever so slightly. Hopefully, the second intruder wouldn't notice. Another white nightgown moved into view, this one quite a bit larger.

It was Virginia. Just like her sister, she placed her candle on the desk and examined the stack of papers.

"Ginny," Caroline whispered as she emerged from behind the curtains.

Virginia gasped. "Dear Lord, Caroline, you gave me such a fright. What are you doing here?"

Caroline strode to the desk. "What are *you* doing here?"

"Isn't it obvious? Since the redcoats are using this library as headquarters, I assumed there would be important information here."

"You're spying? Oh, no, Ginny. You mustn't."

"Why not?" Virginia asked.

Caroline planted her fists on her hips. "Because I'm spying."

Matthias's mouth dropped open.

"No, I should be the spy," Virginia insisted. "I have more experience than you."

"I know," Caroline said. "You were excellent in Boston. But now, it is *my* turn."

Matthias gulped. Virginia had spied before? And now Caroline wanted to?

"It is *my* husband who is fighting the British," Virginia argued. "If this is the only way I can help him, then it is my duty."

"Ginny, you're in no condition to be spying."

"I *hate* that! Just because I'm pregnant, everyone thinks I've become an incompetent dimwit."

"I'm sorry." Caroline touched her sister's shoulder. "But you mustn't take the risk. You have children who need you."

Matthias groaned inwardly. Did they plan to discuss espionage all night? Didn't they know a British soldier could come in at any moment? He had to put a stop to this. He reached for the door latch but hesitated. If the ladies knew about the secret passageway, they would definitely continue to spy.

Virginia adjusted her shawl around her shoulders. "Did you find anything?"

"No. Actually, I was hoping to avoid this sort of activity. I tried my best to learn something at dinner, but Captain Hickman droned on and on about his great military exploits. I didn't believe a word of it."

"I wondered why you were flirting so much. Thank God the children were in the kitchen. They would have been sorely confused."

Caroline shuddered. "I could hardly eat, for his company turned my stomach."

Matthias heaved a sigh of relief, then found himself grinning like a lovesick fool. Caroline was true. Caroline was constant. She wasn't interested in Hickman. She didn't even like the bastard. His smile faded. What the hell was she doing? If she continued flirting and spying, Hickman would either ravish her or arrest her as a traitor.

The floorboard creaked again. The women gasped.

Matthias gripped the door latch. He'd have to protect the women if necessary. And the only weapon he had was Greville's knife.

Caroline blew out the candle. "Come hide in the curtains."

"I'm too big," Virginia answered.

Matthias heard a scuffle of feet and a thump like a sack of potatoes hitting the floor.

The door opened with another candle lighting the room. Footsteps approached the desk.

Edward? Matthias gaped at the sight of the boy. Edward set down the candle and picked up the stack of papers.

Caroline whisked out of the curtains. "Edward!"

He yelped and jumped a foot in the air. The papers flew from his hands and scattered all over the floor.

"Godsookers, Aunt Caroline. I almost wet myself."

"What are you doing here?" Caroline snatched the papers off the floor.

"I'm a spy," Edward announced.

Matthias banged his head on the wall.

"What was that?" Edward asked.

Caroline paused in her search for fallen papers. "I don't know. It sounded like it came from the wall."

"It might be the ghost," Edward whispered.

"There is no such thing as ghosts," Virginia's voice came from behind the settee.

"Mama, what are you doing here?"

"She thought she was going to spy," Caroline said. "But neither one of you is spying. Do you understand?"

"But I want to be a spy," Edward grumbled. "Like Papa."

Matthias rubbed his sore forehead. The father was a spy, too? Was the entire family insane?

"Heaven forbid you should emulate your father." Caroline stacked the papers on the desk. "Do you know he was captured? He was almost hanged, drawn, and quartered."

"Let's not talk about that," Virginia's voice pleaded from behind the settee.

Caroline winced and touched her mouth.

"Why don't we all spy?" Edward asked. "We could make a schedule and take turns."

"No!" Caroline wrapped her shawl tighter about her shoulders. "'Tis too dangerous for you."

"I'm not afraid of Captain *Stickman*," Edward boasted. "He's so bony I could—"

"Enough," Caroline interrupted him. "We've been here too long. We should leave."

Thank God for small miracles! Matthias was beginning to think the threesome would settle down for a game of whist.

"I hate to say this," Virginia responded from behind the settee, "but I—I'm unable to get up."

"What?" Caroline dashed to the settee.

"I need more room to get up," Virginia explained.

Edward snickered. "You mean you're stuck?"

Caroline glared at him. "'Tis not amusing."

Matthias shook his head. *What next?*

Caroline grabbed one end of the settee. "Edward, take the other end."

They moved the settee forward. Edward dropped his end with a clunk. Matthias groaned silently. The British had to be dead drunk not to hear them. Caroline and her nephew heaved Virginia to her feet, then moved the settee back.

"Come, let's get out of here." Caroline grabbed the lit candlestick. Virginia and Edward each took an extinguished one, and the threesome scurried from the room.

Matthias waited awhile to see if any more would-be spies showed up, perhaps the stable boy or barnyard cat. Nothing would surprise him now.

He snapped the peephole door shut, then opened the bookcase door to enter the library. Unfortunately, it was too dark to read the papers on the desk.

He peeked out the curtains and waited for the guard to pass. Then he opened the curtains and returned to the desk. Yes, with the moonlight he could make out the words. *Damn.* Caroline had restacked the papers with some pages upside-down. Those women were asking for trouble.

He righted the papers and put them in order. Most were simple requisitions for supplies, but one was important—a schedule for the supply barges on the Black River. He grabbed a clean sheet of paper and quickly copied the information. Then he shut the curtains.

As he returned to the passageway, he folded his copy and slipped it into his coat. It was still his mission, one way or another, to stop the supplies from getting through.

But right now, he had a more pressing mission to pursue—the demise of the Munro family's secret vocation. He doubted Edward would spy again. His mother and aunt would forbid it. And hopefully, Virginia would realize how unsuited she was to the task. But Caroline—that feisty firebrand would be the devil to stop. She had to be dissuaded immediately.

And he was just the man to do it.

Chapter Sixteen

Caroline shoved a chair against her bedchamber door. No, not good enough. It hadn't stopped Haversham from entering two weeks ago. And tonight there were redcoats on the third floor. Drunken redcoats, which probably made them even more dangerous. It was too risky to give them a sleeping potion every night. They might start to suspect.

She dragged a table to the door, then stacked two wooden chairs on top. It would have to do. Hopefully, she wouldn't need the knife hidden beneath her pillow.

As she paced about the room, the candlestick beside her bed cast lurching shadows on the walls, disjointed and unsettled. Just like her nerves. She hated to admit it, but she had failed. Her first attempt at espionage had yielded nothing.

She strode to the window and gazed at the half-full moon, shrouded in misty clouds. Too many had died for freedom to give up now. Too many like Roger. Tomorrow she would continue. She shuddered at the thought of further flirtation with Captain Hickman.

A soft tap sounded at her door.

She gasped. Should she answer or pretend to be asleep? She dashed to the candle to blow out the flame, then hesitated. No, it was better to see the enemy.

Another knock, a little louder. "Caroline." A man's voice.

She dug under her pillow and pulled out the knife.

The door jiggled. "Caroline, let me in."

He sounded familiar. Could it be? "Who is it?"

"Who the hell would you expect? Does the name Haversham sound familiar?"

"Oh." She exhaled with relief and dropped the knife on the bed. "Just a minute."

She dashed to the barricade and lifted the first chair down. So the mysterious butler had finally returned. She grasped the second chair and paused with it in mid-air. What could he possibly want? Another kiss before vanishing for a fortnight? Did he have any idea how much she had worried about him? As if she didn't have enough to worry about. How dare he appear and disappear without warning or explanation? And the worst part—he made her heart long for impossible things. Love and joy, when reality offered only fear and danger.

She set the chair on the floor. "What do you want, Haversham?"

"Inside, dammit."

"I'm not at all certain I want to see you."

He answered by shoving against the door.

"Wait." She dragged the table away from the door. "We shouldn't make too much noise. And I must say it is a bit rude of you to barge into my room like this."

He stepped inside and shut the door. "Would you welcome me if I were Captain Hickman?"

"Ha! If you've come to insult me, you can leave at once." When she turned, she thought for a moment that he was leaving, but he merely pushed the table back against the door.

He stepped toward her, his eyes narrowed. "We need to talk. Actually, I need to talk. You need to listen."

Was he angry? Why? She was the one with a legitimate complaint. He had said he would return in a few days, not a few weeks. She lifted her chin. "You shouldn't be here. I'm not properly dressed."

His gaze swept down to her bare feet, then slowly inched back up. "If you're so concerned with propriety, why were you wandering about the house in your nightclothes?"

She blinked. "I . . . you must be mistaken."

A muscle rippled in his jaw as he clenched his teeth. "It was a mistake, Caroline, for you to go to the library and rifle through the captain's papers."

She gasped. How could he possibly know? "That—that's ridiculous."

"Ridiculous is your sister and Edward attempting the same thing."

How did he know? She stepped back. "No, that's silly."

"Silly is hiding behind the curtains. The guard outside could have seen you."

She retreated another step. "How do you know all this?"

"I know everything. I know you're planning to spy on the redcoats. I know you flirted with that damned captain at dinner." He advanced toward her again.

"There's no harm in a little . . . harmless flirtation."

He motioned to the table. "If it was so harmless, why do you feel obliged to barricade yourself in?"

"A simple precaution in case he misinterprets my behavior."

Haversham's eyes flashed with anger. "Hickman said you were almost in his lap. How do you expect him to interpret *that?*"

"He's exaggerating." She rubbed her forehead, trying to make sense of it. "You talked to Hickman?"

"No, but I know he plans to seduce you."

"How could you know that?"

"I know *everything!*"

"Well, hallelujah!" She raised her hands in the air. "Jehovah himself has visited me in all his glory. Will you please explain how you know *everything?*"

He shrugged one shoulder. "I work in mysterious ways."

"Ha!" When she swatted a hand at his chest, he grabbed her wrist. "Let me go." She tried to pull away from his grasp, but he held fast.

"No. Not until you swear to give up spying."

"I don't answer to you. I don't even know who you are. A butler? I highly doubt it. And you said you would be back in a few days, but it has taken more than two weeks. Why should I trust anything you say?"

"Because I care about you, dammit!" He pulled her into his arms.

She shoved against his chest, but he wrapped his arms around her, holding her tight. *He cared about her?* Tears stung her eyes. Haversham had come back, and he cared about her.

He cradled her head against his chest, and she felt the vibrations of his quickly pounding heart. Obviously, he was agitated. *Because he cares about you.* She leaned into him and let the warmth of his body seep into her. His arms encircled her like a sheltering cocoon, safe and protected.

"Caroline." He rubbed his chin against her brow. "I missed you."

"I missed you, too," she whispered. His embrace was heaven. "My God."

"Are you referring to me?"

She scoffed. "You arrogant—"

"Go ahead. Call me a demented buffoon. I was a fool to think I could stay away from you."

"I was afraid I'd never see you again." She blinked to keep from crying. "I was afraid you had joined the army."

"Would that be so terrible?"

"Yes!" She pulled away from him, then grabbed the shawl off her bed and wrapped it around her shoulders. "I don't want to lose anyone else to the war."

"You won't lose me."

With a silent groan, she wandered to the window. Roger had sworn he would come back, too. Since Haversham knew other soldiers in the area, he might already be engaged in some sort of military activity. She'd be a fool to set herself up for more heartache. "'Tis late. You should go."

"I will leave once we have reached an agreement." He paced toward her. "I forbid you from spying."

"Forbid?"

"Yes, and I expect you to obey."

She gave him a wry look. "Obey?"

He opened his mouth, then shut it with an exasperated expression. "'Tis a shame that *you* cannot join the army. Then you would learn to follow orders."

She shrugged. That was highly doubtful.

He eased closer to her. "Will you cease with your spying as a personal favor to me?"

The entreating look he was giving her was clearly intended to melt her heart. She wasn't about to let him know how well it worked. She smiled sweetly at him. "Will you cease with your bullying as a personal favor to me?"

He winced. "I'm not a bully."

"Good. Then we have that settled. You may go."

His mouth dropped open, then snapped shut. "We have nothing settled." He crossed his arms, frowning at her. "I cannot leave until you agree to stop spying."

"Then you will be here a long time."

"You are a trying woman, Miss Munro."

"I'm an independent woman. That sounds much better than the term *spinster*, don't you think?"

"Honestly, I'm amazed you haven't been snatched up."

Likewise. She glanced at him. The rascal was too handsome for words.

"Of course most husbands would expect a wife who could *obey*."

Her mouth twitched. "I'm not interested in most husbands."

His eyes glinted with determination as he studied her. "You said you were engaged once before? To a soldier who died at Brandywine?"

She wrapped her shawl tighter around her shoulders. "I'd rather not talk about him."

"Do you still mourn for him?"

"This has nothing to do with Roger."

"Is he the reason you insist on risking your neck? Are you doing it out of love for him?"

"'Tis not love!" With a groan, she propped her elbows on the windowsill and covered her face.

"Then you don't . . ."

When Haversham paused, she wondered why she had blurted out the truth. Was it another case of her saying things that she shouldn't? No, it was more than that. There was a part of her that yearned to share her darkest secrets with him. She had to know—would his feelings for her survive if he knew her worst sin?

"If you don't feel love for him," he murmured, then he drew in a sharp breath. "Guilt."

She nodded, lowering her hands.

"I understand guilt all too well." He touched the ivory-inlaid handle of a knife wedged beneath his belt. "These are difficult times. We have to make terrible decisions, and then we have to live with—"

"I killed him." She closed her eyes briefly. There, she'd said it. Would Haversham leave and never come back?

"Your . . . betrothed? I thought he died in battle."

"He did. But it was my fault."

"How? Did you personally bayonet the man?"

"I might as well have."

"Tell me what happened."

She took a deep breath and paced across the room. "It was after the victories at Trenton and Princeton. Everyone was excited. We actually believed the war would be over soon."

"I remember."

"There was a young man in our village, Roger Dooley, who asked to court me. I told him . . ." It had seemed so inspired and patriotic at the time. How could she have been so foolishly irresponsible?

"What?"

She wandered toward the bed. "I told him I could only love a man who was willing to fight for freedom." She wrapped her arms around a bedpost and leaned against it. "Roger left the next day to join the army. Brandywine was his first battle. And his last."

Haversham grimaced, but remained silent.

"You can imagine how his family reacted. They accused me of murdering their son. And they were right." Hot tears burned her eyes. "If only I had kept my blasted mouth shut."

Haversham strode toward her. "You are not to blame. A man makes his own decisions in life."

She blinked to keep the tears at bay. "That's what my brother, Fergus, said. He told the Dooleys in rather colorful language to leave me alone."

"Good."

"No. Everyone started gossiping about a feud between the Munros and the Dooleys. Roger's brother picked a fight with Fergus, and Fergus broke his nose."

"I think I like your brother."

"I like him, too." Her attempt at a smile crumbled into a sob, and a few tears rolled down her cheek. "The Dooleys were placing horrible notices about me in the local newspaper. My father told Fergus to ignore it, that it would pass, but Fergus disagreed, and they had a terrible argument. Father smashed a chair, he was so angry. Fergus ran off to join the frontier militia and hasn't come back. He left because of me."

"Caroline." Haversham pulled her into his arms.

"I destroyed two families," she whispered.

"No." He rubbed her back. "Your fiancé and your brother made their own decisions. You're not responsible for them."

As much as she wanted to absolve herself of all guilt, she knew in her heart she was partly to blame. The burden would always be there, but it felt a little lighter for having shared it.

And something miraculous was happening. Haversham knew her worst sin, and he hadn't run away. He was still here. Defending her. Supporting her. His chest felt warm and strong. Dependable. Comfortable. It moved gently each time he breathed.

She wiped her cheeks dry. "Father thought the Dooleys would calm down if I left. So I went to Charles Town to live with my sister."

He burrowed his nose in her hair and whispered in her ear, "Then you came to me."

She felt a prickling sensation shimmer down her arms. "I was afraid you would think ill of me."

"Never." He nudged her hair back with his nose and kissed her behind the ear. "You're a beautiful, kind, and clever woman."

He still cared for her. Her heart swelled. "Haversham." She wrapped her arms around his neck.

"Caroline." He trailed kisses across her brow.

Good Lord, this was the man she wanted. He incited such fierce emotions. She felt as strong as a conqueror, yet ached to surrender. She was powerful and vulnerable at the same time, hot and cold all at once. Her skin chilled with gooseflesh, yet a burst of heat shot from her chest down to her belly.

He nibbled a path down her neck.

"Haversham." She shivered as his tongue tickled her. "For pity's sake, I'm still calling you Haversham. Do you have a given name?"

With a frown he stepped back. "Call me . . . Thomas."

"Thomas." She sighed. "Please don't become a soldier."

He winced. "I thought you could only love a man who is willing to fight for freedom."

"It sounds good in theory, but the reality is too frightening and painful."

"That's how I feel about your spying."

"I have the right to risk my own neck." She noticed for the first time he was in his stockings. "What happened to your shoes?"

"They walked off." His eyes twinkled as he stepped closer. "Shall we continue with our previous activity?"

"How did you know what I was doing downstairs? If you were in the library, I would have seen you."

"I liked the position we were in before." He pulled her shawl off and dropped it on the bed.

"You're ignoring me."

"On the contrary, you're all I'm thinking about." His arms encircled her waist.

"You must have been hiding in the library."

"No." He turned her so her back was nestled against his chest. "Ah, I like this."

His hands, splayed upon her belly, radiated heat through the thin cotton shift. He moved a hand toward her bosom and stopped with the fullness of her breast resting on his thumb.

With a shiver, she glanced down. Her nipples had tightened, the hard buds straining against her cotton shift. Good Lord, she looked like a wanton woman!

She lunged from his grasp, snatched her shawl from the bed, and covered herself. "I—I . . ." She searched her mind for something to say. *I refuse to behave wantonly? I fear too much that I want to?*

She didn't dare look at his face. Her cheeks burned. "I was . . . uncomfortable. It must have been the buttons on your coat." *Blast!* What a stupid thing to say. He'd simply remove his coat. In fact, he might take her words as an invitation to disrobe completely.

He smoothed a hand over the buttons on his jacket lapel, then curled his hand into a fist. "The devil take it, they're flat. How could you feel them?"

"Well, they're . . . hard."

"Dammit, woman. You want to see something hard?"

"There's no need to growl. 'Twas naught but a wee—"

"*Button?* I'll show you—" He took a deep breath. "This is not the right time." He strode to the table and yanked it away from the door.

"You're leaving?"

"Yes." He reached for the door latch. "No more spying, Caroline. That's an order." He let himself out.

An order? With a snort, she shoved the table back against the door.

Thomas Haversham. It was highly aggravating that she knew so little about him, when he knew so much about her. How *did* he know what had transpired in the library? How did he know Captain Hickman's intentions?

As far as she knew, the redcoats didn't know he existed. And the way he moved about in the dark in his stockings could only mean he intended to keep his existence a secret. Where was he going now? And what was he doing?

Oh, she intended to keep spying, whether he liked it or not. And while she was exposing secrets, she would discover all there was to know about the mysterious, so-called *butler*, Thomas Haversham.

She needed to know. For she was falling totally and irreparably in love with him.

Chapter Seventeen

Tuesday, September 26, 1780

When the first rays of sun poured through her window, Caroline sat up in bed and discovered the first clue. Dusty footprints on her floor. Obviously, Thomas had walked on some filthy floors in his stocking feet. *Odd.* She couldn't recall seeing a dirty floor in the house.

She grabbed her clothes and followed the dusty trail out the door and down the hall. It stopped next to a wall twenty feet from the nursery door. *Strange.* Perhaps Thomas had removed his stockings and proceeded in bare feet. Had he ventured into the nursery?

The children were just waking as she entered the nursery. "Happy birthday, Edward. Did a man come in here last night, the man who put out the fire in your bed?"

Edward yawned. "No."

Charlotte rubbed her eyes. "You mean the ghost?"

Edward glared at his sister. "Mama says there's no such thing as ghosts."

"Let's dress, so we can go down for breakfast." Caroline strolled into her sister's room and dropped her clothes on the bed. "Good morning, Ginny."

Virginia groaned. "Morning, already?"

"Yes. Did you convince Edward not to spy?"

"Yes." Virginia rolled out of bed. "I think so."

Charlotte dashed into the room and went behind the screen to use the chamber pot.

Caroline pulled off her nightclothes and slipped into a fresh shift. "What about you, Ginny?"

Virginia glanced at the screen, signifying she didn't want her daughter to hear too much. "I promise to be in bed where I belong every night."

"Good." Caroline leaned against the bed to pull on her stockings. "I don't know how, but we were observed. The butler knows everything."

"*What?* You mean Haver—?" Virginia paused when Charlotte emerged from the behind the screen and washed her hands in the china bowl. "You talked to him?" Virginia helped her daughter dress.

Caroline's cheeks grew warm as she tied the garters around her stockings. "He came to see me. Rather late."

Virginia handed Charlotte her shoes and stockings. "Sweeting, put these on in the other room."

Charlotte gave them a curious look. "What's going on?"

"I just need to talk to my sister." Virginia escorted her daughter to the door, then hurried to the chamber pot behind the screen. "I thought Haversham was gone."

"So did I." Caroline pulled a petticoat over her head and

tied the tabs at her waist. "But he arrived at my bedchamber out of the blue."

"Why?" Virginia poured water from the pitcher into the china bowl to wash her hands.

"He saw us in the library and ordered us not to spy anymore. Can you believe the gall of the man?"

Virginia gave her an alarmed look. "How did he see us?"

"I don't know." Caroline tugged a gown over her head. "But I mean to find out."

Virginia moved behind her and took hold of the laces. "He's not a Loyalist, is he?"

"No." Caroline held on to the bedpost as her sister tightened the laces. "He knows Continental soldiers in the area and discovered the location of our father. He must be sympathetic to the cause."

"He may be more than sympathetic." Virginia tied the laces.

Caroline winced. Was it too late? Had she fallen for a soldier? "I have doubts that he was ever a butler."

"I agree." Virginia slipped on one of Jane's old lying-in gowns. "He's a bit mysterious, and no doubt you find that intriguing, but I have to wonder if it is wise for you to see him."

Caroline took the comb from the bedside table and dragged it through her hair. "I admit there is a great deal I don't know about him, but I believe I can trust him. He—he says he cares for me."

"Already?" Virginia's eyes narrowed. "How often have you been alone with him?"

"A few times."

"In your bedchamber?"

"He behaved himself. Somewhat." The warmth in her cheeks reminded Caroline how poorly she disguised her feelings. "Here. Let me tighten your laces."

Virginia turned her back. "He *is* a handsome man."

"You . . . noticed?"

"I'm expecting, not blind. I also have some experience in the wonders of physical attraction." Virginia rubbed her swollen belly. "And the results."

"I—I haven't gone that far."

"Good. I don't want to see you hurt again." Virginia glanced back, a thoughtful look in her pale green eyes. "There could be more to him than you realize."

"I told him about Roger. Thomas knows how strongly I feel about avoiding soldiers."

"Men aren't always what they seem. Remember how Quincy pretended to be a fop?"

"Don't worry. Everything will be fine." Caroline tied the laces, then helped her sister with her stockings and shoes. Ginny had reached the point she could no longer see her feet, much less reach them.

Since the redcoats' arrival, the children ate their meals in the kitchen. Charlotte and Edward skipped down the hallway, then waited at the stairs. As Caroline ambled beside her slow-moving sister, she noticed once again how the dusty trail ended abruptly by the wall.

There it was. A hairline crack in the wall, so fine she hadn't noticed it before. She traced it with her finger. It continued through the chair rail down to the floor.

"Are you coming?" Ginny asked at the top of the stairs.

"I forgot something. Go ahead. I'll catch up." Caroline watched her sister and the children descend the stairs.

The crack in the wall outlined a door, but how to open it? There was no visible latch, so there must be a hidden one. She ran her fingers beneath the chair rail. Yes, she felt a lever of some kind, small and metallic. She pulled and heard a *snick*.

The right side of the door swung out; the left swung inward. Interesting. It swiveled on a rod, so there were no visible hinges from either side.

She peeked inside and spied a steep staircase going down. It was too dark to investigate without a light. She knelt to take a closer look at the top landing of the stairs. Yes, footprints in the dust. Thomas Haversham had come this way.

A door closed nearby, and she heard male voices approaching. It had to be the foot soldiers who roomed on the third floor. She pushed the secret door shut 'til she heard the click.

Footsteps rounded the corner. Two soldiers stopped when they saw her.

She smiled. "Good morning, gentlemen."

One stepped forward and offered his arm. "May I escort you to breakfast?"

"Yes. Thank you." Caroline's heart pounded as she accompanied the soldiers to the dining room. She had discovered Haversham's secret. Where did the staircase lead? To the library, she would wager. And very soon, she'd know for sure.

Early in the morning, Matthias arrived at Snow's Island. Instead of the usual lone welcome from Simon, there were ten soldiers to greet him. The population had multiplied overnight.

"Matt!" Richard approached him. "We've been waiting for you."

Matthias dismounted. "I take it Marion's back?"

"Aye, and he wants to see you." Richard eyed him with a frown. "What happened to your clothes?"

Matthias brushed flour off his coat sleeves. "I slept in the mill on a mattress of flour sacks."

"Why?" Richard smiled. "Did the vixen try to bite you?"

"No, the house is full of redcoats."

Richard's smile faded. "Is Aunt Jane all right?"

"Yes. Where's Marion?"

"This way." Richard led him through a maze of tents.

"Did he receive my report?"

"Yes. Major Munro is . . . assisting him."

Matthias figured this was his cousin's tactful way of saying Marion could hardly read. When Richard pointed out the tent, Matthias entered and found Marion and Major Munro seated at a table with a stack of papers in front of them.

"Captain Thomas." Marion glanced up. "I've been looking at your report."

Major Munro stood and skirted the table with a hand outstretched. "I thank you for finding my daughters."

"My pleasure, sir." Matthias shook his hand, careful not to wince from the Scotsman's tight grip.

Marion leaned back in his chair. "I see you captured supplies at Kingstree without any casualties. Well done."

"Thank you, sir." Matthias was uncomfortably aware that the Scottish major was inspecting him closely. "Without the ferries and bridges, the British have been forced to rely on barges. I have their schedule here." He removed the folded paper from his coat.

"Good lad." Major Munro snatched the paper from his hand and passed it to Marion. "How did ye acquire the information?"

"The redcoats have taken over my home, a plantation on the Black River, midway between Charles Town—"

"Wait." Major Munro raised a hand to interrupt. "Did ye no' write that my daughters were staying at yer home?"

"Yes, sir, they are, but they're safe."

The major frowned. "I'll be the judge of that, laddie."

"They are unharmed, sir. My mother is there also. I wouldn't have left them if I thought it too dangerous."

"Enough." Marion waved the schedule in the air. "How did you acquire this?"

"Captain Hickman has commandeered the library as his headquarters. I went in at night and copied the schedule."

"How many soldiers are there?" Munro asked.

"There were six, but now there's only the captain and two infantry. Of course, whenever a barge comes, the number will increase."

Marion frowned. "Weren't they suspicious of you?"

"They never knew I was there, sir. The house has a secret passageway they know nothing about."

Marion exchanged a look with Major Munro, then rose to his feet. Planting his palms on the table, he leaned forward. "You can access their headquarters unseen?"

"Yes, sir," Matthias replied with an uneasy feeling.

Marion circled the table. "Can you keep your presence there a secret?"

"You're sending me back?"

"Of course. 'Tis too good an opportunity to pass up. You'll need to choose a courier to deliver your messages." Marion stopped in front of him. "Can you do it?"

Matthias took a deep breath. "Yes, sir." He understood the penalty for spying, but the odds of dying in battle were just as bad. At least he'd be there to make sure Caroline didn't risk her neck.

Marion whisked a paper off the desk. "Considering the risk you're taking, I'm promoting you to a major."

Matthias blinked. "Thank you, sir, but hiding in a secret passageway is hardly a heroic act."

"It is when you're that close to the enemy. Particularly in your case." Marion handed him the paper.

Matthias stared at a crude likeness of himself. At the top of the printed handbill, the title read, *Wanted for Treason and Murder—Matthias Murray Thomas.*

Damn it to hell. There was a reward on his head.

"Congratulations. I dinna know ye were such a valuable man." Munro took the handbill and set it on the desk. "Do my daughters know who ye are?"

"No, sir. I . . . never told them." Matt's face grew warm.

Munro narrowed his eyes. "What *did* ye tell them?"

"As little as possible, sir."

"A good strategy," Marion said. "He must be careful. Good luck, Major."

"Thank you, sir." Matthias exited the tent. A wanted man. A spy. He'd be lucky if he saw his twenty-ninth birthday.

This was terrible timing. He couldn't continue to see Caroline when he was a wanted man. She'd suffered enough from losing that Roger fellow. But how could he avoid seeing her when he had orders to spy at the house?

"Well?" Richard asked. "What happened? You're staring at the clouds."

Matthias looked at his cousin. "I have to go home."

"But the redcoats are there."

"That's my new assignment. I'm to spy on them."

Richard sucked in a long breath. "That's dangerous."

"There's more. There's a price on my head."

Richard nodded. "I know. I saw my father yesterday. They posted one of the handbills on his church door."

Matthias closed his eyes briefly. How had the British figured out who he was? "You know the way to Loblolly. Will you be my courier?"

"All right. Where and when?"

"The orchard. The peach tree that was hit by lightning." This was Tuesday, Matthias thought. "Come every Wednesday and Saturday evening."

"I'll come, too," Major Munro announced behind them.

Matthias turned. How long had Caroline's father been there?

Munro continued, "I want to know the way to yer house in case my daughters need my protection."

"I'll be there," Matthias said. "I can protect them."

The Scotsman removed a pipe and pouch of tobacco from his coat. "Do ye think so, laddie?"

"If one of the redcoats lays a hand on Caroline, I'll shred the bastard and feed the pieces to an alligator."

"Och, that's good." The major packed tobacco into his pipe. "But ye seem to have forgotten I have more than one daughter. Did Ginny have the wee bairn yet?"

Matthias felt his face grow warm. "No, sir. And her children are fine."

"Thomas is a Welsh name, aye?"

"Yes, sir."

The major stuck his pipe, unlit, in his mouth, then stuffed the pouch of tobacco back into his coat pocket. "I've always thought the Welsh were too serious. Make good poets and preachers, though."

Matthias snorted. What ridiculous hogwash.

Richard lit a stick in the nearby campfire and handed it to the Scotsman. "You may be right, sir. My father is a preacher."

Matthias scowled at his cousin. "It is nonsense."

Richard smiled. "I've always thought you were a bit too serious, Matt."

"Go to hell."

Munro lit his pipe, then tossed the stick into the fire. "Any Scots in yer family, Thomas?"

"Yes, sir. On my mother's side. Murray."

"Good." Munro pointed his pipe at Matthias. "And if ye lay a hand on Caroline, should I shred you to pieces?"

Matthias blinked. "That will not be necessary, sir."

Jamie Munro's eyes twinkled with humor. "Ye mean ye doona plan to touch her?"

Matthias had a bad feeling the man had been baiting him all along. "I mean that I will behave honorably, sir."

Munro nodded. "See that ye do, Major."

"Major?" Rich turned to Matthias. "You were promoted?"

"Aye, he was," Munro answered for him. "If I have to kill him, 'twill look verra impressive on his gravestone."

Chapter Eighteen

After making an excuse of not feeling well, Caroline left the children and Virginia in the kitchen, enjoying the birthday pudding Dottie had made. It was early afternoon and she had delayed long enough. The secret door on the third floor begged to be investigated.

As she scurried up the stairs, she heard the tinkling sounds of the harpsichord. Agatha was in the front parlor entertaining Jane and the redcoats. Good. There would be no one on the third floor.

She lit a candle in the nursery using the tinder wheel. In the hallway, she located the hidden latch and pulled. She squeezed through the opening and closed the door. Its tiny click sounded ominously final. What if all the doors were similarly hidden? She might have trouble finding an exit. Her thoughts raced ahead, imagining skeletons of other explorers who had failed to find their way out.

"Don't be silly," she murmured, and held her candle aloft. The small landing gave way to a narrow staircase which descended into darkness.

Slowly she moved down the stairs. Dust lay thick on the steps, coating her shoes and causing her nose to itch. How well could a person remain hidden if he sneezed?

On the first floor, she spotted the door that must open to the library. At eye level there was a rectangular sliding panel. She winced when it opened with a scrape. Why didn't Thomas grease this?

She peered into the library. Yes, this explained everything. Thomas had been spying on them. *Spying.*

"Oh, no," she whispered. Thomas Haversham might be a real spy. That would explain why he disappeared for weeks at a time and moved about the house in the dark in his stocking feet.

"Damn." She was not one to normally curse, but this situation certainly warranted it. A spy? That was even more dangerous than being a soldier. How could he do this when he knew how she felt?

She snapped the peephole shut. The grating sound made her grit her teeth. Thomas was flirting with disaster. It would be like losing Roger all over again.

But worse. Her feelings for Roger didn't compare to the yearning that squeezed her heart whenever she thought of Thomas. With Roger, she had been flattered that a man, any man, had wanted to court her, and she'd allowed him to kiss her out of curiosity. How small and childish it seemed to her now. Poor Roger. He had deserved better than that.

And now Thomas was engaging in dangerous activity. How could she bear it if anything happened to him? With her heart heavy, she trudged to the end of the corridor.

When she opened the door, she recognized the small

room lined with cupboards. She had emerged next to the dining room.

A jab of anger coursed through her that Thomas had ordered her not to spy, when he was obviously engaged in the activity himself. Even more irritating was the fact that he wasn't very good at it. The secret corridor afforded him the means, but he wasn't properly maintaining it. The doors and peepholes all squeaked. And the dust caused him to leave footprints wherever he went. She'd followed his trail and discovered the hidden passageway far too easily. If he continued to leave clues like that, he would be discovered in no time.

She would have to convince him to stop. He wasn't cut out for espionage. In the meantime, she would have to protect him the best she could.

The rest of the afternoon, she worked like the devil. She mopped the floors of the secret passageway from top to bottom. Without windows, the air became stifling hot. By the time she reached the first floor, she was drenched with sweat. She left the mop and pail in the china room and dashed to the kitchen.

Dottie looked her over. "Good Lord, girl, you look ill. Are you running a fever?"

"I'm fine," Caroline assured her. "Could I have a bit of grease? The door to my room creaks."

With a small jar of bacon grease, Caroline headed back to the corridor and greased all the hinges and latches she could find. She scurried to her room, grabbed a clean set of clothing, then descended the grand staircase. She planned to change clothes after bathing in the kitchen. Just as she reached the back door, it opened.

Jane and Agatha sauntered in from the garden. Caroline hid the jar of grease beneath the bundle of clothes in her arms.

Jane gasped. "Are you all right, dear?"

Agatha stepped back. "She has some dreaded disease, I know it. She'll give it to us all."

Caroline grimaced. Did she look that bad? "I believe I should excuse myself from supping with you this evening."

"Very well, dear." Jane's brow furrowed with concern. "I hope you'll feel better soon."

"I'm sure I will." Caroline hurried out the back door to the kitchen.

After a hot bath, she dressed and took a tray of food up to the nursery. Eating with her family was so much better than dining with Agatha and the redcoats. Thank God she no longer needed to flirt with Captain Hickman in order to obtain information. She could use the secret passageway instead.

As the evening advanced, her nerves tightened with anticipation. The night was ripe for spying.

Matthias arrived at Loblolly just after sunset. He moved stealthily toward the kitchen and peered in the window. Only Dottie and Betsy were inside.

He waited for the guard to complete his pass, then strolled into the kitchen. "Good evening, ladies."

Dottie rose to her feet. "Boy, what are you doing here? You should be safe in the swamp."

"This is my new assignment." Matthias rolled a barrel against the door. "I'm to spy on Captain Hickman."

With a frown, Dottie shook her head. "Sounds like a good way to get your neck stretched to me."

Betsy shuddered. "I hate having to serve them."

"Look at it this way." Matthias sat at the table. "With the enemy this close, we can know what they're doing, then use that information to defeat them."

Betsy twisted her apron in her hands. "I'm afraid of them. I hate being afraid of them."

"Drink this to steady your nerves." Dottie poured a foul-smelling concoction into a pewter mug and handed it to the maid. "You have to be strong, girl. Don't give them the pleasure of knowing they can frighten you."

Betsy nodded and lifted the mug.

Matthias wrinkled his nose. "That stuff stinks. Do you have anything to eat that smells better than a dead skunk?"

Dottie snorted and plunked a plate in front of him. "You think blocking the door will keep you safe? If they can't get in, they'll be suspicious."

"You can tell them you needed privacy, that you were bathing." Matthias eyed the roasted beef, stewed mushrooms, beefsteak pie, beets, carrots, bread slathered with butter, and baked plum pudding. "I see my mother is feeding the redcoats well."

"Yes, sir. Your mama told me to treat them as honored guests." Dottie poured him a mug of ale, then eased into a chair with a tired groan. "Working me to death. At least Miss Munro has promised to help us tomorrow."

He gulped down some ale, relieved to hear Caroline would be cooking instead of spying.

The kitchen door jiggled against the barrel as someone tried to open it.

"Damn." Matthias stood.

Dottie slid his plate in front of Betsy. "Go to my room. We'll tell you when it is safe to come out."

Matthias closed himself in Dottie's room and looked about. No door for an escape, but the window was big enough to climb through. He listened to the sounds—the barrel being moved, voices, then the barrel being shoved back.

Dottie called to him, "'Tis safe. Come out."

He opened the door and froze. The hell it was safe.

Seated in the spot he had just vacated was Jacob, his father's illegitimate son. All his life Matthias had known there was another. Another son a few months older than himself. The servants whispered about the other one, though never in his mother's presence.

And in all those years, he had never been in the same room with the other one. It had been an unspoken agreement between his parents. Keep the mistress and bastard out of sight, so Mother could pretend they didn't exist.

"Jacob's come for his supper." Dottie set a plate in front of the stranger. "Come and finish your food, Matt."

He hesitated, frowning. "No thanks."

"Go on." Dottie pointed to the bench. "Sit and eat."

The other one rose. He picked up his plate and a lit lantern he'd brought with him. "I can take this back to my house. Thank you, Dottie."

"Don't be ridiculous. 'Tis over a mile away." Dottie glared at the two men. "You're eating here, Jacob. And so are you, Matt. This is *my* kitchen, and you'll do as I say."

Jacob set his plate and lantern on the table. Still standing, he scowled at his food. Betsy poured him a mug of ale.

He was a tall man, Matthias noted, as tall as himself, and apparently intelligent. When Father had been captured in Charles Town, Mother had allowed Jacob to take over the business of running the plantation. It had embarrassed her to ask him, but with no one else available, she'd had no choice.

Dottie moved Matt's plate across from Jacob. "Are you coming?"

"Aye." Matthias approached the table.

Without glancing up, Jacob took a seat and began his dinner.

Matthias sat and bit into his beefsteak pie.

"That's better." Dottie settled in her chair at the head of the table.

Matthias ate quietly. He speared the carrots with his fork, avoiding the beets. As he chewed, he noticed Jacob shoveling his beets to the side. He didn't like them, either? No matter. Probably half the population of South Carolina hated beets.

Dottie propped her feet up on a stool. "Matt has come to spy on the redcoats."

Matthias flung his fork on the table. "Dammit, Dottie. Why don't you announce it in a Charles Town newspaper?"

"Jacob can be trusted." Dottie glanced at the other man. "Am I right?"

"Yes, ma'am." Jacob sliced his roast beef with a knife. "Don't you worry about getting caught?"

Matthias picked up his fork. "No. I'll be fine."

They ate in silence for a while.

Betsy refilled their mugs. "Seems to me the safest way to spy on the redcoats is from the servant passageway."

Matthias nodded. "That's what I plan to do. I can listen at the peepholes."

Jacob drank some ale. "Those peepholes are small. Your range of vision will be limited."

Matthias shrugged. "I can see well enough."

"I have a device that can see around corners."

Matthias paused with a bite of roasted beef halfway to his mouth. "How?"

"It uses magnifying lenses and mirrors. Father and I designed it. We call it a corner telescope."

Matthias lowered his fork. *Father and I.* So Jacob shared Father's interest in mechanical devices. Matthias had always been interested in living things—plants, animals, and people. The lure of metal or glass had never made sense to him. But apparently it did to Jacob.

"In fact," Jacob continued, "I have several items that might interest you. Would you care to see them?"

Matthias hated to admit it, but a tool that enabled him to see around corners could come in handy.

"I guess you don't." Jacob said when Matthias remain silent.

"He does," Dottie announced. "Don't mind him. He's been in a sour mood of late. I need to give him another restorative."

Matthias glared at her. "I am not sour."

"You look a little powdery to me." Betsy swiped at his arm. "Is this flour?"

"I slept in the mill last night."

"No wonder you're so grouchy." Dottie nodded at him with a knowing look. "You need a good night's sleep."

"I am not grouchy," Matthias growled.

"I have a spare bed," Jacob offered. "The one I slept in as a child. I use the room as a workshop now, but you're welcome to sleep there."

Dottie raised a square, plump hand. "There, you see. 'Tis all settled."

"It is not," Matthias protested. "I accepted this mission knowing full well what will happen to me if I'm caught. I will not involve anyone else."

Jacob set down his fork and knife. "I can make my own decisions."

For the first time, Matthias made eye contact with the other one. He was momentarily taken aback by the sharp intelligence in Jacob's brown eyes. "I work alone."

Jacob's jaw tightened. "Do you find the prospect of living with a slave offensive?"

"Enough." Dottie gave them each a stern look. "Matt, you need a safe place to stay. Your brother has been—"

"He's not my bro—" Matthias stopped himself.

A reddish hue spread across Jacob's face. He scraped back his chair and stood. "I don't have to listen to this."

Matthias gritted his teeth. "I have no right to endanger you."

Jacob's eyes glinted in the firelight. "You have no right to enslave me, either, but does that stop you?"

"That's enough." Dottie scowled at them. "You don't have to solve the problems of the world. You only have to sleep in the same house without killing each other. Can you do that?"

Matthias shrugged. "I can." What choice did he really have? He stood and faced the other one. "Can you?"

Jacob's jaw moved as if he were grinding his teeth. "Yes." He grabbed his lantern and strode to the door. With his free arm, he scooted the barrel out of the way.

Matthias edged to the side of the door. "Wait 'til the guard passes."

"You can wait. I have no reason to hide. See you at my house." Jacob sauntered across the garden at a leisurely pace.

Matthias watched him walk away. Father must have given him those clothes. Jacob was well dressed, his long black hair pulled back and braided in a queue.

"Here." Dottie offered him a jug and a parcel wrapped in cotton.

"What is this?"

"Rum and cake. The two of you hardly ate. I figure you'll be hungry again soon."

Matthias accepted the items. When the guard passed, he dashed across the garden to the cover of trees. Then he snaked through the woods to the path by the river. The air, thick and muggy, was filled with the irritating whine of locusts.

He spotted Jacob's lantern ahead of him. Damn his luck. He'd have to share a house with the living proof of his father's unfaithfulness and his mother's humiliation.

CHAPTER NINETEEN

Jacob stopped and waited for Matthias to catch up. "What do you have there?"

"Cake and rum," Matthias muttered.

"Ah. Dottie thinks we need to be drunk to survive the night?" Jacob climbed the steps to his house.

Matthias was familiar with the whitewashed exterior of the house. He'd seen it before when visiting the mill, but he'd never been inside. A part of him was curious—this was the location of his father's other life. Another part felt guilty. His mother would cringe if she knew he was here.

The interior was surprisingly normal, as if a real family had lived there, although he supposed Jacob had been living alone after the death of his mother.

Matthias deposited the jug and cake on a pinewood table. "Have the redcoats been here?"

"They came to the front door, looked inside, then left. Apparently, they don't think a slave has anything worth stealing." Still holding the lantern, Jacob opened a door on the right. "I'll show you the workroom."

Inside, Matthias scanned the crowded room. Tables lined the walls, covered with metal, wire, glass, and tools. A narrow bed, squeezed between two tables, jutted out into the center of the room. It was the two stools, sitting side by side, that caught Matt's attention. Jacob and Father must have worked on projects together.

Jacob shoved some tools aside to set the lantern down. "I know it appears a mess." He grabbed a few books off the bed and set them underneath. "But the sheets are clean."

Matthias eyed the books. "How did you learn to read?"

"Father taught me. And he let me borrow books from his library."

Matthias gritted his teeth. Father had hired a tutor for him and then sent him to college. He recalled his father's parting words—*I have done my duty. See that you do yours.*

Father had done his duty, marrying the heiress Jane Murray and having a son. But this—Matthias looked about the workroom—this was where Father had lived.

He cleared his throat. "Where is the telescope?"

"Here." Jacob passed him a short metal object.

It looked like a normal telescope except that the wider end curved into a ninety-degree angle. Matthias tugged on the smaller end, and the telescope lengthened in three stages of decreasing circumference. He strode to the open doorway and peered through the lens. Not only could he see around the corner, but objects were magnified.

"This is excellent." He snapped the telescope back into its shorter size. "Do you mind if I borrow it?"

"No. Help yourself to anything here that looks like it might be useful." Jacob selected another item. "This lantern is equipped with shutters on all four sides. Each side can be opened or shut."

"That sounds promising." Matthias tried the lever on one of the shutters. "I like this. I can direct the light downward if I wish."

"Yes. Of course if you leave all the shutters closed for too long, the flame inside will die out," Jacob said. "If you need another machine, describe what you want to do, and I'll see what I can come up with."

"Why are you helping me? Are you a patriot like . . . my father?"

Jacob snorted. "I like to solve problems with machines. 'Tis not patriotism, merely intellectual curiosity."

"You don't care who wins the war?"

"Why should I?" Jacob walked toward the door. "Your freedom won't mean a damned thing to the slaves, will it?"

"I understand your dislike of your condition, but—"

"*Dislike?*" Jacob thumped two pewter mugs on the table. "You don't understand at all."

"No, I don't." Matthias approached the table. "How can you care about my father when he's the one who owns you?"

Jacob's eyes glimmered with strong emotion. "I grew up loving him. But I was a young child and didn't know I was a slave. Then afterward—I don't know. Part of me misses him terribly. Another part wishes he'll rot in prison." He sighed. "Love and hate at the same time. You must think I'm strange."

Matthias swallowed hard. "No, not really." All these years he had thought he was alone in his feelings. He had craved his father's attention, wanting more than anything for his father to be proud of him. At the same time, he had detested his father for betraying his mother. And he'd hated the way his father had mistreated the slaves.

He unwrapped the cake Dottie had given them. "I wonder if this is any good."

"Let's try it." Jacob fetched a knife and two saucers. Then he pulled the cork from the jug and sloshed some rum into a mug.

"None for me." Matthias sat at the table. "I need my wits about me tonight."

"You plan to spy?" Jacob handed him a jug of cider.

"Yes." Matthias filled his mug. "I should make it clear. I don't want anyone in the Great House to know I'm here."

Jacob cut two pieces of cake. "Not even your mother?"

"Especially her. Knowledge about me could be dangerous. The British have posted a reward for my capture."

With a grimace, Jacob sat across from him. "I have to say it strikes me as ironic. A slave owner who is willing to die for freedom."

"I don't own you. My father does."

"Our father." Jacob reached for a piece of cake just as Matthias did.

Their eyes met briefly before they each grabbed a piece. They ate in silence.

Caroline gripped the candlestick tighter and took a deep breath to steady her nerves. It was time to spy.

She entered the secret passageway from the third floor and shut the door behind her. On her way downstairs, she noted with pride how clean the passageway was. She stopped in front of the library peephole and grasped the small knob in her hand. *Wait*. The light from her candle might be visible through the hole.

She blew it out and placed the candlestick holder on the floor. With the corridor pitch black, she skimmed her fingers up the door to the knob. Thanks to her earlier coating of grease, the peephole glided open without a sound. She peered inside.

Captain Hickman was seated at the desk, a glass of liquor in his thin hand. A candle on the desk illuminated the scene.

"You wished to see me?" Jane spoke from beyond Caroline's view.

"Come in, Mrs. Thomas." Hickman motioned to the settee across from the desk. "Please sit down."

Caroline wrinkled her nose. How kind of the captain to offer Jane a seat in her own house. Jane wandered into view and perched on the edge of the settee.

Hickman sipped from his glass. "How long do you expect your husband to be away on business?"

Jane's mouth tightened. "Quite some time, I'm afraid."

"You are correct. Before my arrival here, I took the liberty of checking the records in Charles Town. It seems your husband is one of our prisoners."

Jane clutched her hands together. "Was there a reason you wished to see me, Captain?"

"Yes, Mrs. Thomas. I believe, given the circumstances, that you and I should become friends."

Remaining silent, Jane watched the redcoat with wary eyes.

Hickman rose to his feet. "Excellent brandy you have

here." He wandered out of Caroline's view and returned with a decanter and empty glass. "Would you care for some?"

Jane hesitated before answering. "Yes. Thank you."

He poured her a small portion. "I hear your husband is quite ill. Dysentery, don't you know. Quite common amongst prisoners." He offered her the glass.

She accepted it, using both hands to hold the glass steady.

The captain leaned on the edge of the desk. "I could arrange for your husband to receive medical attention, perhaps even be moved to more comfortable accommodations."

"I would appreciate that." Jane took a small sip.

"I was hoping you would. I was preparing to write the request when it occurred to me how helpful you could be."

Jane paled. "In what way?"

"Information. There's a criminal on the loose, wanted for treason and murder. I'm sure you would like to see justice done. Wouldn't you, Mrs. Thomas?"

"Who is he?" Jane whispered.

Hickman grasped a stack of papers and thumbed through it. "I have the handbill here somewhere. Ah, here it is. The man's name is— Well, isn't this interesting?" He dangled the handbill in front of Jane's face. "Matthias Murray Thomas."

Jane gasped. Her hand shook, spilling brandy on her skirt. Caroline covered her mouth to keep from making a noise.

"A shame to spill such good brandy." Hickman dropped the handbill on his desk. "Is it a good likeness?"

Jane set her glass down on a nearby table. "I wouldn't know."

"Come now, Mrs. Thomas. You must know something about the man. No doubt you are related."

Jane remained silent, her hands clutched together.

Hickman glowered at her. "Your husband will probably die if I forget to send the request."

"I understand." Jane stood and strode toward the door.

"Don't be a fool, Mrs. Thomas. I'm offering to help your husband. If you don't help me, I will find the information elsewhere."

"Then that is what you will have to do." The door swung shut, signaling Jane's departure.

Hickman sat with a huff, and Caroline glared at his back. No doubt he had enjoyed tormenting Jane.

Poor Jane. She could save her husband by turning in her only son? It was too cruel. Caroline was tempted to march into the library and clonk the captain on the head with her candlestick.

A knock sounded at the door.

"Come in." Hickman tucked the handbill about Matthias Murray Thomas under his stack of papers.

Booted footsteps approached the desk. It was the foot soldier named Pugsley. Edward called him Ugly Pugsley.

"All is secure for the night, sir," Pugsley reported.

"Good. I'll be retiring then." Hickman stood, and with his glass of brandy in hand, he ambled from the room. The soldier followed and closed the door.

Caroline considered what to do next. Wherever Jane's son was, he needed to know about the bounty on his head. Then he could take appropriate measures, perhaps leave the Carolinas all together.

The candle still burned on the desk, where Hickman had

forgotten to blow it out. She could take a peek at the papers, even examine the handbill about Jane's son.

She twisted the latch to open the door. To her surprise, an entire section of bookcase swung into the corridor. *Amazing.* No one would ever suspect this was a door.

She entered the library and pulled the door nearly shut. At the desk, she inspected the papers. On top was the half-written request to supply Jane's husband with medical attention. Blast that Hickman.

The sound of booted footsteps echoed outside the library. Caroline gasped. She had to leave. Now.

She lunged back to the bookcase door. *Damn!* The door had shut completely! The weight of all the books must have pulled it shut. And she had no idea how to open it.

The footsteps stopped at the door.

She dove under the desk.

The door creaked open. Footsteps approached the desk.

"Ah, there you are," Captain Hickman said. "So kind of you to join me."

CHAPTER TWENTY

Matthias slipped into the china room and closed the door. He set the lantern on the table and opened one of the shutters partway. The flame inside flickered and grew, casting a shimmering orange glow on his mother's crystal glasses. A mop and pail in the corner caught his eye.

Betsy must have been cleaning in here.

He opened the door to the servants' passageway and immediately noticed the spotless floor and clean walls. So this was where Betsy had done her cleaning. He'd have to thank her later. But why would she leave a candlestick on the floor by the library door? And the peephole was open.

He closed himself inside the passageway and set the shuttered lantern on the floor next to the candlestick. A faint light shimmered through the peephole.

A man's voice sifted through the opening. "Ah, there you are. So kind of you to join me."

He peered through the peephole and saw Captain Hickman standing by the desk, looking toward the library door.

A woman's voice answered, "I was feeling a little restless

and thought a walk in the garden would calm me." Agatha Ludlow sauntered into Matthias's view. "Perhaps you would join me for a moonlight stroll?"

"I'd be delighted, my dear," Hickman replied.

But something else caught Matthias's eye. He blinked. Surely that wasn't . . . Yes, under the desk was a huddled form in white. His innards clenched. It had better not be Caroline! He'd wring her neck. If the British didn't do it first.

Agatha allowed her shawl to slide down her arms, revealing an extremely low-cut gown. "I'm not interrupting your work, am I?"

"No, not at all." The captain smiled as his gaze lowered. "I only returned to extinguish this candle I left burning." He leaned over to blow out the candle.

Matthias squinted. Their figures were barely visible in the moonlight that filtered through the open curtains.

"Are you afraid of the dark?" Hickman asked.

Agatha answered with a throaty chuckle. "Not if I'm with a fearless warrior like you."

Gah. It was enough to make him lose his supper. Matthias watched them walk away, the door creaking shut behind them.

This was the perfect time to try the corner telescope. The magnifying lens would help him identify the person under the desk before he or she made a quick exit out the library door.

As he lengthened the telescope, a movement drew his attention back to the peephole. The person crawled out from under the desk, then moved so quickly that all he could see was a white blur coming straight toward him.

He held his breath, waiting for the person to get close enough to identify. The faint smell of magnolia blossoms reached his nostrils.

Caroline. Damn it to hell!

"Blast! Where is it?" she whispered as she rummaged along the bookshelf.

What was she looking for? He remembered the candlestick on the floor. And the open peephole. She was looking for the door latch!

He jammed the telescope down to its shortened length. "Bloody hell."

She gasped on the other side of the door. He peered through the peephole just in time to see her eyes on the other side.

She squeaked and jumped back.

He wrenched open the bookcase door at the same time that she ran for the library door. Just past the desk, he caught up with her and grabbed her from behind.

She squirmed and kicked.

He cursed softly as her heels made contact with his shins. "Stop it, Caroline."

"Haversham?"

"Yes." Setting her on her feet, he loosened his grip so the telescope in his hand wouldn't bite into her ribs.

"How dare you! You gave me a terrible fright." She burst from his grasp, twisting to face him.

Her sudden movement wrenched the telescope from his hand. It hit the rug with a clunk.

"Wait!" He grabbed her shoulders. "Don't move. It might have broken."

"What?"

"Stand still. There could be broken glass." He squatted before her and searched the floor.

"What are you looking for?" she asked.

"I dropped a tool I intended to use." His hand brushed over a bare foot, then rested on her other foot.

"It is not sitting on my foot, Haversham."

He circled her ankle with his fingers. The skin felt thin and delicate, like butterfly wings.

"And it is most definitely not wrapped around my ankle. If I were touching your tool, I'd be aware of the fact."

With a smile, he slid his hand up to her calf.

"Stop that, Thomas. Your tool did not fall *up* my leg."

He caressed the skin behind her knee. "Are you sure?"

"Of course." She jiggled her leg to dislodge him. "The law of gravity clearly states that all objects must fall in a downward direction."

He dragged his fingers back down to her ankle. "You obviously haven't heard of the natural law of attraction."

"No. How does that one work?"

"It causes certain objects to defy gravity."

She snorted. "How could anything go up?"

"Believe me, it is happening as I speak."

Her toes tapped the floor as she considered his words. "Oh, I know what you mean. I've seen it before."

His hand stilled. "You have?"

"Yes. I once saw a magnet attract a nail and move it upward. It was very interesting. But I can only imagine it happening with very small objects."

He gritted his teeth. "It is *not* small."

"Oh, it would have to be. Something too heavy could not possibly rise. The demonstration I saw was with a very small nail, more of a tack, actually."

"Bloody hell." He grabbed the telescope off the floor and stuffed it in his pocket.

"Did you find your tool? Where?"

"Between your legs, dammit." He straightened and nabbed her by the arm. He was sorely tempted to prove he was much larger than a tack, but with his luck, the redcoats would catch him with his tool hanging out. "Let's get out of here."

"Wait." She dug in her heels as they passed through the bookcase door. "Show me where the latch is. I need to know how to open this door."

"No, you don't." He hauled her into the dark passageway and shoved the door shut. "Your spying days are over. Do you understand?"

"You cannot order me about, Thomas. I won't have it."

"I won't have you risking your neck! I saw you, Caroline. You were under the desk with that damned captain hovering right over you." Matthias knelt to find the lantern and lifted the shutters halfway up on one side.

"That's an interesting lamp," she observed.

He glanced at her. The light illuminated the bottom half of her thin shift, clearly delineating her legs. He swallowed hard. He was a great deal larger than a tack.

"Can you control the amount of light on each side?"

"Yes." He straightened slowly. "Caroline. Listen to me. You must stop spying."

"I told you, you cannot give me orders. Besides, these corridors give me the perfect opportunity—"

"How did you find the passageway?"

She folded her arms below her chest. Perhaps she felt the gesture was defiant, but all he could see was how her movement tucked in her shift beneath her breasts. They rested upon her forearms, round and full.

"I discovered it thanks to you. It was so dirty in here, you left a trail of dust directly from the third-floor entrance to my bedchamber."

Damn. He should have noticed that, but it had been dark. "Do the other would-be spies in your family know?"

"No, I told no one. And I cleaned up the evidence you left behind. Really, Thomas. You are not suited for this sort of work."

"What?"

"It was so filthy in here, the dust could have made you sneeze. How would you remain hidden then?" She turned to the bookcase door and slid the peephole shut. "And this squeaked so badly, they would have heard you. I worked all afternoon mopping the floors and greasing things."

"Thank you. You've been a great help, but your work is over now."

"I am not the maid! And you're missing my point." She crossed her arms again in the gesture that made it so difficult for him to concentrate. "I am clearly the best choice for a spy."

He dragged his gaze from her breasts. "Excuse me?"

"I'm much more suited for espionage than you."

"Why? Because you're more *tidy*?" He stepped toward her. "Do you understand the danger involved?"

"Of course. I almost died when the captain came in."

"I almost died when I saw you." Matthias planted his

hands on the wall on each side of her, caging her between his arms. "I'll tie you to a bedpost if I must." He leaned closer. "In fact, that notion appeals to me greatly at the moment."

"Don't be silly." She pressed her hands against his chest to keep him from coming closer. "Oh, I can feel your tool. May I see it?"

"Good God." He dug his fingers into the wall.

She slipped her hand inside his coat.

He groaned at the sensation of her roaming fingers.

"Ah, I found it." She tugged the telescope from his coat pocket. "How does it work?"

He lowered his hands and took a deep breath. "You look through the smaller end. I planned to use it to extend my range of vision through the peephole."

"How clever." She turned her back to him and opened the peephole door. "Oh, dear. You realize your tool is crooked?"

He winced. "It is designed to look around corners."

"Oh, I see." She placed the narrow end to one eye.

He touched one of her red ringlets and rubbed the silky hair between his thumb and forefinger. She didn't seem to notice.

She sighed. "This instrument of yours is not functioning properly."

"Believe me, I'm ready when you are."

"The shaft is too short—"

"Bloody hell!" He wrenched the telescope from her hands. "You can lengthen the shaft." He extended the telescope to its full length. "See?"

She gave him an injured look. "You needn't yell at me just because I don't know how to handle it." She took the instrument from him and jammed it back into its shorter length. "I just yank on the end here?"

He ground his teeth. "I have had all I can bear."

"Is something wrong?" She turned to face him as she repeatedly lengthened and shortened the telescope.

"Would you stop playing with my equipment?" He snatched it from her hands and snapped the peephole shut. "We have something serious to discuss." He set the telescope on the floor next to the lantern.

"If this is about spying, I refuse to quit. *You* should be the one to quit. I told you that I have no wish to involve myself with a soldier. A spy would be even worse."

He placed his hands on the wall once more. "You're already involved with me."

She shrugged. "All the more reason why you should stop."

He moved closer to her. "Do you care about me then?"

She swallowed audibly. "Perhaps."

"I think you do." He leaned forward 'til his face brushed against her cheek. The sound of her breathing grew more rapid. "You're so soft."

"Dottie has been insisting that I try all her creams and lotions."

"My compliments to the chef. You smell delicious." He drew her earlobe into his mouth. She tasted as good as she smelled.

She trembled. "Perhaps we can spy together. Or take turns."

"Hmm." He nibbled a path along her jaw to her mouth.

Her breasts pressed against his chest with each breath. "Then you agree? We will share the corridor?"

He skimmed her lips with his own. "Let's share everything."

"Yes," she murmured in response and wrapped her hands around his neck. Her warm body leaned into him.

He pressed her back against the wall and invaded her mouth. This time she welcomed him with her tongue. She followed his moves with such eagerness, he knew she would be no shy virgin in bed. Caroline. His sweet Caroline.

With his fingers, he traced the neckline of her nightgown to the drawstring, then gently pulled. The ribbon came undone. With a gentle tug on her neckline, the opening widened. His fingertips grazed along the upper curves of her breasts. He followed their path with his mouth.

She moaned and raked her hands into his hair.

He unbuttoned the top button of her nightgown. His heart pounded harder. His manhood grew harder. And the damn buttons became harder to open.

What was he doing? She deserved better than a cold, hard floor. Could he make her forget where she was? He kissed her hard on the mouth as he fumbled with the buttons.

Three more undone and his patience wore out. He pulled away from the kiss and peeled back her nightgown. He heard her gasp.

She was beautiful.

The dark pink nipples tightened as he watched. "Good God."

Suddenly, as if she just remembered to breathe, she inhaled deeply and her breasts swelled. "Thomas, we shouldn't."

He cupped a breast with his hand. "Just a taste. Please." He bent down and kissed the warm, white skin. So full and firm, and so delicious. He kissed her again, closer to the nipple. Her fingers dug into his scalp. As her breathing grew more erratic, she moved against his mouth.

"Thomas," she whispered.

He took her nipple into his mouth. A tremor ran through her body that almost exploded in his own. Her body arched.

He heard a thump.

"Ow!" She let go of him.

He straightened. "Are you all right?"

She glanced at the wall. "I banged my head on the knob to the peephole."

"I'm sorry." He felt the back of her head. "I don't feel a lump."

"I'm all right. 'Twas naught but a small knob."

He groaned. Not that again. "A small knob? A tiny twig, a wee button, a small *prick*?"

She eased away from him with a wary look. "Why are you angry all of a sudden? I'm the one with a sore head."

And he was the one with aching balls. Night after night. Not to mention the swollen member she never felt. "Caroline—"

"The bump knocked some sense into me." She pulled her nightgown close to cover her breasts. "We should stop this . . . behavior before it is too late."

"It *is* too late. The time has come for you to see the truth."

"What are you talking about?"

"This!" He grabbed her hand and rammed it against his swollen manhood. "This is me, Caroline. I swell like this every time I'm near you. And I'm bloody close to exploding right now."

CHAPTER TWENTY-ONE

The man was huge.

"Aagh!" Caroline jerked her hand away. "How could you? That was inexcus—" The fierce determination on his face gave her pause. She stepped back.

He moved forward.

She pressed a hand against her chest. Her heart thundered in her ears. Was he seriously considering . . . here in the passageway?

He removed his coat and laid it on the floor.

Good Lord, he was more than considering it. He was planning on it. With a surge of panic, she ran for the stairs.

"Caroline. Wait."

When she reached the first landing, she glanced back. Thomas had grabbed the lantern and was coming after her. Not running, but moving with a fast-paced stride.

She dashed up the rest of the stairs to the second floor, then sprinted down the corridor to the next staircase. She glanced back. The glow of his lantern was visible as he approached the second floor.

She raced up the long, narrow staircase to the landing on the third floor. In the dark, she fumbled along the wall, searching for the latch to open the door. There. Coated with grease, it slipped in her hand, refusing to turn. *Blast!*

Breathing heavily, she wiped her hand on her shift. What was she doing? There was no reason to panic. Even if he followed her to her bedchamber, she could simply refuse him entry. Thomas was a gentleman. He would leave her be.

But if she let him in . . . A night in the arms of Thomas Haversham? She shivered, recalling how gently he had touched her. And the way he had taken her nipple into his mouth . . . She gulped. Perhaps he was less than a gentleman. But she had liked it. She had never felt so excited, so alive. She was tempted to give herself to him, but could she do it without losing her heart?

A light suddenly pierced the dark stairwell. Her breath caught. What should she do? Play it safe or— Gooseflesh prickled her arms. She turned and spotted him at the foot of the stairs. He set the lantern down, then stood there, looking up at her.

Her heart swelled with longing. She closed her eyes and took a deep breath. *You mustn't fall prey to desire. He's a spy. It will kill you to love him and then lose him.*

She opened her eyes. He was ascending the stairs, noiselessly in his stocking feet. Light from the lantern below outlined him in silhouette, but his face remained in shadow. So little she knew about him. And yet, so greatly she yearned for him.

She turned her back to him, but she could feel him coming. *Good Lord.* She rested her forehead on the door when she realized the truth. She wouldn't refuse him.

She wanted him.

"Caroline," he whispered behind her.

The sound seemed to penetrate the skin on her back and sizzle down her spine. It stopped at the apex of her thighs and hummed, waiting for more.

"Why did you run away? I would never hurt you."

She pressed her palms against the door. She'd never experienced this before, an overwhelming desire to be with a man. It was more powerful than she had ever imagined.

His breath tickled her neck. "I want to make love to you."

She dug her fingers into the wall. Just the sound of his voice made her ache for him. She squeezed her thighs together. "Thomas."

"Is that a yes?" He brushed her hair over one shoulder and kissed the nape of her neck.

"Yes," she whispered.

He wrapped his arms around her and pulled her against him. She inhaled sharply at the bulge pressed against the small of her back. When he nuzzled her neck, she tilted her head and leaned against him.

He unfastened more buttons until her gown fell open to her waist. "You're so beautiful," he whispered as his hands covered her breasts.

She shuddered. He kneaded her gently, then teased her nipples with his thumbs. She bit her lip to keep from moaning, but a small whimper still escaped.

"Look how you respond to me." He tugged gently on the hardened tips.

With a moan, she pressed against his swollen manhood. She wanted him something fierce.

He hissed in a breath. "Good God, woman." He slid a hand down the opening of her nightgown, past her waist and over her belly.

She gasped. His hand was on her curls. "Thomas?"

"It's all right." With one hand he gently massaged her curls while his other hand teased her nipples.

Her body trembled, her knees threatening to give out. "I don't think I can stand . . . ah!" She fell forward and caught herself, her palms against the wall. Good Lord, his hand was between her legs. His fingers. Her knees buckled.

He grabbed her around the waist and turned her to face him. "Hold on to me."

When she wrapped her arms around his shoulders, he lifted her and pressed her back against the wall.

"Put your legs around me." He adjusted his hold with his hands on her rump.

She winced. She was so exposed in this position. But then she could hardly make love without giving herself completely, her body and her heart.

Tears burned her eyes. She had never thought she would allow herself to become so vulnerable. "Thomas." She touched his face.

He turned his head to kiss her palm. "Sweetheart." He kissed her lips. "There are soldiers nearby. Try not to scream."

Scream? Why would she? She gasped when his hand slipped between her legs.

"You're so wonderfully wet."

Good Lord. How embarrassing. "I'm sorry."

"'Tis good." He nuzzled her neck. "It means you want me."

She did. She whimpered as he gently explored her. Now that the initial shock had passed, she found herself wanting more. Greedily needing more. Her heels dug into his back as she pressed herself against him.

"I can no longer wait." He adjusted his hold on her.

The door suddenly swiveled open, and they fell through, crashing onto the floor.

"Oh!" She lay stunned.

"Damn." He quickly moved off her. "Are you all right? Did I hurt you?"

"I—I think I'm all right." Wincing, she sat up.

He jumped to his feet and helped her stand. "I must have moved the latch somehow. I'm sorry."

"I used too much grease on it." She shook out her gown and looked about nervously. Luckily, the redcoats were remaining in their rooms.

"We'll go to your room. I'll fetch the lantern." He stepped back through the door and headed down the stairs.

Her room? With trembling hands, she buttoned her nightgown. Was she really going to have an affair with him?

"Who's there?" Charlotte's voice, high-pitched and frightened, came from the direction of the nursery.

Caroline spotted the white blur of her niece's nightgown. "Don't worry, Charlotte. 'Tis only me."

"Aunt Caroline? Did you see the ghost?"

"No, sweeting. There's no ghost."

A larger shape in white appeared at the nursery door. "I told you there's no such thing as a ghost," Edward said.

"Then why were you too frightened to come to the door?" Charlotte asked.

"I wasn't frightened," Edward protested.

Caroline spotted Thomas through the cracked door. He had closed the shutters on the lantern and was waiting in the dark on the landing.

"Will you read my book to me?" Charlotte asked. "Mama's asleep, and I'm afraid the ghost will come."

"I'll light a candle for you," Edward offered, and disappeared inside the room.

"Go inside. I'll be along soon," Caroline said. When her niece headed back to her bed, she leaned close to the opening where Thomas waited. "I'd better go. Edward cannot be trusted with candles."

"I'll see you tomorrow night?" Thomas whispered back.

"Yes." She pressed the door closed 'til she heard the click. Tomorrow night, they would join forces to spy on the British.

As she padded toward the nursery she realized her mistake. Thomas would interpret her agreement differently.

He intended to spend tomorrow night in her bed.

"I just adore a garden in the moonlight." Miss Ludlow lowered herself gracefully onto the stone bench. "Don't you, Captain?"

"Yes." Ezra Hickman eyed the clear night sky and wondered if the nearby partisans were up to mischief. "Perhaps you can help me, Miss Ludlow."

"Call me Agatha, please."

He smiled at her. "And you may call me Ezra."

"How may I be of assistance, Ezra?" She allowed her shawl to slip off her shoulders.

He propped a foot on the bench and leaned forward, his elbow on his knee. The position afforded him an ideal view of her low neckline. "Did you know the owner of this plantation is a prisoner in Charles Town?"

"Mr. Thomas? Oh, my." Agatha pressed a hand against her bosom. "Jane told me he was away on business."

"Aye, the business of treason. You didn't know the Thomas family was in league with the rebels?"

"No! Goodness, I would have never come here if I'd known. I certainly wouldn't have pursued Jane's son."

"Do you harbor any feelings for him?"

"No, of course not. 'Twas Loblolly I found attractive." She touched Ezra's ankle and smoothed her hand up his stocking. "I assure you, I am loyal to the king."

He figured she knew he could have a person arrested, even executed, if he so desired. Her décolletage and roaming fingers excited him, but the sense of power that surged through him was an even stronger aphrodisiac. "You must tell me all you know of the Thomas family."

"As you wish." She continued to caress his leg. "They own a lovely town house in Charles Town. And Loblolly is a rich plantation. It was my desire to be mistress here that caused me to consider Matthias. I don't even care—"

"Matthias?" Ezra leaned forward. "The son is Matthias Murray Thomas?" No wonder Jane was willing to let her husband rot in prison. She was protecting her son.

Agatha nodded. "I don't actually like—"

"Where is he?"

She shrugged helplessly. "I don't know. I believe he was studying in Williamsburg."

So Jane had neglected to tell Agatha the whereabouts of her son. Ezra smiled to himself. All he had to do was lure Matthias back home. Then he could capture the traitor and collect the reward. "How many sons does Jane have?"

"Only Matthias. He's the heir to the plantation."

"I see." Ezra glanced back at the Great House. Once Matthias Murray Thomas was convicted of treason, his land could be confiscated, perhaps even awarded to the brave soldier who had brought the traitor to justice.

If he worked it right, he could have the money and Loblolly. "It *is* an excellent plantation."

Agatha sighed. "It was all I ever wanted. But now I'll have to return home. I want nothing to do with rebels."

He lifted her hand to his lips. "If you stay and help me, you might still be mistress of Loblolly."

She leaned forward 'til her breasts pressed against his leg. "I'll do anything you ask, Ezra."

Chapter Twenty-Two

The next morning, Caroline wound up the mechanical jack to keep the suckling pig rotating over the kitchen fire. "What a handy device, Jacob. Did you and your father build it?"

"Yes," he answered as he munched on a piece of bacon.

Seated across from Jacob at the kitchen table, Edward buttered a biscuit. "May we see the mill today?"

"Edward, you know we cannot." Virginia sipped some coffee. "We told Dottie we would help her in the kitchen today. Finish your breakfast so we can get to work."

Edward made a face to protest his fate. Charlotte pinched off a tiny piece of biscuit and slowly placed it in her mouth. Edward followed her example.

Caroline exchanged an amused look with her sister. The children obviously planned to make breakfast last as long as possible.

She moved to the pump by the stone sink to wash the vegetables she'd picked at sunrise. After a sleepless night, she had decided the best remedy was hard work. If she was exhausted enough, she would sleep.

She rinsed the dirt off a turnip, chiding herself for her flawed logic. She'd worked hard the day before, mopping the secret corridor, but sleep had still eluded her.

For the first few hours, she'd tossed in bed remembering all the deliciously wanton things Thomas had done with her. But then she'd recalled her purpose for cleaning the passageway. Her father, brother, and brother-in-law were risking their lives in the war. And Jane's son was wanted for treason. How could she think about something as fleeting as physical pleasure when lives were at stake?

Jane's son needed to be warned about the handbill. Caroline had had the perfect opportunity to tell Thomas, but she had failed. She'd let her desire override her duty.

And she'd failed to even consider the consequences of her desire. The possibility of pregnancy was all too real. She glanced back at Charlotte and Edward still eating their biscuits at a snail's pace.

Unexpected tears came to her eyes, and she turned back to the sink. All right, so she wanted a child of her own. And a husband who loved her. And a home. After Roger's death, she had tried to bury that dream. She wasn't even sure she deserved to be happy after what she'd done.

Now that Thomas Haversham was in her life, he made her long for the impossible. She recalled his words that morning in the pergola when he'd tried to sever their relationship. The timing was wrong, he'd said. She blinked back tears. As much as she hated to admit it, he was right. She couldn't fall in love and have children now.

"Dottie!" Betsy barged into the kitchen with a tray of dirty breakfast dishes. "Mrs. Thomas needs you."

"What's wrong?" Dottie asked.

Betsy dumped the tray on the table with a noisy clatter. "It was terrible. He's an evil man, he is."

"Calm down, Betsy," Dottie ordered. "I have to know what's wrong, so I can take Miss Jane the right medicine."

"She's frightened out of her wits!" Betsy shouted, then took a deep breath. "They were eating breakfast when Captain Hickman asked Mrs. Thomas to take a walk with him. He said he wanted to pick the perfect tree. And when she asked him for what purpose—" She shook her head. "I hate him. God help me, I hate them all."

Jacob rose to his feet. "What did the captain say?"

Betsy wiped away a tear. "He said she would watch her traitorous son, Matthias, hang."

Jacob cursed softly.

Charlotte whimpered, and Virginia pulled her close.

Caroline balled her fists. So Hickman had discovered that Matthias was Jane's son. "I suppose Miss Ludlow told him who Matthias was."

Betsy nodded. "I went to her room this morning to help her dress, but her bed wasn't slept in. She must have spent the night with—"

"We understand." Virginia covered her daughter's ears.

Dottie selected several small bottles from a shelf. "I'll fix something for Miss Jane."

"I should be going." Jacob strode toward the door, then hesitated. "Betsy, could I have more breakfast to take with me?"

"Oh, that's right. You have— Just a moment." Betsy quickly packed some food.

Caroline wondered if someone was staying with Jacob. It

would be a good place for Thomas to hide. After Jacob left, she removed her apron and excused herself.

"Jacob?" She caught up with him just past the kitchen garden.

He stopped. "Yes?"

She lowered her voice. "Is Haversham staying with you?"

Jacob blinked. "I—I cannot say."

"There's no need to deny it," she whispered. "I know he's here. I met him in the secret passageway last night."

Jacob's eyes widened. "What were *you* doing there?"

She looked around. No one in sight. "I was spying. And I heard some information about Jane's son. I need to tell Haversham."

Jacob's eyebrows lifted. "This should be interesting."

"Is he there with you?"

"Yes, but he told me no one from the Great House was supposed to know about him."

"*I* know about him."

Jacob scoffed. "So you say."

The guard, Pugsley, came into view as he was making his rounds. Caroline walked silently beside Jacob until they had passed the guard. When they reached the path by the river, she felt safe to talk again.

"Do you know Haversham very well?"

"Not really," Jacob answered. "I'm a slave, so I never spent much time with the white folk. Mrs. Thomas was never comfortable around me."

"Why not?"

"No one told you?" Jacob's face reddened. "Her husband, Mr. Thomas, is my father."

"Oh." Caroline tried not to look shocked. This explained a great deal—why Jacob was educated and lived in a nice house. "Then you and Matthias are half brothers."

Jacob snorted. "As if he would ever admit to it."

Caroline sighed. Poor Jacob, caught between two worlds. "At least you have Haversham for a friend."

Jacob's eyes twinkled with humor. "I hear he's a terrible butler."

"Aye, he is." Caroline nodded. "But at least he's not wanted for treason. I only hope Matthias will have the sense to leave the Carolinas."

"I doubt it. Everyone knows he's as stubborn as a jackass. You can remind Haversham of that when you see him."

"Well, if you think it will help." Caroline lifted her skirt to ascend the steps to Jacob's house.

She stepped into the sunny parlor and stopped short. In the kitchen area, Thomas was leaning over a bowl, bare from the waist up, his dark brown hair loose and pushed behind his ears. He splashed water on his face, then cupped more water in his hands.

Straightening, he deposited the water on top of his head. It streamed down his hair to his shoulders, then divided into rivulets. He raised his arms to stretch, and the drops of water meandered in a sinuous path around the muscles that bunched and flexed.

"Pardon me." Jacob squeezed past her. "You're blocking the door."

"Jacob?" Thomas grabbed a towel and turned.

Caroline barely heard Jacob's response. Water had drizzled down Thomas's neck to his chest, where a mat of dark curls had trapped the moisture. The drops of water sparkled in his chest hair, and down below, the hair narrowed into a line that disappeared into his breeches.

"Good morning, Caroline." He wiped his face with the towel, never taking his eyes off her.

The movement brought her attention back to his face, and she wondered how his dark whiskers would feel against her fingertips. He rubbed the towel on his chest in a slow, circular motion. She sucked in a deep breath. The top buttons of his breeches were undone. *I swell like this every time I'm near you.*

"You shouldn't be here." He dropped the towel on the table, then slowly fastened the buttons of his breeches.

Her cheeks grew warm. "We brought you breakfast."

"Lord Almighty," Jacob muttered. "You two can gawk at each other all day, but I have work to do." He shoved the basket of food into Caroline's hands. "I'll fetch him a shirt."

While Jacob strode off to a room on the right, Caroline approached the table and set the basket down. Thomas picked up the bowl and tossed the water out the back door.

Without a word, she emptied the basket. Betsy had packed bacon and sausage, sandwiched between two tin plates. Wrapped in a thick cloth, the biscuits still felt warm. She located a jar of peach preserves and some silverware. Thomas was so close with his bare arms and chest, she kept her eyes carefully focused on what she was doing.

He set a jug and two pewter mugs on the table. "Would you like some cider?"

"Yes." She took a deep breath, reminding herself why she had come. "I heard something important last night. I should have told you immediately, but I was . . . distracted."

With a smile, he filled a mug, then handed it to her. "What is it?"

"Matthias Murray Thomas is wanted for treason. The British have put a price on his head."

Thomas's smile faded. "How did you find out?"

"I was watching through the peephole. Captain Hickman has one of the handbills on his desk."

Thomas paused with a mug of cider halfway to his mouth. "Did you see the handbill?"

"Not close up, but I saw him show it to Jane. She refused to tell him anything. Can you get word to Matthias?"

Thomas nodded and took a drink. "Anything else?" He sat at the table and bit into a piece of bacon.

Caroline sat across from him. "Agatha Ludlow must have informed Hickman that Matthias is Jane's son. Hickman was tormenting Jane at breakfast, telling her to select a hanging tree for her son."

"Bloody bastard," Thomas whispered.

Caroline leaned closer. "Will Matthias listen to you? How well do you know him?"

"Well enough." Thomas smiled slightly as he cut up the sausages. "I hear he's a marvelous fellow."

Jacob snorted as he came back into the room. "Here's a clean shirt." He draped it over the back of another chair, then went to his desk.

Caroline drank some cider. "You must convince Matthias to leave the Carolinas."

"He's not the type to run from danger." Thomas popped a slice of sausage into his mouth. "Nor will he leave his mother to face danger alone."

"But if he's far away—"

"No." Thomas lifted his mug for a drink. "He's a soldier. He'll obey his orders no matter what."

She groaned. "Then it is true? The man is mule-headed?"

"What?" Thomas plunked the mug on the table. "I believe the correct term here is *brave*."

She crossed her arms, frowning. "I heard he's as stubborn as a jackass."

"*What?*" Thomas rose to his feet.

Jacob chuckled.

"Who the hell—" Thomas started, then glared at Jacob. "I see. Very clever."

She noticed a scar on his left shoulder that appeared fairly recent. "How did you injure your shoulder?"

"An accident." Thomas sat down and stuffed more sausage into his mouth.

He was being deliberately vague, blast him. Caroline stood. "I should be going now. You will pass the news on to Matthias?"

"Aye." Thomas ripped open a biscuit. "Meet me in the orchard tonight."

She blinked. Was he intending to seduce her there? "I—I don't believe I can."

"Why not?" He spread peach preserves on his biscuit.

She cast a wary glance at Jacob, and lowered her voice. "I've been giving our relationship a great deal of thought, and you were right about the timing being wrong. I intend to keep spying with you, but that is all."

"Caroline." He stood. "Don't—"

"I'm sorry." She dashed to the front door.

He caught up with her. "Caroline."

"I cannot lie with you under an apple tree," she whispered.

"I agree." He gave her a wry look. "We have no apple trees. But you have your choice of peach, pear, plum, or crabapple. Of course I'd like to try all four."

She snorted. "And it doesn't occur to you that I might . . . bear fruit? We have to be sensible. I have no home now. I'm only staying at the Great House out of Jane's kindness. And the redcoats could kick us out at any moment."

He took hold of her shoulders. "I would take care of you."

"How? You're living in secret. And you're a spy. You could be captured—"

"I know the timing is bad. We—we'll slow down. We don't have to stop."

She blinked back tears. How could she admit how little control she had whenever he kissed her?

"I'll be in the orchard at sunset, by the peach tree that was struck by lightning," Thomas announced.

She groaned inwardly. "I have no idea where such a tree is, and I don't intend to look for it."

"Jacob can take you." Thomas glanced over at Jacob, who was working at his drop-leaf desk. "You know which tree I'm talking about?"

"Aye," Jacob replied.

Caroline sighed. "I am not meeting you there."

"Then you've agreed to give up spying?" Thomas smiled. "I'm meeting my contacts there tonight."

"What?" She narrowed her eyes on Thomas. "Very well. I'll be there."

"What is this?" Jacob's examined a paper on his desk.

"Oh, that's mine." Thomas retrieved the paper. "'Tis the schedule for the supply shipments. Another barge will be arriving tomorrow. I intend to steal it."

"Steal it?" Caroline strode toward him. "Can I help?"

"No." Thomas gave her a stern look. "The partisans will help me. You'll have no part in it."

She planted her hands on her hips. "I will not be pushed aside. I'm just as good a spy as you are, Thomas Haversham. You'll see." She pivoted and marched out the door.

In the fading twilight, Matthias spotted two figures approaching through the orchard. His cousin Richard was a tall man, but even so, his form was dwarfed by the larger man beside him. It had to be Major Munro.

"Promise me you won't squeal," he whispered to Caroline.

The dying rays of the sun lingered golden red in her curls, distracting him from his train of thought. Good God, she was beautiful. He wanted to pull her into his arms and kiss her all over.

She gave him a skeptical look. "Why would I squeal?"

He frowned at her. To hell with her wish to cease their relationship. It was true the timing was wrong, but that didn't mean he could simply extinguish his desire like blowing out a candle. If anything, the flame was burning hotter than ever.

"We're not that far from the Great House and the guards," he explained. "We have to be quiet."

She huffed. "Do you think I'm dense, Thomas?"

No, he thought she was magnificent. The war wouldn't last forever. He would wait. And never give up.

"Is Francis Marion coming?" Jacob leaned against a nearby peach tree, studying the men in the distance.

"No. 'Twill be my courier Richard and—" Matthias stopped when Caroline gasped.

"No squealing," Matthias warned.

"My father?" She turned to Matthias. When he nodded, a smile blossomed on her face that stopped his heart for a second.

"Thank you!" She kissed his cheek, then dashed through the trees headed for her father.

Matthias sighed. She wouldn't thank him when she realized his true purpose for inviting her here. He couldn't make her stop spying, but her father could. One word from Major Munro and Caroline's days of espionage would be over.

The huge Scotsman broke into a run. He caught his daughter in his arms and spun her about, her feet off the ground as if she were no older than Charlotte. With a laugh, Caroline wrapped her arms around his neck and held tight.

At first Matthias smiled, but slowly a hollow feeling seeped into his pores. Would he ever see his father again? If he did, it wouldn't be a happy reunion like this. He couldn't recall his father ever embracing him.

He glanced at Jacob. Had Father been affectionate with him? Had they laughed together on their stools, side by side, in the workroom?

Jacob observed the reunion in the distance, his face harsh with emotion. "In case you didn't know, our father is dying."

Matthias blinked. He waited for a sense of loss to affect him, willed it to happen like the dutiful son, but nothing. Nothing but cold, hard anger toward the man who had betrayed his wife and used his power as slave owner to force young maids to his bed. "I guess you'll get your wish that he rots in prison."

Jacob pushed away from the peach tree. "That's all you have to say? Are you that eager to inherit the land? And the slaves? Hell, you could even own your own brother."

Matthias gritted his teeth. He should have never come back to this godforsaken place. "What makes you think I want any of it?" Without another word, he strode toward his cousin.

"Are you all right?" Richard asked, slapping him on the shoulder.

Matthias winced. "I'm fine. Where are your horses?"

"Simon is nearby, guarding them in the woods."

Matthias motioned to where Caroline stood, still in her father's embrace. "May I introduce Caroline Munro?"

"I'm delighted to meet you, Miss Munro." Richard bowed and flashed Matt a smile that conveyed his approval. "My cousin has been singing your praises."

"Indeed?" Caroline wiped tears from her face. "Thomas is your cousin?"

Frowning at his cousin, Matthias shook his head. Then he extended a hand to Caroline's father. "Thomas Haversham, sir. I am pleased to meet you."

"Haversham, ye say?" Jamie Munro crushed Matt's hand in a brutal handshake.

Matthias figured his smile looked more like a grimace. "Yes, sir."

"And who is yer friend behind you?" Munro asked.

Matthias glanced over his shoulder, surprised that Jacob was still there.

"You must be Jacob." With a smile, Richard shook Jacob's hand. "I've always wanted to meet you."

"You're . . . Richard? The cousin?" Jacob asked.

"My parents would be happy to meet you," Richard continued. "You should come for dinner."

"I . . ." Jacob withdrew his hand. "I don't usually leave the plantation."

"Jacob, is it?" Jamie stretched out a hand. "I'm Major Munro, Caroline's father."

"How do you do?" Jacob shook his hand.

Matthias glanced at the sky. The last of the sunlight was fading away. "We should take care of business. Major, could I speak to you in private for a moment?"

Jamie Munro looped an arm around his daughter. "Why in private, *Haversham?* Ye wouldna be keeping secrets from my daughter now, would you?"

Matthias could feel the man's eyes focused on him, sharp as daggers. He took a deep breath. Caroline would hate him for this, but he couldn't allow her to jeopardize herself. "Your daughter has taken a foolish notion into her head, sir."

Caroline gasped.

Matthias continued, "She believes she should be allowed to spy upon the British. I have forbidden it, of course, but she refuses to obey."

"I see." Major Munro tilted his head to look at his daughter. "Is this true, lass, that ye refused to obey such an order?"

Her gaze dropped to her feet. "Aye."

"That's my girl." Jamie kissed the top of her head.

Matthias's mouth fell open.

With a grin, Caroline hugged her father. "Thank you."

"My daughters can make their own decisions," Jamie announced.

Matthias found his voice. "Sir, it is far too dangerous."

"Ye think my daughter doesna ken it is dangerous? Do ye think she's lacking in intelligence, then?"

"No. But I will not allow her to endanger her life."

"Ye know it is dangerous, lad, but ye do it all the same. Why should Caroline be any different?"

Matthias gritted his teeth. "She is a woman, sir."

"Aye, and I'm certain ye've noticed it on more than one occasion." Jamie released his daughter and moved closer. "A word of advice, laddie. Ye're treadin' on slippery ground here. Ye should start back steppin' fast before ye drown yerself in a bog."

Matthias lowered his voice. "Sir, I'm trying to take care of her."

"Why?"

Why? What did the major expect? An admission of love? A lump in Matt's throat choked any hope of a response. God help him, he did love her.

Jamie leaned closer and whispered, "Are ye courting my daughter with a pack of lies, son?"

"I'm not courting her at all." Matthias raised his voice so Caroline could hear. "Your daughter has made it clear that there will be no relationship between us other than friendship. Isn't that so, Caroline?"

"Yes, it is," she whispered.

Thank God he couldn't see her expression in the dark. It was painful enough just to hear the words.

"Do you have any news to report, Ma— Mr. Haversham?" Richard asked.

"Yes," Matthias replied. "A new shipment of supplies is scheduled to arrive by barge tomorrow. With the help of a few partisans, I believe we could lighten their load."

"When do ye want to do it?" Jamie asked.

"'Twill have to be tomorrow night," Matt replied. "They'll leave the next morning."

Richard muttered a curse. "Impossible."

"Aye," Jamie agreed. "Marion is taking half the group to Georgetown for a raid tomorrow night. Richard and I will be taking the rest to Lenuds Ferry on the Santee. We canna afford to lend you any men."

Matthias paced away, dragging a hand through his hair. "I don't see how I can do it on my own."

"Ye're no' alone," Jamie replied. "Ye have two good helpers right in front of you."

Matthias spun around. "No! Caroline and Jacob will not take part."

"I'll be glad to help," Caroline said.

"I will, too," Jacob added.

"There. Ye have yer team." Jamie extended a hand to Matthias. "Good luck."

How had he lost complete control? Matthias shook the Scotsman's hand in a daze. Jamie Munro hugged his daughter, then left with Richard.

"All right," Caroline said in a breathy, excited voice. "What is the plan for tomorrow night?"

"You'll be safe in your bed asleep." Matthias stalked back toward Jacob's house.

"No, I won't," she answered. "I'll be helping you."

Matthias picked up his pace, ignoring her.

Caroline snorted. "Who made you the leader, anyway? Jacob and I will do it together. Right, Jacob?"

"I believe we could."

Matthias pivoted to face them. "You will not."

Caroline edged around him and kept walking. "Did you hear something, Jacob?"

"Bloody hell." Matthias clenched his fists and followed them to Jacob's house.

CHAPTER TWENTY-THREE

Thursday, September 28, 1780

"If one of those soldiers touches her, I'll kill him," Matthias muttered as he squinted through the telescope. From his vantage point, across the river and high in the branches of an oak tree, he could see the entire scene.

Jacob waited at the base of the tree, hidden behind some bushes. As planned, they had spent the day building a raft and preparing a false cargo. Then they had sailed the laden raft across the river and hidden it behind a thick clump of cattails.

That afternoon, three British soldiers had arrived with the supply barge, increasing the number of soldiers at Loblolly to six. Captain Hickman would not be a problem. Thanks to Agatha Ludlow, he would not be venturing from his bedchamber tonight.

Still, the Loyalist captain was taking no chances. He had ordered all five of the remaining soldiers to stand guard throughout the night. As the sun slipped over the horizon, they built a fire.

Right on schedule, Caroline sauntered toward them, a jug of rum in each hand. The soldiers scrambled to their feet, and she smiled at them. The setting sun blazed off her red curls.

Matthias gripped the telescope tighter and cursed softly. "I should never have agreed to this."

"'Twas an excellent notion, drugging them," Jacob whispered from the base of the tree. "Much better than your plan to capture them all and tie them up."

"We could have done it." Matthias watched Caroline sit at the soldiers' campfire. The men pushed and shoved, each vying for the honor of sitting next to her.

Jacob snorted. "They have us outnumbered. Besides, an overt attack would cause trouble for your mother. 'Tis much better to do this secretly."

Matthias agreed in theory. The soldiers would never admit that they had fallen asleep while on duty. And the next morning, the supplies would appear untouched. The barge would continue its journey to Cornwallis, the soldiers unaware they had been robbed. Still, it was bloody annoying to watch Caroline flirting with the enemy.

The soldiers guzzled down the rum that Dottie had laced with her sleeping potion. One of them passed a jug to Caroline. Her laughter carried across the river, jolting his nerves. There were five of them. They could gang up on her.

She lifted the jug to her mouth. He hoped she wasn't swallowing any of it. He had urged Dottie to make it very strong, hoping the soldiers would pass out quickly.

With the sunset, the pink-tinted clouds faded to murky

gray, but the campfire lent enough light for him to see. The men continued to drink. Their voices drifted across the river as they entertained each other with bawdy songs. One by one, they toppled over.

Relieved, Matthias climbed down the tree. "Let's go."

They poled their raft across the river. As they tied off beside the larger barge, Caroline approached them on the pier.

"Here." Matthias handed her the shuttered lantern. "Light this from the fire."

They set straight to work. Matthias and Jacob pried off the tops of barrels and crates. Just as he suspected, the British were transporting food, muskets, and gunpowder—all items the militia sorely needed.

A simple robbery would not suffice. The British would know if crates and barrels were suddenly too light. So they planned to exchange the British cargo for their own worthless one.

The soldiers snored peacefully by the fire while Matthias and his team made the switch. When the raft had taken all the weight it could, they poled it downriver to the gristmill and unloaded the loot.

Matthias lifted a barrel of gunpowder. "I'll be right back." He ran to Jacob's house, deposited the gunpowder on the back porch, then returned to find Caroline and Jacob still storing the stolen loot in the mill.

When they were done, they returned to the enemy camp for another load. Once the British barrels and crates were empty, they filled them with counterfeit cargo, then hammered the lids back on.

"Let's go." Matthias helped Caroline onto the raft. She settled on a burlap sack filled with flour. Jacob and Matthias poled the raft downstream.

They left the light of the campfire behind. A crescent moon hovered over them, partially concealed by wispy clouds. The mill clung to the riverbank, an immense black shadow, its huge wheel groaning as it slowly turned and slapped the water. They passed the load they had left at the mill, planning to come back for it later.

Caroline opened the shutters of the lantern completely. "It went well, don't you think?"

"Yes." Matthias swatted at a mosquito that buzzed by his ear. "You're certain this cabin is deserted?"

"It was a few weeks ago. The partisans had burned the ferry, and the owner claimed he was ruined. He left . . . on our horse with all our belongings."

"I see." Matthias recalled burning the ferry himself.

"It shouldn't be far." Caroline yawned. "We were on foot and not moving very quickly."

Soon, the lantern light picked out the remains of the burned ferry. Matthias and Jacob maneuvered the raft to the north riverbank, tied it off, then grabbed some items to carry to the cabin. Caroline accompanied them, carrying the lantern.

"Wait here." Matthias dropped his sack outside the door and pulled the knife from his belt. He pushed the door open and peered inside. Empty. Almost. Four golden eyes stared down at him from a shelf. He set the lantern on a table. "We have a few uninvited guests."

"There they are." Caroline pointed. "Raccoons. The rascals will get into the food." Stifling another yawn, she located a broom. "I'll try to shoo them away."

The men returned to the raft. Matthias came back with an armload of muskets.

"They're gone!" Caroline announced with a smile. "I chased them out the back door." Her smile faded as she stumbled back and steadied herself by leaning on the broom.

"Are you all right?" Matthias deposited the weapons on the floor.

She rubbed her brow. "I feel a little . . . tired."

"I knew it." Matthias grabbed her just as the broomstick clattered onto the floor. "You drank some rum, didn't you?"

"I . . . didn't mean to . . ." Her head rolled against his shoulder. Her body went limp.

"Damn." He lifted her in his arms.

Jacob strode in with two buckets full of gunpowder. "What happened?"

"She's out." Matthias carried her to the narrow bed in the corner. "We'll have to take her with us when we go back for the second load." He adjusted her skirt to cover her ankles. "I'm not leaving her alone in this condition. She cannot protect herself."

Jacob set the buckets down. "Why don't you tell her the truth?"

"I wish I could, but I'm a wanted man. 'Tis safer for her not to know who I am."

"I was referring to your feelings."

Matthias crooked a finger in his neck cloth to loosen it. "She knows that I care about her. Come, we have a job to finish."

Jacob followed him out the door. "If you care about her, then you should tell her the truth."

Matthias groaned. Ever since the meeting in the orchard he had managed to maintain a business-like attitude around Caroline. And she had done likewise. "She doesn't want to be involved with a spy. And she's right. As long as I'm involved with the war, I shouldn't court a woman." He reached the raft. "Take the other end of this crate, will you?"

"You could do as she suggested and go away. The two of you." Jacob lifted his side of the crate with a grunt. "And when the war is over, you could come back to live at Loblolly."

Matthias trudged alongside Jacob, carrying the other end of the crate. "I'm not sure she could be happy at Loblolly. I'm not sure I could, but then, I don't have a choice."

Jacob gave him a surprised look. "Don't you want to run the plantation like our father did?"

"No!" Matthias dropped the crate inside the cabin. "Not like Father. *Never* like him."

Jacob's eyes narrowed. "You have a problem with our father?"

"Of course I do. Don't you? The man *owns* you." Matthias stalked toward the raft. He hefted a burlap sack over his shoulder and paced back to the cabin.

Jacob grabbed a small crate and followed him. "I have good reason to be angry, but why would you resent Father? I used to watch you and Richard playing in the garden. You had the ideal childhood."

Matthias dropped the sack on the floor of the cabin. Ideal childhood? He'd been plagued with nightmares and guilt. He'd felt ashamed of his father and grandfather, yet had tried in vain to gain their approval. "My father wanted nothing to do with me. He was happy to send me away for an education. But you, he taught you himself."

With a snort, Jacob set down his crate. "You complain? I would have given anything to go to college like you."

"I would have given anything if he had loved me. Or at least loved my mother." Matthias strode out the door toward the raft.

"I get it," Jacob said softly. "You're jealous."

"What?" Matthias spun around. "Are you crazed?"

"You're jealous because he wanted my mother, not yours. He wanted to be with me, not you."

Matthias clenched his fists. How dare the bastard throw that at his face? Jealous? No, he was furious. "Why would I want to spend any time with that sorry excuse of a father? He forced young maids into his bed. They couldn't refuse him because he *owned* them. He was a bloody *rapist*!"

"Don't talk about him like that!" Jacob stalked toward him, his hands fisted.

"He raped them," Matthias hissed. "He raped your mother."

"No!" Jacob grabbed Matt by his shirt and pulled him forward. His eyes blazed with anger as he raised a fist. "He loved my mother. And she loved him. He loved her long before he was ever forced to marry your mother."

"You can defend him? He cheated on your mother. He cheated on mine."

Jacob's breathed heavily, his fist trembling in front of Matthias's face. "Damn you."

It suddenly struck Matthias that he wasn't alone. He wasn't the only son who had suffered from the sins of his father. "Are you going to hit me?"

Jacob pushed him away. "You can have a slave flogged for striking his master."

"I am *not* your master!"

"You will be soon enough."

Matthias closed his eyes. Why couldn't his bastard of a father live forever? Loblolly was the last place on earth he wanted to inherit. Bloody hell, Richard was right. He was using the war as an excuse. It wasn't the war that was keeping him from moving on with his life. It was his home.

He opened his eyes and studied the man before him. Tall, strong, determined, intelligent. And loyal. Jacob had cause to hate Father, but he defended him. And Father had loved Jacob more. Father had loved Jacob's mother more. God help him, Matthias realized the truth. He *was* jealous.

He took a deep breath. "As soon as I can, I'll free you."

"What?"

Matthias bent over to pick up a crate. "You heard me." He strode to the cabin. *Please don't thank me.* It would be humiliating to be thanked for common decency. He plunked the crate down on the floor. When he turned, Jacob was standing in the doorway, his brown eyes glimmering with moisture.

"Free them all," he said softly.

Matthias slipped past him, headed for the raft. "The plantation cannot survive without them."

Jacob followed him. "There might be a way to manage it. I've given it a great deal of thought."

"I have no choice." Matthias picked up a sack and trudged toward the cabin. "I made a vow to my grandfather on his deathbed that I would continue his damned legacy." Matthias dropped the sack on top of a crate. "I'm bloody well trapped. As trapped as any slave."

Jacob snorted and plunked down his sack. "Am I supposed to feel sorry for you?"

"You don't have to feel anything. You'll be free to go. It will be *my* problem." Matthias returned to the raft.

"I could help. We could come up with an alternative—"

"I am not freeing them. It would be the death of the plantation. Would you have my mother homeless? Have me break my vow to my grandfather?" He hefted the last sack on his shoulder.

"Is your vow more important than freedom? I thought you were fighting for freedom."

Matthias adjusted the sack on his shoulder. "There's nothing I can do." He trudged toward the cabin. Trapped. Trapped in a life he didn't want by a vow he hadn't wanted to make. He dropped the sack on the table.

Jacob stopped beside him. "You're not what I expected you to be."

"Neither are you." Matthias slid his hands under Caroline and scooped her into his arms. "Let's go back for the second load."

In silence, they returned to the raft. Matthias laid Caroline down on the planks, using his coat to cushion her head. They poled back to the mill.

"Why don't you take her to my house?" Jacob suggested as

they loaded the raft. "She'd be better off in a bed than being hauled about all night."

Matthias shook his head. "I won't leave her alone."

"Then stay with her. I can take this load to the cabin. And I'll guard it 'til the partisans come tomorrow to pick it up."

Matthias swallowed hard. Spend the night alone with her? He'd certainly be able to protect her.

But who would protect her from him?

CHAPTER TWENTY-FOUR

Caroline's eyes slowly focused. Sunlight gleamed off a pile of metal parts heaped on a table. She blinked. Where was she? This didn't look like her room in the Great House. She breathed in the fresh, clean scent of her pillowcase. It certainly wasn't the ferryman's filthy cabin.

She sat up and quickly lowered her feet to the floor.

"Aah!" Something jerked beneath her feet.

"Aah!" She responded with a gasp of her own and leaned back onto the bed, tucking her feet up beside her. She squinted at the moaning man. "Thomas?"

He lay on the floor beside the bed, his knees drawn up, his face red. A hissing sound emerged from his gritted teeth. "God . . . bless . . . America."

"Are you're injured?"

"Bloody . . . hell, woman. You stepped on me."

"I—" Caroline noted his hands cupping his groin. "I suppose that hurts?"

The look he gave her indicated she had uttered a gross understatement.

"I'm sorry. I didn't know you were there. Why are you there? Where are we?"

"Jacob's house. My bedchamber." Thomas rolled onto his side. "Dammit. You practically stood on me."

"I said I was—" She eyed his hands at his crotch. "Must you touch yourself there? It is very distracting."

He moved his hands, glaring at her. "Then you touch me. I want to know if the parts are still working."

She scoffed. "Why are you sleeping on the floor?"

"I was protecting you." He sat up, wincing.

"And why was I sleeping in your bed?" Caroline grimaced, realizing the sun had been up for some time. "Ginny will be worried sick."

"You didn't tell her about last night's mission?"

"No, I thought that was a major point to being a spy— keeping things secret."

"You're right." He eased to his feet.

She noted his feet were bare. And so were hers. His shirt was neither buttoned nor tucked in. His hair was loose about his shoulders.

He picked up his blanket and pillow from the floor and tossed them on the bed. "What will you tell your sister?"

"I suppose I'll have to say I . . . spent the night with you." Warmth spread across her cheeks.

"That's probably for the best. 'Tis true, after all, and you're not a very good liar."

Splendid. Ginny would think she was having an affair. "Are my shoes here somewhere?"

"Underneath the bed. I removed them so you would be more comfortable."

She glanced up at him and found him staring at her. "And my stockings?"

"I removed them so you would be more comfortable."

"Then . . . you must have untied the garters?" *On her thighs.* Her face blazed hotter.

"They were too tight. I wanted to make you—"

"More comfortable?" she finished his sentence.

"Yes."

Thank goodness she hadn't worn panniers or he would have continued his quest for comfort up to her waist. Was it her imagination or was the blue in his eyes more intense than usual? "And the laces on my gown?"

"I loosened them so you could breathe easier."

"I see. How thoughtful of you."

"It was the least I could do." He shrugged one shoulder. "The point may be moot, since we don't intend to use the equipment, but in case you're interested—" He leaned toward her.

"Yes?"

"My male parts are still working. Perfectly."

"Oh." Caroline sat still, stunned for a moment, then jumped to her feet. "Well, I should be going now." She located her shoes with her stockings tucked neatly inside. "Is Jacob here?"

"No. He stayed at the ferryman's cabin to guard the supplies."

"Oh." So she was alone with Thomas and his perfectly working male parts. She unrolled a stocking and motioned to the door by tilting her head. "Do you mind?"

He raised his eyebrows. "You need help?"

"No, I want you to leave."

"Oh." He grabbed his shoes and stockings and padded to the door.

Caroline noticed the weapons by the door. "Are these crossbows?"

"Yes, mechanical ones that Jacob designed." Thomas paused at the door. "If you need me, I'll be close by." He exited, shutting the door behind him.

She dashed to the chamber pot in the corner, then quickly pulled on her stockings and shoes. But what about her laces? She couldn't go back to the Great House with the laces to her gown loose. As much as she hated to admit it, she would need Thomas's help.

She slipped into the parlor just as he entered the back door with a pitcher.

"I brought you some water." He poured it into a crockery bowl.

"Thank you." She washed her face and hands while he put on his stockings. "Could you . . . lace up my gown for me?"

"Of course." He circled behind her.

He tugged at the laces, and she clutched the edge of the table to keep from stumbling. Every touch of his fingers melted her resolve to avoid further involvement with him. How could she work alongside him when all her senses yearned for him?

His fingers grazed her spine as he tied a bow. "There, you're done."

No, she was undone. She eased away from him. "I need to go. Good night. I mean, good morning."

"I'll walk with you." He jammed his feet into his shoes. "I want to see if the supply barge has gone."

"All right." She wandered toward the door. "I—I don't remember very much from last night. I was trying not to swallow any of the rum, but I suppose I did."

"Aye." Thomas tied his hair back with a ribbon. "You passed out at the ferryman's cabin. We brought you back here." He strode toward her, pulling on his coat.

They strolled along the river path. Clouds gathered thick overhead, blocking out the sun. A breeze rippled the surface of the river. She wondered if it was going to rain.

"Do you wish me to bring you a meal at noon?"

He smiled. "Thank you, but no. I need to meet up with the partisans to tell them where to pick up the supplies we stole. Jacob will be stuck there until they do."

"I'm glad you're his friend. He seems so lonesome."

Thomas's smile faded. "We have much in common. Caroline, if you ever need your father, you can find him at Snow's Island, where Lynches River joins the Great Pee Dee."

"All right. Thank you."

"This way." Thomas led her to the grove of loblolly pines. Situated on a knoll, the pines offered them cover and an excellent view of the river and front lawn.

He pulled down a low branch and peered through a window of fragrant short needles. "The barge is gone."

"Good. Then they never noticed anything was amiss." She scanned the ground, looking for Edward's hiding place.

"What are you looking for?" Thomas asked.

"Our musket and horn of gunpowder." She brushed a pile of needles aside 'til her fingers grazed the cold metal of the barrel. "'Tis still here, in case you ever need one."

Thomas crouched beside her. "A Brown Bess?"

She nodded. "We brought it with us. It seems like a long time ago, though I know it is not." She scooped up pine needles and heaped them on top of the musket.

Thomas helped her bury the musket and gunpowder. "A great deal has happened in the last few weeks."

"Yes." She had sworn to avoid soldiers, to avoid any heartache to do with the war, yet she had become a spy. And fallen in love with another spy.

Sticky resin coated her fingers, and she wiped her hands on the hem of her gown. How could she have allowed this to happen? She glanced at Thomas and her heart stilled. It was too late. He was the one. God help her, she couldn't imagine not loving him. Her soul cried out for his.

As if he heard her, he met her gaze. Desire flared in his eyes. "Caroline."

Should she fight it or surrender? It was tempting, so tempting to pretend the war didn't exist, that they would be safe for years to come. But it wasn't true.

The ground vibrated beneath her.

"What's that?" Thomas jumped to his feet and peered through the pine branches. "Bloody hell," he whispered.

"What is it?" She joined him.

A group of horsemen emerged from the woods across the lawn and galloped toward the front door. Dressed in green jackets, they sported tall helmets that accentuated their tall height. "Who are they?"

"Tarleton and his dragoons." Thomas turned to Caroline. "He's known to like the ladies. Stay away from him."

She nodded. "I hope he doesn't intend to stay long."

"The horses look worn. He'll want to feed and rest them

a bit. Damn, is that—" Thomas pulled his telescope from his pocket and peered at the men. "Bloody hell."

"What's wrong?"

Thomas cursed softly. "Greville." He jammed the telescope to its smaller size and dropped it in his pocket. "Dammit. Tarleton will go inside to talk to Hickman, and I won't be able to hear it."

"I can do it. No one will think it odd if I go in the house. And I'll be safe in the secret passageway. They won't know I'm there."

Thomas gave her a worried look. "You don't know how ruthless these men can be. Tarleton is called the Butcher, and with good reason."

Caroline swallowed hard. "It needs to be done. I'll tell you what they said later."

Thomas grimaced. "Fine. I'll meet you tonight in the passageway. And Caroline—"

"Yes?"

"You're beautiful in the morning." He grabbed her shoulders, planted a kiss on her brow, then slipped away into the woods.

"Who's in charge here?" Tarleton demanded as he entered the library. His eyes narrowed on Ezra. "You look familiar."

Ezra stood at attention. "Captain Hickman, sir. We met before. At Camden." He glanced at Pugsley, who stood gaping at the famous lieutenant colonel. "Pugsley, take care of our guests."

"Yes, sir!" The guard saluted and dashed from the room.

Tarleton paced across the library, leaving a muddy track with his boots. "I remember. You're that . . . Loyalist fellow." He lounged on the settee, smearing mud on the blue damask. "We've been chasing Marion and his pack of traitors all night. God, I'm parched. Pour me a drink, man."

"Yes, sir." Ezra strode to the sideboard. "The partisans made a strike last night?"

"Yes. At Georgetown." Tarleton removed his brown plumed helmet and dropped it on the settee beside him. "The bastards slithered into the swamp like a swarm of cowardly snakes. Did they come by here? Did you see anything?"

"No, sir." Ezra presented him with the glass of brandy. "It was quiet here. We had a shipment of supplies by the dock. I had five guards posted there all night."

"And they saw nothing?"

"Nothing, sir. The supplies left this morning without incident."

"Hmm." Tarleton took a sip of brandy, then set the glass on a nearby table. "You've had no trouble at all with the partisans?"

"No, sir. We've been very careful."

Tarleton rose to his feet. Even without the tall helmet, he towered over Ezra. "The partisans are all over this area. Why haven't you captured any of them? You wouldn't be *protecting* them, would you?"

Ezra gulped. "No! I assure you, sir, I am loyal to the king. And I have devised a plan for capturing the wanted partisan, Matthias Murray Thomas."

"Why him in particular?" Tarleton's mouth twisted in a sneer. "You want the reward money?"

The reward and the plantation. Ezra focused on Tarleton's cold, dark eyes. "I want to serve my king."

"I always wonder about you Loyalists. Loyal to the king, but willing to kill your neighbors." Tarleton grabbed his helmet off the settee. "If you discover where the patriots are hiding, you will tell me first. Understand?"

"Yes, sir."

Tarleton stepped close. "You can have Thomas, but Marion is mine."

That evening, Caroline crept silently down the secret passageway to the china room. She placed her candlestick on the table in the center of the small room. How sad the shelves looked with half the crystal missing.

During the midday meal, Captain Hickman had once again asked Jane the whereabouts of her son. When she refused to answer, he had gathered up some of her prized crystal glasses and smashed them into the fireplace. Then he had announced he would spend the afternoon questioning the inhabitants of the local village. He had returned at sunset, still in a foul mood.

Caroline paced around the table. Poor Jane was worried sick about her husband and son. It was difficult for Virginia, also. With her baby due any day now, she despaired of ever hearing news about her husband, Quincy.

The door to the china room opened. Caroline exhaled with relief when Thomas slipped inside the room. Dressed in black, he moved about like a shadow.

"Did you see the partisans?" she whispered.

"Yes." He lifted one shutter of the lantern and looked at her. "Your father sends his love."

"Thank you. Did Jacob make it back home safely?"

"Aye." Thomas slipped off his shoes. "Did you hear what Tarleton said this morning?"

"He told Hickman that he chased Marion all night, and Hickman claims he has a plan to capture Jane's son."

"Indeed. Well, let's see what the bastard is up to now." Thomas strode into the passageway and set the lantern on the floor close to the library peephole.

She quickly joined him, then he closed the shutter on the lantern, casting them into complete darkness. When he opened the peephole, a rectangle of light acted as a beacon. She eased closer. He was warm and smelled of soap. When he bent over to look through the peephole, she noticed the wet gleam of his hair. He must have just bathed.

She had remained dressed this evening to help them maintain a business-like relationship. But now, as she tried to sidle up close to him, her skirt and numerous petticoats proved to be an encumbrance.

Voices sifted through the peephole—Captain Hickman and the guard, Pugsley, but she found it difficult to distinguish their actual words. She leaned closer. As intent as Thomas was on the peephole, she hoped he wouldn't notice that her bosom was pressed against his arm.

When he turned his head slightly, she could feel his warm breath against her cheek. His gaze dropped to her low neckline, then returned to her face, lingering on her mouth. Her lips felt suddenly dry, too dry, and she moistened them with her tongue. He closed his eyes with a pained expression.

A sudden noise burst from the library. Thomas turned back to the peephole, and Caroline concentrated on her sense of hearing. It sounded like someone was pounding a fist on the furniture.

"I cannot have Tarleton questioning my loyalty!" Hickman shouted. "I must find a way to make Mrs. Thomas talk."

"Well, you can hardly blame her for protecting her son," Pugsley muttered.

"Her precious son is a murderer," Hickman snarled. "I cannot threaten her with the fate of her husband much longer. Sooner or later, she'll learn the truth. The old fart is already dead."

Thomas straightened with a jerk.

"Really?" Pugsley asked. "When did he die?"

"A few days ago. The news came in yesterday with the supply barge."

Thomas turned and leaned back against the wall. Caroline could hear his breathing, fast and agitated. No doubt he knew Mr. Thomas personally and found the news disturbing. Her heart filled with sorrow for Jane. Poor Jane would need to know the truth, so Hickman could no longer use her husband as a means to torture her.

"Did you learn anything from the villagers?" Pugsley asked.

Caroline peered through the peephole. Pugsley was sitting on the blue settee facing the desk.

"No, they were totally uncooperative." Captain Hickman strode by, a glass of brandy in his hand. "It seems the British soldiers in the area have been sampling the local wares without their consent."

Pugsley snorted. "You mean they're rogering the wenches?"

"Aye." Hickman perched on the edge of his desk and calmly sipped from his glass.

Caroline caught her breath. The redcoats were assaulting the local women?

"You might expect the fathers to object," Hickman continued, "but the women themselves were screaming at me."

"Humph." Pugsley sneered. "Most unladylike."

"Exactly." Hickman set his glass down and picked up a handful of papers. "They insisted I take these formal complaints to Cornwallis himself. As if I'd waste the general's time with the rantings of a few silly women."

Caroline dug her fingernails into the wall. Her blood pounded so hard in her head she could hardly hear.

Pugsley shook his head in disgust. "The women here in the colonies don't know their place."

"Indeed." Hickman held the letters of complaint over a lit candlestick 'til they caught fire.

As the flame grew, so did the heat in Caroline's veins. She snapped the peephole shut, then opened a shutter on the lantern so she could see. She stalked toward the door to the china room. By God, she would show these bastards just how tough an American woman could be.

Chapter Twenty-Five

His father was dead, dead in a British prison. Matthias breathed deeply, willing himself to remain in control.

Dead. Somehow, he had thought his father would survive, that nothing could actually kill the old bastard.

Dead. He'd never see his father again. No more awkward meetings. No more painful memories. No more possibility of reconciliation. It was if a book had ended in mid-chapter. No resolution. No good-bye. Nothing.

Dead. How would Mother feel? Would she mourn or secretly bless the day that the man who had betrayed her over and over could never hurt her or humiliate her again.

Jacob would mourn. Damn, he would have to tell Jacob.

Matthias clenched his fists and slowly relaxed them. He needed to retain control. He was a soldier fighting for liberty. His passion for the cause was perhaps the only thing he had ever shared with his father.

Next to him, Caroline stiffened with a gasp. She shut the peephole, opened a shutter on the lantern, then rushed toward the door.

"Caroline," he whispered, catching up with her as she slipped into the china room. "What's wrong?"

"I'll kill them," she hissed.

"What?" He grabbed her shoulder and turned her toward him.

"Let go." She shoved his hand off her.

He'd never seen her this angry before. "What happened?"

She grasped the candlestick off the table. "I could clonk them on the head while they sleep."

"Have you lost your mind?" He wrenched the candlestick from her hand. "You cannot attack them."

She paced around the room. "I'll slip one of Dottie's potions into their food and make them ill." She opened the door to the dining room.

He shut it and seized her by the shoulders. "Dammit, Caroline. What is wrong?"

With a strangled sob, she pulled away from him. "Didn't you hear them? They're raping the women in town. The British soldiers are raping them."

"Oh." No wonder she was upset.

"Oh? Is that all you can say?" Her voice rose in anger.

"Quiet." He glanced back. The door to the secret passageway was still open.

Her eyes shimmered with tears. "We have to do something."

"I know you're upset." She snorted, but he continued, "Listen to me. Killing them now will bring repercussions against this house and the nearby villages. The British could retaliate by killing everyone, including women and children. We must remain calm."

She glared at him, her eyes narrowed.

"We have to remain focused on our mission. We can't hurt them right now, but we can use them."

She clenched her fists and made a sound of frustration. "I know you're right, but I'm so . . . *angry*."

"I can see that." He took a deep breath. "I don't think you should spy anymore. You're too . . . emotional for this kind of work."

"Too much like a woman, you mean?" Her voice sounded strained.

"I didn't say that."

"I'm fighting for freedom, Thomas, just like you. Freedom to make my own choices without some tyrant of a man dictating to me."

He grasped her shoulder. "I'm not a tyrant. I'm trying to protect you."

"I don't need your protection."

"Well, you bloody well have it whether you like it or not. Don't you know I'm in love with you?"

She gasped.

He released her. *Bloody hell.* Of all the stupid things to say. She moved away from him.

He shook his head. Damn, he had terrible timing. She was far too angry to leap into his arms and declare that she loved him, too.

He swallowed hard. She was awfully quiet. She might not have anything to declare. He loosened the black cravat around his neck. What if she didn't love him?

He opened his mouth to speak, then changed his mind. It was better if she didn't love him. He was a wanted man. With all probability, he would soon follow his father to the grave.

"Wait here. I'll fetch the lantern and take you to bed." He winced. "I mean, your bedchamber." Good God, he might as well dig his own grave and jump in.

He slipped back into the passageway and picked up the lantern. Back in the china room, he found the door to the dining room standing ajar.

Caroline had left.

Sunday, October 1, 1780

Pugsley sped into the library. "He's come back!"

"Who?" Ezra Hickman hurried to the window. Green-coated men on horseback charged toward the house, the plumes of their brown helmets waving in the breeze. Tarleton? His last visit had only been two days ago.

"See to the men and their horses," Ezra ordered.

Tarleton marched into the library. Pugsley saluted, then hurried from the room.

"How many inhabitants in this house?" Tarleton demanded.

Ezra stood at attention. "Five females, including an indentured servant. Two children. Another female in the kitchen."

"Any men?"

"No, sir. Just myself and two foot soldiers. There are slaves, of course, but they live a distance from here."

"Then it is as I suspected." Tarleton stopped in front of Ezra. "You are a traitor."

With a gasp, Ezra swayed on his feet. "Sir, I am loyal.

My sole desire is to destroy the rebels. I have long craved the honor of joining you and your men so I could prove myself—"

"Enough," Tarleton cut him off, slashing a hand through the air. "Did you think no one would notice what you did to the last supply shipment?"

"The supplies? Sir, they passed through here safely."

"Oh, they arrived, all right, but the barrels of gunpowder were filled with ashes! And the sacks that were supposed to be potatoes and corn were full of rocks and pine cones!"

Ezra gaped. "I . . . I don't understand."

"Cornwallis is livid. He ordered a full investigation."

"It . . . it must have happened in Charles Town."

"No. When the shipment left, it was in order. *This* was the only place the supplies docked on the way."

Ezra gulped. "But I had five guards out there all night."

"Did you inspect the supplies yourself?"

"No. I—I never touched them. I thought it best not to tamper with them." Bile rose in Ezra's throat. He could end up swinging from a tree over this.

"There is evidence the barrels were pried open." Tarleton stepped closer 'til he was inches from Ezra's face. "There is something rotten going on between Charles Town and Camden, and I believe the stench starts here. We will hold you responsible."

"I will investigate the matter thoroughly. It will never happen again. You have my word."

"Would that be the word of a Loyalist or a traitor?" Tarleton stepped back. "I'll be watching you, Hickman." He swiveled on his booted heel and marched from the room.

Ezra strode to the sideboard to pour a glass of brandy. His

hand shook so badly, he splashed brandy all over the embroidered doily.

"Damnation!" He clunked the decanter down. Someone had played a trick on him, and if he didn't figure out who the bastard was, he would pay the price himself. It had to be some sort of partisan plot. Were the ladies here in on it?

He paced across the room. Those damned women. He'd get the truth out of them one way or another.

He paused in mid-stride. Did he even need to know the truth, as long as he found someone to blame? Anyone would do, as long as it saved his neck.

Jane Thomas probably knew what had happened. Hell, her son might be behind it. If only this Matthias Murray Thomas could be found, he could take the blame.

Yes, this Thomas fellow was the answer to all his problems. Ezra strode to the sideboard and poured himself a drink, relieved to be once more in control. "Pugsley!"

"Yes, sir." The guard scurried into the room. "Tarleton is gone, sir. They didn't stay very long."

"I know. Gather the women in the front parlor at once. I wish to speak to them."

"Yes, sir!" Pugsley raced off.

Ezra sat at his desk, enjoying his brandy. He'd let the women wait 'til they were as flustered as a pack of hens with a fox invading the henhouse. They'd be so nervous, one of them would be sure to squawk.

He had finished his brandy by the time Pugsley returned. "They're all there, sir, waiting in the parlor."

"Good." Ezra straightened his cravat, then strode into the parlor with Pugsley close behind.

The pregnant woman sat on the rose-colored settee, flanked by her children. The servant, Betsy, stood behind them. Mrs. Thomas sat in a Windsor chair, her face drawn and ashen. Next to her, Miss Munro occupied another chair. She narrowed her green eyes and glared at him.

Ezra returned her hard look. No doubt she was a Colonial sympathizer. It would be a shame to hang her by that pretty neck. He skimmed his eyes over her, assessing her worth. No, she was worth keeping alive. His groin tightened at the thought of Miss Munro with her fiery red hair and patriotic passion struggling with him in bed.

A trill of high notes brought his attention to the harpsichord. Agatha Ludlow, seated at the instrument, gave him an encouraging smile. He bowed his head. At least he could be sure of Agatha. She wanted dearly to please, and please him she did every night.

He pivoted suddenly and paced toward Mrs. Thomas. "This is your last chance. Tell me the location of your son, Matthias Murray Thomas."

She raised her chin. "I can honestly tell you, I do not know."

"Don't expect help from your husband. The traitorous bastard is dead."

Mrs. Thomas flinched. "I . . . I know nothing."

With a sudden move, Ezra leaned over Miss Munro. "You know, don't you? You know where the partisans are, and you're going to tell me."

Her eyes widened, surprised by his abrupt change of strategy. "I don't know."

"Did you think I wouldn't find out what you did to the supplies?" His voice rose in anger. "You think it was clever to sabotage my career? You're messing with the wrong man, bitch."

Her face paled.

Ezra straightened, still glowering at Miss Munro. "You will tell me the location of the partisans." He withdrew his flintlock and pointed it at Mrs. Thomas's head. "Or I shoot."

A series of gasps circled the room. The little girl squealed and dove into her mother's lap. The young boy jumped in his seat. Agatha's hands slipped on the harpsichord keys, producing a jarring noise. Miss Munro's eyes filled with tears. She gave Mrs. Thomas a beseeching look, begging for guidance.

Ezra watched the drama unfold. Hell, this was better than the theater in Charles Town, and the fact that he was the director of this scene gave him a satisfying sense of power. Live puppets, that was all they were, and he alone could pull the strings.

Miss Munro opened her mouth to speak, then closed it with a pained grimace. Indecision. Ezra's pulse accelerated. The wench might actually know something.

"No!" The boy, Edward, leapt to his feet. "Leave them alone! They don't know anything. 'Tis the ghost you want."

"Edward, please." His mother tugged at the boy's coat.

"A ghost, you say?" Ezra couldn't help but be amused. His little play even had comedic overtones.

"Yes." Edward sat. "He can go through walls."

Ezra smiled and turned his attention back to Miss Munro. He paused, his smile fading. The fear in her eyes had not diminished with the boy's outburst, but increased.

"Miss Munro," he whispered. "Do you have something to tell me?"

She glanced at Mrs. Thomas as if asking permission to talk.

The older woman shook her head and whispered, "No."

"So you are willing to die for your son, Mrs. Thomas?" Ezra stepped toward her, gratified to see a tear roll down her cheek. He paused with the flintlock aimed between her eyes. Just a few more seconds of terror was all he wanted.

"Since you desire death, you shall have it." He returned his flintlock to his belt. "You're under arrest for harboring a traitor to the crown."

"Pugsley." He swiveled to the foot soldier. "You will escort Mrs. Thomas to her bedchamber and lock her in. You will nail boards across her balcony door so she cannot escape. She will receive only a crust of bread each day and enough water to keep her alive."

Ezra turned back to Mrs. Thomas. *Good.* The tears were streaming now, her chin trembling. "I will have handbills printed and distributed that spread the news. If Matthias Murray Thomas wishes to save his mother from a slow death by starvation, he will turn himself in."

Mrs. Thomas whispered, "I would rather die."

Anger surged through Ezra once again. These damned women would not get the better of him. "Then you are fortunate, madam, for you may have your wish!"

CHAPTER TWENTY-SIX

Matthias inserted an arrow into the crossbow and pulled back the lever. The gear shifted with a metallic click. A little too loud, but it was still quicker than loading a musket. He aimed and pulled the trigger. The arrow sped through the air with a whoosh, then quivered from its impact in an oak tree.

"Not bad." Jacob approached from the slaves' quarters.

Shielding his eyes from the afternoon glare, Matthias spotted the slaves in the distance, covering their roofs with a layer of hot tar. "That stuff must stink for miles."

"Aye, but it will keep the rain out."

Matthias wandered toward the oak tree. "And the barrels of gunpowder?" His barrel of stolen gunpowder had been divided into four smaller barrels. He'd wanted each barrel coated in tar to make them waterproof, but since the smell might be noticed by the redcoats, Jacob had disguised their activity by having the slaves treat their homes.

"Ready to go." Jacob motioned to the arrow as Matthias yanked it free. "At least you're hitting the tree now."

With a snort, Matthias pointed to the side. "I was aiming at the bottle."

Jacob winced.

Matthias paced back. "This new plan is more dangerous than the last one. We may have to kill some redcoats. If you'd rather not participate, I'll understand."

Jacob stiffened with his jaw firmly set. "I am taking part. They killed our father."

Not knowing what to say, Matthias simply nodded. He had told Jacob the bad news two nights ago. The night he had foolishly confessed to loving Caroline. He inserted another arrow in the crossbow and pulled back the lever. "I'm a good shot with a musket. Why do I keep missing the damned bottle?"

"Let me see it." Jacob reached for the crossbow. "Oh, no wonder. This is the first one I made. The alignment is off. Try one of the other two. They're much better."

They headed for Jacob's house when Caroline burst out the back door.

"There you are! I came as soon as I could." She breathed heavily as if she had run all the way from the Great House. "I had to wait for Hickman to leave for town. The other soldiers are busy guarding Jane, so I knew it was finally safe for me to come here."

"Guarding Jane?" Matthias repeated her words, dumbfounded. "Why?"

"It was horrible!" Caroline cried, then took a deep breath, visibly attempting to calm herself. "Hickman called us into the parlor, then demanded that Jane tell him the whereabouts of her son. When she refused, he asked me where the patriots were hiding. When I didn't answer, he . . . he . . ."

Matthias pulled her into his arms and felt her body trembling. He'd never seen his brave Caroline so afraid.

Her voice came out in muffled spurts, pressed against his linen shirt. "He pointed a . . . a pistol at her. At Jane. I was afraid he would shoot her if I didn't talk."

Cold fury coursed through Matthias, turning his blood to ice. "He threatened to shoot my—"

"She's all right." Caroline pulled back to look at him. "But Hickman arrested her. He plans to starve her to death unless her son turns himself in."

Matthias stiffened. His mind froze for a moment, too stunned to think.

"Bastard." Jacob spat on the ground.

"Can you send word to Matthias?" Caroline asked.

Matthias swallowed hard. "He could give himself up."

"No!" Jacob shook his head. "He'd be executed, and there's no guarantee that Hickman will spare Mrs. Thomas or any of the ladies. With him gone, who will protect them?"

"We have to do something!" Caroline cried. "Can we rescue her?"

Matthias mentally shook himself out of his daze. "Where is she being held?"

"In her bedchamber. There will be one guard at her door at all times. The other guard is boarding shut her window and balcony door." Caroline's face lit up with a sudden thought. "The secret passageway! Is there one to her room?"

"No. There are none on that side of the house." Matthias glanced at Jacob. "But we could make one."

Jacob raised his eyebrows. "And not be heard?"

"We'll do it immediately after the other plan has succeeded. That one will serve as a distraction."

Jacob nodded slowly. "It could work."

"What other plan?" Caroline asked.

"Don't worry about it," Matthias assured her. "We're taking care of everything."

Her emerald-green eyes shimmered with frustration. "You made plans without me?"

She was beautiful when angry. Matthias chastised himself for even noticing at a time like this. "What we're planning is far too dangerous for a woman."

Caroline clenched her fists. "I am not a weakling. I'm just as brave and clever as you."

Matthias nodded. "I know you are."

"And I can be trusted," she added.

"I know that, too."

"Then let me help you!"

Matthias groaned inwardly. He was as frustrated as she was.

Jacob cleared his throat. "I thought I saw Tarleton and his troop come by."

Matthias dragged his gaze from Caroline to Jacob. "When?"

"This morning," Jacob answered.

"Did you hear their conversation?" Matthias asked Caroline.

"No. He came and went very quickly. And then Captain Hickman ordered us to the parlor. He accused me of messing with his supply shipment and sabotaging his career."

"Then he knows about the switch we made. Tarleton must have told him, and Hickman suspects *you* may be behind it." Matthias gave her a pointed look. "All the more reason for you to stay out of this. He's watching you."

Caroline folded her arms across her chest with a stubborn lift to her chin.

"The British will hold Hickman accountable," Matthias continued.

"That would explain his actions," Jacob added. "He hopes to save his skin by passing the blame to someone else."

Caroline sighed. "I hope Matthias will learn how much his mother is suffering for him."

Matthias winced inwardly. "If all goes well, she will be free in two days."

"And I'll be ready to help, whether you like it or not." Caroline headed back into Jacob's house, slamming the door behind her.

Matthias winced.

Jacob shook his head. "Why don't you two admit that you love each other?"

"I did. She didn't. End of story."

Jacob snorted. "'Tis obvious that she loves you. She's willing to die by your side."

A flame of hope flared in his chest. "You don't think that is merely a passion for the cause?"

"I must have inherited all the intelligence in the family."

Matthias scoffed. "Strange words from a man who designs a crossbow that cannot shoot straight."

"Perhaps it is your poor eyesight. After all, you appear to be blind."

Matthias yanked at his neck cloth, loosening the knot. Once again, his actions had backfired. His initial escape had caused many to lose their homes when the British had retaliated. His burning of bridges and ferries had caused the British to take over Loblolly. And his last plan, the disguised theft of the supply barge, had ricocheted back to place his mother in further jeopardy. It seemed no matter what he did, he made matters worse. "I can see what I've done, Jacob. I'm not blind. I'm cursed."

Caroline was better off without him.

Tuesday, October 3, 1780

Hidden in the branches of a cottonwood tree on the north bank of the Black River, Matthias watched for the arrival of the supply barge. When it came into view, he scrambled to the ground, grabbed his crossbow and quiver of arrows, then sprinted upriver to the ferryman's cabin. The tar-covered barrels of gunpowder lay on the bank of the river, tied together with a rope at two-foot intervals.

Across the river, on the south bank, Jacob waved to signal his readiness. Matthias tied the end of the rope to an arrow and inserted the arrow into his crossbow. He aimed for an oak tree across the river.

He missed. *Damn.* He examined his crossbow. He must

have picked up the one that was misaligned. But how? There had been only two crossbows in the house. He had assumed they were the good ones and that Jacob had put away the bad one.

There was no help for it now. He would have to aim to the left of his target and pray for the best. Across the river, Jacob retrieved the end of the rope and pulled.

The rope unwound, dragging the small barrels into the river. Matthias tied his end around the base of a sturdy tree. Jacob did the same and soon, the four black barrels of gunpowder bobbed in the center of the river.

The two men dashed upriver to where they each had a small fire ready to ignite. With a spin of a tinder wheel, Matthias sent a shower of sparks onto the pile of dead leaves. Soon, the fire blazed nicely. Across the river, he noticed a small black plume of smoke. Jacob's fire.

Matthias inserted an arrow into his crossbow—an arrow with a flammable tip of Jacob's design. He peered around a tree and waited for the barge.

It came slowly up the river. A redcoat stood at each corner, a total of four, each one stabbing his long pole into the riverbed to move the barge along. In the middle of the barge, an officer sat on a chair, sipping from a canteen. As he lowered his arm, sunlight glimmered off his rings and the silver gorget around his neck. A large plume on his tricorne rippled in the breeze.

As they neared the floating barrels, one of the soldiers pointed. The officer rose from his cushioned chair and sauntered to the fore of the barge. Meanwhile they drifted closer and closer to the four barrels.

The officer raised a quizzing glass to examine the barrels. Suddenly, he straightened with a shout.

Matthias lit his arrow. Patience, he cautioned himself. *Timing is everything.* The barge collided with the barrels.

Whoosh! A ball of fire erupted from the south bank as Jacob shot his first arrow. Matthias pulled the trigger, then immediately loaded the next arrow and lit it.

A loud explosion deafened his ears, followed by a second one. *Good.* They had both found their marks. He glanced up to take aim and paused, momentarily stunned by what they had done. Flames engulfed the front of the barge. And he could hear the soldiers. Some were shouting in anger; others screamed in agony.

Bloody hell. But what choice did he have? He couldn't rescue his mother with live redcoats about. *This is war.* Man's imitation of hell, complete with the fiery furnace.

Just as he pulled the trigger, he saw Jacob's second arrow fly through the air. Two more explosions rocked the barge. The officer was flung into the air and landed with a splash in the river. The plumed tricorne flew to the side. Smoke billowed up to the sky, thick and black.

Through the smoke, Matthias spotted a redcoat jump into the river, holding his musket over his head as he swam for the north bank. The other redcoats, he assumed, were dead.

He kicked dirt onto his small fire, then ran upriver 'til he came to a huge oak tree with thick lower branches. It was an easy climb and soon he was positioned high above the river. He had left a thick rope coiled in the tree, one end tied around the trunk.

He removed an arrow from his quiver. This one Jacob had

designed with a large hole in the metal shaft. He threaded the end of the rope through the eye and knotted it tight. Then he shot the arrow across the river. It found its mark in another oak tree just opposite him. He pulled the rope taut and tied it off, noting with satisfaction that the rope sloped downward to the other tree.

He spotted the redcoat, running up the path, his musket in hand.

Matthias rested his crossbow on top of the taut rope, grasped each end with his hands, and pushed off from the tree. With his legs dangling free, he slid down the rope, crossing the river in mid-air. A quick glance downriver and he spotted the barge, a floating fire with clouds of black smoke.

A shot rang out, the musket ball whizzing past his back as he flew across the river. The redcoat had spotted him. When he reached the other bank, he dropped to the ground and glanced back. The redcoat was climbing the oak on the other side.

Boom! A huge explosion shook the ground, knocking Matthias off his feet. The fire must have found a stash of gunpowder on the barge. He glanced downriver as he regained his feet. The barge had become a huge bonfire. The air surrounding it wavered with heat.

Across the river, the redcoat had managed to stay in the tree, although he appeared to have lost his musket.

Matthias scrambled up the tree on his side. He yanked his knife from his belt and began sawing at the rope.

The redcoat pulled off one of his white cross belts and looped it over the rope. He shoved off from the tree.

"Damn," Matthias muttered as the redcoat hurtled

through the air straight toward him. One last chop with his knife and the rope broke.

With a yelp, the redcoat plunged into the river. Matthias jumped down from the tree, grabbed his crossbow, and sprinted upriver.

Another gunshot exploded behind him. He dove behind a tree and peered through the cover of leafy branches as the thud of pounding feet came toward him. It was the officer. He had survived and come ashore on this side.

Matthias reached into his quiver. The last arrow. He clicked it into place and waited. *Timing is everything.*

He heard the man's labored breathing as he ran forward. Matthias stepped from behind the tree and pulled the trigger. The officer fell.

"Halt! Damn you!" It was the second redcoat, the one who had fallen in the river. His tricorne and wig gone, his uniform dripping, the man charged toward Matthias.

Matthias drew his knife.

A swoosh of air blew past him.

The redcoat jolted to a stop, then slumped to the ground, an arrow imbedded in his chest.

Matthias looked around, but saw no one. He approached the fallen redcoats to make sure they were dead.

"Are you all right?" Jacob ran toward him. "I heard gunfire."

"I'm fine." Matthias motioned to the second redcoat. "Thanks to you. You may have saved my life."

Jacob frowned at the arrow, then pivoted slowly, gazing into the woods.

"Something amiss?" Matthias asked.

"Yes," Jacob answered. "I didn't shoot that arrow."

Matthias scanned the woods around them. "Whoever he is, he appears to be on our side."

Jacob hunched down beside the body and examined the arrow. "It looks like one that I made."

"The third crossbow. Damn, that explains it."

Jacob glanced up. "What do you mean?"

Matthias lifted his bow. "This is the misaligned one. Remember how I missed that first shot?"

Jacob straightened. "But there were only two bows in the house this morning. I thought you must have discarded the bad one."

"I thought *you* had." Matthias strode upriver toward the mill. "Our mysterious helper has the missing crossbow."

Jacob accompanied him. "Who could he be?"

"I don't know." The mill came into view, then Jacob's house. Matthias jerked to a halt as a chill swept through him. "God, no." *Not Caroline.*

"What?" Jacob pivoted, searching the woods for something wrong.

"Caroline passed through the house. She could have taken it."

"The crossbow?" Jacob gave him an incredulous look. "I cannot imagine her killing anyone."

Matthias pounded his thigh with his fist. "Bloody hell! I told her to stay out of this."

"But whoever did it saved your life."

"I could have killed that man myself. God help me, I'm good at it now." Matthias shoved a loose strand of hair out of his face.

A vision of Caroline flitted through his head——her arms crossed, her chin lifted in defiance. *I'll be ready to help, whether you like it or not.* And the last time they had spied on Hickman, she had threatened to commit murder. Sweet Lord, what ungodly effect this war had on people, turning the innocent into killers.

"Matthias." Jacob jabbed him on the shoulder. "Come on. We still have work to do."

CHAPTER TWENTY-SEVEN

In the nursery, Caroline finished reading out loud the last page of Charlotte's book.

Edward jumped off his bed. "Thank God that's over."

"Shh." Virginia motioned to his sleeping sister. "Don't wake her. She barely slept at all last night."

"Poor Charlotte," Caroline whispered as she returned the young girl's book to a bookcase against the wall.

"Aye." Ginny pulled a quilt up to Charlotte's shoulders. "That scene in the parlor frightened the wits out of her."

"It scared me, too." Caroline shuddered. Poor Jane, alone in her room. This was her second day without food, although according to Betsy, Jane did have some of her favorite candied fruit hidden in a drawer.

Caroline skimmed her fingers over the selection of books, wishing there was something she could do. An untitled book caught her eye and she opened it. The beginning pages were filled with handwriting, a crude, childish script, signed Matthias with a backward S.

His journal, began in his childhood. Caroline snapped

the book shut and shoved it back onto the shelf. Where was this Matthias when his mother was starving to death?

A boom sounded in the distance.

Caroline whirled to face her sister just as a second explosion followed the first. "What was that?"

Ginny bit her lip. "Gunpowder. Or cannon fire?"

Edward ran to the door. "'Tis the Continental Army, come to push the bloody lobsterbacks into the sea!"

Caroline followed him. "It could be the partisans." Or it could be Thomas and Jacob and their secret plan. Two more explosions roared in the distance.

"Let's go and look," Edward whispered.

"I'm coming, too," Ginny said.

Caroline opened the door as her sister waddled toward them. "Are you sure you shouldn't rest?"

"I feel fine today. Not tired at all." Ginny hurried through the door. "Edward! Don't run ahead of us."

When they reached the front porch of the Great House, Caroline spotted Captain Hickman and both the foot soldiers down by the riverbank. Agatha Ludlow was strolling toward them, her peach-colored parasol ruffling gently in the breeze. In the distance, a column of black smoke billowed into the air.

Edward raced to the river. Caroline and Ginny were halfway there when he sprinted back.

Edward grinned. "The supply barge is ablaze!"

"Oh, my," Ginny whispered.

Caroline ran to the pier and looked downriver. The barge was totally consumed with fire, the air around it shimmering with heat. The smell of burning wood was accented by other strong odors, black pitch and gunpowder, and what she feared was burning flesh.

"How dreadful." Agatha flicked open a delicately painted fan of thin chicken skin and fluttered it in front of her face. "I wager I can feel the heat from here."

Captain Hickman turned to Caroline, his face red with anger. "What do you know of this, Miss Munro?"

She blinked. "Nothing. I . . . Perhaps they had an accident with the gunpowder on board."

"This was no accident. Pugsley, Bertram!" the captain yelled at his soldiers. "I want every inch of the riverbank inspected. Look for survivors. And if you see anyone suspicious, shoot to kill."

"Aye, sir!" they shouted in unison and darted down the path toward the mill.

Caroline swallowed hard. Hopefully, Jacob and Thomas would keep out of sight.

Hickman shook his head and muttered, "Dammit. There will be hell to pay for this."

Virginia and Edward reached the pier.

"What a disgusting odor." Agatha fanned herself harder. "I only hope that horrid smoke doesn't reach the house. I would hate for that smell to infect my gowns."

Caroline exchanged a look with her sister. Men had probably lost their lives in the explosion, and Agatha was concerned about her clothes. Her gaze wandered to the Great House. *Jane.* No one was in the house to guard her.

She cleared her throat. "I could close the windows."

"Oh, would you?" Agatha gave her a beseeching look. "How kind of you."

Caroline grabbed Edward's arm as she stepped off the pier. "Come and help me."

Edward tugged away. "I want to watch the fire."

"Edward." Caroline gave him a pointed look.

"Come along, Edward." Virginia nabbed him by the arm and accompanied Caroline back to the house. "What are you planning?" she whispered.

"You can close the windows on the front porch while you keep watch for me," Caroline whispered back. "Let me know if any of the soldiers come back."

"Of course." Virginia smiled. "Jane's guards are gone."

"Exactly. I'm going to take some food to her." Caroline took off running, leaving her sister and nephew behind. She dashed through the house and then burst into the kitchen.

Dottie was at the table, shelling peas. "What is happening out there?"

"The supply barge is on fire." Caroline ran to the shelves and grabbed a loaf of bread and a wedge of cheese. "Jane is unguarded. I mean to pass some food to her."

"Excellent! Here." Dottie handed her a cloth sack and a bottle of cider.

With a sack full of food and drink, Caroline darted back into the house and up the stairs.

"Jane!" She jiggled the latch to Jane's door. It was locked. "Jane, can you hear me?"

The sound of footsteps approached the door. "Caroline, is that you?"

"Yes. I have some food for you."

"The door is locked. Is the guard not there?"

"The soldiers are by the river." Caroline yanked once more

on the door handle, then thumped her fist against the wood in frustration. There had to be a way.

"What were those explosions outside?"

Ignoring Jane's question, Caroline dashed onto the balcony to examine the door there. A series of boards had been nailed across the glass-paned door to keep Jane from exiting, but the gaps were wide enough to pass something through.

She looked toward the river. *Blast!* If Hickman turned toward the house, he would see her. She squatted down, hoping the balcony railing provided enough cover.

A repetitive hammering sound came from within the house. Was Jane pounding on the other door?

Caroline wrapped her hand in her skirt and shattered a pane of glass near the floor. "Jane! Over here."

Jane's face appeared between two slats of wood. "Be careful. Someone could see you."

The hammering grew louder.

"What is that noise?" Jane asked.

"I was going to ask you." Caroline removed the bottle of cider from her sack and passed it through the hole in the door.

Jane grabbed the bottle. "I believe it is coming from upstairs. Oh, my Lord!"

"What?" Caroline pressed against the glass door, trying to see. She heard a metallic, scraping sound.

"Two metal stakes ripped through my ceiling," Jane said. "And now, two saws are cutting through the wood."

Thomas and Jacob! Caroline grinned. They were safe. And rescuing Jane. She stuffed the rest of the provisions through the hole. "Jane, listen to me. Take this sack and pack it with whatever you wish to take with you."

"I . . . I'm leaving?"

"Yes! Hurry!" Staying low, Caroline hurried back into the house.

She scurried up the narrow staircase to the third floor. As she ran to the east end of the house, the scrape of the saws grew louder. They must be in the small storage room across the hall from her room. She tried the door. It opened an inch before ramming into a piece of furniture.

The sawing stopped.

"Thomas?" she whispered.

"Dammit, Caroline." The sawing resumed. "What are you doing here?"

"I want to help."

The sound decreased to one saw. Footsteps pounded to the door and Thomas peered through the opening, his face ruddy with exertion. "You have helped more than enough already!"

Caroline blinked. "What did I do?"

His eyes flashed with anger. "If you want to be useful, go and saddle three horses."

"Yes, of course." Caroline shut the door and ran toward the stairs. Why was Thomas angry with her?

"Aunt Caroline?" Charlotte appeared at the nursery door, a frightened look on her face. "I woke up and I was all alone."

"Come with me." Caroline grabbed her hand and ushered her down the stairs and onto the front porch.

The little girl ran into her mother's arms.

Virginia hugged her as she spoke to Caroline, "Did you succeed? Does Jane have food?"

"Yes. Thomas and Jacob are rescuing her."

"Zounds," Edward whispered. "Aunt Jane is escaping?"

Caroline nodded. "They need my help. Can you keep the redcoats from coming in until after they've left? And Edward, I need you to go inside and close all the windows."

"We'll take care of everything," Virginia assured her. "Go on."

Caroline ran out the back door to the stables. The first horse, feeling her excitement, shook its head, making it more difficult to put on the harness.

"Shh. Good boy." She rubbed his nose. The action soothed her own nerves along with the horse. While saddling the third horse, she heard the creak of the stable door.

Thomas slipped inside. "Are the horses ready?"

"Yes." Caroline cinched the last saddle. "Did you rescue Jane?"

"Aye." He took the reins of the three horses and led them toward the door. "Thank you."

"I'm happy to help. Did you cause the explosions?"

He gave her skeptical look. "Why ask? You were there, weren't you?"

"I was in the nursery."

"We'll discuss it later." He scowled at stable door. "Will you check outside?"

Caroline peeked outside. "No one in sight."

Thomas exited with the horses.

"Where are you going?" she asked.

"The less you know, the better."

Caroline planted her hands on her hips. "Am I untrustworthy all of a sudden?"

"Go back to the Great House. We'll talk later."

Caroline glared at his back as he led the horses into the woods. For a man who claimed to love her, he was treating her in a most unfriendly manner. She followed him, winding through the trees.

He glanced over his shoulder, frowning at her. "There's no need to guard my back. I can take care of myself."

Guard his back? She opened her mouth to question him when she spotted the others. "Jane! Jacob!" She ran forward and embraced them both. "I'm so happy you're all right."

Thomas helped Jane mount a horse, then tied her pack to the saddle horn. He glanced briefly at Caroline. "Go back to the Great House before they notice you're missing."

Caroline frowned. "Fine."

Thomas started to mount, then abruptly pulled her against him. "Stay out of trouble." He kissed her hard, then turned away to mount his horse.

Caroline touched her mouth as they rode away. His kiss had been an odd mixture of desire and anger. Was he angry that she'd avoided him after his confession of love?

She wandered back to the Great House. On the front porch, Virginia and Charlotte rested on a bench. Edward sat on the front steps with a sour look on his face. In the distance, the pillar of smoke had dimmed to a wispy gray.

"Is Jane safely away?" Virginia asked.

Caroline nodded. "Yes, thank God."

"That's good." Virginia sighed. "Hickman will be furious. He may try to blame us."

"You were on the porch here in plain sight," Caroline assured her. "And Edward and I were gone only a few minutes to close windows. Right, Edward?"

"Right." He nodded.

Caroline turned her attention to the riverbank. Captain Hickman was standing there with Agatha Ludlow. Pugsley and Bertram trudged toward him with a dead body, then dropped it on the ground at the captain's feet.

Agatha squealed in horror and scurried toward the Great House, her parasol waving erratically. Hickman's voice, loud and angry, drifted toward them on the breeze.

Edward glanced back. "Come on, Mama, let me go. Then I can tell you what I learn."

"No, Edward, you're staying here."

Edward glowered at his mother. "I'm not afraid of a dead body. I've seen them before."

Virginia smoothed her hand over her swollen belly. "Good Lord, what a time to be raising children."

"This is horrid!" Agatha paced toward them. "Simply horrid!"

"What has happened?" Caroline asked.

"A disaster!" Agatha ascended the steps to the front porch. "I thought Loblolly would be safe from the war, but I was wrong. Those disgusting rebels are all around us. I'm seriously considering returning to Charles Town."

Caroline tried again. "I meant what is happening with the barge?"

Agatha shrugged. "Nothing. 'Tis burned and the men are dead. Where is Betsy? I'll need her to pack my things."

"The soldiers they found, how did they die?" Edward asked. "Were they burned in the fire?"

Agatha wrinkled her nose. "What a horrid curiosity for a child . No, they were shot with arrows, murdered by those evil partisans." She marched into the house.

Arrows. Caroline remembered the crossbows in Jacob's house. And she had seen Thomas practicing with one. No wonder he and Jacob had not wanted her involved. This was not a matter of hiding in secret passageways or exchanging pinecones for potatoes.

She shuddered. Thomas and Jacob would be hunted men now. The British would not rest until they were dead.

"Well done, Major Thomas," Francis Marion announced after Matthias had given him a brief recounting of the day's events. The partisan leader bowed his head to Jane. "I am relieved you have been safely delivered, madam."

"Thank you." Jane struggled to stand up from the log where she'd been sitting.

"Careful, Mother." Matthias steadied her. "You're still weak."

"You're a major now?" she whispered. "Why didn't you tell me?"

Matthias shrugged one shoulder. "It didn't seem important."

She touched his face. "Your father would have been proud." She glanced at Jacob. "He would have been proud of both of you. Thank you for saving me."

Jacob blushed and studied his feet. "You're welcome."

"We could use more men like you, Jacob, if you're interested." Marion slanted a look at Matthias. "Unless your master objects."

Matthias winced at the title *master*. "Jacob can do as he pleases. I consider him a free man."

Jacob's eyes glinted with moisture.

Richard patted him on the back. "Would you like to come with me, cousin? I'm taking Aunt Jane to my father's house on the Pee Dee." He lowered his voice. "And we'll have some papers drawn up for Matt to sign."

Jacob nodded. "I'd like that."

"Fine." Richard turned to Marion. "Permission to leave, sir?"

Marion nodded. "Godspeed." He bowed to Jane and made his leave.

Matthias helped his mother to mount once again. "What is in this bag of yours?"

"A change of clothing and all my jewelry," Jane answered. "I didn't want Hickman to get his hands on it. Don't forget about the silver. 'Tis hidden in the bathing room."

He squeezed her hand. "All will be well, Mother. Someday it will be safe to go home again."

"'Tis only wood and brick, Matthias. It is love that makes a home. If you are fortunate enough to find love in this life, you must grab it and never let it go."

He snorted. "This is not the time for matchmaking."

Jane shook her head. "There is nothing stronger than love. You must trust in it."

"I'll see you soon, Mother." He swatted the horse's rump, and Jane's horse trotted off after Richard and Jacob.

"Ah, there ye are, lad," Major Munro approached him, accompanied by a young man. "I have someone I'd ye to meet."

Matthias extended a hand to the stranger. "Matthias Thomas, at your service."

"A pleasure." The young man shook his hand. He glanced at Major Munro, his blue eyes twinkling. "Aye, ye're right, Grandpa. He's the right man for Caroline."

Matthias groaned inwardly. More matchmakers. "And your name is?"

"Josiah Stanton, son of Quincy and Virginia."

Matthias studied him with a frown. He looked to be about twenty years of age. "I didn't think Virginia was old enough—"

"Adopted son." Josiah grinned. "Quincy bought me in Boston when I was a lad of nine years."

"Oh. Then you have news of Quincy?"

Josiah laughed. "We have more than news. Can you take us to see Ginny?"

Matthias snorted. "You realize there are redcoats there? We just killed a few of them and burned their bloody barge, so they're looking for someone to hang."

"We know." Jamie gave him a wry look. "But since ye were able to sneak yer mother out, we were thinking, lad, that ye can sneak us in."

CHAPTER TWENTY-EIGHT

"Wait here," Matthias whispered. He eased along the wall of the kitchen and peered into the window.

In front of the fire, Dottie was resting in her favorite chair. Caroline sat at the table, mending a pair of stockings. Betsy was unloading a tray of dirty dishes.

He motioned to others. They approached quietly, their black clothing rendering them almost invisible in the dark. He had insisted they wait for the sun to set before embarking on this foolish plan.

He leaned close to Jamie. "I suggest we have your family reunion in the kitchen. The nursery would be too difficult to reach and much harder to escape from."

"All right, lad," Jamie agreed. "Lead the way."

At the front corner of the kitchen Matthias paused for the guard to complete his pass. "Now," he whispered, and darted to the door.

Caroline looked up. "Thom—"

He held a finger to his lips to warn her.

Her eyes widened as three men entered behind him. With

a gasp, she stumbled to her feet. "Quin!" She slapped a hand over her mouth, then lowered her voice to a whisper. "Quincy! You're alive!"

"Caroline." He grabbed her in a quick embrace. "How is Ginny? Can you bring her here?"

"Oh, my God." She touched his shoulders as if to verify he was real. She glanced at the other men. "Josiah! Papa!" She lunged toward them, laughing.

"Caroline." Josiah enveloped her in his arms.

Matthias rolled a barrel to the door, glancing back to make sure Josiah's embrace was of the platonic sort.

"Josiah!" Caroline brushed back his long brown hair. "Look at you. I vow you're still growing."

"And you're even more beautiful." With a grin, Josiah lifted her and swung her in a circle.

Matthias jammed the barrel in place beneath the door latch. Beautiful? Was that how a man talked to his aunt?

"I can't believe it!" Caroline hugged her father. "You're all safe and sound."

"Has Ginny had the baby yet?" Quincy asked.

"No." Caroline grinned at him. "She'll be so happy to see you."

"Can ye bring her and the wee ones to the kitchen?" Jamie asked.

"Yes, of course." Caroline rushed to the door.

Matthias moved the barrel. "Be careful that you are not seen."

Caroline touched his shoulder. "Thank you, Thomas."

He shrugged. "'Twas the least I could do."

"Where is Jacob? Is he all right?"

"Yes. Caroline, you must return the crossbow to me. Hickman suspects you, so he might search your—"

"What crossbow?"

He studied her face. She looked genuinely confused. "You didn't borrow a crossbow?"

"No." She stepped closer to him and whispered, "What has happened, Thomas? Why have you been angry?"

He brushed her cheek with his knuckles, reluctant to explain his suspicions. "Forgive me." If she hadn't shot the redcoat, then who the hell did? "Do you want me to come with you?"

She reached up to squeeze his hand. "I'll be fine. Pugsley was sent to report the burned barge, so there's only one guard left." She slipped outside.

Matthias shoved the barrel back in place.

"She calls you by your last name, Major Thomas?" Quincy asked, a suspicious glint in his eye.

Jamie glared at him. "No' courting, are you? I've seen how ye look at each other. Ye doona think my daughter deserves the truth now?"

Matthias faced them, aware of the heat in his face. "'Tis for the best. I'm a wanted man. If Hickman knew that she had knowledge about me or the partisans, he would not hesitate to abuse her for the information."

Quincy's eyes narrowed. "I'm a wanted man, too. But I'm honest with my wife."

Matthias gritted his teeth. As far as he was concerned, Quincy Stanton was not doing an adequate job of protecting his wife and children. "What took you so long to get here? I believe your wife is due any day now."

"I am aware of that." Quincy scowled at him. "With the blockade in place, we had to come ashore south of Savannah and make our way over land. We arrived at the hunting lodge on the Pee Dee only to find it burned to the ground."

Josiah nodded. "We feared the worst 'til we found a partisan who took us to Snow's Island."

"And there they found me," Jamie continued the story. "I was able to set their worries to rest."

"Have you men had a decent meal lately?" Dottie asked.

Jamie snorted. "I've been living on roasted potatoes for weeks."

"Sit." Dottie motioned to the table. "Betsy, pour them some ale."

Conversation dwindled while the men dug into roasted beef and minced meat pies. Matthias grabbed a pie and returned to the door. When he heard footsteps, he peeked outside.

Caroline carried a sleepy Charlotte in her arms. Edward was in shirt and breeches, but barefoot. Virginia was in a night shift with a woolen cloak thrown about her shoulders.

He opened the door. "Quickly," he whispered. "And keep your voices down."

"What is this big surprise you promised us?" Virginia muttered to her sister. "It had better be worth it. I hate going up and down those stairs."

Caroline bustled them into the kitchen, and Matthias rolled three barrels across the door.

"Papa!" Edward ran to his father and leapt at him.

With a laugh, Quincy caught him. "Not so loud."

Charlotte, now wide awake, wiggled out of Caroline's arms. "Papa!" She ran toward him.

Quincy gathered her up as he strode toward Ginny.

She stumbled, and Caroline steadied her.

"Am I dreaming?" Virginia pressed a hand to her chest.

"Ginny." Quincy stopped in front of her, his arms filled with their children and his eyes glimmering with unshed tears.

"'Tis really you." Ginny reached a trembling hand toward him.

Caroline retrieved the children from Quincy's arms. "Look! Grandpa and Josiah are here, too."

Edward and Charlotte ran toward them. Jamie lifted the boy in the air, while Josiah twirled a laughing Charlotte around.

Quincy pulled Ginny into his arms. "I'm here, Ginny. I love you."

She burst into tears. "I was so afraid." She wrapped her arms around his neck.

Quincy held her tight. "I missed you, sweetheart. I've wanted to see you for so long, but—"

"I know." She touched his face. "They want to arrest you. You sweet man, you shouldn't have come."

"I had to, Ginny." He kissed her.

Caroline turned away, wiping a tear off her cheek, and Matthias was tempted to pull her into his arms.

With tears streaming down her cheeks, Virginia glanced at her adopted son. "My brave Josiah. Thank you for coming. And Papa." She stiffened with a gasp.

"What's wrong?" Quincy asked.

A puddle formed around her feet. "The baby is coming."

A series of exclamations circled the room.

"Not so loud." Matthias held up his hands to hush them. "Are you sure, Mrs. Stanton? This is not the best time."

She gave him an incredulous look. "Try telling that to the baby."

Quincy snorted. "He has a lot to learn."

Matthias frowned. "She doesn't have any control over the matter?"

"Och, lad, ye canna order a baby back in." Jamie looped an arm around his daughter's shoulders. "Ye'll be just fine, Ginny. We have a nice fire here and water."

"And a midwife," Dottie added, headed toward her room. "I've delivered many a baby over the years. Come along, Ginny. And you, too, Caroline and Betsy."

Quincy held on to his wife as she waddled toward Dottie's room.

Dottie frowned at him. "Where do you think you're going?"

"I've been separated from her for five months," Quincy growled. "I'm not leaving her side."

Dottie snorted. "Then be prepared if she starts cursing you."

All the women and Quincy disappeared into Dottie's room. Matthias frowned at the closed door. If Ginny screamed during her labor, it might bring the guard to the kitchen door.

"Can I go, too?" Charlotte asked. "I want to be with my mama."

"In a while, perhaps." Jamie sat in the chair by the hearth and pulled the young girl into his lap. "But first, I want to hear all about you."

Charlotte took a deep breath and launched into a detailed description of her life at Loblolly and how her brother tormented her. Josiah returned to the table and finished his dinner. Edward sat beside him and bit into a meat pie.

Matthias waited at the door, uncertain what to do. He drummed his fingers on barrels. "Will this take very long?"

"Aye. Sit down, lad." Jamie replied. "It could take hours."

Hours? Matthias strode to the windows and shut the curtains. "The guard might wonder why the kitchen remains lit so late at night."

"If he knocks on the door, we'll hide while Edward tells him that his mother is giving birth," Jamie said. "The guard will want nothing to do with a birthing, so he'll leave us alone."

"I'm not so sure. We just destroyed their barge, and they have some dead soldiers with our arrows in them. Hickman suspects Caroline already." Matthias paced across the room. "This is bad timing."

"Grandpa?" Charlotte tugged at Jamie's neck cloth to get his attention. "Will it be a boy or a girl, 'cause I really want it to be girl so I can have a sister."

"I doona know, lass." Jamie brushed back her curls. "But if he's a boy, ye'll be bigger than him."

With a smile, she nestled her cheek against Jamie's shoulder.

Caroline peeked out the door to Dottie's room. "Could one of you set some water to boil?"

Matthias strode toward her. "Is the baby coming?"

She looked amused. "Yes. Eventually. I thought we might like some coffee. 'Twill be a long night." She closed the door.

A long night. Matthias grabbed a kettle and filled it from the pump. He placed it on a hook over the fire, then added more wood. After he had made everyone a cup of coffee, he resumed his pacing.

"Take a seat, lad." Jamie sipped from his mug. "Ye'll wear out yer shoes."

Matthias sat and gulped down some coffee. A low moan drifted from Dottie's room, and she emerged, shutting the door behind her.

"Is something wrong?" Matthias asked.

"No, 'tis going well." Dottie rummaged along her shelves and selected a bottle. "Here, this will help with the pain."

Matthias sighed when she went back into her room and shut the door.

"The wee lass is asleep," Jamie whispered. "Is there a place I can lay her down?"

"I'll fix something." Matthias lined up some sacks of flour on the floor and covered them with a tablecloth.

Jamie deposited Charlotte gently on the makeshift pallet. "Would ye care to lie down, Edward?"

Edward made a face, then turned to Josiah. "Tell me about the pirates on the high seas."

Josiah grinned. "I haven't met many of those, but I can tell you about the battle for the *Serapis* with John Paul Jones."

Edward's eyes lit up. "How many ships did you sink?"

Matthias sat at the table to listen, but Josiah's story grew more and more farfetched in his attempt to entertain the boy. Apparently, Josiah had personally shot every cannonball that hit its mark during the battle—an amazing feat that required him to be on every ship in the fleet at the same time.

The smell of Jamie's pipe tobacco permeated the room. Moans continued to emerge from Dottie's bedchamber, each one sounding more intense than the last.

Matthias clenched his fists. Why was it taking so long? At least Edward didn't seem aware of his mother's suffering, so enthralled was he by Josiah's outrageous tales.

Caroline rushed from Dottie's room, fetched an apron from a drawer, and tied it around her waist.

Matthias jumped to his feet. "Is everything all right?"

"Yes." She wrapped a towel around her hand and grabbed the kettle.

"It has been four hours."

"It takes time." She headed back to Dottie's room.

Matthias followed her. "How long?"

Caroline shrugged. "'Tis hard to say, but it is progressing faster than it did with Edward or Charlotte."

"How long did it take me?" Edward asked.

"About fourteen hours." Caroline reached for the door latch.

"*Fourteen hours?*" Matthias grimaced. "Why does it take so long? Either the baby is coming or it isn't."

Caroline sighed. "Can you find a bottle of rum, Thomas?"

"Aye." Matthias rushed to the table and grabbed a bottle. "Is it to help with your sister's pain?"

"No." She smiled. "'Tis for you." She slipped into Dottie's room and shut the door behind her.

"Damn." Matthias thumped three mugs on the table and poured some rum for Jamie, Josiah, and himself. He was refilling his mug when Caroline ran from the room, collected a stack of bed linens and towels from a cupboard, then dashed back. She shut the door without reporting a single word. How the hell were they supposed to know what was happening?

Matthias rose to his feet and paced across the floor. He didn't like not being in charge.

Jamie chuckled. "Ye're wearing a rut in the stones, man. Take a seat."

Matthias glowered at the man as he sat calmly puffing on his pipe. "This is *your* daughter who is suffering."

"He reminds me of Quincy," Josiah observed.

"Aye." Jamie removed his pouch of tobacco from his coat pocket. "Seems to me he's practicing for fatherhood himself."

Matthias snorted. "Don't be ridiculous."

"I think you're right, Grandpa." Josiah grinned. "If he's going to act like a father, he might as well be one."

Matthias glared at Josiah as he paced by. "This is the worst possible time to have children."

"Ginny is surrounded with family and friends." Jamie pointed his pipe at Matthias. "Ye should remember that, lad. 'Twould be the same for Caroline. A woman is not alone when she has family."

Matthias halted. Were his fears ungrounded? Virginia was receiving the best of care while surrounded by loved ones. If he had children with Caroline, she and the children would always have family. Even if he died, they would not be alone.

But if he died, she would be left a grieving widow. How could he bring such suffering upon her? Then again, death was inevitable for everyone. Shouldn't they seize every moment of joy that was possible while they could?

He swallowed hard and meandered around the room. Jamie tapped the tobacco out of his pipe and packed in another load. Edward gave in to his exhaustion and lay down beside his sister.

Matthias glanced at the sleeping children. *Children*. With Caroline. Would she agree?

He wandered across the room. The moans from Dottie's room grew louder. The women's voices sounded urgent.

Jamie and Josiah jumped to their feet. Matthias grabbed the bottle of rum and gulped some down. This was it. The baby was coming, and his decision had been made.

A woman's cry erupted, followed by the wail of a baby. Jamie and Josiah laughed and slapped each other on the back.

Betsy peeked out the door. "'Tis a boy! A healthy boy."

Matthias sighed with relief. Yes, joy was possible in the midst of war and chaos. He would waste no more time.

"Och, another grandson." Jamie beamed with pride. "And a fine set of lungs he has."

Josiah leaned over the children and nudged their shoulders. "Edward, Charlotte, we have a baby brother."

Edward yawned. "What's his name?"

"I don't know yet," Josiah replied.

"Why is he crying?" Charlotte asked.

"I expect he's tired and a wee frightened," Jamie answered.

The door opened and Caroline emerged with a white bundle of screaming humanity. "Here he is."

Matthias took note of the squirming blanket, then looked at Caroline. Her hair curled about her brow, damp with perspiration. Dark smudges under her eyes indicated she was near exhaustion. And damn if he didn't think she was the most beautiful woman he'd ever seen.

"His name is James Quincy," she announced with a smile.

"Och, now there's a fine name, though I doona know about that Quincy part." Jamie tugged back the blanket to have a look.

Josiah laughed. "He has red hair."

"Aye, he's a handsome lad," Jamie observed.

"Ha!" Caroline passed the baby to her father. "You would say that. He looks like you."

"Aye, verra handsome." Jamie sat so the children could see their new brother.

Matthias wandered closer.

"Ooh, he's naked," Charlotte said.

"Of course he is, bufflehead," Edward muttered. "Did you think he'd come out with clothes on?"

Charlotte lifted her chin. "I like him better than you. *He* is nice to me."

Edward slanted a suspicious look at his baby brother. The baby's cries dwindled into whimpers.

"Ye should watch yer tongue, young Edward," Jamie warned. "This lad may be bigger than you someday."

Edward gulped.

Jamie passed the baby back to Caroline. "How is Ginny?"

"She's fine. Tired, but happy." Caroline smiled at Matthias. "Would you like to see the baby?"

Matthias stepped back. "I can see him from here." He eyed the wiggling, whimpering bundle. So much energy. Somehow he had thought babies slept all the time.

Quincy strode into the room. "Is everyone done admiring my new son?" Charlotte ran up to him and latched on to his leg, and he picked her up to hug her. "I have the most beautiful children in the world."

"We'll have to leave soon," Josiah warned him.

"Let me see Ginny first." Jamie strode into Dottie's room.

Charlotte clung to her father's neck. "I still have your book, Papa."

"That's my girl." He kissed her brow. When Edward sidled close, he patted his son on the back.

"Do you have to leave?" Edward asked.

"I'll stay close by for a few weeks," Quincy replied. "But eventually, I have to get back to my ship." He set Charlotte on her feet. "Stay here for a moment, while I see your mama again."

When Charlotte's bottom lip trembled, Josiah said, "You can help me with the baby. Can I hold him, Caroline?"

"Of course." Caroline passed him the baby, and Josiah sat on a bench by the table.

"Let's make sure he has all his fingers and toes," Josiah said, and the children sat on either side of him to inspect their new brother. Caroline gazed at them with a tired smile, then sank into the chair by the fire.

Matthias swallowed hard. This was it. But what should he say? Did he dare confess who he really was?

Anyone associated with the wanted traitor Matthias Murray Thomas would be a target for torture and murder. No, he couldn't tell Caroline his name. Not yet. He could only pray she understood and loved him no matter what name he assumed. After all, hadn't Juliet loved Romeo in spite of his name?

He winced. The best analogy he could think of was a tragedy? He cleared his throat. "Caroline?"

"Yes?" She looked at him with her emerald-green eyes.

He wiped his damp palms on his breeches. "Could . . . would you step outside with me for a moment?" He could propose to her in the orchard. Or maybe the pergola.

With a sigh, she closed her eyes. "My feet are tired."

"I understand, but I have something important to discuss with you."

She waved a hand in his direction. "Let the war rest. This is a night for celebrating life." Her eyes opened and she glanced at the baby. "This was my third time to help with a birthing, and it never ceases to amaze me."

"Caroline." He moved in front of her. "I need to talk to you. Now. Enough time has been wasted."

She frowned. "Then speak."

"Not here. Come walk with me."

"I cannot. Ginny might need me. Or the baby."

"Dottie and Betsy can take care of them."

She gestured to the children. "And I need to return the children to the nursery."

"Betsy can take them." Matthias gritted his teeth. Damn, it shouldn't be this hard. "Caroline, come with me to the orchard to see the bloody trees."

"I don't think I like your tone."

"The devil take my tone! If you won't cooperate, I'll have to do it here." He bent down on one knee and took her hands in his.

Her eyes widened. "Thomas? How much rum did you drink?"

"Bloody hell, woman, I'm not drunk. I'm asking you to marry me."

CHAPTER TWENTY-NINE

Caroline gasped. Had she heard him correctly?

"Aunt Caroline!"

She jumped when Charlotte suddenly grabbed her arm.

"Aunt Caroline, say yes!"

Josiah chuckled. "Charlotte, leave her be. She has to decide for herself."

Charlotte returned to the bench and took a seat beside Josiah and Edward. All three of them watched with expectant faces. No wonder Thomas had wanted her to leave. Their audience was enjoying the show. Even the baby grew quiet.

Thomas squeezed her hand. "I cannot promise you much," he whispered. "I cannot even say how much longer I'll be alive. But I can promise that as long as I draw breath, I will love you. As long as my heart beats, it is yours."

Her eyes filled with tears. There was no guarantee of a long life, so shouldn't they cherish every moment they could find together?

Charlotte leapt to her feet. "*I'll* marry you!"

Josiah hushed her, and the young girl slumped back on the bench.

A tear escaped down Caroline's cheek. "Thomas, I love you, too."

His eyes glimmered with hope as he straightened and pulled her to her feet. "Then you will say yes?"

Caroline nodded and gave him a shaky smile. "Yes."

He let out a gush of air and grinned. "*Yes.*"

"Hurrah!" Charlotte jumped to her feet and ran toward Dottie's room. "Mama, Mama, Aunt Caroline's going to marry!"

Edward grimaced. "Are they going to kiss now?"

Josiah laughed. "I believe so. Let's give them some privacy." He rose and sauntered toward Dottie's room with the baby in his arms and Edward at his heels.

"I thought they'd never leave," Thomas muttered with a glare in their direction, but as soon as he focused on Caroline, his smile returned.

She wiped away tears with trembling fingers. Good Lord, he had a way of looking at her like he was worshipping every freckle that marred her face. She wanted to melt in his arms, ooze into his pores, and crawl under his skin. She wanted to be a part of him forever.

He kissed her brow, then her damp cheeks. "My uncle is a minister. We'll go to him tomorrow."

She blinked. "Tomorrow?" She was struck with the enormity of what she'd agreed to. This man would be her husband. She hardly knew him. In fact, she'd met him only a month ago. And she seriously doubted he was ever a butler. "I . . . Ginny and the children might need me tomorrow."

"I'm not waiting." He nabbed her by the elbow and led her to the kitchen door.

"Where are we going?"

"Does it matter?" He rolled the barrels away.

"What about my father and Josiah?"

"They know the way back. They don't need me." Thomas cracked the door and peered outside. "Let's go."

Cool, crisp air pinched her cheeks, a welcome change from the stuffiness of Dottie's bedchamber. She ran alongside Thomas to the shelter of the pergola. There, encased in leafy darkness, the scent of earth and night-blooming flowers surrounded them.

She breathed deeply. "I believe autumn has arrived."

He placed a finger on her lips and whispered, "The guard."

Bertram trudged by, barely visible in the moonlight, though by the slump of his shoulders she knew the boy was half asleep on his feet. It had been a long day and night for them all.

Thomas's arms enveloped her, holding her close. His clothes smelled of wood smoke. She nestled her cheek against his broad chest, feeling entirely safe even with Bertram nearby. Thomas's hand ventured past her waist and slowly caressed her bottom. Her mouth fell open. The rascal. He knew she couldn't voice an objection with a redcoat close by.

Whether it was exhaustion or elation, she didn't know, but she didn't feel like objecting. On the contrary, she felt wildly free. Ginny had given birth to a healthy baby; Ginny's husband was alive and well; Thomas had declared his love for her; and very soon, she would be marrying him. So many glorious reasons to celebrate!

Reaching around him, she gave his buttocks a squeeze and nearly giggled out loud when he jumped.

"You want to play, vixen?" he whispered in her ear, then grabbed her hand and led her through the pergola.

"Where are we going?"

"Jacob's house."

Caroline's heart leapt up her throat. Jacob wouldn't be there tonight. Was Thomas planning a wedding night before the wedding?

Her heart raced. Did he not realize how exhausted she was? And dirty? Her clothes were stained with blood, and she felt like a horrid mess.

Thomas escorted her to the back entrance of the pergola and into the orchard.

"Wait." She dug in her heels. "I'm filthy. I should return to the kitchen and bathe."

"You can bathe at Jacob's."

"But I have no clean clothes there." She caught a glimpse of white teeth as he grinned. The rascal. Her lack of clothes only strengthened his resolve.

"Come on." He guided her through the orchard to the woods. "We'll get a few hours' sleep, then leave early in the morning. By midday, we'll be married."

She gulped. "So quickly?"

He halted. "Are you changing your mind?"

"No, I definitely want to marry you, but I've hardly had time to adjust—"

"I'm in a hurry." He resumed walking, tugging her along with him.

"I gathered that, but this is an excellent example of a problem I foresee in our future."

"We will have no problems."

"Of course we will."

"If we have one, I'll fix it, and then, there won't be a problem."

She scoffed. "*You* will fix the problem? Shouldn't *we* fix the problem?"

He gave her an exasperated look as they emerged onto the path by the river. "Why are you fussing about a problem that doesn't even exist?"

"You're missing the point. I see marriage as a partnership."

He stopped. "I'll be responsible for you, Caroline."

"I'll feel just as responsible for you."

"But I can take care of myself."

"So can I."

His grip on her arm relaxed. Slowly he trailed his fingers down to her hand. "I believe you can. You are an amazing woman."

"Thank you." She entwined her fingers with his.

"I would like to wed tomorrow. I see no reason to wait." He watched her with a hopeful expression.

Tomorrow. She took a deep breath. The smell of exploded gunpowder and burnt wood still hovered along the river, a potent reminder of the risk Thomas had taken that day. It would be foolish to waste what little time they might have.

She nodded. "Yes. Tomorrow."

They resumed their walk to Jacob's house at a more leisurely pace. Moonlight sparkled off the Black River.

Downriver, Caroline noticed a black patch in the water. It was the blackened husk of the barge, still floating on the river. "They found the bodies, you know."

Thomas glanced at her. "How many?"

"Five. Hickman believes two were killed in the explosion and one drowned. The other two were shot with arrows." She waited, but Thomas said nothing. "I can see why you didn't want me involved."

He sighed. "We made the incident as dramatic as possible to keep Hickman and his men removed from the house. Otherwise, the rescue could not have succeeded."

"I see." She walked alongside him for a moment in silence. Exhaustion bore down on her, and she yawned.

"What else did Hickman do?" Thomas asked.

"He sent Pugsley to report the incident to General Cornwallis. He was extremely agitated, screaming at everyone, even Agatha."

Thomas nodded. "He's afraid he'll be held responsible."

"If they ever find out *you* were responsible, there will be a price on your head."

Thomas was silent.

They neared the mill. It crouched on the river's edge like a huge black crow with a metal beak jutting out over the water. The wheel groaned and slapped the water as it slowly turned.

She yawned again as she climbed the steps to Jacob's front porch.

Thomas opened the door. "I should tell you. There already is a price on my head." He entered the house and went straight to the hearth to light a fire.

Caroline remained by the door, stunned.

"I'll heat some water so you can bathe." He grabbed a pot and a kettle and filled them at the pump.

A wanted man. She slid the bolt on the door and wandered to the fireplace. She was marrying a wanted man tomorrow.

He hung the pot and kettle over the fire. "Would you like some cider?"

"Thomas, we should leave this area. We could go to my home in North Carolina."

He uncorked a jug and poured two glasses. "I will not abandon the cause of freedom."

"I'm not asking you to. But couldn't we have a brief respite?"

"Perhaps." He smiled as he brought her a glass. "I would love to spend some time alone with you."

With a blush she accepted the glass. She sat on the wooden settee and sipped her cider while Thomas hauled water from the pump to the tub in Jacob's room. Finally, he took the pot and kettle and added boiling water.

"'Tis ready," he called.

She entered Jacob's room. It was sparsely furnished, but charming. An oil lamp flickered on the small bedside table. A quilt of blue and white adorned the four-poster bed, while a hooked rug of the same colors lay on the floor.

Thomas motioned to the neatly folded stack on the bed. "There's a linen towel there, and some clean clothing." He headed for the door. "I'll leave you alone now."

"Thomas, I—I need help with my laces."

"Oh, of course."

She swiveled and held her breath while he untied the laces to her gown. "And the corset, if you don't mind."

"Not at all." His voice sounded hoarse.

She held the gown to her bosom to keep it from slipping down, while his fingers worked their way up her spine, tingling her skin. He finished, but remained standing behind her. She could hear his breathing, harsh and fast.

"Thank you."

"You're welcome." He hesitated, then left the room, closing the door behind him.

She took a deep breath and peeled off her clothes. On top of Jacob's clothespress, she found a bar of soap. Magnolia-scented, the soap that Dottie made. She climbed into the tub, quickly scrubbed herself clean, then leaned back and closed her eyes. What a long day it had been.

Just a few minutes of rest, she thought, sinking deeper into the warm water.

A knock sounded on the door. "Caroline, are you all right?"

With a gasp, she sat up. Goodness, the water had turned cold. She must have dozed off. "Just a minute."

She scurried to the bed, toweled dry, then examined the clean clothes Thomas had left. A man's shirt and stockings? The shirt ended a few inches below her hips. Without garters, the large stockings flopped around her ankles. How could she walk into the parlor with her legs exposed?

She searched the room 'til she found a clean sheet, then wrapped it around her waist and tied the ends. Taking a deep breath, she ventured into the parlor.

The fire in the hearth drew her attention first. It illuminated a makeshift pallet Thomas had made on the floor, several quilts and two pillows. Side by side.

She spotted him at the table. A lit candlestick flickered between two pewter mugs and plates.

"Come and eat." He stood and held out a chair for her.

She smiled at the simple fare he had prepared for her—cheese, bread, and a few figs. "Thank you."

He poured some cider into her mug. "I know you're tired, so I made a place for you to sleep."

"Thank you." She glanced at the pallet with its two pillows. "I suppose you're tired, too."

"Aye, it's been a long day. And I still smell of smoke and gunpowder." He took the kettle from the hearth and walked toward Jacob's room. "I'll heat up the water and take a bath." He smiled at her as he closed the door.

She nibbled on some cheese as she looked around. Thomas's plate was empty. He must have eaten while she was dozing in the bathtub. Her gaze drifted once again to the pallet. Did he intend to sleep with her?

She yawned. She was far too exhausted to get indignant or even worried. Thomas had to be exhausted, too. The man had blown up a barge, battled redcoats, rescued Jane, witnessed a birthing, and proposed marriage in one day.

Her husband. With a weary smile, she padded over to the pallet. She untied the sheet around her waist and covered herself up from her feet to her chin. Within minutes, she felt herself drifting off.

It was too hot. She slowly opened her eyes to gaze sleepily at the fireplace. The fire had burned down to a pile of glowing embers. She blinked, coming more fully awake. There was a body pressed against her back. Thomas's bare arm was wrapped around her, and he'd flung a leg across hers. It was like being embraced by a furnace.

She nudged gently at his leg, and with a moan, he rolled onto his back. She listened to his soft breathing for a while, then quietly turned to face him. His hair was loose, the dark strands spread across his pillow. She glanced at his eyes to make sure they were shut, then admired his profile in the dim firelight. Straight nose, strong jaw and chin, interesting dark whiskers.

Would they be prickly or soft? She skimmed a finger over them. Prickly. She glanced back at his eyes. Still shut.

Propping herself up on an elbow, she let her gaze drift over his bare chest. There were interesting mounds and dips, outlining the muscles along his abdomen and the contour of his hipbones, so different from her own. He wore no stockings, so his calves were bare and sprinkled with dark, curly hair. His breeches were partially unbuttoned, and a line of hair emerged from them and led up to his belly button. His chest was broad and muscular. Between two copper-colored flat nipples, dark brown hair curled. Prickly or soft?

She tested it with her fingertips. Soft. She skimmed her fingers across the thick mat 'til she reached the thin line that led to his navel. It was so smooth and silky, she soon ended up with a finger in his belly button.

"Don't stop there."

With a gasp, she jerked her hand away. His eyes were open and he was watching her. "I'm sorry. I didn't mean to wake you. Go—go back to sleep." She lay down, dragging the sheet to her chin and squeezing her eyes shut.

She heard a rustling sound beside her and sneaked a peek. He was propped up on an elbow, looking at her. She closed her eyes again. Her skin tingled, just from the knowledge that he was studying her. Would he touch her? Caress her breasts like he had the other night? Take her nipples into his mouth?

Heat blossomed in her cheeks, then skittered down her chest and belly to her core, where it sizzled and made her squeeze her thighs together. He had touched her there before. God help her, she wanted it again.

She opened her eyes.

He smiled. "Do you know how beautiful you are? I could look at you for hours."

Stop looking and start touching! She licked her lips.

His gaze dropped to her mouth. "Caroline?"

"Yes."

He leaned closer, studying her intently. "Yes?"

She nodded. "Yes."

He touched her cheek as he leaned forward and kissed her once, twice, before pulling her into his arms. She wrapped her arms around him as he rolled onto his back, taking her with him.

He raked a hand into her hair. "Kiss me."

She skimmed her fingers along his whiskers, then brushed her lips across them, enjoying the ticklish sensation. He turned his mouth to meet hers and kissed her so thoroughly, she was caught by surprise when his hand squeezed her bare rump.

She broke the kiss, gasping.

"Sit up."

She did. He dragged the shirt up her body and over her head. Instinctively, she covered her breasts.

"Don't." He moved her hands away. "You're beautiful."

"Thomas—"

"Lie down."

"You seem to be ordering me about."

"I'm about to explode."

Her gaze dropped to the bulge in his breeches. It was bigger than ever. "I suppose you're feeling a bit rushed."

He snorted. "I'll manage. Meanwhile, allow me to re-phrase my request. Will you please recline so I may kiss your breasts?"

"Oh. Well, if you put it that way." She lay back.

Smiling, he brushed her hair away from her face. "You can give me orders, too."

"Really?" She smoothed her hands up his arms to his shoulders, enjoying the bulge of his muscles. "I wouldn't know what to say."

"You can say kiss me." He kissed her cheek. "Lick me." He ran his tongue up the length of her neck.

She shuddered.

"Touch me." He fondled her breasts. "Taste me." He lapped at her nipple with his tongue.

"Yes." She arched against him.

"Ravish me. Make me scream." He sucked her nipple into his mouth.

"Oh, Thomas." She raked her hands into his hair. "Yes. Do that. Make me scream."

He lifted his head. "Are you sure?"

"Yes. I have a strange desire to . . . scream."

He smiled as his hand smoothed over her belly. "It will require a full assault on your senses."

Her heart raced. "Yes."

"And a thorough ravishing of your entire body."

Moisture pooled between her legs. "Yes."

His hand slipped between her legs and he inhaled sharply. "Slick and sweet. I think you're ready."

"Get on with it!"

"Is that an order?" He pulled the sheet off her legs.

She squeezed her legs together. As much as she wanted to scream, she was still a bit shy about lying before him completely naked.

He smoothed a hand up her thigh. "You're so beautiful." Smiling, he leaned over and kissed the red curls at the juncture of her thighs.

She gasped. "Thomas! Surely, that's not . . . allowed."

With a grin, he stroked his fingers along her inner thighs. "I thought you wanted to scream."

"I—I do."

"Then let me touch you, and kiss you, and lick you."

She gulped. Surely he didn't mean to . . . She jolted when his fingers slipped between her legs. More moisture seeped from her.

His movements were shocking; his fingers bold. She clutched the quilt in her fists and shook her head. It was more than she could bear.

Her thighs fell open, and soon she was writhing along with his incessant fondling and rubbing. Her heart thundered in her ears. Good Lord, he hadn't exaggerated. This was a full assault on her senses. A calculated attempt to drive her insane.

She gasped when he inserted a finger inside her. He had

warned her about that, too. A thorough ravishing of her entire body. The man was relentless, and she loved it. She needed more. More. "Thomas, please."

"Don't scream yet." He moved between her legs and lifted her knees, opening her entirely to his view.

"Is—is that entirely necessary?" Good Lord, he would know what she looked like better than she did.

He leaned over and kissed her swollen, wet flesh. She jerked in response. Was such a behavior allowed? Surely he had crossed the line. But all thoughts dissolved as he continued to taste her and stroke her. Explore and suckle her. An incredible rising tide gripped her and carried her up and up, then shattered all around her.

She screamed. Wave upon wave pounded through her. Slowly she became aware of her ragged breaths. She opened her eyes and saw two Thomases peering down at her.

"I cannot see straight." She rubbed her eyes.

He grinned and kissed her brow.

She pressed a hand to her racing heart. "I had no idea. I think I'll like being married."

"I know I will." He pulled off his breeches and tossed them aside.

She gasped. Good Lord, he was huge. And so stiff. "You—you didn't use some of Dottie's ointment, did you? The one that promotes swelling?"

"What?"

She sat up. "I think you used too much."

"Caroline, this is me."

"How? I've never seen such mammoth proportions. 'Tis not natural." She scooted away.

"How many fully aroused men have you seen?"

"Well, none, but you weren't that big the other day."

"I wasn't this aroused. And I happen to have more than a small *prick*. Now can we proceed?"

She frowned at him and crossed her arms.

He pointed to the quilt. "Lie down."

"You're giving orders again."

His voice started low with clenched teeth, but rose with increasing volume and frustration. "Please be so gracious as to recline for me, Miss Munro. I need inside you before I explode!"

"Now that's reassuring! Unfortunately, I highly doubt you can get inside me. I could never accommodate such a huge— I would have to be the size of a bloody cavern!"

He laughed, then winced. "Don't make me laugh right now."

"I'm not trying to. I find nothing amusing about the prospect of being torn asunder."

"I won't hurt you. Well, it might hurt a little, but believe me, I'll do my best to give you pleasure."

She gave him a doubtful look. "Everyone knows only the man enjoys intercourse."

"Where did you hear that?"

She shrugged. "I'm not really sure, but I've heard it said."

"By unfortunate women with dullard husbands. Trust me, I'm going to give you pleasure."

She gave his manhood a suspicious look.

"Trust me." He pulled her closer. "You liked what I did before, right?"

"Yes."

"Then you'll like this." He slid his hand to the back of her neck and kissed her. He explored her lips and mouth slowly and thoroughly. He caressed her back with butterfly strokes of his fingertips 'til she tingled all over. And wanted more.

He pushed her gently onto her back and lay beside her, his body pressed against her. His manhood strained against her belly, sending flutters to her woman's core. With a moan, she raked her hands into his hair. He nuzzled her neck, scraping her slightly with his whiskers.

He caressed her breasts, then suckled them. Heat pooled between her thighs once more, and she found herself wanting him, wanting him to take her and fill the aching emptiness.

When he touched her core, the burst of sensation was so enticing, she opened her thighs. He moved between her legs and reached down to position himself against her.

She gulped.

"Wrap your legs around me." He pressed against her.

She winced. "It hurts."

"I'm sorry." He entered her slowly, then stopped. A smile spread across his face. "You're a virgin."

She huffed. "Did you think I wasn't?"

"I thought you were, of course, but I just now realized I would be the only man inside you. I really like that."

She rolled her eyes. "Congratulations. Can we get this over with?"

"As you wish." He plunged in.

"Aagh!" She hit his shoulder. "That hurt!"

"I'm sorry."

Sure you are. She gritted her teeth. She felt ripped in two, seared with heat, and stuffed like a sausage. Slowly, the burning pain seeped away, and still he lay over her, propped up on his elbows, not moving.

"Are you all right?" she asked.

"I'm fighting for control," he whispered in a strained voice.

"Why? I'm not struggling with you."

He shook his head. "Timing. Timing is everything."

What on earth was he mumbling about? She patted his back. "It will be all right." And hopefully, soon it would be over and done with.

He slowly pulled himself back 'til only the tip of his manhood teased her.

She sucked in a hissing breath. Suddenly, she no longer wished for him to finish quickly. Or even finish at all.

His eyes glimmered a steely blue. "I'm in control now." He pushed back in.

"Oh, my."

He continued, and Caroline realized he was correct. He was giving her pleasure. A great deal of pleasure, and this time it was even better, for the pleasure was shared.

She wrapped her arms around him. "Oh, Thomas. You have excellent timing."

CHAPTER THIRTY

Matthias jerked awake, mentally shoving aside the nightmare that had haunted him since childhood. Sitting up, he glanced to the side.

Caroline slumbered quietly beneath the blanket he had fetched for the two of them. Her fiery curls, gleaming in the morning light, spread upon the pillow like a halo. How would she react when he confessed his true identity? Would she be delighted with the wealth of Loblolly, or would she be as appalled as he was over the prospect of owning slaves?

He jumped to his feet and pulled on his breeches. Regardless of how Caroline felt, he needed to take her and her family to his uncle's home, where they would be safe from Hickman. It might be difficult to move Virginia and her baby, but what choice did he have? Once it became public record that Matthias Murray Thomas had married Caroline Munro, the entire Munro family could be in danger.

He pumped fresh water into a pitcher. The best way to keep them safe would be to keep his false name, but then the wedding would be false. He couldn't do that to Caroline. How angry would she be when he confessed?

With a sigh, he soaped up his face. She'd said she loved him. He had to believe it.

While he was shaving, she awoke. She sat up and glanced around.

"Good morning." He wiped his face dry.

A blush colored her cheeks. "Good morning." She quickly donned Jacob's shirt.

"I thought we'd go see how your sister is faring."

"I—I need to go to my room first and put on a proper dress." She stood, tying the blanket about her waist like a skirt. "I look very strange. I hope no one sees me."

"I think you look beautiful." He touched her cheek. "I am honored to be your husband."

Tears glimmered in her eyes. "I—I'm a little overwhelmed. I never knew it would be so . . .'"

"Wonderful?"

"Frightening. I feel like I've lost my heart. If anything should happen to you—"

"Nothing will happen. I love you." He kissed her quickly. "Now, we have a wedding to go to."

She nodded, her eyes clouded with worry. "I hope so."

After she ran to Jacob's room to bundle up her dirty clothes and use the chamber pot, he led her outside and they ambled along the river.

He glanced at her, wondering why she was so quiet. Shouldn't a bride be happier on her wedding day? "You're not ashamed of making love to me, are you?"

"No, of course not. I'm grateful we had that time together."

He reached for her hand. "Caroline, we have our whole lives together."

Her eyes glinted with pain. "Yes, I know."

That was it. His throat constricted with the realization. She was defining their "whole lives" as a limited number of days. He'd admitted he was a wanted man, and she thought he would end up hanging from a rope. How could he convince her she was wrong when she could be right?

And he wasn't the only one in danger. If Hickman had any idea how involved she was with the partisans, he wouldn't hesitate to hang her as a traitor.

Matthias tightened his grip on her hand. "Caroline. Whatever happens, always remember that I love you."

Her eyes glimmered with unshed tears. "You feel it, too? That something dreadful will happen?"

"No. Nothing will happen. I won't allow it."

Her sad smile seemed to indicate that he was somewhat simplistic, but that she still loved him.

"I think I should take you and your family to North Carolina."

Her eyes lit with hope. "Oh, yes! We could go to my parents' home. 'Twould be the safest place for Ginny and the children."

"Aye." Matthias nodded. And the safest place for Caroline, too, although he would have to leave her there to rejoin the army.

He felt the horsemen coming first. The ground vibrated beneath his feet. He pulled Caroline behind the cover of trees, then peered through the branches and spotted green coats. Tarleton. And Greville was riding in the rear. They stopped in front of the house. "Come, I want to hear this."

"Careful." Caroline hurried alongside him. "Someone might see you."

"Pugsley left yesterday, remember? Bertram is probably sound asleep, and the dragoons are staying on the front lawn." Matthias dashed to the servants' entrance with Caroline close behind him. They entered the secret passageway, and he eased open the peephole.

Tarleton strode across the library, his boots clunking on the wooden floor, then sounding muffled as he traversed the imported rug. "Your man Pugsley gave us a disturbing report. Five soldiers dead, an entire shipment destroyed."

"Yes, sir." Hickman stood at attention, his face pale. "It was most unfortunate."

Tarleton stopped in front of the captain and looked him over. "Fortunate for the rebels, wouldn't you say?"

"Yes, sir." Hickman cleared his throat. "Would you care for some refreshment, sir?"

Tarleton whirled about and slammed a fist on the desk. "I would care for an explanation! What the hell are you doing here that the last two shipments were sabotaged?"

"I . . . I had nothing to do—"

"Nothing! Now there's the truth of the matter. You do *nothing* here, do you, Captain? You spend your time in this house drinking the fine wine and bedding the women."

"It is the fault of the partisans, sir. They're all around us, but hide in the swamp like a pack of cowards."

"And you haven't captured any of them?" Tarleton's eyes

flashed with anger. "I have to wonder why you're so poorly motivated."

"I'm working on it, sir. I have a plan in motion as we speak. Soon I will have one of the traitors in my grasp."

"*One?*" Tarleton cocked an eyebrow, clearly unimpressed. "I have a better plan, one that could eliminate a large group of rebel sympathizers all at once." He marched to a window and gazed out onto the front lawn. "I've received reports that the people of Kingstree have been supplying the partisans with food. This afternoon, my men are attacking the village."

Matthias flinched, and not just because Caroline's fingers dug into his arm. He noted her stricken face, then refocused on the scene in the library.

Even Hickman looked a bit surprised. "You mean to kill the townspeople, the women and children?"

"Does it offend you?" Tarleton glanced over his shoulder. "'Tis a simple matter, Captain. Whoever helps the traitors is then a traitor also."

"Yes, sir."

Tarleton sauntered toward him. "Consider all those rebellious little children, eager to grow up and shoot at us. Why not nip the problem in the bud?"

"Excellent thinking, sir."

"And when we're done, I'll send someone here to pick up that *one* traitor you have promised to deliver."

Hickman nodded. "Yes, sir."

Tarleton strode toward the door. "Let's hope that one traitor isn't you."

So Tarleton suspected Hickman of sabotaging the supply

barges himself. Matthias had a glimpse of Hickman's pale face before shutting the peephole door.

"We have to do something," Caroline whispered as they hurried to the china room. "We cannot allow that butcher to massacre women and children."

"I'll ride straight to Snow's Island," Matthias said. "We'll evacuate the people of Kingstree."

"Is there time?"

"There should be. Tarleton said the plan was to attack this afternoon. Caroline, this will delay our wedding."

She shook her head impatiently. "Don't worry about that. There are innocent people to save."

"As soon as the townspeople are safe, I'll return for you and your family. Pack your things and be ready. We will marry tonight."

She grabbed his coat in her fists. "Be careful."

He covered her hands with his own. "I'll be fine."

Her eyes gleamed with tears as she stepped back from him. "Good-bye, Thomas. I love you."

"I love you, too. And this is *not* good-bye." He planted a kiss on her worried brow, then hurried to the stables.

Jacob was there, unsaddling a horse. "You're going somewhere?"

"Aye." Matthias took Jacob's saddle and hefted it on the back of a fresh horse. "Tarleton is attacking Kingstree this afternoon. I'm going to Snow's Island so we can evacuate the people."

"I'll go with you."

"I prefer you to stay here. The women might need you."

Jacob frowned. "You're expecting a skirmish with the British. You think I don't know how to fight."

"I trust you to protect the women and children. As soon as I return, I'm taking them all to my uncle. Caroline and I will be married."

Jacob raised his eyebrows. "Did you tell her who you are?"

"Not yet, but it won't matter." He hoped.

Jacob snorted. "Right. So am I invited to the wedding?"

Matthias shrugged one shoulder and led his horse out. "I suppose. If you want." He mounted the horse, aware that Jacob was glaring at him. Damn, he was giving the man his freedom, what else did he want?

Ezra Hickman's hands shook so badly he spilled brandy on his white breeches. Damnation. He raised the half-full glass to his mouth and downed the contents. Nothing. No soothing comfort to his fears. He ripped his cravat loose as cold sweat dripped down his neck. How could he prove he was loyal?

His only hope would be to capture a partisan who could take the blame. He needed to deliver Matthias Murray Thomas, and fast.

Ezra dashed up the stairs to Jane Thomas's room. The silly woman should be desperate enough to talk now. He fumbled in his coat pocket for the key to the door. There was no sound from within. Was she already dead? This was her third day of confinement.

He ventured into the quiet room. "Mrs. Thomas?"

Rays of sunshine shot through the gaps on the boarded window and balcony door, casting fractured beams of light to fall across the large four-poster. A huddled form lay under the blankets, still and lifeless.

"Mrs. Thomas, wake up. It is time to talk." He pulled back the blankets. *Pillows.*

He yanked the blankets off the bed. It was empty.

"Mrs. Thomas!" He scanned the room.

Sunlight sparkled off shards of broken glass by the balcony door. The glass crunched under his boots as he knelt down to investigate the hole in the door. Certainly not large enough for an escape. He spotted a crock on the floor. He picked it up, uncorked it, and sniffed. Cider. Someone had been passing her food. Someone in this house.

"Damnation!" He hurtled the crock against a wall. It crashed, leaving a dripping stain of cider.

Was the woman hiding? He peered under the bed and found a large wooden circle. Then he noted the scattering of dust on the rug. Sawdust.

He looked up. "No!" The hole in the ceiling led to the third floor. Jane Thomas had made her escape right under his nose. "No, dammit, no!"

Tarleton would string him up from the nearest tree and laugh as he struggled for his last breath. The incompetent Loyalist who couldn't even control an old woman!

Ezra charged up the stairs to the third floor and flung open the doors 'til he found the room where she'd escaped. The bastards had left their saws and rope behind.

"Hell and damnation!" Blood pounded in his ears. He

picked up an old lopsided chair and smashed it against the wall. Who had done this? Had Matthias himself sneaked into the house to rescue his mother? There were two saws here and the crock of cider below. Whoever this villain was, he had accomplices.

The other women in this house. Damn them, damn them all. No wench was going to send him to the gallows.

In the hallway, he caught a glimpse of skirts. "Halt!"

The woman turned.

He charged toward her. "Agatha? What are you doing here?"

She edged toward the stairs, her face pale. "I—I heard strange noises. Are you breaking furniture?"

"Jane Thomas has escaped."

Agatha's eyes widened. "How did she manage that?"

"I mean to find out. What do you know of it?"

"Nothing! I—I should go now and finish packing. I just spoke to Bertram. He agreed to take me as far as Fort Watson."

He stiffened. "You're not leaving. We have plans, remember? We're taking over Loblolly."

Agatha eased closer to the stairs. "I want to leave. 'Tis too dangerous here. I'll feel safer in Charles Town amongst the British."

"You don't think I can protect you, do you?" Ezra balled his fists. "You think I'm a failure!"

Her bottom lip trembled. "Please, don't hurt me. Let me go."

"Fine, then, bitch! Go on and desert me when I need you."

She gasped and scurried down the stairs.

Ezra drew in a long, shaky breath. His plans were crumbling around him, but he wouldn't go down without a fight. He marched toward the nursery and flung open the door.

Caroline Munro started. The little girl seated next to her on the bed grabbed a pillow to hide her face. The boy jumped from his bed and eased toward his aunt.

"Was there something you wanted, Captain?" Miss Munro rose to her feet.

"What do you know of Jane Thomas?"

Miss Munro raised her chin. "I know you are slowly starving her to death."

"Indeed?" He stepped into the room. "And you wouldn't be the one passing her food through the balcony door?"

"I know nothing about that."

"You're a liar. I know you helped Jane Thomas escape."

She blinked with surprise. "Escape? Jane is gone?"

He ground his teeth at her lame excuse for acting. "I know you helped them. That makes you a traitor. Do you know what happens to traitors, miss?"

"It wasn't her!" Edward blurted out. "It was the ghost."

Ezra snorted. "A ghost wouldn't need a saw to pass through a ceiling."

Miss Munro smoothed back her hair as if unconcerned, but her pale face indicated otherwise. "When do you believe this escape took place?"

"I would say yesterday while my men and I were occupied with the explosion."

"The children and I were in the kitchen. My sister gave birth yesterday and I was there helping her. You may ask Dottie or Betsy. They can confirm it."

"They lie as poorly as you do, Miss Munro. Trust me, I will prove my loyalty to the crown, and if I have to string up a pack of women and children to do it, then I will."

Satisfied with the white, stricken faces of Caroline Munro and her nephew, Ezra left the nursery to the sound of the little girl's sobs.

CHAPTER THIRTY-ONE

"Ye disappeared with my daughter last night," Jamie Munro announced as he rode beside Matthias.

"We had some urgent matters to discuss." Matthias felt his face redden. For the past five miles, the Scotsman had glowered at him. Never had a short journey felt so long.

"Aye, I have no doubt ye were feeling a wee urgent. Tell me, lad, what exactly did ye discuss?"

Matthias hoped the village of Kingstree would suddenly appear around the next bend. Marion had put him and Major Munro in charge of the evacuation. Richard, Quincy, Josiah, and a dozen more men rode behind them. "I asked Caroline to marry me."

"That's great news," Quincy said.

Jamie Munro huffed. "He dinna ask me for permission."

Matthias took a deep breath. "I believe you told me that she's allowed to make her own decisions."

"Aye. So was she smart enough to refuse you then?"

Quincy and Josiah snickered.

Matthias gritted his teeth. "No, she wasn't."

"Are ye calling my daughter a dimwit?"

Matthias slanted an impatient look at his future father-in-law. "She's as clever as her father."

Jamie's eyes twinkled. "I like grandchildren. Do ye think ye can manage that, lad?"

"Yes, sir. It will be my pleasure."

"'Tis my daughter ye should be pleasing. If ye can. Ye're no' one of those minute men from the north, are ye?"

"Excuse me?" Quincy scoffed. "I've given you four grandchildren."

Jamie shrugged. "Aye. I've about decided to accept you."

Quincy snorted. "Welcome to the family, Major Thomas."

"Aye," Josiah added. "Congratulations."

"Thank you." Matthias slowed his horse as they rounded the bend. The road in front of them was narrow and straight, tightly hugged by thick vegetation on each side.

Jamie came to a halt, holding up a hand to alert the horsemen behind them. "Ye suspect a trap?"

Matthias scanned the trees. "Let's divide and meet in Kingstree. Richard and I will take a group to the left."

"Agreed." Jamie veered to the right, motioning for Quincy, Josiah, and six of the men to follow. They had just entered the forest when musket fire erupted.

"Take cover!" Matthias yelled.

More shots rang out. Two men fell. The horses reared and whinnied as men scrambled for cover. Choking smoke surrounded them. Shouts of *huzzah* echoed around them, signaling the British advance. His men panicked, knowing they were outnumbered.

"Disperse!" Matthias hollered as he weaved amongst the men and their agitated horses. Their group of seventeen partisans had no chance of victory in a conventional battle. It was better to lead the British on a chase into the nearby bogs of the treacherous Tarcote Swamp.

Fifteen partisans, Matthias corrected himself. The two men who had fallen in the road were not getting up.

"Go!" he shouted, relieved to see Jamie Munro and his group riding safely away. The musket fire ceased, followed by an ominous silence. Tarleton must have given the order to mount and give chase.

"Come on!" He waved at Richard, and they charged through the trees.

The pounding of horse hooves followed them. Tarleton and the dragoons were hot on their trail.

He headed for the Tarcote Swamp. He and Richard had hunted and fished there as boys and knew every path.

Silently, they skirted the bogs. A few times, they backtracked to leave false trails into pools of muck. The British continued to hunt for them. He could hear their shouts and curses echoing through the swamp.

He led them to a path, then guided his horse into a creek. Upstream, he emerged on the other bank. As he hid behind a tall thicket of swamp titi, Richard joined him.

He noted the sweat on his cousin's ashen face. "Are you all right?"

Richard shook his head. "No."

"What—" Matthias heard the sound of horses. Tarleton and his troop dashed along the path on the other side of the creek, passing them by. Their white pants and green coats glistened with black mud. Matthias spotted Greville in the rear as they charged out of sight.

"Thank God they're gone." Richard slid from his horse and crumbled to his knees.

"What's wrong?" Matthias dismounted, and when he grasped his cousin by the shoulders, warm blood oozed onto his fingers. "Richard, no."

A dark stain blotched the back of Richard's coat where a musket ball had ripped into his shoulder.

"You will not die from a bloody shoulder wound," Matthias growled. "Do you hear me?"

"I'm not dead. Yet," Richard mumbled.

"You're not dying *ever*!" Matthias removed his coat and bundled it under his cousin's face. "Dammit, Richard. Why didn't you say you were wounded? I wouldn't have led the British in circles for so long."

"As long as they were following us, the others had time to escape."

"Shit, Richard. Why do you have to be so noble?" Matthias yanked his shirt over his head and pressed it against the wound. "You're not dying on me. That's an order. We'll fetch medicine from Dottie. You'll be all right. You're going to my wedding, remember?"

Richard's eyes fluttered shut.

Caroline took the children to the kitchen for the midday meal. Virginia and the baby were asleep, so she cautioned the children to eat quietly. The minutes dragged by as she worried about Thomas. Would the partisans evacuate the towns-people in time, or would they do battle with the British? Was Thomas in danger? Her father? Quincy or Josiah?

The door to the kitchen opened, and she jumped to her feet. "Oh, Jacob."

"Not happy to see me?"

"I'm happy you're back. Let me fix you a plate."

The door opened again, and she spun around. "Betsy."

Grimacing, Betsy shut the door. "That pig Pugsley is back. He and the captain want their dinner served soon."

"Are they waiting in the dining room?" Dottie asked.

"No," Betsy answered. "They went to the library to talk first. Pugsley insisted."

It must be important, Caroline thought. "Will you excuse me a moment?" She headed to the door.

"Be careful," Jacob warned her as she left.

She dashed to the Great House and tiptoed into the secret passageway. With the peephole cracked open, she listened.

"How did the general take the news?" Hickman asked.

"Cornwallis was upset, naturally, but too dignified to scream about it like Tarleton," Pugsley responded. "I have to tell you, sir, that Tarleton believes you are responsible for the failed supply shipments. He called you a traitor, sir."

Hickman collapsed in a chair. His shoulders slumped as he rested his head in his hands. "I could hang for this. How am I supposed to prove my loyalty?"

Pugsley frowned at his commanding officer. "Perhaps you won't have to. They came up with a plan. I heard it all."

Hickman straightened his shoulders. "Tell me."

"Tarleton thinks you're leaking information to the local

militia. So his plan was to come here and tell you a falsehood. Did he say something about an attack?"

Caroline pressed closer to the peephole, her heart pounding.

"Yes," Hickman replied. "He said he was going to attack Kingstree this afternoon and kill the townspeople."

Pugsley nodded. "He thinks you will alert the partisans so they can charge to the rescue."

Hickman snorted. "Ridiculous."

Caroline's breath caught.

Pugsley continued, "Since Tarleton expects the partisans to show, he'll be waiting for them."

She pulled back from the peephole, her stomach twisting as the horrible truth sank in. *Thomas has ridden into a trap.* And her father, Quincy, and Josiah might be with him.

"So, you see," Pugsley said. "Your problem is solved. When the partisans fail to arrive, Tarleton will know for a fact that you are loyal to the crown."

"My God, what a relief!" Hickman shouted.

Caroline cupped a hand over her mouth as bile rose in her throat.

"Of course, Tarleton is hoping you're guilty," Pugsley continued. "He wants a chance at Marion. If the partisans come, the townspeople will be spared. 'Twill be the partisans who will die."

Caroline slumped against the wall. *No, not Thomas.*

Hickman's voice sounded far away. "I want you to go to Kingstree after dinner. I have to know what happened."

She had to know, too. Caroline shut the peephole with trembling fingers. *Thomas. Father. Quincy. Josiah.* Too many loved ones. She had to know if they had survived.

She ran back to the kitchen. Her mouth opened, but the words wouldn't come. No, impossible to lose them all in one day.

"Caroline?" Jacob rose to his feet. "What's wrong?"

"Good Lord, child, you're as pale as death," Dottie said. "Do you need a restorative?"

She shook her head. The children looked up at her with worried faces, and she forced a smile. "Everything's fine. I might need to go somewhere for a few hours, but I'll return soon." She backed toward the door. "Jacob, can I speak to you outside?"

"What's going on?" He joined her as she hurried toward the stable.

She quickly explained the situation. "You know the way to Snow's Island, right? You can take me?"

"Of course." Jacob helped her saddle two horses.

The journey to Snow's Island passed in a daze. Thomas. Father. Quincy. Josiah. Had she lost one of them? All of them?

When they crossed Lynches River, the water rose up to her skirts. Sweat trickled between her breasts.

Her stomach knotted. "I think I'm going to be sick." Soon she would know. She urged her horse to follow Jacob's up the sandy bank.

A soldier in plain homespun appeared from behind a tree and leveled a musket at them. "You have business here?"

"We have family." Jacob dismounted. "This is Caroline Munro." He helped her down from her horse.

"You're related to Major Munro?" the soldier asked her.

"He's my father. Do you know him? Is he all right?"

"Aye. This way." The soldier took the reins of their horses and led them around a dense stand of giant cane.

"What about Thomas, Quincy, and Josiah?" she asked. "Are they all right?"

"They're fine. You mean the major, right?" the soldier asked.

A sob caught in her throat. Thomas was alive. "M-my father is a major." Tears streamed down her cheeks.

"Aye. Your father is over there, by the graves." The soldier pointed to a clearing where men were digging two holes in the ground.

"Oh, God." Caroline pressed a hand to her mouth. Two bodies lay on the ground, blankets drawn over their heads. Her father, Quincy, and Josiah were helping the gravediggers.

"Papa!" She darted toward him, and Jacob followed.

Jamie enveloped her in his strong arms. "Lassie, what are ye doing here?"

She quickly relayed the conversation she had overhead. She looked at the covered bodies of the two who had died and felt a pang of guilt that she had been so relieved to find her loved ones safe. "If only I had known earlier about the trap, I could have warned you."

"Aye." Jamie wiped sweat from his brow. "At least Hickman will take the blame for this."

"How is Ginny?" Quincy asked. "And the baby?"

"They're fine." Caroline hugged him and Josiah. "Is Thomas nearby? I want to see him."

"I believe he's with his cousin." Jamie placed a hand on Jacob's shoulder. "I should tell you that Richard was wounded. He's all right. They've taken the bullet out."

Jacob winced. "Can I see him? Where is he?"

"In one of the tents." Jamie motioned toward the camp. "Ye see the one where young Simon is standing?"

As Jacob strode toward the tents, Caroline rushed to catch up with him. The smell of smoke, sweat and horse dung hovered about the camp. The men, seated about campfires, looked at her with sad, grimy faces.

More guilt nagged at her. She'd been eating fine meals, sleeping in a real bed, trying to pretend the war was far away, when all along it was so close, with men who fought for freedom in spite of hunger and exhaustion. Men who had lost their homes, their families; men who had nothing left to lose but the dirty rags on their backs.

"The boy by the tent is so young," she whispered to Jacob. "Doesn't he have a home?"

"No. This is Simon's home."

"You and Richard have become good friends?"

Jacob nodded. "He's the only family I have who will admit to it."

"You're related? I thought he was related to Thomas."

Jacob groaned. "Simon, can we go in?"

"Aye." Simon lifted the flap to the tent and gave Caroline a doubtful look. "Are you sure you want to see this, miss?"

"I'll be fine." Caroline ducked under the flap.

A mixture of blood and alcohol immediately accosted her sense of smell. It took longer for her eyes to focus in the dim light. Richard lay on a cot. A doctor was bandaging his shoulder. A pile of bloody rags lay on the ground, next to a bucket of blood-tinted water. Thomas wasn't there.

"How are you?" Jacob asked his cousin.

"I'm drunk," Richard lifted a canteen to his mouth.

The doctor tied off the bandage. "He'll be fine as long as a fever doesn't set in. He was telling me about a local woman named Dottie who makes potions and such."

"Yes." Jacob nodded. "I could bring some medicine."

"Good. I think he'll need it." The doctor excused himself and left the tent.

Caroline patted Richard's hand. "You'll be fine. We'll make sure you have all the medicine you need."

Richard smiled grimly. "I'm afraid I may miss your wedding."

"Don't worry about that. I'm just grateful you're all right." Caroline straightened. "Has anyone seen Thomas?"

"Major Thomas?" Simon asked.

"No, Thomas Haversham."

Simon wrinkled his nose. "I don't know him. But I know a Thomas Barrett and—"

"Wait." Caroline held up a hand. "Did you say *Major* Thomas? Matthias Murray Thomas? Is Jane's son here?"

"You could say that." Richard took a gulp from his canteen, then offered it to her. "You might want some of this."

"No thank you." Caroline tensed as a surge of anger swept through her. "Jane's son has been here all this time? How could he stay here when his mother was being held prisoner?"

"He did go home," Simon declared.

"When? I didn't see him." Caroline planted her fists on her hips. "And where was he when his mother was starving to death? Jacob and Thomas had to save her. How could he let other men rescue his mother?"

"The wages of sin," Richard murmured, and helped himself to another swig of rum.

Simon glared at her. "Major Thomas is a hero."

"I beg to differ." Caroline lifted her chin. "Where is this Matthias? I'd like to give him a piece of my mind."

"You'll find Major Thomas outside," Richard explained. "He wanted to be alone. He blames himself for my injury. And he blames himself for the death of those two men."

"Why would he—" Caroline studied Richard, then Jacob. They knew something, she could tell by the way they avoided her eyes. A cold shiver crept into her bones.

She needed to see Thomas. Now. She threw open the tent flap and marched outside. She scanned the campsite, searching the dirty, scarred faces.

Her Thomas was here. He had to be. He loved her. And she trusted him. She'd given him her heart.

"There he is." Simon followed her outside and pointed in the distance.

She spotted Thomas Haversham, far away in a grove of trees. His back was to her as he leaned against the trunk of a loblolly pine. The slump of his shoulders spoke of his despair. Poor Thomas. She moved toward him to give him comfort.

"Major Thomas!" Simon shouted. "There's someone here to see you."

Caroline halted. *No, don't turn around. Don't be a liar. Don't break my heart.*

He turned.

Chapter Thirty-Two

"Caroline? What are you doing here?" Matthias strode toward her.

She stepped back, her face pale and stricken.

What was wrong? He noted Simon's confused expression. *Major Thomas*, the boy had called to him. *Damn*. She knew who he was.

She backed away, her eyes glistening with tears.

"Caroline." He moved toward her. "We need to talk."

She shook her head. "I don't talk to strangers."

"We're hardly strangers."

"No?" She lowered her voice. "Tell me, Matthias Murray Thomas, do you normally bed a woman *before* introducing yourself?"

He sucked in a breath. "No. You're the first."

"Lucky me." She pivoted and stalked away.

He followed her. "I don't blame you for being angry."

She snorted and kept walking.

"I apologize. I know I should have told you sooner."

She swiveled to face him. "Why didn't you? Why weren't you honest with me?"

"I— At first, I wanted to know if your attraction to me was real, that it had nothing to do with wealth."

She gave him an incredulous look. "You thought I was hunting for a rich husband? Like Agatha? How could you?"

"I didn't know you then. How was I to know you could be trusted? You were lying about your identity, too."

Her eyes narrowed. "I confessed the truth. Why didn't you?"

"I didn't want to lose you. You said you wouldn't involve yourself with a soldier."

"So that justifies lying to me?"

"I was always honest about my feelings."

She huffed. "And I'm supposed to trust you on that?"

"Yes, dammit. I wouldn't have proposed marriage if I didn't love you."

As a tear coursed down her cheek, a pang of guilt pierced his heart. He had lived with his lie for so long, he had ceased to understand how badly the falsehood would hurt Caroline. How could he convince her he was true when all she could see was a living, human lie?

Her whispered voice was laced with pain. "You let me call you by the wrong name when we made love."

"Thomas is my *last* name—close enough. I wasn't offended."

Her eyes flashed with emerald fire. "How generous of you. I would certainly hate to offend."

Dammit, everything he said was coming out wrong. "Can we put this behind us? Please?"

"What are you asking? That I forget our relationship was built on a lie?"

"Our love is not a lie! Caroline, does it really matter? We're alive, and we love each other."

"It matters to me! I trusted you. I trusted you to be honest. And you would have been honest if you trusted me."

He tugged at the cravat around his neck. "I'm a wanted man. It was better for you not to know."

"Why? Did you think I would turn you in?"

"Not on purpose, but you did warn me on more than one occasion that you have a loose tongue."

She flinched and stepped back. "You have a low opinion of me, Matthias Murray Thomas. And my opinion of you is even lower. Good day." She pivoted and marched away.

Virginia sat up in bed. "Caroline, what happened? Dottie told me that you and Jacob left suddenly."

Caroline wandered into Dottie's bedroom off the kitchen. "I learned that Tarleton had set a trap for the partisans. I was afraid for Father, Quincy, and Josiah, but I saw them. They're alive and well."

"And your Thomas? How is he?"

Caroline blinked away the tears. She'd cried all the way back from Snow's Island. Now she was determined not to waste another tear on him. "He's . . . gone."

Virginia gasped. "He was killed?"

"No." Caroline slumped on the edge of the bed. It felt like he had died. Thomas Haversham was gone, and a stranger named Matthias had taken his place. How could she love a man she didn't know? "I lost him."

Virginia narrowed her eyes. "What do you mean?"

"He lied."

"Who? Thomas?"

"He lied to me! He was never a butler." The baby woke with a cry, and Caroline groaned. "I'm sorry. I'll get him." She trudged toward the cradle and lifted the newborn in her arms.

Virginia loosened the drawstring at her neck. "We always suspected Thomas was more than a butler."

"Yes, but I thought he was at least honest about his name." Caroline cooed to the crying baby, "Sweet little Jamie. You won't grow up to break a little girl's heart, will you? You won't seduce her with lies 'til she's too blind to see the obvious? You won't be a *scurvy jackass*, will you?"

"Give him to me." With an exasperated look, Virginia reached for the baby. She settled Jamie at her breast, and his cries ended abruptly. "Now, tell me everything."

"What's to tell?" Caroline collapsed on the bed and stared at the ceiling. "I was a fool to believe him. After all, he was a miserable excuse for a butler. He was obviously acquainted with members of the militia. And he knew all about the secret passageway."

"Secret passageway?"

Caroline winced. Was Thomas right to worry about her loose tongue? *Blast him!* He still should have trusted her. She sat up. "I am so vexed with him! I wager he was laughing behind my back all this time."

"He always seemed rather serious to me."

Caroline's eyes misted with tears and she shook her head. "I refuse to shed another tear for him. I'll never see him again."

"So it is over?" Virginia frowned. "Have you suddenly forgotten that you love him and agreed to marry him?"

"This is not *my* doing! He's the one who lied. He's not Thomas Haversham. He's Matthias Murray Thomas."

Virginia gasped. "He's Jane's son?"

"Yes! He's a blasted major in the army."

Virginia's mouth twitched. "A successful soldier and owner of this plantation. How dreadful. No wonder you have rejected him."

"'Tis not amusing."

"Caroline, he's a wanted man. I would expect him to protect his identity."

"Not to me! Not when we—" Caroline lowered her head into her hands.

"You feel betrayed?" Virginia whispered.

"I—I gave him everything. I felt so . . . exposed. Why couldn't he do the same?"

"I'm sorry, sweeting. You still love him, don't you?"

Caroline wiped a tear from her cheek. "Yes. No. I don't know."

"Has he ever said he loves you?"

Caroline nodded. "Several times."

Virginia smiled. "That's good. I was married to Quincy for months before he could admit that much."

Caroline gaped. "You're in jest. The man was obviously in love with you."

"Obvious to everyone but him. And me. You cannot expect a courtship or marriage to sail along without an occasional storm. If you love each other, you will persevere."

"But I don't even know him. I know nothing about Matthias."

"Then take the time to get acquainted." Virginia nudged her sister with her foot. "He's still the man who loves you. The man who wants to marry you."

"You think I was wrong to fuss at him?"

"Goodness, no. He deserved it." Virginia switched the baby to her other breast. "He should come crawling on his knees, begging you to forgive him."

Caroline sighed. "It feels so strange, thinking about him as Matthias now. I hope he's as miserable as I."

"Hell's bells, you look miserable." Richard gazed at him with blurry eyes.

Next to his cousin's cot, Matthias perched on the end of a log that served as a makeshift chair. "I don't think I've ever seen you so drunk."

"They keep filling my canteen with more rum. You want some?" Richard offered the canteen with an unsteady hand.

Matthias helped himself to a drink. "Do you know one of the men who died had a wife and two children?" He recalled the man he had met on the Pee Dee while looking for Major Munro's daughters. The children had lost their home because of him, and now, they had lost their father. "I asked him to join the partisans. He's dead because of me."

"You didn't shoot him."

"I might as well have."

"Bullshit." Richard grabbed the canteen. "You're just wallowing in self-pity. If I wasn't injured, I'd knock your teeth in."

Matt's mouth fell open. "You're more drunk than I thought."

"You're more stupid than I thought."

Matthias took a deep breath and rose to his feet. "I'd better go. I refuse to clobber an injured man."

"That's noble of you." Richard gave him a wobbly salute that missed his brow and bounced off his nose. "Where are you going? Your wedding?"

Matthias paused, a tent flap gripped in his hand. A pain shot through his chest. "She left me."

"Oh, right. She found out you were lying to her."

Matthias dropped the flap. "'Tis for the best."

"So you're giving up that easily?"

Easily? There was nothing easy about this. "What kind of life can I give her? I cannot go home with a price on my head. Everything I have done has only made matters worse. The homes on the Pee Dee were destroyed because of the escape I initiated. The British took over my house because I burned all the ferryboats. Hickman imprisoned my mother because of me. Two men have died because I led them into a trap. And you were injured. Hell, you wouldn't even be here if it weren't for me."

"That's not true."

"You were raised a Quaker. You never would have joined the army if you hadn't been following in my footsteps."

"Damn you!" Richard struggled to sit up. "You think I haven't a mind of my own? I decided to join the army. I defied my father and his beliefs. It was my decision, and you cannot steal it from me."

Matt stared at his cousin a moment. "Very well. It was your decision. Now lie down before you do yourself harm."

"Why? If I start bleeding again, will it be *your* fault? Do you take responsibility for the entire world?"

"I must take responsibility for the consequences of my actions."

"You cannot have it all. I want my share back, dammit." Grimacing, Richard reclined against the bare pillows. "As for our escape from the British, even if you hadn't initiated that, the partisans would have still rescued us. It was the British who made the decision to destroy homes, not you. When you burned bridges and so forth, you were simply following orders and good ones, I might add. It was not your decision to imprison your mother. In fact, you rescued her. You're not cursed, Matt. You're full of shit."

He snorted. "That's pithy. I'll have it put on my gravestone." He turned back to the tent entrance. "Get some rest."

"I'm not done. God willing, I'll never be this drunk again, so you'd better listen."

Matthias groaned

"You're afraid to get married," Richard declared.

"Not true. I was planning to marry today."

"Then why did you give up?"

"I didn't give up. Caroline rejected me."

"You gave up. You didn't go after her."

Matthias clenched his fists. He had wanted to go after her, but then he had told himself she was better off without a wanted man for her husband. He'd convinced himself he was backing off for her sake. Because he loved her.

But dammit, how could he live without her? Why was he fighting for freedom if he wasn't free to be with her? "I have to get her back."

"That's more like it." Richard took another swig of rum. "But what will happen when the war ends and you go back to being a wealthy plantation owner. And slave owner. How will Caroline like that? How will *you* like it?"

"It doesn't matter what I like. I made a vow to my grandfather that I would take care of the plantation."

"I know what you saw, Matthias. You wrote about it in your diary. You drew a bloody picture of it."

"You read my journal? Dammit, Richard. That was none of your business."

"I wanted to know why you were having nightmares. You would never talk about it."

"Shut up and rest before you start bleeding again."

"You hated how your grandfather treated the slaves. You hated the way your father forced the women into his bed. You hated how much it hurt your mother."

"Bloody hell, enough!" Matthias strode toward the cot and glared at his cousin. "All right, you want the truth? Before I met Caroline, I had planned never to marry. I was going to be the last owner. No more heirs. No more vows."

"For God's sake, Matt. Why are you making yourself miserable over a vow to our grandfather when you have no respect for him?"

Matthias paced across the small tent. "I wanted to keep my word. And I need to keep the plantation for my mother. She's been accustomed to wealth all her life. I cannot ask her to live in poverty."

Richard leaned back against the pillows, frowning. "I think she would prefer to see you happily married with children than live like a queen all alone."

Matthias rubbed his brow. For years, he had avoided Loblolly and its responsibilities. He had tried to pretend Jacob didn't exist. He'd tried to ignore the fact that someday he would inherit slaves. And all those years, he had been running from the truth. No wonder he was so adept at lying. He even lied to himself. "I'll deal with it."

"Good." Richard handed him the canteen. "Talk to Jacob. He has some good ideas, and he wants to help. Loblolly is his home, too."

"All right." Matthias swallowed some rum and handed the canteen back.

"You'll apologize to Caroline?"

"I'll get her back if I have to belly crawl through the swamp to do it."

"Good." Richard gave him an ironic smile. "You'll be a married man. Might as well get used to begging."

CHAPTER THIRTY-THREE

After breakfast the next morning, Caroline searched the bookcase in the nursery. "Shall we find something to read?"

"I want to read Papa's book," Charlotte insisted.

"I'm sick of that book." Edward stretched out on the floor, setting up the pewter army figures. "And I'm sick of that mean Captain Stickman."

"I agree with you there." Caroline patted her pocket to make sure her knife was there. She wasn't sure how safe it was for her and the children to remain at Loblolly. Agatha had left for fear of further violence, taking Bertram with her. Pugsley had not yet returned from Kingstree.

Only Hickman remained. Could she handle him on her own? Perhaps she should ask Dottie to slip a sleeping potion into his next meal. Then they could tie him up.

Thomas, or Matthias as she now tried to think of him, had promised to take them all to North Carolina, but she doubted he would return now. She would have to take care of her family herself. She groaned at the thought of Virginia traveling so soon after childbirth.

In the bookcase, a narrow book with no title caught her eye. The journal of young Matthias Murray Thomas. She had noticed it before, but it had possessed little meaning for her then. She ran her fingers over the faded, frayed cover.

Take the time to get acquainted, Ginny had said. What better way to understand the man she loved? Her breath hitched. God help her, she *did* love him.

Sleep had been nigh impossible last night. To be close to the children, she had slept in Virginia's bed in the nursery. Memories of the night before had invaded her thoughts and left her restless and yearning for more.

Thomas . . . rather, Matthias had made love so passionately. Surely he loved her. And her heart didn't care what his name was. He was simply her beloved.

She opened the diary. The childish scrawl and lopsided signature tugged at her heart. She thumbed through the pages. The entries grew longer and more detailed as he aged. He wrote about his days with Richard and the nights they sneaked out to go fishing.

It was a good childhood, Caroline thought until she turned a page and saw it. A hideous painting in watercolor spread over two pages. A brown alligator with a black man in its jaws. Swirls of red paint covered the entire picture. Blood in the sky, blood in the water.

"My God." Had Matthias actually witnessed such a horrid scene? She turned to the page after the painting.

April 10, 1759
   Grandfather took me to the new field he is having cleared. He always tells me to be proud because it will all be

mine someday. I saw the slaves. They were up to their knees in the muddy swamp. Grandpa says the swampland will make good farmland once it is drained.

It looked like a log. It was so still. We all thought it was a log, but Micah got too close. The alligator attacked. Micah screamed and tried to escape.

Grandpa took me away. He was so angry. He said a good slave was too expensive to lose. I looked back and the slaves were crying.

I'm not sure I like Grandpa anymore.

Caroline blinked back her tears. "Dear God."

"What's wrong?" Charlotte asked.

Caroline closed the book and placed it back on the shelf. "Memories." She glanced at her niece. What dreadful memories would these children carry with them the rest of their lives? The sight of Hickman pointing a pistol at Jane? The sight of the cabin on the Pee Dee engulfed in flames?

The door to the nursery burst open. Charlotte squeaked.

Caroline spun about. "Oh, Betsy, you gave us a fright."

Betsy regarded them with a grim expression. "Pugsley is back."

"Already?" Caroline strode to the door. "Can you stay with the children for a little while?"

"Yes." Betsy lowered her voice to a whisper. "I'll keep them safe. I won't let the redcoats hurt anyone. Not anymore."

Caroline nodded. "I'll be right back." She hurried to the library peephole. Silently, she slid it open.

"Are you sure?" Hickman's voice rasped.

"Yes," Pugsley answered. "The inhabitants of Kingstree

said there was gunfire outside their village yesterday afternoon."

Hickman collapsed into the chair behind the desk. "Go on."

"They found two dead partisans in the road. Apparently, Tarleton and his men chased down the others." Pugsley paced to the sideboard. "Some of the partisans survived, for they returned later to retrieve the bodies of their comrades."

Hickman slammed a fist down on the desk. "Damnation! How did the partisans know about Kingstree?"

"I don't know, but Tarleton will believe he has proof that you're a traitor. They could be coming to arrest you."

Hickman surged to his feet. "But I'm innocent!"

Pugsley returned to the desk with a glass and the decanter of brandy. "Do you need a drink?"

Hickman ripped the decanter from Pugsley's hand and hurled it toward the bookcase.

Caroline jumped to the side as crystal shattered around the peephole. Shards of glass flew into the passageway. Her heart thumped wildly. It had to be a coincidence. Hickman didn't know she was there.

She needed to leave. A shard of glass crunched under her foot.

"Did you hear something?" Pugsley asked.

"Yes," Hickman answered. "What was it?"

Caroline gulped. Were they looking at the bookcase? The peephole was wide open. Would they see it? Could she shut it without them noticing? She reached for the knob.

Footsteps came toward her. "Sir, look at this!" A man's hand jabbed through the hole.

Caroline jumped back with a gasp.

"There's someone back there," Hickman growled.

She swallowed the scream that filled her throat. Hickman would come after her. And the children.

She scurried up the stairs to the nursery. "We must leave. Now. Grab whatever you want to take with you."

Ezra tossed books onto the floor, clearing the bookshelves. "A ghost. I should have listened to that boy. He kept talking about a damned ghost who could walk through walls."

"Aye, this explains everything." Pugsley ran his fingers along the dark polished wood, searching for a hidden door latch. "Someone has been spying on you."

Ezra paused. They were wasting their time hunting for a latch. The spy had to be entering from somewhere else. "The dining room is back there. And the china cabinet." He had seen that small room before when he had taken the crystal and smashed it. "Let's have a look."

Minutes later, they were examining the china room.

"Here, sir." Pugsley outlined a crack in the wall with his finger. "There's a door here."

Ezra probed the area for a hidden latch and found it under a chair rail. The door swung open. A passageway lay before them, littered with shards of glass. He peered through the peephole and spotted his desk. "The bastard. He's been watching us all this time. Or *she* has." Was Caroline Munro behind this?

"We could arrest everyone in the house," Pugsley suggested.

"They would claim ignorance. We need proof." Ezra noted the stairs. "Are they on the third floor?"

"Yes, sir."

"Then we set fire to the grand staircase. They'll have to use this staircase to escape."

Pugsley's eyes widened. "But if they don't know about this staircase, they could be trapped and burn to death."

"The price they pay for proving their innocence." Ezra smiled. "I wouldn't worry about that, Pugsley. Caroline Munro will use this staircase to save the children. And we'll be waiting outside the dining room to arrest her as a spy."

"I see. Excellent plan, sir."

"Yes." Ezra nodded. "And the best part of it—I can clear my name with Tarleton by foisting the blame on her. Innocent or guilty, she's going to die."

Caroline stuffed a pillowcase with a spare set of clothing for her and the children. In her pocket, the knife rested against her hip.

"May I bring the tinder wheel?" Edward asked.

"Yes," Caroline answered, watching him jam the device into his coat pocket. "It may come in handy later." When they were camping in the woods with no home.

"I like it here." Charlotte frowned, her father's book clutched to her chest. "Will we ever come back?"

"I don't know. For now, we're going to North Carolina to live with your grandmother. Doesn't that sound nice?" Caroline gave the children an encouraging smile as they hurried down the hall.

"What about Mama?" Charlotte asked.

"She'll come with us." Caroline winced inwardly. Could a day-old baby survive such a journey?

Betsy met them at the top of the stairs. She, too, had a bundle in her arms. "This is all I have in the world. The redcoats destroyed my home and my family."

Edward scowled. "I hate the redcoats. I want to join the partisans and fight with Josiah."

"You're too young." Caroline headed down the stairs. "Hurry now. Quietly."

"I smell smoke," Betsy whispered behind her.

Caroline reached the second-floor landing and gasped. Billows of smoke drifted up the stairs.

"The house is on fire!" Betsy shouted.

Charlotte squealed and dropped her book.

"Wait here." Caroline covered her mouth and nose and descended a few steps. A wall of heat stopped her. Through the smoke, she spotted the flames, devouring the base of the stairs. She scurried back up the landing.

The terror on the children's faces ripped at her heart. "Don't worry. We'll get out," she told them to reassure herself as much as them.

"I know!" Betsy yelled. "We'll go down the servants' staircase and out the back door. Hurry!" She charged up the stairs to the third floor. The children ran after her.

Caroline glanced out the window of the second-floor landing and spotted Hickman and his foot soldier by the servants' door. Pugsley had a musket in his hands, the bayonet gleaming in the afternoon sun. A trap. Hickman wanted them to use the secret passageway.

"Wait!" She charged up the stairs. "Betsy, wait. We have to find another way."

Betsy stopped. "What other way is there?"

"We'll . . ." *Think, Caroline, think.* "We'll go to the balcony on the second floor. The front of the house."

"And what? Jump? 'Tis too far."

"I know where there's a rope. Go! Go to the balcony." Caroline passed her bundle to Edward, then ran to the room where Matthias and Jacob had rescued Jane. She gathered up the rope and darted down the stairs to the second floor.

Waves of heat rose up from the ground floor. The smoke was so thick, she covered her mouth and hurried to the balcony. Fresh air welcomed her and she breathed in relief to see Betsy and the children waiting.

"We'll climb down using the rope." She tied one end around a column.

Betsy tossed their bundles over the balcony.

"'Tis too far," Charlotte whispered. "I'm afraid."

Edward pounded his fists on the balustrade. "I hate the British! I *hate* them. They burned our home and our cabin. And now they're burning—"

"Edward!" Caroline grabbed him by the shoulders. "I need you to go first. Show your sister how easy it is."

Edward nodded. Caroline and Betsy held him steady as he climbed over the balustrade and took hold of the rope. With his feet pressed against the column, Edward eased himself down the rope to the ground.

Caroline knelt in front of her niece. "You see how it is done, Charlotte? 'Tis simple."

"I'm afraid!" Charlotte's face paled to a deathly white. "Where's Papa's book? I dropped it. I don't have Papa's book."

"You don't need it. Your Papa is fine."

"I want Papa's book!"

Caroline straightened. She could hardly fling her niece over the balcony. The heat from the house was growing stronger, like a giant oven, and they stood just outside it. How long before the floor collapsed beneath their feet?

"Betsy, go next," Caroline ordered. She spotted Edward running toward the river. Where on earth was he going?

Betsy had almost reached the ground when Pugsley and Hickman rounded the corner.

"Halt!" Pugsley leveled his musket at the servant. "Don't move!"

Betsy yelped and fell to the ground.

"Don't be ridiculous!" Caroline shouted from the balcony. "Do you expect us to stay in a burning house?"

Hickman muttered a curse, then glanced at Pugsley. "Lower your weapon."

Caroline hunched down in front of her niece. "Charlotte, we have to go. I want you to climb onto my back now." She breathed with relief when Charlotte obeyed. She prayed she had the strength to get them both down the rope.

"I'm afraid," Charlotte's voice whimpered in her ear.

"I won't be able to hold you. You'll have to hold on tight." She regretted her words when Charlotte gripped her neck with enough force to choke a mule. *"Not that tight."*

Charlotte wrapped her little legs around Caroline's waist. Caroline eased over the balustrade. Her niece's breaths puffed rapidly against her ear. She grasped the rope. The rough texture bit into her palms.

The instant she stepped off the balcony, her shoulders strained with the weight. Her hands burned. She gritted her teeth and lowered them down.

When her feet reached the ground, she dropped to her knees. Charlotte slipped off her back. She stumbled to her feet, flexing her sore fingers. The house wavered before her eyes, encased in a cocoon of heat. An orange glow illuminated the front windows. The fire had spread to the front parlor. A low roar emanated from inside, punctuated with sudden snaps. Poor Jane would never see her house again.

And Matthias—he had lost his home. His father. He probably believed he had lost her. With tear-filled eyes, she grabbed her niece and their bundle of clothing and moved away from the house.

"A clever escape." Hickman stalked toward her. "But you're still under arrest for treason."

She swallowed hard. "You have no proof."

"You were using a secret corridor to spy on me."

"What secret corridor?" She motioned to the burning house. "I believe you have set your proof on fire."

Hickman's eyes flared. "Bitch. You'll pay for this."

Glass exploded as the front windows shattered from the heat. Charlotte buried her face in Caroline's skirt.

She wrapped an arm around Charlotte and looked toward the river. What was Edward doing? Her blood froze when she spotted him on his knees in the grove of loblolly pines.

She dropped the bundle of clothes. *No.* He had dug up the horn of gunpowder. "Edward, no."

He leapt to his feet, the musket in his arms.

"Edward, no!" she screamed.

He charged toward them, raising the musket to his shoulder. "I hate you! I hate you!"

"Meddlesome child," Hickman muttered. He pulled his flintlock from his belt and took aim.

CHAPTER THIRTY-FOUR

Caroline spotted a man darting from the trees toward Edward. She shoved Hickman to the side just as his pistol sparked and fired.

The man and Edward hit the ground rolling. She watched, terrified, waiting to see if either of them would stand up.

"*Bitch!*" Hickman slapped her so suddenly, she tumbled back on her arse. Pain lanced her cheek.

"I want that man alive!" Hickman bellowed.

Pugsley sprinted toward Edward and his rescuer. He stopped beside them with his musket ready.

Jacob slowly stood and helped Edward to his feet.

Hickman stalked toward them. "You. What is your name?"

Jacob glared at the redcoats.

Caroline rose to her feet. Charlotte clung to her skirts. In the distance, she saw Betsy disappearing into the woods.

Hickman kicked Edward's musket aside and studied Jacob. "You're the slave that lives by the mill, aren't you? You just interfered with my business. I wonder what else you're guilty of."

Jacob's throat moved as he swallowed hard. He shoved Edward toward Caroline.

Hickman stepped closer to him. "If we investigate your cabin, what will we find? Bows and arrows? Gunpowder? You've been sabotaging my supplies, haven't you?"

"Edward! Charlotte!" Virginia's frantic voice shouted behind them. "Where are you?"

Caroline swiveled to see her sister coming around the burning house. Dottie followed her, carrying the baby.

"Mama, we're here!" Charlotte ran toward her mother.

Virginia fell to her knees, sobbing.

Caroline grabbed Edward and whispered in his ear, "Saddle the horses and escape!" She pushed him toward his mother.

Hickman strode toward her. "You're not leaving, Miss Munro."

Caroline stood still as she watched the children reach their mother. She prayed Virginia would do as she asked.

"Touching." Hickman eyed the reunion impatiently, then dragged Caroline back toward Jacob. His bony fingers dug into her arm. "'Tis a shame I'll have to arrest this woman as a traitor. She's been spying on me, and the penalty is death."

Caroline's eyes blurred with tears. She glanced over her shoulder and saw Virginia and her children hurrying around the burning house. Would it be the last time she ever saw them?

"Let her go," Jacob said. "She's done nothing."

"How would you know the extent of her guilt unless you were guilty yourself?" Hickman asked. "Tell me, are you prepared to confess in her stead?"

Caroline shook her head. "No," she whispered.

Jacob glanced at her briefly, then squared his shoulders. "I am your spy. I worked alone."

Hickman scoffed. "I don't think so. No matter what you claim, I believe Miss Munro was helping you. And someone else, I wager. Matthias Murray Thomas. Where is he?"

"I don't know the man."

"Liar!" Hickman let go of Caroline and seized Jacob by the shirt. "He owns the plantation. He owns you! You should be happy to turn him in."

Horse hooves thundered toward them. Caroline moved back slowly as two of Tarleton's men rode up. One pointed a pistol at Hickman.

The other spoke, "You're under arrest, Hickman. We have orders to take you to Tarleton immediately."

"That won't be necessary, Greville. I have the spy right here. He has already confessed."

"Is that true?" Greville eyed Jacob, then glanced at the burning house. "What the hell is going on here?"

"This spy was using a secret corridor behind the library to eavesdrop on my conversations," Hickman explained. "He set fire to the house to cover up his crime, but I caught him."

"You confessed?" Greville asked Jacob.

"Yes." Jacob shot Caroline a pointed look.

Her heart pounded in her ears. Did he have some sort of plan?

"I'm sure he didn't act alone," Hickman continued. "Miss Munro helped him. And I believe he can tell us the whereabouts of another accomplice, Matthias Murray Thomas."

"Now that I would like to know. I have unfinished business with that bastard." Greville dismounted. "There are four of us soldiers, all together. Surely we can persuade this man to talk."

Jacob grabbed Pugsley's musket and wrenched it from his hands. He hurled the bayoneted weapon toward one of the horses. The horse reared, tossing the mounted greencoat to the ground.

Jacob sprinted toward the river in the direction of the mill. The soldiers gave chase.

Caroline hesitated, then turned and ran toward the stable. She hoped Jacob wouldn't feel she was abandoning him, but she couldn't take on four soldiers without help.

When she reached the stables, she found three horses saddled and ready to go.

Virginia had tied an apron around her shoulders, creating a safe, attached cradle for the baby that left her hands free. The baby nestled quietly against his mother's chest. She was mounted on the first horse with Charlotte seated behind her.

Virginia stifled a sob as tears slid down her cheeks. "Oh, thank God! I thought they wouldn't let you go. I was so afraid—"

"Shh." Caroline reached for her sister's hand. "There's no time. You must leave."

Seated on the second horse, Dottie spoke, "We're going to the Pee Dee. Matthias's uncle is there. And Miss Jane."

"Good. Travel slowly and be careful." Caroline strode to the third horse. "Get down, Edward, and sit behind Dottie."

"Aren't you coming with us?" Edward asked as he dismounted.

"I cannot. I need help to save Jacob."

"Where is Betsy?" Dottie asked as Edward settled behind her.

"I don't know. I saw her slip into the woods." Caroline swung up onto the horse and took the reins. "I'll find her later. For now, you must go." She dug in her heels and headed for the orchard. Glancing back, she saw Dottie and her family ride into the woods. Thank God they would be safe. Now if she could only save Jacob.

First, she would have to remember the way to Snow's Island. She had traveled the route before in a daze. Had it only been yesterday? She followed the trail until it forked. Which way had Jacob gone?

She heard the sound of horses coming fast. Friend or foe? She steered her horse behind a thick growth of swamp holly. Two horsemen sped by—Matthias and the younger boy, Simon.

"Wait!" she screamed. "Matthias, stop!" She charged after them, shouting.

Simon glanced back. With a yell, he reined in his horse.

Matthias pulled to a stop. "*What?*" His grim expression softened with surprise at the sight of Caroline.

She caught up with them. "Thank God you're here! I need you."

Matthias turned his horse toward her. "Does this mean you forgive me?"

"Yes. I mean, no." She shook her head. She was babbling like an idiot.

"Someone hit you?" He eased his horse closer. "*Who is he?*"

She touched her cheek. There was a murderous glint in

Matthias's eyes, so fierce it left her speechless. How could she have ever thought this man was a servant? He exuded strength and authority; he could kill without hesitation for the right cause. He was exactly who Jacob needed right now. "You need to save Jacob. Hickman arrested him as a spy. I'm afraid Hickman will torture him 'til he tells them where to find you."

Matthias sat back in his saddle. "How many are there?"

"Four. Hickman, Pugsley and two soldiers from Tarleton's troop."

Matthias glanced at his young companion. "We'll save time if we don't go back for more men. Can you take one of them?"

Simon snorted. "I'll take two."

Matthias turned to her. "Stay out of this. Go to Snow's Island and wait for me."

"I will not!"

"I cannot bear to lose you! 'Twill be bad enough to lose Jacob. He—he's my brother."

"You can save him," she assured him. "Go!"

He nodded once, then urged his horse into a gallop. Simon followed. Caroline waited a moment, then trailed behind them at a slower pace.

Soon she could see the large plume of smoke billowing up into the blue sky. She followed Matthias into the woods on the far side of the house.

He had already dismounted and was staring at the smoldering husk where his grand home had once sat.

"I should have warned you. I'm sorry." She pulled her horse to a stop beside them.

He scowled at her. "Dammit, Caroline. Why couldn't you do as I ask?"

"You didn't ask. You ordered."

He raised his arms to grab her as she slid from her horse. "If I ask nicely will you go away?"

She touched his cheek. "I'll try to stay out of danger, but don't expect me to leave you. I cannot."

He took her hand and kissed the palm. "I love you, Caroline. I will always love you."

"I love you, too . . . Matthias."

"Was it Hickman who hit you?" When she nodded, he stepped back with determined glint in his eyes. "Are you ready, Simon?"

"Aye, sir." The youth gripped his musket.

Matthias adjusted the knife in his belt, grabbed his musket, then sprinted through the woods toward the river. Simon ran after him.

Four against two. They might need her. She removed the knife from her pocket and followed them.

Matthias and Simon were close to the river, hiding behind a thicket of palmetto and swamp holly. In the distance she saw the mill and four soldiers.

"I'm taking Hickman," Matthias whispered.

"I'll take one of Tarleton's men," Simon whispered back. "The one with the broken nose looks familiar."

"That's Greville. I'm taking him, too."

"You mean from the time we were captured?" Simon asked. "I thought he was taken prisoner."

"He escaped. I should have killed him when I had the chance."

"Where is Jacob?" Caroline whispered.

Matthias glanced back with a muttered curse. "What are you doing here?"

"Have you seen Jacob?" she repeated.

"Aye." Matthias grimaced. "But we cannot save him until we are rid of the soldiers. Let's go, Simon."

Matthias and Simon separated and inched forward. Caroline remained hidden behind the palmetto, searching for Jacob. The four soldiers had their backs to her as they watched the mill. Two of them were dripping wet as if they'd fallen into the river. She glanced at the river where the wheel was turning slowly.

She gasped. *Jacob.* They had tied him to the waterwheel. His ankles and chest were lashed to one of the spokes. His arms, stretched out along the circumference, were tied at the wrists in a hideous imitation of a crucifixion.

She stared, desperately searching for a sign that he still lived. Yes, his chest was moving. He was breathing. But for how long? Soon he would plunge into the river as the wheel made its turn.

Shots rang out. She saw Hickman and one of Tarleton's men fall. The other two soldiers scrambled for cover and returned fire.

They could continue to shoot at each other for too long, and Jacob needed rescuing now. She had a knife, and she knew how to swim and climb. Her mind made up, she lifted her skirt and removed her petticoats, stockings, and shoes.

Keeping low, she crept toward the riverbank. Cool mud oozed around her toes. She clenched the knife in her teeth and eased into the murky water. Soon she could no longer skim the riverbed with her bare feet. The river was deep, dredged to allow the waterwheel room to rotate.

Jacob was moving with the wheel in a clockwise fashion, nearing three o'clock. She swam toward him, hoping to meet him before he was swept under. Her skirts tangled around her legs, slowing her progress.

Jacob's face was swollen with bruises, his mouth bloody where the British had attempted to batter information from him. His eyes widened at the sight of her. "What are you doing?" He glanced about. The men were still occupied with their shooting.

Unable to answer with the knife in her mouth, she steadied herself against the wheel. She grabbed each spoke as it descended toward her. His left hand reached her first. She grasped the ropes and slipped the point of her knife between his wrist and the wheel.

Furiously, she sawed at the rope. His fingers dipped into the water. Time was running out.

"Caroline, let go."

She heard him taking deep breaths to prepare himself. His wrist descended into the water. Still, she held on and sawed at the ropes.

Her eyes met his. "I won't leave you." She took a deep breath and went under. Hanging on to the rope, she was sucked down, down into the dark water. She could hardly see, but she could feel. The rope was giving way. She sawed at it desperately. Her lungs burned.

At last! The rope floated away, leaving Jacob's hand free.

She kicked for the surface and broke through. After a few gasps for air, she paddled toward the edge of the wheel. *Please, Jacob, still be alive.* She waited for him to emerge.

The minute she spotted his feet, she grasped the rope and attacked it with her knife. She heard his gasp for air.

"Jacob! Thank God." She leaned onto him and slipped a leg over the spoke where he was tied. She sat up, straddling the spoke like a horse. The wheel pulled her out of the water.

With his free hand, Jacob tugged at the ropes around his chest. "Caroline, don't," he gasped. "'Tis too dangerous."

"I'm fine." She sawed at the ropes, riding the spoke as it approached nine o'clock.

Ten o'clock. She began to slip. She hung on to the rope and sawed.

Eleven o'clock. The rope broke, and his legs were free.

"Take my hand!" Jacob extended his left hand to her.

She grabbed his hand as her body slipped off the spoke and her legs dangled in mid-air. The spoke inched toward twelve o'clock.

Jacob groaned, burdened with her entire weight, made worse with her wet skirts. She jammed the knife handle in her mouth, then used her free hand to grip his belt. As the wheel slowly turned, she eased her left leg over the spoke, so she was once again straddling the wooden beam.

He pulled her toward him, and she slipped her knife under the rope around his chest.

Two o'clock. She sawed at the rope.

Three o'clock. The rope broke. Jacob fell downward, banging against the wheel, his feet splashing into the water below. He was hanging from the wheel, suspended by his right hand.

Four o'clock. Caroline allowed the downward movement of the wheel to send her sliding down the spoke toward his hand. She went to work sawing on the last rope. Soon they would be immersed once again.

"Caroline, don't. Save yourself."

"I'm not leaving you." She slipped off the spoke into the water.

She heard Jacob drawing a deep breath. His head disappeared.

She took a deep breath and joined him.

Chapter Thirty-Five

He had never enjoyed killing before, but when Hickman fell, Matthias experienced a burst of satisfaction. The bastard deserved it for terrorizing women and children, starving his mother, and hitting Caroline.

He darted to another clump of bushes and reloaded his musket. Simon's first shot had felled one of the greencoats. Greville and Pugsley remained. They took cover and discharged their weapons. Smoke betrayed their location, and Matthias took another shot.

A second shot rang out. Simon. The boy was doing well. If only Jacob could last 'til this was over.

He moved silently toward the enemy. If Simon kept them busy, he could circle behind them and take them by surprise. As he approached the bank on the far side of the mill, a glimpse of red appeared behind some tall grass. It was Pugsley, crawling on his belly toward the next cluster of swamp holly. A wide oak tree grew behind it.

Matthias slipped behind the oak tree and waited. *Timing*

is everything. The soft scraping noise drew nearer. He spotted Pugsley's black boots dragging through the grass.

He lay down his musket and eased around the tree. Pugsley had risen to his knees behind the holly, his musket raised to the shoulder.

Matthias pounced, grasping Pugsley's musket in his hands and ramming it against the man's throat. The redcoat squirmed and kicked. Matthias clenched his teeth and squeezed harder. He couldn't afford to let Pugsley cry out.

The squirming stopped, and the body sagged against him. Matthias swallowed hard and released him. He could berate himself later. For now, Jacob was still in danger.

The gunshots continued, indicating that Simon and Greville were still alive. Matthias collected his musket and Pugsley's and moved toward the riverbank, keeping low. Greville's green coat made him hard to spot. He must have removed his helmet.

Voices came from the river, and Matthias glanced at the wheel. *Caroline.* He blinked, hoping the sight would disappear. No, she was still there, straddling the wooden beam where Jacob was tied. Stunned, he watched her ascend into the air. Panic struggled with admiration. She was crazed. She was amazing.

"We meet again," Greville spoke behind him.

He heard the click of the hammer. *Damn.* Greville was ready to shoot. Matthias slowly straightened with his back to the enemy, his fingers grazing the handle of his knife. Timing wasn't in his favor this time. He'd be shot before he could throw the knife. He could only hope that Simon could see them.

"The partisans are on their way," he lied. "You should escape while you can."

"I plan to escape," Greville said. "But I want my knife back first. And I want you dead."

Matthias gripped the knife in his hand. "Be careful what you wish for."

A shot exploded. Matthias spun around as Greville cried out. A musket ball had skimmed his arm, causing him to drop his musket.

Matthias threw the knife, and it thudded into Greville's chest. Greville slumped to his knees, a dazed look clouding his eyes.

Thank God Simon had taken a shot. Matthias lunged forward to retrieve Greville's musket.

Greville grasped the knife handle in his hand. "My father gave it to me," he whispered, then collapsed onto the ground.

Matthias glanced back at the river. Jacob was hanging from the waterwheel by his right hand. He disappeared beneath the water, and Caroline followed him.

"No!" Matthias ripped the knife from Greville's chest and charged into the river. He swam toward the wheel, then took a deep breath and dove.

They were hard to see in the murky water. Caroline was clinging to the rope, sawing at it with her knife. He pushed her hands aside and inserted his sharper knife. She kicked her legs and swam for the surface. With one sharp slice, he severed the rope and pulled Jacob away from the wheel.

His body was limp. Panic squeezed at the last of Matthias's breath. Dropping his knife, he grasped Jacob under the shoulders and swam for the surface.

Caroline was there, treading water. "Is he all right?"

"No," Matthias gasped. He swam for the bank with his

brother in his arms. Caroline helped him drag Jacob out of the water.

"Jacob!" He slapped at his face. "Breathe, dammit!" He flipped him over and shoved at his back. How could he lose him now? "Don't die on me, Jacob! Don't leave me."

Water spewed from Jacob's mouth. He coughed and gasped for air.

"Jacob." Caroline brushed his hair back from his brow. "You're all right. You're safe now." She glanced at Matthias with tears in her eyes. "And you're safe, too."

"Is it over?" Jacob murmured. "Are they gone?"

"Yes," Matthias answered. "Can you stand?"

Caroline gasped.

Matthias looked up.

Hickman was standing before them, a flintlock pistol in his hand. Blood stained his coat, seeping from a stomach wound. His hand trembled slightly. "Matthias Murray Thomas, I assume. I've been waiting for you."

"It is over," Caroline said. "Leave us be."

"I have just enough strength to kill one man before I die." Hickman aimed his pistol at Matthias. "And I mean to take you with me."

A swooshing sound split the air, followed by a thunk.

Hickman jolted, then crumbled to his knees and fell forward on his face. An arrow protruded from his back.

Matthias jumped to his feet. "Who's there?"

Betsy emerged from the woods, a crossbow in her hands, her eyes glazed with a distant look. "The redcoats killed my family. All of them."

The crossbow tumbled from her hands. Her gaze drifted

to Hickman's body, and she stepped back as if shocked at what she had done.

Matthias moved toward her. "It was you, wasn't it? You saved my life before?"

Her gaze traveled to Matthias, but appeared unfocused. "They killed my family. They kill everyone. I had to stop them."

"Betsy?" Simon ran from the woods. "Betsy, is that you?"

She turned at the sound of his voice.

Simon gasped with a choking sound and dropped his musket. "Betsy. 'Tis me, Simon."

She shook her head. "You're dead. You're all dead."

"I escaped and joined the army. I didn't die. I thought *you* were dead."

Betsy blinked and focused on Simon's face. "Simon? You're alive?"

Simon ran toward her with such force that his embrace knocked them both to the ground. His laughter mixed with the halting sound of Betsy's sobs.

He grinned at Matthias. "She's my sister!"

Caroline sniffed. She picked her petticoat off the ground and wiped her nose with it. "Is it really over?" she asked for the tenth time.

Matthias rolled a stocking up her leg. "Yes. Are you all right now?"

She dried her face. "I think so." Betsy's reunion with her brother had started the flow of her tears. Then when she realized that everyone she loved had survived the latest ordeal, her tears had degenerated into sobs. She inhaled a deep breath and let it out slowly. "I've had a bad day."

Matthias fastened the garter around her thigh. "I would call it a good day. We're all alive."

"Yes, but 'tis not a day I would care to repeat."

"You need some rest. We'll go my uncle's home—"

"Oh, I do need to go there. My sister and Dottie are headed that way with the children."

"Good. Then they'll be there when we arrive." He slipped on her shoe. "You know, I'll be tempted to take liberties with you tonight. Perhaps we should marry first."

Caroline studied Matthias. He knelt beside her in soggy clothes with his dark hair loose about his tanned face, a handsome man, a fierce soldier who was gently helping her dress. He plucked her other stocking from the ground. She hid a smile at the sight of her delicate underclothes in his strong, calloused hands.

All her anger over his deception had dissipated in the face of death. Life was too short and too precious to waste in anger. And even though she had sworn to avoid the war and avoid soldiers, she had learned the painful lesson that none of them was safe. None of them could hide. They could only cherish each moment they had together.

He glanced at her. "You will marry me, won't you?"

"Marry a soldier? I don't know. I had my heart set on marrying a butler."

His mouth twitched. "Only because you wish to order me about."

"Perhaps." She wiggled her bare toes at him. "You do make a fairly decent maid."

"Yes, madam." He slipped on her other stocking. With a slow smile, he smoothed it up her leg. "In case you're interested, I provide a full range of services."

She snorted. "I have sampled your services before."

"That was only an appetizer." He tied the garter above her knee. "Would you care for the next course?" He caressed the inside of her thigh.

She slapped at his hand. "Not now. The setting is hardly romantic."

He withdrew his hand with an injured look. "But I am always on call, madam."

"Have you forgotten there are a number of dead bodies lying about? It rather dampens the mood. At least for me."

He glanced over his shoulder. "Damned redcoats, always interfering. We'd better leave before Tarleton comes looking for his men." He took hold of her hands and pulled her to her feet.

She stepped into her petticoat and raised it to her waist. With her damp skirt bundled in her hands, she asked, "Can you tie the laces for me?"

With a groan, he stepped behind her. "I'd much rather be taking clothes off. There. Done."

She smoothed down her wet skirts. "I must be one horrid-looking bride."

"Then you agree to marry?"

"Yes, of course. But don't let it go to your head. It may be the last thing we ever agree on."

With a grin, he led her down the path to the Great House. What was left of the Great House. Simon and Betsy were there, their arms still around each other. Jacob stood there with the horses.

Caroline gazed at the smoking ruins. Only the brick chimneys reached out of the ashes toward the sky. "I'm sorry about your home, Matthias. Do you plan to rebuild it someday?"

He shook his head. "I should feel sad, but I don't. It was never a life I wanted."

"It is still your property," Jacob reminded him. "What about your oath to your grandfather?"

"*Our* grandfather," Matthias said. "My exact words were his land would be in good hands. And since I'm a wanted man, I believe your hands are the best choice. I've heard you have some ideas?"

Jacob blinked. "Yes, I do. But you realize I'll want to free the slaves?"

"I'm counting on it."

"Thank you." Jacob's grin faded. "How will you live?"

"I suppose I'll have to start over. I may need some of the silver hidden in the kitchen, if you don't mind." Matthias turned to Caroline. "Will you have a poor man for a husband?"

She laughed. "I thought you were poor when I fell in love with you."

Betsy grinned at her brother. "I may be poor, but I feel like the most fortunate person on earth. I have my brother, alive and well."

Matthias extended a hand to Jacob. "I am fortunate also to have a brother."

Jacob grasped his hand, his eyes glimmering with tears.

Caroline smiled. "We have family. And love. What else could we need?"

"Liberty." Matthias pulled her into his arms. "And we'll be taking that soon enough. Trust me."

She leaned her cheek against his shoulder. "I do."

A former tap dancer and high school French teacher, *New York Times* bestselling author KERRELYN SPARKS has always searched for creative ways to express herself. A prolific reader since childhood, she discovered that writing her own stories provided the ideal way to combine her love of comedy, language, and history. And what a relief that the voices in her head have led to a paycheck instead of a padded room! A native Texan, Kerrelyn lives with her husband and children in the Greater Houston area.

Visit www.AuthorTracker.com for exclusive information on your favorite HarperCollins authors.

Give in to your impulses . . .
Read on for a sneak peek at four brand-new
e-book original tales of romance
from Avon Books.
Available now wherever e-books are sold.

THE MAD EARL'S BRIDE

By Loretta Chase

WANTED: WIFE

By Gwen Jones

A WEDDING IN VALENTINE

A Valentine Valley Novella

By Emma Cane

FLING

A BDSM Erotica Anthology

By Sara Fawkes, Cathryn Fox, and Lauren Hawkeye

An Excerpt from

THE MAD EARL'S BRIDE
(Originally appeared in the print
anthology *Three Weddings and a Kiss*)

by Loretta Chase

Gwendolyn Adams is about to propose to an
earl. On his deathbed. Because she comes
from a long line of infamous heir breeders,
she is being offered up as the last chance to
save a handsome aristocrat's dying line.

The Earl of Rawnsley is in for the shock of
his life: a surprise bride. No one asked him
what he wanted, but if he may die, he most
certainly does not want to spend his last
days breeding . . . no matter how tempting
and infuriating Gwendolyn may be . . .

"The name is Adams," she said. "Gwendolyn Adams."

He scowled. "Miss Adams, I should like to know whether you are trying to convince me to marry you or to kill myself."

"I merely wished to point out how pointless it is, in the circumstances, to quibble about our respective character flaws," she said. "And I wished to be honest with you."

A wicked part of her did not wish to be honest. She realized he was worried about his male urges clouding his judgment. The wicked part of her was not simply hoping the urges would win; it was also tempting her to encourage them with the feminine tactics other girls employed.

But that was not fair.

They had turned into the narrow drive leading to the stables. Though the rain beat harder now, Gwendolyn was aware mainly of the beating of her own heart.

She did not want to go away defeated, yet she did not want to win by unfair means.

She supposed the display of her limbs—however much her immodest mode of riding had been dictated by the need for haste and the unavailability of a sidesaddle—constituted unfair means.

Consequently, as they rode into the stable yard, she headed for the mounting block.

But Rawnsley was off his horse before she reached it, and at the gelding's side in almost the same moment.

In the next, he was reaching up and grasping her waist.

His hands were warm, his grasp firm and sure. She could feel the warmth spreading outward, suffusing her body, while she watched the muscles of his arms bunch under the wet, clinging shirtsleeves.

He lifted her up as easily as if she'd been a fairy sprite. Though she wasn't in the least anxious that he'd drop her, she grasped his powerful shoulders. It was reflex. Instinctive.

He brought her down slowly, and he did not let go even after her feet touched the ground.

He looked down at her, and his intent yellow gaze trapped her own, making her heart pound harder yet.

"The time will come when I will have no power over you," he said, his low tones making her nerve ends tingle. "When my mind crumbles, little witch, I shall be at your mercy. Believe me, I've considered that. I've asked myself what you will do with me then, what will become of me."

At that moment, one troubling question was answered.

He was aware of the danger he was in. His fears were the

same as those she felt for him. His reason was still in working order.

But he continued before she could reassure him.

"I can guess what will happen, but it doesn't seem to matter, because I'm the man I always was. A death sentence has changed nothing." His hands tightened on her waist. "You should have left me in the mire," he told her, his eyes burning into her. "It was not pleasant—yet Providence does not grant all its creatures a pretty and painless demise. And I'm ready enough for mine. But you came and fished me out, and now . . ."

He let go abruptly and stepped back. "It's too late."

He was in no state to listen to the reassurances, Gwendolyn saw. If he was angry with himself and didn't trust that self, he was not likely to trust anything she said. He would believe she was humoring him, as though he were a child.

And so she gave a brisk, businesslike nod. "That sounds like a yes to me," she said. "Against your better judgment, evidently, but a yes all the same."

"Yes, drat you—drat the lot of you—I'll do it," he growled.

"I am glad to hear it," she said.

"Glad, indeed. You're desperate for your hospital, and I'm the answer to your maidenly prayers." He turned away. "I'm desperate, too, it seems. After a year's celibacy, I should probably agree to marry your *grandmother*, Devil confound me."

He strode down the pathway to the house.

An Excerpt from

WANTED: WIFE

by Gwen Jones

TV reporter Julie Knott has been dumped
two weeks before the wedding. But when she
follows a story to the backwoods of New Jersey,
she finds a new marriage proposal, one born
of logic. Can they keep their relationship
simple, or will love come crashing in?

Andy Devine Seeks a Wife
Landed, Financially Secure 40-YR-Old Male
Seeks Healthy, Athletic Female
For Marriage and Family.
Must Submit to Full Disclosure and
Be Willing to Work Hard.
Generous Monetary Compensation
If Terms of Contract Are Not Met.
Interviews Will Be Held at the Iron Bog Firehouse,
Main Street, Iron Bog,
Friday, 27 August, 1:00–4:00 PM.
Please Bring ID.

"You," Andy Devine said. "I want you for my wife."

As that statement traveled the neuron pathway to the part of my brain that would absorb, interpret, and decide how to answer, I couldn't help but think of all the bizarre things I've seen. A dog on a high wire balancing an egg on his nose, a three-legged goose, a woman who ate nails, a man surgically altered to look like Chewbacca, a woman living in a refrigerator, an old man who hoisted a truck when it rolled atop his grandson's leg, a couple whose house had two rooms filled to the ceiling with pennies. I've seen heroism and lunacy, oddity and insanity, but up until that moment, none of it had made my jaw drop. Because up until then, none of it had involved me.

So "*What?*" was all I managed to reply.

To which he reiterated, "I want *you* for my wife."

I smiled, clearing my throat. He had to be playing with me. "I'm flattered, Mr. Devine, truly I am, but what's your real answer?"

He leaned in, his proximity sending numbing signals to my brain. "The same."

I laughed. "You're joking."

"When I'm joking," he said, moving even closer, "you'll know it."

Denny lowered his camera. "Excuse me," he said to Andy Devine, "but are you for real?"

"Pardon?" he answered, unblinking.

"Okay, never mind," Denny said, realigning the camera. "Go on."

I slapped my hand over the lens. "Shut that thing off. Are you insane?"

Denny lowered it. "I ought to be asking you the same thing. It's the best offer you've had in years."

I scowled at him, returning to the subject at hand. "Mr. Devine—a word." Then I promptly crossed to the other side of the room. When I turned, Denny had sunk into a folding chair and my would-be suitor was standing before me.

"Yes?" he said, calmly attentive.

A part of me was so flabbergasted I hardly knew where to begin, but I retained enough professionalism to override anything. "I'm a TV reporter, Mr. Devine, not a candidate for your fiancée. I'm here to cover a story, not to become one. So as tempting as your offer may be, I have to decline."

He lifted a brow. "Why, Ms. Knott, are you patronizing me?"

That threw me. "What? No!"

"Because I detect a hint of condescension."

"Then you're imagining things." My hands were sweating. I swiped them on my skirt. "I'm just stating a fact."

His gaze dipped seductively. "So you don't think I'm worth considering."

"Mr. Devine, don't take—" Suddenly I was struck by the line of his jaw, so angular and forthright that I swear he could be a judge or a juror or anyone who's supposed to be capable of impartiality, and yet . . . there was something about it, in his emerging beard and how it sloped toward his mouth, that was so indefinably sexy it knocked all sense out of me. I was fighting a losing battle, and I knew it.

I cleared my throat and began again. "Look, I don't want you to take this personally, but—"

"I won't," he said. "In fact, I've gone out of my way to make sure personalities have nothing to do with it. I need a wife to help run the farm and have our children. And if she does, she'll share equally in all the rewards and benefits. All I ask is that she's healthy, able to have children, and willing to work hard. You, Ms. Knott . . ."—he looked me over—". . . appear to meet all the criteria."

The man was astounding. "But you know nothing about me!"

"What do I need to know beyond what I can see?"

"How about what's inside me, what my interests are, if I'm honest, how I take my coffee—Christ!" I stabbed my fingers into my hair, a comb tumbling out. "Why, if I even *like* you, for Pete's sake!"

He plucked the comb from the floor. "Do you like me, Ms. Knott?" he said with the barest of smiles, the bit of tortoise-shell plastic pinched between his fingers.

I snatched it from him, shoving it into my hair. "That's not the issue and it never was."

He leaned in. "My point exactly."

An Excerpt from

A WEDDING IN VALENTINE
A Valentine Valley Novella
by Emma Cane

It's the wedding all of Valentine Valley has been
waiting for, and once again the town works its
magic in this brand-new novella by Emma Cane.

Heather Armstrong is looking forward to
a weekend away at her best friend Emily's
wedding, but when she learns that her
previous one-night stand is Emily's brother,
the weekend takes an unexpected turn.

Heather Armstrong gasped as the plane dropped down between the Colorado mountains, which were painted myriad shades of green below the tree line, barren and brown at the top, awaiting the next winter's snow. The ground seemed to rush up, and only when they touched down at the small Aspen airport did she let her exhilaration at her first mountain landing subside back into wedding excitement. She was about to be a bridesmaid in the June wedding of an old friend, Emily Murphy.

As she waited for a call from Emily, she wandered the airport. It bustled with people dressed casually for the outdoors, many carrying cases for fishing equipment, a pastime this valley was known for in the summer. She'd always preferred being a people watcher, observing from the background rather than commanding attention herself. It was one of the reasons she'd never enjoyed being in charge of a restaurant's kitchen and had opened her own catering business. But now her people watching skills made her halt in her tracks as she caught a glimpse of a familiar figure.

A man wearing a cowboy hat slouched in a chair near the main doors, as if he, too, was waiting for someone. His head was bent over a book, and she couldn't quite see his face. A feeling of unease shivered up her spine and made her so wary that she backed up to where she was partially hidden around a corner. Peeking out again, she studied his pale blond hair beneath the hat, the checked Western shirt that snugly outlined his broad chest, the long legs encased in faded jeans above worn cowboy boots.

The bang of dropped luggage drew his attention, and he looked up. Heather recognized him instantly, and with a gasp, she retreated behind the safety of the wall. His name was Chris, and that was all she'd known when they'd been snowbound together in the Denver airport seven months before. Late-night drinks at the bar and mutual attraction—make that lust—shared with Chris had turned her into a person she'd never been, a daring flirt who'd ended up in bed with a cowboy. They'd spent two wild days together, exploring and laughing and connecting on an intimate level that had surprised her with its depth, considering they'd been strangers and all. Though she'd left him her number, assuming they'd see each other again, he'd never called. She'd felt like an idiot, a slut, and whatever other bad names she'd called herself over the following months. Gradually she'd accepted the "adventure" as a risk she'd obviously wanted to take, and had learned from. She wasn't cut out for one-night stands. She felt too much, expected too much. A man pursuing such a brief affair wanted only that and nothing else.

Today had been the first day airports hadn't made her think about him, she thought bitterly. Tough luck for her.

To find some peace, she'd chalked the experience up to a valuable lesson. Other women had done stupid things in college, but not her. She'd been too focused on her business degree, and then culinary school, the future her goal. She was little lured by frat parties and wild drinking. She'd had a boyfriend or two, of course, serious engineering and business students, and that same pattern had continued throughout her twenties. Never time for an intense relationship—until Andrew four years before. She'd thought everything so perfect, so wonderful, and hadn't even seen that he was pulling away from her, that their sex life was full of desperation more than real passion. Everything on the surface had been too good to be true. The breakup with him was probably what had launched her recklessness that snowy night in Denver.

But Chris's face had haunted her a long time, lean and sculpted, his blue eyes almost startling in their intensity. She hadn't been with another man since him, had been ready to change her life, find a new place to start over, to forget her past and find more peaceful surroundings.

FLING
A BDSM Erotica Anthology
by Sara Fawkes, Cathryn Fox, and Lauren Hawkeye

WELCOME TO FETISH WEEK

Unleash your kinky side with three tales of BDSM
romance in an exclusive Mediterranean sex
resort from three hot erotica writers, including
New York Times bestseller Sara Fawkes.

Take Me by Sara Fawkes

The minute sexy hotel manager Alexander Stavros spots shy,
sweet Kate Swansea at the Mancusi resort, he can tell she's
begging for release. This Dom is the perfect man to help her
. . . if she's willing to let go of her inhibitions and enjoy the
ride.

Teach Me by Cathryn Fox

There's nothing Luca Mancusi loves more than lingerie. So
much so, he's made it his business. Fashion design intern Josie
Pelletier is supposed to be negotiating a deal with him, but as
talks heat up, he can't wait to teach her the ways of business
. . . and BDSM.

Tame Me **by Lauren Hawkeye**

CEO Marco Kennedy can't help being drawn to Ariel Monroe. When he follows the pop star abroad to the Mancusi resort, she agrees to a deal: He'll win her as a sub through pleasure . . . or he'll disappear from her life. Ariel's game . . . just as long as she doesn't lose her heart too.

Available now from Avon Red
Wherever e-books are sold